WHAT IF...

A DIFFERENT TIME,
A DIFFERENT PLACE?

CHARLES JACKSON

CSN Books
San Diego, California 92119

WHAT IF...?

ISBN: 978-1-59352-385-5

Published by:

CSN Books
7287 Birchcreek Rd.
San Diego, CA 92119
Toll-free: 1-866-757-9953

www.csnbooks.com

Printed in the United States of America.

ACKNOWLEDGMENTS

I would like to thank my Lord and Savior, Jesus Christ. He has blessed me so much throughout my life and especially this project. He has loved me, forgiven me, and upheld me as I did my best to be the hands of His work. Without Him, I am nothing.

I would also like to thank my wife Sandie, who has stood by me throughout my life and has always been supportive and loving through good times and bad. I appreciate her wisdom and how the Holy Spirit speaks to me through her.

My children, Kori, her husband Mike, Jake, his wife Amanda, and Barrett have been my encouragers throughout the writing of this book. Many times I doubted my abilities to complete such a task, but they assisted in review and suggestions and moral support over the years it took to complete this book.

Finally, I would like to sincerely thank Gary and Julie Kirk, my publishers. They have been extremely patient with me, holding my hand as I walked through unchartered territory. Because of this process, I have not only published a book, I have also gained two more Christian friends.

INTRODUCTION

I grew up in a Christian home, however, the characters in the Bible always seemed abstract and in some ways almost unreal. I had trouble relating to the dress, culture, and political atmosphere of the times. The idea for this book came to me when I was teaching a high school Sunday school class. I always tried to present the lessons in a way the young people I was teaching could see that the characters in the Bible were real and that these events actually happened! The "stories" in the Bible were not just fables; they were actual historical events, and my goal was to help the students identify with and relate to the real characters in the Bible.

I soon dismissed the idea of writing the book for several reasons; however, God had different plans. He would not allow this idea to leave my mind. I fought Him for 20 years, and if you don't already know, that is a fight that no one ever wins. I eventually resolved to pursue my calling and write the book.

The original inspiration for this book was God. I believe that He is the source of everything good, however, I did not really write this as a religious book in the traditional sense. *What If...?* does refer to God and Jesus Christ and you will find nothing immoral or irreverent in its content. It is my hope that you will find this story entertaining and thought provoking.

The original intent for this novel was to cause you, the reader, to think about a significant historical event in a different way more than my concern to be scripturally correct. If you are a believer, hopefully, you will be blessed. If you are not a believer, I pray that it will make you think about life in a different way. Life with God is much better than life without Him.

Charles Jackson

CHAPTER ONE

Mary Reubenowitz was a sweet girl. There is no other way to state it. She was kind, gentle, and always considerate of others. She loved children and enjoyed volunteering to work in the nursery at church. People would routinely say that they couldn't believe how a heart as big as hers could live in such a petite body. Her sincere respect for senior citizens was only exceeded by her deep religious convictions.

Having received the unanimous vote of her peers to be captain of the cheer squad could have left her with an ego as big as all outdoors, but she remained humble. Everyone knew that Mary was the prettiest girl in school. She wasn't the painted, sexy type of pretty. She had a natural beauty that didn't require makeup. Mary was the type of girl that could catch a pass while playing touch football, fall into a mud puddle, and still look good! However, when she did get dressed up, she looked amazing! Not just a pretty face, Mary was also an honor student. She had a 3.98 GPA. However, her most cherished honor was being selected by the National Family Life Council as the chairperson of 'Teens for Abstinence'. This organization's sole purpose was to convince single people all over the world to abstain from pre-marital sex. This position demanded a significant amount of time for Mary and would require her to travel for speaking engagements all over the country. Notwithstanding, Mary remained humble and sincere. Feeling blessed and dutiful, she always put her accomplishments in perspective by giving honor and glory to God.

Joseph Goldstein was in the middle of his junior year on top of the world. He had it all. Selected as an all-state quarterback, he had already set state records in total passing yards, touchdown passes, and was third in the state in rushing. Scholarship offers from countless major universities were pouring in. In addition, he had led his baseball team to two consecutive state championships as a pitcher with an ERA of 0.95 and a batting average of 425. All of the newspapers in the state were predicting that Joe would lead both the football and baseball teams to state victories in his remaining years in high school. Several professional teams were scouting him to go directly from high school to the major league. With a GPA of 4.0 and standing at 6' 4", 180 lbs. with dark hair and soft, kind eyes, Joe was a strikingly handsome young man. Every girl in his school wanted to go out with him and expended much time and effort in order to accomplish their goals. However, whenever they flirted with him, he would only say, "I would never do that to Mary, I love her too much."

It had always been Mary. She and Joe had grown up together. They lived across the street and their parents were the best of friends. Having been born only two weeks apart, they literally shared cribs as babies. Joe had never known life without Mary and had been with her every day of his life except for two weeks last summer when Mary had gone with their church youth group on a mission trip to South America. Joe had been scheduled to go as well. However, Joe's father owned a construction business and had broken his leg working on a house. So Joe volunteered to remain at home and help his dad with the business until he could get back on his feet.

Those two weeks were the longest of Joe's life! He was lost without his best friend. He had never gone a day without seeing her. They had shared holidays, sicknesses, and even played on the same soccer team as children together. They had been in the same classroom in the first and second grade. When they were finally separated in the third grade, Mary cried so long that the teacher had to take a picture of Joe and put it on Mary's desk!

It was understandable. Joe had always been there for her. He had protected her from bullies as children. No one dared harm Mary or it was Joe to face. As teenagers, Joe was Mary's moral support when the other girls were mean to her out of jealousy.

Mary counted on Joe and he liked it. He took great pride in being her rock. He would do anything to make her smile. All he ever wanted to do was make her happy. His accomplishments meant nothing to him unless Mary was there to share them with him.

Mary felt the same way about Joe. She supported him throughout his entire life. Whatever Joe decided to attempt, Mary was there for him. One time in junior high, Joe decided that he was going to break the pole vault record in track. He had never even tried it before! Mary read up on the techniques and training procedures for the event and actually coached Joe on how to accomplish his goal. In the fall of his eighth grade year, he broke the record by six inches! He gave the trophy to Mary.

They were the perfect couple who complimented each other in every way. Best friends at first, they had been in love longer than anyone could remember. It was just a matter of time before they got married and everyone knew it.

It was January and time for the annual New Year's Resolution party at the Goldstein's. The Holiday Season was over and the kids were getting ready to go back to school. Actually, it was just another excuse for the Goldsteins and the Reubenowitzs to get together. It seemed as if they "made excuses" to have a party at least twice a month. Birthdays, holidays, sidewalk sale days at the mall...it didn't matter; the two families loved being together.

This party was particularly special because it marked the official beginning of Mary's tenure as the chairperson for 'Teens for Abstinence'. Joe was proud of her but wasn't looking forward to her weekend trips away from him. She assured him that it would be OK and that she was doing God's work. He accepted the explanation and was trying to be supportive but really hated the fact that they would be apart occasionally. Mary wasn't fond of the idea either. She knew that she was doing the right thing; but she hated the fact that Joe wouldn't be there for her. They both resolved to make the best of it and allow God to do His work.

School was to resume tomorrow and Mary and Joe couldn't wait. They had worked hard to get a good education as well as build an excellent reputation for themselves. The remainder of this year and all of their senior year was going to be fun! Unless something major happened in the classroom, they were also going to be valedictorian and salutatorian. There were rumors that they both had been given full ride scholarships to Harvard. However, Joe and Mary would never confirm or deny this rumor; they only smiled and said that no matter where they went, they would go together. They were a shoe-in for homecoming King and Queen next year. Everyone always said that Joe treated Mary like a queen anyway. Joe was known to be a "perfect gentlemen" to Mary and received some pretty brutal teasing in the locker room about him and Mary remaining virgins. It hurt, but his honor and Mary's purity meant more to him than any accolades he could have received from his peers if he had succumbed to temptation. Besides, he always told himself that the guys were just jealous since none of them had the fortitude to remain true to themselves and God.

Jacob Reubenowitz (Mary's dad) was a pharmacist and owned Witz's Drugstore in their hometown of Pleasantville, Montana. It was the largest family-owned and operated drugstore in the state and "Big Jake" (as the locals called him) was known to have the best prices in the area. Jake was a big man with a bear-like handshake. He could be intimidating but wasn't. His heart was as big as an eagle's nest. It was not uncommon for Jake to allow people to charge medicine to their account but somehow the bill would "get lost" or the computer would "go haywire" and the account would read "paid in full." Jake would grumble out loud and then smile and laugh that deep down belly laugh that made everyone feel good. His wife Ruth worked the front part of the store. She managed the day-to-day operation and worked side-by-side with the employees. She was not above taking out the trash or cleaning the restrooms and the employees loved her attitude. She was always cheery and pleasant in a contagious sort of way. It was not uncommon for friends and neighbors to stop by the store to visit with Ruth "just for a dose of Ruthy" as they called it. Everyone always left the store in better spirits.

No child EVER left the store without a piece of candy; "on the house" as Miss Ruth (as the children called her) would say. She would tell the kids that they would be doing her a favor if they took the candy because it would be keeping Big Jake from eating it. The exact opposite of Jake physically, she was extremely petite and very pretty. She and Mary were often confused as sisters by people who didn't know them. When Big Jake would "catch" Miss Ruth giving away candy, he would chase her around the store while she shrieked with fake terror much to the delight and amusement of the customers and employees. When he caught her (she would have to slow down or that would never happen), he would pick her up, swing her around, and then sit her on top of a shelf, cabinet or refrigerator! Then she would act angry (smiling all the time) and demand that he lift her down. Big Jake would reply that she was not getting down until the candy had been paid for. After a minute or two of fake argument, Ruth would agree to pay for the candy herself. Big Jake would reply with a hardy and triumphant, "Fine!" Miss Ruth would then plant a big kiss on Big Jake and he would yell at the top of his lungs, "PAID IN FULL!" As he lifted her gently to the floor, everyone would cheer and someone would always ring the bell at the counter. It was one of those traditions that everyone loved.

Abraham Goldstein (Joe's dad) was a contractor. A quiet, shy, unassuming man, he had gotten into the business before he and Eve had married. He had been a carpenter working on a construction crew for a builder in town. His talent and work ethic had quickly gotten him promoted to foreman. After they got married, Eve convinced him to go out on his own and start his own company. After much prayer and consideration, they started "Dream Builders." It was tough at first. Abraham worked out of his garage all by himself. The hours were long and cash flow was tight. He couldn't afford any employees so he served as delivery boy, construction crew, and bookkeeper. Eve helped whenever she could and turned out to be "a fairly good carpenter" to use Abraham's words. As time went on, his reputation for quality and fairness created more opportunities than he could imagine. His business boomed when he constructed the new Witz's Drugstore and he now employs twenty people. Eve has since hung up her hammer and spends her days keeping books for the company and preparing bids...all of that business stuff.

Eve was a "knockout" as Abraham described her. In fact, Joe used to tease his dad saying that he had "overachieved" when he landed Eve. Abraham would smile and say that he had caught her on a bad day; thank God! Eve was the opposite of Abraham in that she was outgoing and had never met a stranger. She was always the life of the party and everyone loved her.

Notwithstanding, she was totally crazy about Abraham. When they were together, it was easy to tell that they were deeply in love. They seemed to be lost in each other as if no one else was around. Joe would watch this over the years and was sure that it would be this way with he and Mary—he knew it!

CHAPTER TWO

Joe was so anxious to see Mary that he could hardly contain himself. It had been two days since he had dropped her off at the airport to fly to Washington DC for her first speaking engagement as chairperson of 'Teens for Abstinence'. She had left right after school on Friday night and was scheduled to hit the ground Sunday evening at 6:00. Joe had been at the airport since 4:00 just in case the plane arrived early! Joe kept asking the agent at the gate if the plane was on time, if there were any problems with the plane, even if she had spoken with the pilot! The agent was very nice and patient with Joe and reassured her that Mary was just fine. Joe missed her terribly.

When the plane finally landed, Joe literally leaped in the air and hugged the agent! Everyone in the waiting area cheered because by now, Joe had told everyone around about Mary and even showed them a few pictures of her! When she finally walked through the security area, Joe ran up to her, picked her up, and swung her around as if she were a doll. He hugged her so tight that she could barely breathe, but she didn't mind a bit as she missed him as well. All of Joe's "new friends" in the waiting area applauded and cheered. Mary asked Joe, "Who are all of these people?" Joe replied, "This is your new fan club!" Mary turned as red as a fire truck and gave Joe a playful slap on the shoulder as the "fan club" laughed and enjoyed the moment.

As they headed down the terminal to baggage claim, Mary was excited to tell Joe about the events of the weekend. Her meetings on Saturday morning had gone very well. She had been introduced to her assistant chairperson, Gary Blackburn from Sacramento, California, who Mary described as a tall, good looking senior with blonde hair and was "very tan." Gary's whole purpose in the organization was to support Mary in whatever she needed and be available to stand in for her in the event that she couldn't attend a function. Mary also had a "secretary," Karen Miller from Houston, Texas. Karen was a beautiful athletic type of girl who was extremely outgoing and likeable. She had that deep southern accent that immediately made everyone like her. Karen was in charge of the details of event scheduling, hotel arrangements, transportation... and she was very good at it. She had already scheduled the next three events, February 4th in Salt Lake City, February 25th in Chicago, and March 25th in Fort Lauderdale for a six-day event to reach the students on spring break.

The next morning Mary could barely speak as time for her presentation drew closer. She had to speak to an audience of about 500 people! Not only were there so many people, but they were very important to the success of the organization. The audience consisted of major corporate and private contributors for the funding of 'Teens for Abstinence' as well as many influential politicians who would be voting for federal supplemental funding as well. She had worked hard on her presentation putting together facts, graphs, and charts showing how teenage pregnancy had become a major problem in the United States. Her presentation focused on how complete abstinence was the only way to insure against pregnancy and disease. In addition, she presented papers and documentation from several noted psychologists and social scientists proving that teenagers who practiced abstinence had increased self-esteem, and when they did get married, had a much lower divorce rate than did teenagers who were sexually active prior to marriage.

When she concluded her speech, she received a standing ovation. As she stood there nodding in humble appreciation to the ovation, she caught a glimpse of a small commotion coming from the back of the room. As she focused on the activity, the applause turned into cheers as she realized that the president of the United States was striding down the main aisle directly at her with a host of secret service agents in tow! He skipped up the stairs two at a time and clasped her hand with both of his hands smiling warmly at her. He was deeply impressed with her research and her commitment to the project. The president commended her on her speaking abilities and jokingly asked her not to run against him in the up-coming election! All she could do was say, "Thank you" as she stood there in total astonishment. As he waved to the crowd he whispered in her ear, "I'm proud of you, if you need anything, please call Jim." Jim was one of the aides that she had dinner with the night before. Jim had been standing right behind the president and stepped right up and handed a business card to Mary. A dark object flashed by that distracted her for just a second. She locked eyes with Jim and immediately felt cold. He had an air about him that Mary didn't like. He was charming; maybe too charming. With that, the presi-dent turned and walked swiftly off the stage. Mary stood there in total shock at what had just happened. After what seemed like hours she gathered herself and waved to the still-cheering crowd. Tears ran down her cheeks as she walked off the stage.

The backstage area was swarming with people. Karen was talking with a bunch or reporters and Gary was shaking hands with several politicians and other influential people. Mary just stood there taking it all in when Gary caught a glimpse of her out of the corner of his eye. He immediately excused himself and ran over to Mary. He gave her a big hug and planted an innocent kiss right on her cheek! This caught Mary off-guard which caused her to blush so much that her cheeks were as red as cherries. Karen laughed at the abrupt complexion change which didn't help Mary's face to return to normal any quicker. The reporters joined in the harmless laughter while one made the comment that if a simple kiss on the cheek made her blush, she must be the right person to represent this organization.

When the laughter and good-natured teasing died down, Karen related to Mary and Gary that a press conference was scheduled in 15 minutes in the lobby for them with local and national TV coverage. This was going to be on National News. Mary collected herself and pulled Gary and Karen aside and told them, "We need to talk about what we are going to say to the press. I have never even been to a press conference let alone hold one! Do I talk? Do I take questions? Should I do a song and dance?" Mary was frightened and Gary and Karen knew it. Karen felt awful because she was the one who had agreed to it. She had gotten caught up in the moment and hadn't quite thought it through. Gary was frantically reviewing Mary's notes from her speech to attempt to find some highlights and important points for Mary to share with the reporters but there wasn't enough time. Mary was just going to have to wing it and this made her very nervous. It was one thing to stand up in front of a crowd with a prepared speech, but it was quite another thing to face a bunch of journalists who were professionals at asking questions.

As the three of them stepped into the lobby, the reporters darted toward them all screaming questions at the same time. Cameras were going off so frequently that the three of them couldn't see past the dozen or so microphones that were jammed in their faces. It was total confusion! Mary could scarcely hear herself think let alone discern any of the questions. Karen and Gary moved in tightly on each side of Mary and grabbed her hands to give her some moral support. Mary felt totally helpless but something deep inside her took over causing her to bow her head and pray silently. "Father, I am in way over my head. I don't know how to handle this crowd and I don't know what to say to them but I know that You are in control. Please give me the proper words in response to their questions and allow Your glory to rise above anything else in this room. Amen."

When she open her eyes, not only had the crowd calmed down, it had become so quiet in the lobby that the noise on the street could be heard through the two sets of doors leading to it. As Mary looked around, the reporters seemed to be reverently waiting for some clear sign to proceed while Karen and Gary were stuck in some kind of stupor. Karen acted as if she couldn't blink and Gary's mouth was so far open that it looked as if his jaw was on his chest. Mary smiled at the reporters and said, "Thank you for giving me a moment to talk to my Boss, He is really good at getting me through times like these." The reporters smiled but remained silent. Mary looked at Karen and told her to breathe. She then turned toward Gary and said, "Gary, close your mouth." It was not so much what she said to her companions, but how she said it. There was a confident type of kindness in her voice that caused a few chuckles from the crowd. All at once, everyone seemed to relax and Mary said, "Does anyone have any questions?"

After about ten minutes of questions such as, "How did you get selected for this position?," "What are your plans to make this succeed?," and personal questions about family, school and such, the reporters seemed satisfied. "One final question," a voice from the back shouted. "Do any of you have a significant other?" Karen stated that she was between boyfriends and Gary said that he was playing the field right now. However, Mary went into a significant amount of detail about Joe before Karen interrupted by saying, "Enough already, we get it, Joe is perfect!" Everyone laughed and Mary blushed. As the crowd began to disburse, a rather unkempt-looking photographer came up to the three of them and asked how he could get in touch with them. Karen gave him their home telephone numbers and e-mail addresses. He then asked for a final picture and requested that they lean in close and put their heads together and smile. He snapped the photo and disappeared into the street.

Joe was grinning from ear to ear as they pulled up into Mary's driveway. The house was dark as it was 10 p.m. and her family was probably already in bed. She had talked all the way home from the airport about her experiences in Washington. Joe was so proud of her that he could barely contain himself and keep quiet about the small surprise that Mary was about to discover. As she glanced at the dark house she said, "It looks as if mom and dad are already in bed; I guess I'll tell them about the trip before school in the morning." Joe smiled and agreed as he jumped out of the car and raced around to open the car door for her. He grabbed her suitcase and they walked up the sidewalk holding hands. He gave her a quick peck on the cheek and said good night as she quietly opened the door.

Just as she reached inside for the light switch, the living room lights came on and a crowd of people yelled, "Surprise!" Apparently the Reubenowitzs and the Goldsteins had found yet another excuse to have a party. Besides the two families, there were several people from church as well as most of Mary and Joe's friends from school. There was food everywhere and a big sign in the living room that said, "We're proud of you, Mary!" The celebration lasted until after midnight.

CHAPTER THREE

Joe rushed into Mary's house early the next morning with a copy of *The Washington Post* in hand. Jacob and Ruth were sitting at the kitchen table having breakfast and Mary was just coming down the stairs to join them. Joe flipped open the newspaper to show them the front page and there was a picture of Mary shaking hands with the president. A very nice article accompanied the picture stating what 'Teens for Abstinence' was about and a short summary of Mary's personal biography as well as her responsibilities in the organization.

Jacob grinned from ear to ear and grabbed Mary as she turned the corner and hugged her so hard she could barely breathe. Ruth smiled at Mary and said, "I'm so proud of you, you are a wonderful young lady." Mary looked bewildered as she had not yet seen the newspaper. Joe flashed it in front of hers eyes for a few seconds and then abruptly closed it and waited for her response. Mary was speechless for a few seconds and then said quietly, "That is an awful picture of me." Everyone, including Mary, burst out laughing as Ruth slid a plate of bacon and eggs in front of Joe. Jacob read the article in its entirety out loud with the flare and drama of a bad stage actor. By the time he was finished, Joe was almost on the floor because he was laughing so hard, Ruth was playfully mocking Jacob, and Mary was blushing terribly. When things calmed down Ruth looked at the kitchen clock, told Mary and Joe to get off to school and reminded Jacob that he was already late for work.

As Mary and Joe walked into the school, Mary was immediately dragged away from Joe by her girlfriends as they were dying to hear about her weekend. She began telling them about everything that had happened as well as her new friends Gary and Karen. Mary went into great detail about meeting the president, her speech, and the tour of Washington DC. After Mary had mentioned that Gary was from California and had blonde hair, Josie excitedly asked, "Is he cute?" Mary replied that she had some pictures of Gary as well as Karen and that they could decide for themselves. After quickly skipping through the pictures of Karen and studying the ones of Gary, Josie exclaimed, "He's gorgeous!" loud enough that several guys who were standing across the hall heard it and looked up hoping that she was talking about them.

Joe looked over at his football teammates and noticed that they were looking at one of those cheesy tabloid newspapers. He didn't think much of it as he assumed that they were reading about the exploits of some rock or movie star. Just as he got to the group, Jimmy snidely quipped, "It looks like Mary has another boyfriend." Joe laughed as he was used to the guys teasing him. However, the other boys weren't laughing and Jimmy's facial expression had darkened. The boys weren't joking as they handed the tabloid over to Joe. As Joe scanned page two, his eyes fell to a picture of Mary and Gary with their heads playfully together and right along next to it was a picture of Joe and Mary taken last fall at the Home-coming dance. The caption under the picture read in bold lettering, "Teens for Abstinence president has tough time juggling boyfriends; is she really practicing what she preaches?"

Joe quickly read the article beneath the picture. It wasn't a long article; only a paragraph. However, it sure made Mary look bad as a role model. It inferred that Gary and Mary had been out on the town in Washington half of the night and made suppositions regarding how they were using the 'Teens for Abstinence' funds for their partying. In addition, it questioned the alleged lack of super-vision for the two kids and implied that the sleeping arrangements for the night were questionable.

Joe was so taken aback that he couldn't move or speak. He felt his face flushing and his legs trembled. His hands were shaking so hard that it was everything he could do to slowly place the tabloid in the front section of his notebook. As he looked up at the boys around him, all of them were staring at him with blank looks on their faces. The only exception was Jimmy. His face had transformed into that type of evil, pompous sort of grin that one only sees on people who are vindictive and jealous. He was so caught up in the potential for scandal that he couldn't contain himself and sarcastically blurted out, "So what do you think of your little virgin now?"

Jimmy had barely gotten the words out of his mouth when Joe grabbed him by the front of his shirt collar and slammed him up against the lockers. The entire hallway became silent as all of the kids stared. Jimmy was up on his tiptoes as Joe had most of Jimmy's weight in his right hand. Joe's face was barely two inches from Jimmy's. He could feel Joe's breath on his cheek and couldn't muster enough courage to look him in the eyes. The smirk had left Jimmy's face and all that could be seen in his eyes now was fear. The other boys backed away as they had never seen Joe react this way to any situation. After what seemed like an eternity, Joe whispered in a voice so low that Jimmy could barely hear him, "Look at me." Jimmy's eyes slowly met Joe's angry coal black pupils as Joe whispered, "Be very careful, you don't want me as an enemy do you?" As Joe let Jimmy down to the floor, a teacher popped his head out of a door across the hall to see what all of the quiet was about and started to approach the two boys but the bell rang and everyone started off to class. Joe whisked past the teacher and Jimmy headed the other way. Joe glanced around and was relieved to see that Mary had already headed off to class and hadn't witnessed the altercation.

Joe didn't hear a word the teacher said in class. All he could think about was what he had read. Surely Mary hadn't done any of those things that the tabloid had implied. But, Gary was a good-looking guy and Mary had mentioned several times how nice he had been to her. However, this was MARY! His best friend and the person he trusted for everything. She would never do anything like that; however, people do change and even fall into temptation occasionally. He even had briefly considered it on occasion. His mind went crazy for the entire hour. Did she or didn't she? He finally came to the conclusion that Mary must be told and the news had to come from him. He would gauge her reaction as to the validity of the accusations.

The bell rang and Joe headed for his locker. Mary met him there and gave him the usual squeeze on the arm. Joe didn't respond as he normally would have and Mary asked if something had happened in English class. Joe shrugged it off and mumbled that they should get to next period. He had decided to confront Mary in study hall before anyone else had the chance to tell her.

As they slid into their seats Ms. Simms went through the same old speech regarding the importance of utilizing this time by studying. However, she would allow quiet conversation if it didn't interrupt anyone who was attempting to study. Joe pulled Mary's chair over to his so that they could sit face-to-face. Mary grinned happily as it was unusual for Joe not to study. She always wanted to talk and he usually needed to study so it was always a treat when Joe decided to blow off study hall. However, she sensed that this wasn't going to be a great conversation by the look on Joe's face. He looked as if he were going to a funeral and she wanted to try and lighten up the mood by asking him who died but thought better of it. All she could say was, "Joe, what's wrong?" Joe didn't respond. He reached into his backpack, pulled out the tabloid and turned it slowly to page two. He slid it over to her desk without a word.

Mary focused on the picture of her and Gary and then the headlines. She briefly glanced up at Joe who was watching her intently. She nervously read the article as tears came to her eyes. When she finished the article she looked up at Joe who also had tears in his eyes. Mary couldn't speak, her lips just quivered. All Joe could say was, "Is this true?" Mary burst into tears and got up and left the room sobbing. Ms. Simms jumped up, glared at Joe, and followed Mary to the restroom. When she caught up with her, Mary was throwing up in one of the stalls. Ms. Simms asked Mary if she was alright but Mary couldn't answer between sobs and gasping for a breath. When she finally calmed down, Mary accepted Ms. Simms' offer to go to the school nurse. Once there, Mary asked if she could go home because she wasn't feeling well. The nurse agreed but told Mary that she wouldn't allow her to drive and that she would take her home.

Joe sat in silence in study hall waiting for Mary to come back. When Ms. Simms finally came into the room, Joe got up from his seat and went to her and asked where Mary had gone. The short reply was, "Home." Joe's heart sank as he walked back to his seat.

22

Ruth was running the cash register at the store when the door opened and in came Delores. She had the gleam in her eye that she gets when new gossip was being spread around town. Delores had the reputation all over town as being the person who knew the gossip, loved to spread it, and enjoyed the notoriety that came with it. Ruth started to ignore her and hoped to get away from the cash register before she checked out. Ruth disliked talking with Delores as gossip was not one of the things that Ruth enjoyed. In fact, she always stood up for the person being discussed even when it appeared to be true.

Delores came right up to Ruth and threw the tabloid containing the article about her daughter on the counter. Ruth spoke up and stated firmly, "Now Delores, I told you before that we do not want to carry that paper in this store, it is not up for discussion and I don't care how much money we could make selling it!" "Now hold on," came the reply. "I'm not here to try and convince you to sell it here, although it would be good for your business since everybody reads it. I'm here to show you an article on page two in which you will be interested." "I would never be interested in that trash," Ruth stated firmly. "Just humor me for a minute," Delores replied with a smirk on her face and shoved the article under her nose.

Ruth's eyes went straight to the picture and then to the headline. As she read the article she could feel Delores' eyes straining to read it with her and waiting for a reaction. Ruth finished the article, composed herself and slowly peered into the waiting glare of Delores. As her face flushed, she looked Delores squarely in the eyes and asked, "What do you make of this?"

Joe spent the rest of the day in a fog. He shuffled his way to each class, plopped down at his desk and stared right through the teacher, his mind wandering between Mary, the article, the picture of Gary, his parents, Mary's parents, and back again. He lost track of the lectures and for the first time in his life, didn't care. Joe spent his lunch break sitting alone in the gym. It was quiet up on the top row.

As he was sitting there reliving some of his childhood memories of he and Mary, he heard the door open slowly and the voice of his best friend Allen whispering, "Joe, are you in here?" Joe made no reply. The door gently closed and then the sound of footsteps across the floor and up the bleachers. Joe peered through his fingers at Allen as his friend came closer.

The look on Joe's face and the redness in his eyes immediately told Allen that something was wrong. "What's up?" Allen asked. "I know you don't have a test because we are in the same classes and I know you don't have a game; so why are you sitting here and where is Mary?" Joe didn't say a word. He merely handed the article to Allen who read it over very carefully. When he finished he looked at Joe and said, "You don't believe this junk do you?" "Mary would never do that to you or to herself!" Joe just shrugged and shook his head. After a long silence, Allen said, "Look Joe, you need to talk to Mary about this, there has got to be a good explanation; besides, look at what paper this came out in. They are notorious for fabricating stories!" Joe replied, "I did confront her and all she did was jump up crying and left the room—she didn't say a word to me! What am I supposed to think?"

"You're supposed to think the best of your girlfriend! How long have you two been together? Like forever? How dare you think the worst when you don't even have the entire story? You trust her, remember? If I could, I would smack you upside your head!" Joe muttered something about Allen being right and started to get up to leave. As he stood up, he looked Allen in the eyes and said, "But what if it's true? How do I handle it?" Allen just shook his head and said, "It can't be true, it's MARY!" "Hope you're right," Joe replied as he headed down the bleachers and off to class.

Ruth tapped her fingers on the counter as she waited for the reply from Delores. There was an awkward silence between the two women and Delores didn't like it at all. Of all the potential responses that she had suspected from Ruth, the question of 'What do you make of this?' was not anticipated at all. Delores fidgeted for a few seconds and fumbled through her purse as she mumbled something about coupons. Finally, she looked up at Ruth's glare and replied, "Well of course I don't believe anything that I read in that paper, I just wanted you to know about it before it got spread all over town. After all, you know how people in this town can be!" Then she continued. "I guess I've left those coupons at the house, I'll be back later." She didn't wait for a reply from Ruth and spun around and marched out the door. Ruth's glare never left Delores as she watched her disappear past the front window. Ruth's head fell into her hands and she began to sob.

Jake had walked up behind Ruth just as Delores was leaving. Ruth hadn't heard him come up so she was somewhat startled as she felt a hand on her shoulder. Jake asked, "What did SHE want?" Ruth spun around and her tear-drenched eyes met his. All she could do was to hand the paper to him and point to the article. Jake read it several times and became more and more angry each time. He slammed the paper down and picked up the phone. "Who are you calling?" Ruth asked. "I'm calling the newspaper where that lousy little weasel who wrote that article works. I'm going to track him down like the dog that he is and inflict the kind of pain on him that he has inflicted on us!" "JACOB RUBENOWITZ, YOU'LL DO NO SUCH THING! At least not right now. You're going to stay right here and run this store. I'm going to find Mary before she has a chance to read this trash. She will be devastated. Now you calm down. I'll call you as soon as I find Mary and don't pick up that phone unless it rings!" Jake started to object but caught himself when his eyes met Ruth's. He knew when she meant things and this was one of those times. He turned around and mumbled something about wearing the pants in the family as Ruth headed for the door.

CHAPTER FOUR

The phone rang at the high school and a student's voice answered. "May I please speak to Carol?" Ruth inquired. In just a few seconds Carol's usual cheerful self sang into the phone, "Hello Miss Ruth. How are you doing today?" "Fine, thank you." Ruth was polite, but straight to the point. "Could you please find Mary and have her give me a call right away?" "Sure Ruth, is everything OK?" "I just really need to speak with her as soon as possible. Please have her call my cell phone, thanks." Then the phone went dead. Carol put the receiver down and went straight to work finding out where Mary should be at that time. Ruth wasn't herself and Carol knew it. They had been friends for 20 years and Carol sensed that something was wrong.

In just a few minutes Ruth's cell phone rang. "Ruth, this is Carol. It seems as if Mary has gone home. She got sick in study hall and the school nurse drove her home. Is there anything I can do?" "No, thanks Carol, I appreciate you getting back to me so quickly. I'll run home and check on her. Maybe she has a touch of something. Thanks again." As Ruth closed her cell phone her blood ran cold. She knew her daughter. She was sick alright. Sick because of what she had read in that trash some people called a newspaper. She was too late. Ruth turned around and headed for the house.

Ruth pulled into the driveway and tried to see if the lights were on in the house. She couldn't tell because the curtains were pulled; a sure sign that Mary was home. As she opened the door, she could hear Mary sobbing in her room. Ruth gently knocked and simultaneously opened the door. Mary looked up at her mother and began crying louder. "I didn't do it," Mary muttered between sobs.

Mary knew her mother would have heard the news somehow. This was a small town and rumors, especially bad ones like this spread quickly. "I know honey," Ruth replied. "Don't pay any attention to that filth. That reporter is a slime ball." Ruth sat down on the edge of the bed and began to softly stroke Mary's long dark hair.

After a few minutes of tender-loving care from Ruth, Mary calmed down and began to recount the events that led up to her discovery of the news. Mary carefully detailed the entire morning from the time they entered the school until the moment when they sat down in study hall. Mary did recall that while walking from first period class to study hall one of her friends had mentioned an altercation between Joe and Jimmy but Mary has dismissed it as either rumor or exaggeration. When she came to the part where Joe had asked if it was true, Ruth's mouth dropped open and she looked as if she had been struck by lightning. "How could he even begin to ask such a question? What is the matter with him? After all you two have been through, how could he possibly think that such a thing could even be remotely possible? AND consider the source! He knows about that newspaper. He knows how we feel about it and what it stands for. He even agreed with us when we decided not to carry it in the store! Just wait until I see him!"

Mary agreed that it was uncharacteristic of Joe to react that way and admitted that it was his reaction to the article that hurt her the most. Although the article was shocking and that kind of publicity was unusual for a small town girl, it was those three words that Joe had stated, 'is this true?' that cut her like a knife. She just couldn't believe that Joe would even consider it as a possibility. Tears began streaming down her face again and she fell back into her mother's arms.

Just then the doorbell rang. Ruth had already decided to ignore it but her eyes fell on the clock on the bed stand next to Mary's bed. It said 3:45. School had been out for 30 minutes and she wondered if it was one of Mary's friends checking on her. At Mary's urging, Ruth trudged down the hall, put on a smile and opened the front door. Much to her surprise, it was Joe! The smile turned sour and Ruth blurted out a curt greeting. "Since when do you ring the bell? You normally just walk on in." Joe just stood there dumbfounded. He couldn't say a word. Ruth just waited for him to say something, but nothing came out. Finally, she asked, "Don't you have baseball practice now?" All he could say was, "Didn't go, is Mary here? I need to see her." "She is here, but she doesn't feel well enough to see anyone, especially you." The reply came from a now angry, but composed Ruth. "Please," Joe begged, "I really need to see her for just a few minutes." Just then, Ruth heard Mary's voice, "Mom, be nice." "Oh, come on in," Ruth's voice softened a little. "Thank you," Joe replied as he slid past Ruth and made a beeline for Mary.

He held out his arms as if to get his usual hug as he walked toward her. Mary shifted her weight and crossed her arms, tears glistening in her eyes. Ruth stood defiantly in front of the door and watched with the zeal of a lioness protecting her cub. Joe knew that he had blown this one big time and was ready to admit it. As he dropped his arms in surrender of the hug he knew that he wouldn't receive, he said, "Mary, I'm sorry, I should have never doubted you. I know that you would never do anything like that and that God has intended for us to be together for the rest of our lives. I will NEVER doubt you again."

Mary looked over Joe's shoulder and caught her Mom's eye in the background. There was a tear in her eye, but there was also a smile on her face. She gave Mary a slight nod of approval. Mary's eyes met Joe's for the first time. She could see that he was in pain and it hurt her to see him that way. They just stood there looking at each other for what seemed like eternity. Finally, Mary said in a soft voice, "You hurt me, Joe." Joe replied, "I know, it was terrible of me to even consider it, I am sincerely sorry. Please forgive me, PLEASE?" Mary looked down in fake sadness and caught her mother rolling her eyes in the background. She knew that Mary had already forgiven Joe but was just giving him a hard time at this point. Mary then raised her head and had a huge smile on her face. Joe looked bewildered but he broke out in a hopeful grin. Mary jumped into his arms and he swung her around the room. He held her so tight Mary thought she was going to pass out. She whispered in his ear, "Can't breathe." Joe stopped hugging her so tightly and slowly let her to the ground. Mary kissed him on the cheek and stood there gazing into his eyes. Until that moment, Joe had forgotten that Ruth was taking all of this in. He turned around and looked at Ruth. "Sorry mom," came out of his mouth. He had called her mom since he had been old enough to say the words. Ruth walked over to him and playfully slapped him on the back of the head. "Don't do it again or Jake will hear about it," she said with a snicker. "Oh please, not that!" Joe feigned with a laugh. Mary snickered and said, "OK it's over, how about we make some cookies?" All three of them smiled and headed for the kitchen.

Ruth turned away from the window to check the clock. It was six on the nose. Joe and Mary were in the middle of a flour fight and the kitchen looked as white as the backyard. As Joe was about to cover her head with a cup of flour, Mary caught the concern in her mom's eyes and stopped short of rubbing Joe's nose in the cookie batter. "What's wrong Mom?" she questioned. "I'm just worried about your father; that car is not made to be driven in the snow." She replied. "He's just now closing up the store." Joe observed. "Want me to go get him?" "No, your car isn't any better. He'll be OK," she said with little assurance and continued working on dinner. Just as she turned away from the stove, Joe covered her with the flour that had been meant for Mary! Ruth's hair was as white as a 90-year-old lady. Surprised at first, she quickly broke out in a grin as Joe and Mary were on the floor holding their sides with uncontrollable laughter.

Jake was just locking up the store when he heard a car honk behind him. There sat Abraham and Eve in the company four-wheel-drive. "Hey Jake, how about we go on a picnic down by the lake?" Abraham yelled with a grin. Jake didn't miss a beat as he wiped snow from his glasses, "Too hot and I forgot my swimming trunks!" Both men laughed as Eve rolled her eyes and said," Jake, how about we give you a lift home? That car of yours won't make it around the corner in this snow." "This is a great car," Jake replied. "I'll be just fine. Thanks anyway, I'll see you all at home." He then turned for his car. Eve and Abraham watched as Jake unlocked the car and started it. "Don't leave him," Eve ordered Abraham. "Never intended to," Abraham replied. Jake took a significant amount of time to clean the windows as the ice had built up on them during the course of the day. When he finally dropped the car in reverse, it just sat there and spun. Abraham snickered and Eve slapped him and got out of the car. Jake was busy rocking the car back and forth trying to get it to budge and didn't notice Eve walk up to the window. She tapped sternly on the window which surprised him. "Jake, I'm not asking, I'm telling. Get out of that car and into the truck right now! Don't make me call Ruth!" Jake shot a glance at Abraham and got a shrug that told him he had better give up. Jake shut off the car.

As they pulled into the driveway, Eve and Abraham noticed that their house was dark. They surmised that Joe was probably at Jake's house. Eve announced as she got out of the truck that she was going in to check on Ruth and the kids. Abraham knew better than to object and shot a look at Jake to insure that he wasn't going to protest either. Jake had no intention of protesting the fact that Eve was going to the rescue. In fact, he secretly was thankful for the support. He knew that Eve could relate to Ruth as well as anyone. After all, they had been through a lot together and understood each other very well.

As the three slowly entered the front door, they heard Mary and Ruth screaming in what seemed to be terrible pain. Jake yelled as loud as anyone had heard and ran through the front room into the kitchen with Abraham and Eve in hot pursuit. As Jake threw open the door to rescue his wife and daughter, he couldn't believe what he was seeing. Joe had cornered the girls between the breakfast bar and the refrigerator and was about to break an egg on each of their heads. Joe grinned at Jake and his parents over his shoulder as Ruth and Mary giggled uncontrollably. All three of them were covered from head to toe with flour and the kitchen looked as if a tornado had been through it. Abraham looked at Eve and said, "I guess there's no problem here!" "Oh yes there is!" retorted Eve. "These three have obviously lost their minds!" Everyone broke out in laughter. Just then, Jake said, "Is something burning?" Ruth suddenly came to her senses and ran over to the oven. She flung open the oven door and smoke bellowed out. She grabbed the dinner and put it on top of the stove. "What is it?" Abraham questioned cautiously. "It used to be chicken," Ruth snorted. Then she smiled and announced that Jake was buying pizza if Abraham would use the 4x4 to pick it up.

As Jake reached for his second piece of pizza, he asked about the article in the paper. He figured that Ruth and Mary would have been upset. Ruth laughed and began to recount the events of the day. When she came to the part where Joe had questioned Mary if the article was true, Eve's eyes narrowed at Joe and Abraham's mouth dropped wide open. Jake acted as if he hadn't heard it. Ruth sensed the tension and tried to defend Joe to no avail. This only made things worse as Abraham slowly turned to Joe and stared at him. Joe felt the "heat" of the look from both his parents and decided that it would only be a matter of time before he had to deal with it. He glanced at Mary as he slowly raised his eyes to meet his dad's. Mary had a tear running down her cheek and it broke his heart to see it. Abraham's stare was something he hated. There wasn't anger in his eyes, only disappointment. Joe couldn't stand to look at his dad very long and shifted his eyes to his mom for comfort. It was in the eyes of his mother that he found the anger. Despondent, his eyes fell to Mary. She smiled through her tears and touched his hand under the table. It was then that Abraham broke the silence. "Is that the way we taught you to treat the girl you love?" Eve jumped in with both feet. "Joseph Samuel Goldstein!" Joe always knew the level of trouble he was in by the number of names his mother used to address him. When she called him "Joe" it wasn't bad at all. "Joseph" meant the discipline would be slightly more severe. "Joseph Samuel" indicated that he was in for some major punishment, but his entire name was saved for the grand-daddy of all. He had only heard it a few times during his lifetime and each time he vowed to never hear it again. His heart sank.

Jake knew all of this as well and came to the rescue. "Now hold on just a minute," he stood and spoke in a voice that was just under a yell. "It's MY daughter that the boy has offended. I want to hear from him. Then I will decide what to do!" Joe shivered in his boots as all eyes fell to him. However, he caught a glimpse of Jake who winked at him when no one else was looking. Joe immediately caught on and breathed a sigh of relief. Jake had assessed the situation when he got home and knew that Ruth had come home early to take care of things. Jake surmised that the flour fight was a tension reliever that came after the problem had been addressed. He didn't need to know the details. He knew his wife and daughter. If they had addressed the problem enough to get to the point of destroying the kitchen with a food fight, that was good enough for him.

Abraham leaned back and folded his arms as Eve continued her stare through Joe. "Well?" She asked rather abruptly. Joe muttered, "I'm sorry." "Good enough for me!" Jake interrupted and grinned. "Now wait a minute!" Eve stated earnestly. "It's not that easy. Joe messed up big time and he's not getting off so quickly."

"Why not?" injected Ruth. She had caught on to the game and wanted in. Ruth glanced at Mary who immediately read her mother's mind as only a mother and daughter can do with each other. "I'm totally cool with it." Mary mocked in her best Valley girl impression. Abraham looked at Eve and she returned the stare. Both sat in astonishment. Just then Ruth began to snicker and Mary blushed. Jake busted out in laughter while Joe sat there with his face in his hands trying not to laugh. "What's going on?" Eve demanded.

When Ruth finished telling the rest of the events of the day INCLUDING Joe's sincere apology and the reconciliation between Joe and Mary, Eve and Abraham calmed down and laughed just a little. "This doesn't mean you're totally off the hook," Abraham stated emphatically. "We need to have a talk about trust." Eve went over to give Mary a hug and added, "That's right! How could you not trust this precious little girl? Don't you ever do that again." With that, she slapped Joe playfully on the shoulder. "That's the second time I've heard that today. What do you women do, get together and decide how to gang up on someone?" Joe quipped with a smile. Mary laid her hand on Joe's shoulder and said in a soft but playful voice, "Joe, you have no idea."

CHAPTER FIVE

Joe groaned as he trudged by the window in the front room and peered out into the street. It had snowed all night and there was about ten inches of snow covering the driveway. Normally, this would have made him happy because he knew that school would be delayed or cancelled. However, after the events of yesterday, his parents had decided that it would be "in his best interest" to shovel their driveway as well as the driveways of the Reubenowitz's and each neighbor on both sides of their houses. That was six houses in all! The purpose of this exercise was to allow him time to remember how he had treated Mary during the past 24 hours as well as to encourage him to not jump to silly conclusions in the future. In short, this was his punishment. He had set his alarm for 5:30 a.m. in order to get the snow all finished before school. It was 5:35 and he hoped for a miracle.

"Good morning Joe," Abraham said cheerfully as he walked by on his way to the kitchen for his second cup of coffee. "Morning" the sleepy reply came from Joe. He knew that Abraham had been up since 4:30 as he always had been and that he had completed his daily devotions and was on his way to the kitchen for breakfast. Joe could hear his mother humming as she prepared breakfast for her family. The only redeeming thing about the morning was the aroma coming from the kitchen. Joe smelled bacon, eggs, and biscuits encompassed with fresh coffee as he turned the corner into the kitchen.

Joe just finished the Reubenowitz's driveway and this was the last one. He looked up in the window and Mary was motioning him to come in. Joe glanced at his watch; 9:15 since school had been delayed due to the snow. It was 45 minutes until the bell rang and he needed to allow for 20 minutes for the drive to school, plenty of time.

As he walked in the door, Ruth asked if he was hungry. "Always." "We figured you might be." Mary inserted, "Mom made extra biscuits and gravy, just in case."

Joe quickly came out of his coveralls and plopped down at the table. He had been sweating from working so hard. This, however, had made him cold. He shivered as he sipped the hot chocolate that Mary had made for him. The biscuits and gravy went down quickly and Joe glanced at his watch; 9:30. He had ten minutes before he had to leave for school. No time for a shower. He would just have to wing it until he got home.

"Hey Mary, how would you like to ride to school with a guy that smells like a goat?" Joe chided as he put on his coat. Mary put on her best actress voice and said, "Why Joe, you are so romantic, how could I ever turn down such an irresistible offer?" Ruth rolled her eyes, kissed them both goodbye and shoved them out the door. As they were walking down the freshly shoveled sidewalk, Joe felt a snowball hit him squarely in the back. As he whirled around he saw Ruth standing in the doorway grinning from ear to ear. "You missed some," came the sarcastic reply from Ruth as she pointed to the remnants of the snowball that was on the walk. Joe flashed a smile and started running toward the door. Ruth shrieked and closed the door just as Joe got there. However, she didn't get it locked in time and Joe playfully fought his way in. Mary was laughing uncontrollably as Joe picked Ruth up in his arms and carried her out the door as she kicked and screamed in fake terror.

Just then Eve came out of the house and saw what was going on. She swiftly walked to the curb and yelled, "Joseph Goldstein, you put Ruth down right this second!" Joe looked fiendishly at Mary who knew immediately what was on his mind. She gave him a slight nod of approval and Joe said, "Yes ma'am!" and dropped Ruth right in the middle of a pile of snow! Eve's mouth dropped open in disbelief. Ruth wallowed in the snow pile until she could position herself to stand up. Mary was laughing so hard that tears came to her eyes. Joe just stood there grinning first at his mother and then at the snow covered Ruth. It was in her hair, down the back of her blouse, and in her house shoes. Ruth stood there in shock for what seemed like an eternity. But then slowly a grin came to her face. By then, Eve had crossed the street and was making a bee-line to Joe. Just as she arrived to scold him, Ruth busted out laughing. Eve didn't know how to react. She wasn't sure if she should laugh with everyone else or make some attempt to show some sort of disapproval to Joe. As she was sorting out her dilemma, the answer came in the form of a snowball that whizzed by her ear and landed in the middle of Joe's chest. Eve spun around to see Mary standing behind her with a grin and a second snowball ready to be launched. "Nobody messes with my Mom," the explanation came from Mary. "Care to pick on somebody your own size?" Joe laughed and rushed at Mary in an attempt to tackle her into the snow. However, just as he got there, Mary side-stepped him in much the same fashion as a bullfighter and stuck out her foot. Joe couldn't stop his momentum in time, tripped on Mary's foot, and fell smack dab in the middle of the same snow pile from which Ruth had just crawled. All three women stood over Joe triumphantly laughing and high-fiving. Joe just laid there stunned that he had been taken down by Mary and giggling at the entire situation as well.

Eve glanced at her watch; 9:40. "Guess I'm going to be late for work, and you two better get to school." "Let's get going Joe," Mary said emphatically. "I can't wait to tell the girls how easy it is to take you down. Maybe I should go out for the football team." Joe groaned and climbed out of the snow. He knew he would be in for some major teasing once this incident got around school. Oh well, he could take it. He figured he'd have to anyway, might as well enjoy it. They climbed into the car and headed off to school as Eve and Ruth headed inside.

Mary and Joe swung into the school parking lot with five minutes to spare before the bell rang. Allen spotted them, walked up nonchalantly and asked, "How's it going?" Joe knew immediately that his best friend was referring to the events of yesterday. He and Allen had been friends for almost as long as he and Mary had been together. Allen was that one true loyal friend that he could always count on. Joe owed him an explan-ation. "You were right Allen," Joe stated in a matter-of-fact tone. "I was an idiot. But it's all good now." "No arguments here," Allen replied with a smile. Mary squeezed Joe's hand and smiled as well. Just then the bell rang and the three headed off in different directions. Joe hesitated for a moment and thought to himself while he watched Mary walk down the hall. 'I was stupid for even considering that Mary would cheat on me. I will NEVER doubt her again!'

CHAPTER SIX

The next couple of weeks went by smoothly for Mary and Joe. School was going well and both of them had been extremely busy after school. Joe had been in the gym every other day after class working out with the baseball team getting ready for the spring season. On his off days, he would work with his dad and help out on the carpenter crew for a few hours. Joe enjoyed the diversion of working with his hands alongside his dad and was a natural at finished carpentry. Abraham appreciated the help and Joe appreciated the extra cash he earned working for his dad. Mary was in full swing of preparing for the February 4th through the 6th 'Teens for Abstinence' rally in Salt Lake City. She spent many hours preparing speeches and coordinating with Karen and Gary regarding the activities, press releases, meals, housing, transportation, etc. Mary hadn't realized how big of an operation this was turning out to be. The preliminary response from the high schools in Salt Lake City indicated that there could be well over 500 kids at the rally.

One particular evening a few days before Mary was scheduled to fly out to Salt Lake City for the rally, Joe was at her house helping her work on her opening speech. As they reviewed it, she decided to call Gary and get his input. Joe thought that was a great idea because he needed a break. He headed for the kitchen just as Ruth was finishing cleaning up after dinner. Joe opened the door to the frig and Ruth teased, "Joe, how can you be hungry? We just finished eating." Jacob was in the living room and overheard the conversation. "Leave the boy alone Ruthy, he must still be growing."

He yelled with fake annoyance. Joe grinned at Ruth and grabbed the chocolate cake.

Joe plopped down on the couch next to Jacob and began discussing the basketball game that was being reviewed by the sportscaster on TV. He could overhear bits and pieces of Mary's conversation with Gary in the other room. At one point he heard her giggle, "Gary, you're so bad, I couldn't say that in my speech!" There was further laughter and giggling before Mary hung up with a "see you this weekend" at the end.

Mary walked into the room smiling and Joe asked her about Gary's thoughts on her speech. Mary replied that Gary had some good input and that she was going to make minor changes at his suggestions. "What was that you said to him about something you couldn't put into the speech?" Joe inquired innocently. Mary laughed and turned a little red. "He was just teasing me about inviting everyone to a toga party after the session on Friday," Mary replied. "TOGA PARTY?" Jacob bellowed. "What kind of organization is this!?" "Relax daddy. There's no toga party. Gary was just teasing about how cute Karen and I would look in a toga and he got carried away. It is just harmless fun."

Jacob glanced at Joe who had set the cake down and was staring at the TV. He could tell that Joe didn't like the fact that Gary was flirting with Mary. In fact, Jacob didn't like it either. He didn't know anything about this California boy whom his daughter had been talking about so much lately. All he had seen was a picture of a tall, good-looking tan boy that Mary had taken when they had been in Washington; that picture and the one from the newspaper that no one discussed—EVER. Jacob didn't like this Gary guy but decided to keep his opinion to himself. Besides, he was sure that he was being overprotective of his little girl. He dismissed the notion and joined Joe in watching TV.

Joe sat there in silence and faked apathy about Mary's conversation with Gary. Inside, he was boiling. But he couldn't figure out why. It isn't the first time that some random guy had flirted with Mary. After all, look at her, she's gorgeous! In fact, it happened all the time and Joe always felt a little complimented by it. After all, she was HIS girlfriend. You wouldn't want other guys looking at her saying things like, "Oh man! There's a double bagger," or "Wow, look at that two-legged dog!" But this was different. Gary had gotten under his skin for some reason. Maybe it was because he really didn't know him. Maybe it was how Mary seemed a little infatuated with him. Or maybe it was all that junk that was in that tabloid. As he sat there stewing about all of this, he came to his senses when he heard Mary say, "Joe, penny for your thoughts?" "Huh?" was all he could say as he came back to reality. "I asked you if you would mind taking a look at the revisions to my speech. Is something bothering you?" "No nothing, I was just day-dreaming about baseball practice today. I can't seem to get my curve to break sharp enough. I'll be glad to look at it," he said as he reached for the papers. Jacob caught Joe's glanced and smiled at him. "Nice save." Jacob snickered. Joe turned red and looked up at Mary. She looked quizzically at both of them and shrugged it off. "Must be a guy thing," she muttered and handed the speech to Joe.

Joe read the speech over for seemed like the one hundredth time and had no suggestions to make. As he handed the draft back to Mary the clock in the hallway struck 9 p.m. Joe looked alarmed and checked his watch to see if the time was correct. "Boy, time flies when you're having fun. I've got to get home and study for that calculus test tomorrow. Thanks for dinner, see you all tomorrow!" There was a test tomorrow, but Joe didn't really need to study for it. He had already put in the time after practice and Mary knew it. She sensed something was wrong with Joe and followed him out of the living room to the front door. Joe slipped on his letter jacket and started to open the door. He had pretended to not notice that Mary was right behind him and acted startled when she put her hand on his arm. "No kiss good night?" was the innocent yet inquiring question that she whispered. "Sorry," Joe said and he gave her a quick peck on the cheek and started out the door. Mary grabbed him by the coat and whirled him around with surprising strength and looked into his eyes for what seemed like eternity to Joe before she said, "Joe, what's wrong?" "I don't want to talk about it, I am being really stupid and it embarrasses me to even feel it." Joe muttered. "Even more than the time daddy caught us making out in the driveway last year?" Mary stated in an impish tone. Joe grinned, turned red, and looked at his shoes. "It's just that this Gary dude gets under my skin. I don't know why. He's just another guy on a long list who flirts with you. I just don't like him and I have never even met him. I know it is stupid, but I just can't help it." Joe slowly raised his eyes from his shoes and caught Mary grinning at him. "Joseph Goldstein! You're jealous!" She almost seemed happy about it. "I can't believe it!" She said as she began laughing. "I never thought I'd see the day when you would be jealous over another guy! It's kind of flattering. But I don't want you to feel that way. You have nothing to worry about. I hope you know that. We just work together on this project." "I know," Joe grumbled. "It's just that he seems so charming, and you, your friends, and even Karen go on and on about how good-looking and nice he is. That tan and the whole surfer dude image just gets me." Mary rolled her eyes and snuggled up to Joe. The laughing had stopped and Joe had finally gotten it off his chest. "I know you would never do anything like that Mary. I realize that I'm being stupid about all of this, sorry." Joe said with all the sincerity in his heart. Mary smiled and gazed into his eyes. Joe bent down and kissed her deeply. He then whispered in her ear, "I just love you more than life. You are my reason for being. I couldn't stand to be without you." Mary opened her eyes and said, "Now THAT was a kiss good night. If you keep on doing that, you'll have no worries." "You've got a deal!" Joe replied as he flashed his pearly whites and took off down the sidewalk. Just then a snowball hit him in the back. He whirled around to see Mary standing there smiling at him. "Oh by the way, I love you too," she said in a matter-of-fact tone. "Funny way of showing it," he said as he bent down to pick up a snow ball himself. Mary shrieked and scurried into the house and shut the door just as the snowball hit it. Joe strutted down the sidewalk, grinning all the way home.

CHAPTER SEVEN

As the plane backed out of the space at the terminal and turned to head for the runway, Mary looked out of the window at the people milling around the main portion of the terminal. She took a double take when she saw Joe and a few strangers holding up a banner that said, "Good luck Mary, we love you!" She immediately recognized the handwriting as her mother's. Joe was waving wildly and the strangers had astonished smiles on their faces. Mary turned as red as a beet and sheepishly waved back. She watched until the plane turned the corner and she could no longer see Joe or his newfound friends.

Just then the pilot announced over the intercom, "Ladies and gentlemen, we are fifth in line for take off, please raise your seats forward…." Mary quickly tuned the rest of the announcement out as she had heard it several times throughout her life. She suddenly came back to reality when the flight attendant whisked by on the way to her seat. Mary caught the eye of the lady sitting next to her as she turned away from the window. Mary felt a strange kind of warmth as she peaked into the lady's eyes. It was as if she had met this person before but Mary just couldn't place it. Notwithstanding, there was something very special about this lady. Mary was drawn to this person for some reason which was unusual for her. She was, by nature, very shy around people she didn't know well. "You must be Mary," the lady broke into her trance and said with a smile. Mary looked at her quizzically and the lady said, "You know, Mary, on the banner that the cute boy was holding up in the window?" Mary turned red again and nodded. "Boyfriend?" was the one word question from the lady. "Yes he is." Mary said with a smile. "Seems like a keeper to me, cute and nice. You're lucky I'm not twenty years younger. You would have competition!" The lady laughed confidently. Just then the plane lurched forward as the pilot took off under full power.

As the plane leveled off, Mary reached for her backpack to retrieve her opening speech. She wanted to review it again before the plane landed because she knew she wouldn't have time once they hit the ground. The lady next to her had pulled out a laptop and was waiting for it to boot up. Mary observed that she was probably around 40 years old, nicely dressed in a business suit and was attractive. The lady glanced over at Mary and observed the title of Mary's speech. "Abstinence Is Cool" was written across the top of the outline. "Abstinence from what?" the question rang in Mary's ears as she looked up to see the lady's questioning eyes. "Sex, no sex, no way, until you get married—period," Mary replied. "Interesting topic. Taking a speech class?" "No, I'm giving a presentation in Salt Lake City tonight; I hope the weather at the airport holds off until we land. I heard that the weather forecast is predicting a foot of snow tonight." Mary stated. Just then the lady's computer booted up and Mary saw Witz's Drugs pop up as an icon on her computer.

Mary just stared at the screen. A million thoughts ran through her mind. How could this lady know about her dad's store? She glanced up at the lady with a quizzical look and was greeted with a smile. Mary looked away and nervously began to mumble an apology for being nosey but was interrupted by the lady who said, "I'm a pharmaceutical rep and Witz's drugstore used to be one of my best customers. Have you ever been there?" Mary grinned and said, "I've been there a time or two, my dad owns the store!" "Your dad is Jake Reubenowitz? I've known him and Ruth ever since they opened the store! I thought I recognized you from somewhere. You are little Mary? I guess it's been awhile since I've seen you. I remember you and this little boy running up and down the aisles chasing each other. You two sure kept the customers in stitches. I guess I haven't seen you or your parents for a few years. It sure is a small world. How are your parents?" "They are doing great. The store keeps them busy and we all have had a great year. Joe and I are planning to attend Harvard next year." "Joe? Was Joe the cute boy with the sign back at the airport?" "That's right," Mary proudly replied. "In fact, Joe was the little boy that you saw chasing me in the store when we were little. I've known him all of my life. In fact, his dad built our store." "No kidding! I guess Pleasantville is a small town. It has been so long since I have been there. I wish I could see your folks again. Miss Ruth always insisted that I take a candy bar 'to keep Big Jake from eating it'. In fact I distinctly remember this one instance where I was in a hurry and left the store before selecting a treat. I hadn't gotten down the street more than twenty yards when this little girl came running after me with a candy bar in her hand. "Mommy said that you forgot your candy" you told me as you tugged on my coat. You were as cute then as you are now. I can't believe how time flies." Both Mary and the lady laughed at the coincidence. Both of them took the laugh as an opportunity to return to their work.

After a few minutes Mary looked at the lady and asked, "I'm sorry I don't even know your name." The lady hit the save button on her laptop and smiled at Mary. "My name is Gabriella White, but everyone calls me Gabby because I love to talk. People say that I have the gift of communication. Sometimes my boss tells me that "my gift" is the reason he hired me. He says that using your gifts and talents keep a person sharp and on track. He also says that if you don't use them your skills diminish and you can become lazy and even get off track from your life's purpose. That happened to me once and he had to call me in from the field and spend some time getting my head straight at home. It was the best time I ever spent. I emerged refreshed and ready to take on the world. Has anything like that ever happened to you Mary?"

Mary tilted her head and gazed off into space at nothing in particular as she contemplated the question. "I guess I haven't ever had any experience similar to yours. It does sometimes seem as if there must be something more that I am supposed to do. Don't get me wrong, I have a very fulfilling life and I have been blessed with good health, great friends, a wonderful family and of course there's Joe." "Of course," the smile of approval from Gabby indicated that she thought Joe was a good guy. "But," Mary continued, "I just get the feeling that I have this...this." Her words trailed off and Gabby finished her sentence, "calling?" "Yes, that's it, a calling. You know, something I am supposed to be a part of; something I need to do that will require a great deal of effort on my part."

"Do you think it might be the Harvard thing or maybe 'Teens for Abstinence'?" Gabby asked. "Maybe, but I don't think so." Mary replied. "You would think so, after all, it is a huge responsibility and I am honored to have been selected, but there is this gnawing feeling I get sometimes; maybe I am crazy. I can't believe I'm discussing this with a total stranger. You probably think I'm a mental case."

"Not at all," Gabby assured her. "You see, everyone has a calling. Most folks are just too frightened, insecure or shallow to attempt to seek it out and accomplish it. This life is more than just muddling through it attempting to seek out self-centered passing pleasures. The majority of people just don't get it. However, Mary, I believe that you do." Gabby reached out and took Mary's hand. As she touched it, Mary felt a warmth shoot through her body like she had never felt before. It startled her for just a moment but then she felt a serenity wash over her as if she had slept on a cloud. Mary looked deep into Gabby's eyes and saw kindness and love. She didn't want the moment to end. She couldn't remember ever feeling this good. As she sat there in a trance, Gabby broke the silence. "Mary, I think you get it. I truly believe that you are special. You are in store for something wonderful. You are destined for a task. I just know it. Be patient and wait on God. Seek the Kingdom and God will show you what you are to do."

The moment was interrupted by the pilot over the intercom. "Ladies and gentlemen, we will be landing in approximately ten minutes, please turn off all electrical devices...." Gabby removed her hand from Mary's and said, "I guess we're here." With that she began to shut down her computer and put her stuff away in preparation for landing. Mary followed suit but couldn't help but notice that the warm feeling had left her. She fought the urge to grab Gabby's hand to retrieve the feeling once again but thought better of the idea and restrained herself. She was strangely drawn to Gabby but couldn't exactly figure out why. After a few seconds she dismissed the thought as being anxious for a mother figure to rely on for the weekend's activities in Salt Lake City.

The plane landed without incident and in a few minutes it came to a stop at the terminal. The passengers began collecting their belongings and Gabby stood up to get her travel bag from the overhead compartment. Mary sat there next to the window watching the activity on the runway. As she turned to say goodbye, Gabby was holding out a business card in Mary's direction. "I would love to hear from you sometime. If you ever want to chat, you know old Gabby would love to 'yak' at you!" Mary grabbed the card and stuffed it into her purse alongside her plane ticket and claim checks. She stood up and gave Gabby a hug and said, "I can't tell you how much I have enjoyed talking to you. Don't give me this card unless you mean it because I will call you. I promise." "Please do." Gabby replied. "I love to talk!"

It was their turn to disembark the plane. "Got any luggage?" Mary asked hopefully as they walked down the terminal. "No, I always travel light so I can make a quick get-away." Mary laughed as she stopped at the escalator down to baggage claim. "Good luck with your conference this weekend," Gabby said with a big smile. "I know you'll do great." They hugged again and Gabby turned to walk away. Mary turned toward the escalator and then looked up to catch a glimpse of Gabby but she had disappeared into the crowd. Mary headed for baggage claim.

CHAPTER EIGHT

Mary stood at the luggage claim watching the bags pass her by. She was trying to focus on the events coming up this weekend but her mind kept going back to Gabby. She had never really met anyone like her. Mary couldn't believe that she had opened up so much to a total stranger. That was totally out of character for her. Gabby was such a warm-hearted, gentle-natured individual; and that feeling Mary got when Gabby touched her was amazing but also kind of weird.

Standing there in a daydream, Mary lost track of where she was and what she was supposed to be doing. All of a sudden a man's voice behind her asked, "Excuse me miss, is this your bag?" Mary was so startled that she dropped the envelope with her plane ticket, claim check and other travel papers. When the envelope hit the floor, the papers flew everywhere. Mary whirled around to see a grinning Gary and Karen holding her bag.

Their grins quickly turned into embarrassed looks as they realized how much they had startled Mary. "I'm so sorry!" Gary exclaimed. "I didn't intend to scare you. We saw you from the other side of the carousel and grabbed your bag when we spotted it. I'm really sorry." Karen was already on the floor picking up the papers and stuffing them into the envelope. "Don't worry about it." Mary laughed as she collected her composure. "I was off in outer space and forgot where I was or what I was doing. I just didn't see it coming." Karen was on her feet and reviewing the papers that she had collected. "Plane tickets, claim check, hotel reservation, itinerary, anything else?" she asked in an apologetic voice. "No, that just about covers it, thanks Karen." "It's the least I can do; after all, I was the one who made you drop them in the first place." All three of them laughed as a tension reliever. "Now, how about a proper greeting?" Mary asked as she held out her arms to her new friends. The three of them came together in a group hug.

As the three of them stood there chatting and exchanging pleasantries about family and school Gary suddenly looked at his watch and said, "Wow, it's 5:45 and our conference starts at 8:00. We had better get going." They headed out of the terminal and Karen flagged a cab. "Where to?" the cab driver asked. Karen whipped out a piece of paper with the address including directions to the hotel. "I know how to get there," the driver growled. "Be there in about 45 minutes." "Good," Karen replied ignoring the driver's annoyed attitude. "We can check in, have a quick bite to eat and head over to the conference."

The driver took off and the kids immediately could see that it had been snowing and that the accumulation had already mounted to approximately six inches. Gary being from Southern California wasn't used to seeing this kind of snow and had his nose glued to the window. "What's the forecast?" Mary quizzed the driver. "Snow, snow, and then snow; up to 12 inches by Sunday; after all, this is Salt Lake City in February." The kids looked around and could each read the mind of the other. 'Are we going to be able to get home?' Mary decided to break the silence. "I hope this doesn't hurt attendance at the conference. Some kids are traveling a long way to get here." "Naw," the driver interjected, "we're used to it around here. The roads will be clear quicker than you can say snowman. You know Salt Lake City claims to be able to remove more snow than any other major city in the Northwest."

The driver continued into a long boring monologue about how great the town was and how other cities were trying to copy them. A glaze fell over the kids and they rolled their eyes at each other as the brag fest continued. Just then the traffic began to slow and then came to a stop. "Must be a wreck," the driver stated with authority. "Probably one of those out-of-towners coming in for the conference. They ain't used to driving on the snow around here." They sat there for 15 minutes. Karen could see that traffic was backed up as far as the eye could see. See looked at her cell phone; 6:30, plenty of time if we get going soon she thought. "How far to the hotel?" she asked. "'Bout 30 minutes on good roads, probably about 40 minutes in these conditions." The driver stated without emotion. 'Good, Karen thought to herself. We can get there, check in, freshen up, and head over to the conference. Thank goodness it was at the hotel.' Karen looked at Gary and could tell that he was doing the math himself.

"We're not going to have time to eat!" He realized suddenly. "I'm starving!" "Relax Gary," Karen said calmingly. "I'm way ahead of you. Here eat this." She pulled a granola bar from her backpack and handed it over Mary to Gary. "I think I'm in love. Will you marry me?" Gary quipped playfully. "How can you be so organized?" "It's my job to look after you two. I always come prepared." Karen blushed. Mary had been reviewing her speech and had tuned out the chatting in the cab. However, when Karen handed the granola to Gary she snapped back into real time. "Huh? What? Did someone say my name? I'm sorry I didn't hear you." Gary gave Karen a wink and she took the hint. "Gary just proposed to me? Want to be a bridesmaid?" "What???" was all that Mary could say. After all, they had only been together one time. Gary and Karen cracked up and the driver looked at Mary in the rear view mirror and shook his head in disbelief. Mary smiled and then laughed along with the rest of the car.

Upon arrival, bellhops swarmed over them, grabbed their bags, and led them into the hotel. "Wow, this is a nice place," Mary exclaimed as they entered the lobby. "Nothing but the best for you and my fiancée," Karen said nonchalantly while glancing up at the clock in the lobby; 7:10. "We have 50 minutes before the conference starts. I have to meet the press in 35 minutes and I need for you two to be in the conference room by 7:45. Gary, make sure that Mary has everything she needs including a bottle of water on the podium. Also, please do a sound check on the mike before we get started. I want to make sure everything goes right. This is our first conference with other kids and it has to go well. I suggest we get to our rooms, freshen up and get back down here ASAP. Gary, if you have time, check with the hotel manager and make sure the band is here and ready to go." "Band? What band?" Gary faked amnesia. "I can't think straight on an empty stomach." Karen unzipped her backpack, pulled out a package of peanut butter crackers, and tossed them in Gary's direction. He caught them with one hand and said, "Now I'm sure I want to marry you; what, no soda?!!" "Don't push it." Karen said sternly as she poked him playfully in the chest. "Keep it up and you'll be spending the honeymoon on the couch with a fat lip, now get moving!" Gary and Mary obediently headed for the elevators and the bellhops met them with keys and bags to their rooms.

Ten minutes later, Mary met Gary at the elevator doors. Mary fumbled through her speech in the elevator and took a last look in the elevator mirror to check her makeup. "You look great, relax. You're going to do fine," Gary assured her. "Thanks, that means a lot. I'm just so nervous." Just then the doors opened and there was Karen talking to a bunch of reporters. She caught their eye and motioned for them in the direction of the conference center.

George, the hotel manager, escorted Mary backstage and grabbed a stack of papers that were sitting on a chair. "Here is the itinerary for the night. The band is scheduled to perform for about 30 minutes. We have allotted 15 minutes for your speech. I hope that's enough. That will be followed up with another 45 minutes from the band. I need you or Gary to introduce the band. Most of the kids that are coming will be staying here but approximately one third of them are locals and will be commuting from home. We are expecting about 500 kids. You ready for this?"

Mary stood there in astonishment. She had anticipated a big production because Karen had warned her about it; however, it just began to sink in. There were lights, huge banners, and speakers for the band that were as big as a car if you turned it on its side. Before she could reply to George his walkie-talkie blurted out from under his jacket. 'George, the buses are here; OK to let the kids in?' George grabbed the walkie-talkie and hesitated as he looked to Mary. She nodded at him and he spoke to the voice on the end. "Ready or not, let 'em in." The doors opened and five hundred kids started filing in.

Mary heard Gary's voice on the sound system, "Testing, testing, 1-2-3." He got a thumbs-up from John. Gary flashed a big smile and headed straight for Mary. "Everything's ready. Man, am I excited. Do you want to introduce the band or do you want me to do it?" "Go ahead; I'm going to collect myself for a minute." "You OK, Mary? You're looking a little pale," Gary asked as he placed his hand on her shoulder. "Everything just hit me all at once. I'll get it together. It's just that we have a chance to make an impact on a lot of people tonight. I just don't want to blow it." "Mary, there's a reason that they chose you to run this show. You are great and there is no one out there that can do this like you. Besides, the future wife and I have got your back!" Gary said with a big grin. "Thanks Gary, you're the best," Mary replied as she got up and gave him a big hug. "Hold on there." A voice from the shadows called. "What are you doing hugging my man?!!" Karen came out of the shadows laughing. "We're ready to go. The band is in place waiting for an introduction and the press is in the front row. Who's introducing the band?" "I am," Gary said proudly as he headed for the curtain. All at once he stopped and turned back toward the girls. "What's the name of the band again? My blood sugar is so low that I can't remember." "GET OUT THERE!" Karen almost yelled at him as she threw a pencil at him. He caught it in mid-air and flashed his California smile at the girls and threw open the curtain as the crowd began the first applause of the evening.

As Mary's thoughts bounced from fear to questions and back again, she heard the band start to play. Oh boy, 30 minutes until she had to get up in front of 500 of her peers. She began to worry about what they would think. Would they think that the whole concept was corny and old-fashioned? Would they boo her? Laugh at her? After all, most teens were sexually active. Even in her little hometown, over 60% of the seniors admitted to having had sex. Teenage pregnancies are not uncommon and no longer considered taboo. She was having serious doubts about this whole thing. What had she gotten herself into? She was about to become a laughing stock and would go home totally embarrassed!

Tears began to run down her face as she wallowed in her thoughts. She glanced at her watch. The band had been playing for 20 minutes. She was up in ten more minutes. Suddenly, Mary felt the urge to pray. She folded her notes and bowed her head. 'Lord, you know my thoughts and my fears. You know I don't understand what is going on but I do know that You are in control and that You have placed me in this situation for a reason. I'm not sure what to expect but I commit this evening to You. Please give me the correct words to speak to these kids. I believe in abstinence until marriage because that is Your absolute law. Please help me to become Your instrument in distributing that message, Amen.' Mary didn't open her eyes and although she could still hear the band playing in the background, it wasn't distracting to her. A sense of peace and contentment washed over her like a cool breeze on a hot summer day. She could sense a presence near her. She hadn't felt anything like it before. It was as if some sort of protective shield was surrounding her. The fear melted away. Confidence flooded her inner being as if to make her feel like she could do anything. Her thoughts returned home. The time her mom nursed her through the measles and when her dad taught her how to drive a car all came back to her. She smiled when she remembered when Joe had shown her how to build a birdhouse. Her thoughts turned to the airplane trip. Gabby's face came to mind and her words; "You are destined for a task." Maybe this was her task. At least it was for now. All of a sudden someone walked behind Mary and lightly brushed her hair on the back of her neck. Mary broke out of her trance and turned to see who it was. There was no one in sight. There wasn't even any air moving. 'That's weird' Mary said to herself. 'I know something touched me.' It was too big to have been a bug and she would have heard wings flapping if somehow a bird had gotten into the building.

Her thoughts were interrupted by the sound of Gary's voice over the sound system. "Isn't the band great? They are going to take a short break while we hear from our main speaker for the night. She is here to speak to us about a very serious problem that is affecting families all over the country. This girl is a senior at Pleasantville High School in Pleasantville, Montana. She is captain of the cheer squad, has a 3.98 GPA, is headed to Harvard this fall, and is just about the sweetest girl you would ever want to meet. Oh yeah, and guys, she's HOT! Give it up for Mary Reubenowitz!"

As the kids began to sit down she prayed, "Father, HELP!" Mary opened her eyes and her confidence returned. She felt the same swish against her hair and the back of her neck. She quickly looked back but no one was there. 'Must have been the AC,' she thought. She turned back around and began to address the audience.

"I can't tell you how happy I am to be in Salt Lake City. I have never seen such beautiful mountains and this town is great. Everyone here is so friendly. You need to know that the activities of this weekend are a team effort. There are many volunteers here locally who have helped organize transportation and lodging arrangements.

In addition, the hotel staff has been extremely helpful in making sure that we have everything we need. Finally, there are two very special people without whom this event would never have come to fruition. You have already met one of them, Gary our MC. The other is Karen, who is the mastermind behind everything. Would you all show your appreciation to them? Gary, Karen, come out here please." After the applause died down and Gary and Karen walked offstage, Mary continued. "I want to thank you all for coming here this weekend. It means a lot to me that there are so many of my peers who are opened-minded enough to listen to our thoughts on the very serious subject of pre-marital sex. The rate of sexual activity among teenagers is at an all-time high. More kids are having sex than not. It has become the norm and is expected by the third date by both boys and girls! Teenage pregnancies have stabilized because our society has made it so easy to access birth control and provide government-funded abortions. However, STDs are climbing at an alarming rate. May I have the first slide, please?"

Slide one was a chart of statistics backing up the information that Mary had just stated. Percentages of sexually active teenagers, number of abortions annually, amount of money spent on birth control for teens, percentage increases in STDs, the number of single unwed mothers and their high school dropout rates were among the full page of startling statistics. Mary moved onto the rest of the slides. These slides were pictures of aborted babies, teens with AIDS, other STDs, and pictures of girls before they became pregnant and after they had either had the baby or had an abortion. The pictures seemed to hit home with the kids. There was total silence in the room except for the sound of Mary's voice.

"This is just the tip of the iceberg," Mary stated in a concerned tone. "There are numerous stories out there that cross all racial, economic, and intelligence lines. Everyone is affected. Not only are the kids directly involved, but their families as well. We are in a crisis mode regarding this issue. It is up to us to make changes." Mary's voice began to resonate and become louder. "When did immorality become acceptable? When did selfishness replace self-control? Why aren't people accountable for their actions? When did lustful desires give way to pride and integrity? When did sex become the only way to have fun? Let's show this town that we know how to have fun without having sex! Let's show them how to party! Anybody ready to hear more from the band?"

By now the kids were on their feet screaming and cheering. Mary had whipped the crowd into a frenzy. Her speech had hit just the right chord with the kids. It seemed as if it was something that the kids had longed to hear from a role model. The kind of direction that everyone wants to pursue, but no one has the courage to be the first. The band ran back out on the stage to the roar and appreciation of the crowd. The rumble of the drums, followed by the squeal of the guitar and the melody of the keyboards sent shockwaves through the building. Mary slipped off the stage into a waiting group hug with Karen and Gary. "Homerun!" Gary shouted and Karen whispered, "Great job," in Mary's ear. By now a spontaneous dance party had broken out in the crowd. "Care to practice what we preach about this fun stuff Karen?" Gary smiled at her. "What do you mean?" Karen quizzed. "Let's dance!" "Here?" "No, down there with the other kids, come on!" "Only if Mary goes too," Karen replied. "Have it your way," Gary flashed his biggest smile. He grabbed both girls by the hand and pulled them down the stairs. Mary resisted at first but then felt compelled to follow suit as the crowd caught wind of what was going on and began to encourage Gary. He pulled them into the middle of the crowd where they began dancing first in groups and then with a number of different partners. All kinds of guys were coming up to Karen and Mary and cutting in on each other; and Gary was having the time of his life dancing and living it up with all the girls in the room. Unbeknownst to Mary, Gary and Karen, the reporters in the room were moving around among the kids taking pictures of the more than willing teenagers who wanted to see their picture in tomorrow's paper. Everyone was having a ball.

Mary's mind wandered back to school dances when she and Joe would dance with anyone that asked. They were never jealous and never wanted to hurt anyone's feelings by turning them down. Besides, they had made some great friends with kids in school that they hadn't previously known that well by dancing with them. She wished that Joe was there and for a brief moment flirted with some homesickness. She quickly forgot about that when a nice-looking boy came up to her and said, "Hi I'm Brad, wanna dance?" "Sure," she smiled which caused him to blush as they began moving to the music. Mary was practically worn out when the song finished. Brad looked her in the eye and said, "I need to talk to you sometime this weekend. Do you think you could carve out a few minutes for me?" Mary wasn't ready for this. She wasn't sure if he was some sort of stalker or if he needed to talk about some personal issue. She looked deeply in his eyes and saw sadness. She smiled, which made him blush again, and said, "Find me after lunch tomorrow. We are planning some activities in the sports complex to get a little exercise after the morning session." "Thanks, I'll see you tomorrow." Before she knew it, Brad had grabbed her and was giving her a big bear hug. As Brad put her down, Mary heard Gary's voice over the sound system. "That's just about it for the evening. Let's thank the band. If we're loud enough, maybe they will come back tomorrow!" The crowd went wild with cheers and applause as the band left the stage. Karen and Mary made their way back up to the stage as Gary was saying, "We'll see you all tomorrow at 8 a.m. for breakfast and the first session at 9:00. Boys will be in the Garden Room and girls will be in the Ballroom. Be careful going home. Good night!" Gary, Mary, and Karen waved as they walked off the stage.

George met them as they left the stage. "The band is already in the lobby greeting the kids as they leave. It might be nice if you three to go out there as well." "Good idea," Karen echoed and grabbed Gary and Mary by the hand and started for the stage door. "Wait a minute," Mary hesitated and dug in her heels. "Where are the reporters? I don't want to get into another mess like last time. If the jerk from that tabloid is here, I think I might be tempted to slug him." Gary and Karen knew what she was talking about. Mary had talked to both of them after her fight with Joe over the article that accused Mary of being with Gary. "Relax," Karen soothed. "I've scheduled a press conference for tomorrow night after the closing concert. That's when you'll see the press." "I'm not sure I know what you all are talking about," George interjected, "But I've seen enough of these events to tell you that the press is everywhere. The formal press conference is tomorrow, but you can bet your buttons that they are hanging around in the lobby. It goes with the territory. Didn't you all notice them taking your pictures during Mary's speech and especially when you all headed out into the crowd? The flashes were going off constantly." "I told them in the lobby before the band started to come back tomorrow night. Karen asserted. "I can't believe they stuck around anyway." George looked at the three bewildered teenagers and rolled his eyes. "Imagine that, reporters not listening to a teenager. Why, they don't even listen to the president! Look, tell you what. I'll go in there and clear them out of the lobby. That way, you all can do your thing with the kids without being interrupted, OK?" "Thank you," they said in unison. George wheeled around and headed for the door. "Give me five minutes; I know how to handle these guys."

Mary followed Gary and Karen into the lobby. Her eyes swept the room looking for reporters. No sign of them. Just then George walked up to her and said, "Relax, they are all outside, see?" He pointed to the glass revolving door and Mary could see at least a dozen of them looking in at her. "Thanks, George, you're a lifesaver." Mary smiled at him. "Don't mention it. I understand completely. However, you need to get used to these guys. You are in a high pro-file position and they want to sell their newspapers. I held them off tonight, but they will find you. After all, you have met the president. Not many people can say that." "I know," Mary replied.

Just then, Mary caught a glimpse of a man with his back to her. He was standing in the corner talking to the boy who had asked her if he could talk to her sometime. She couldn't remember his name but he seemed nervous and kept looking away from the man. Mary assumed it was his dad and the boy was embarrassed to have his dad in such a setting. After all, most teens don't want to be seen in public with their parents. However, as the man turned to leave she recognized him in an instant. It was that jerk from the tabloid! The man started for another kid in the lobby and Mary started toward him. She was going to give him a piece of her mind. Just as she got within five feet of him she felt a strong hand grab her arm. It was Gary. "Don't do it," he said. "We can't afford a scene now, we've come too far." By now George had caught sight of what was going on and headed for the reporter. "I told you all to get out of here," he said sternly as he walked quickly toward the slime ball. "Sorry, I must have been in the bathroom," he sneered as he headed for the door. Gary was holding Mary back as she stared a hole in the reporter. He looked at Mary as he continued walking and said in a sarcastic tone, "I see you two are still together; is your boyfriend back home OK with that?" George reached him at that same moment and ushered him quite forcefully to the door.

CHAPTER NINE

Mary awoke to the sound of the telephone; the clock read 6:30. She had been sure that she had left a wake-up call for 7:00. No matter, the phone was ringing. She reached for it clumsily and finally got it to her ear. "Hello?" No answer. Then the phone rang again. She smiled to herself as she realized that it was her cell going off. She grabbed it from the nightstand and saw that it was Joe. "Hi!" she answered in the perkiest voice she could muster at 6:30 in the morning. "Hi Mary, you OK? I was worried last night when you didn't call." "I'm fine Joe. Sorry I didn't call. Everything was so crazy and busy. By the time we got back to our rooms, I figured you would have been in bed and didn't want to wake you like you did me this morning," she giggled into the receiver. "Oh no," the voice on the other end lamented. "I didn't mean to wake you, I'm sorry. So, since you're already up, how did it go?" "It was fantastic! There were over 500 kids at the rally and everyone says that my speech went well. I think we are going to have a great day today." "How's Gary and Karen?" Joe asked in his most innocent voice. Mary knew Joe well enough to realize what he was asking. "Joe, it's fine. We just worked on the project together. Gary AND Karen are just fine and we are JUST friends." "OK, just checking. You can't blame me, after all, you are the prettiest girl in the world and I wouldn't blame him if he made a move. I would if I were him." "Aw Joe, you know I love you, and only you." She then proceeded to tell him all about the band, the snow, and even the incident regarding the reporter in the lobby. They continued chatting until the hotel phone rang.

"Hang on Joe, that's the real wake-up call," she laughed. Joe could hear what was being said in that background. "Hello?" "This is your wake-up call, time to get up and party! I'm starved again, see you downstairs for breakfast." "Gary? Is that you?" Mary questioned the familiar voice. "Yep, I told the front desk I would call you. How's that for being a nice guy?!" "Thanks Gary, quite a surprise, but thanks. I'll see you at breakfast." Mary hung up the hotel phone and spoke into the cell, "Joe? You still there?" "Yep. I heard, you have to go meet Gary for breakfast. Sure was nice of him to wake you up," Joe said sarcastically. "Hope you two have fun." "Joe, don't be like that. That isn't the way it sounds." "Whatever you say," Joe dismissed the discussion. "I'll let you go; can you call me tonight?" "Sure will," Mary said in her sweetest voice. "I love you." "Love you too," came the somber reply and the phone went dead.

Joe stared at the phone for a minute as he replayed the conversation between Mary and Gary over and over in his head. What was it about this guy that bugged him so much? He hadn't even met Gary and already didn't like him. That was not Joe's normal approach to people. He usually liked people for no other reason than the fact that they were God's creation. It took a lot for Joe to dislike someone. If he chose to dislike every guy who had a crush or hit on Mary, he would most likely hate every guy who had ever met her. Most of the time he would take it as a compliment that someone so hot would choose him. He never felt threatened by another guy; and this guy, Gary, hadn't even hit on Mary! What was his problem? However, Joe just couldn't shake this gnawing feeling in his stomach. There was something about this Gary guy that didn't sit well with Joe.

Just then his cell phone rang; it was Allen. "Hey Allen, what's up?" "Hi Joe, a bunch of us are headed to the park to go sledding. You never know when it's going to melt and we won't get another chance to go this year. Do you want to go?" "No thanks Allen, I really don't feel like it today." "Great!" Allen persisted, "I'll be over to pick you up in 30 minutes." "But Allen, I don't want to go!" Joe protested. "What?" Allen said. "You're breaking up a little; something about breakfast. You've got plenty of time to eat. See you in a half hour." Joe continued protesting into the phone until he realized it was dead. He chuckled to himself as he closed his phone.

Allen wasn't going to take no for an answer. He knew Joe would be moping around this weekend. Allen had probably organized the whole thing so that Joe would have something to do today. Joe had been busy playing in the basketball game last night. Joe had a great game; 25 points, 12 rebounds, and ten assists; a triple double. But when Allen had asked Joe to go to Cindy's after the game, Joe declined and went straight home. Cindy's was the local hangout for the kids in Pleasantville. Everyone went there after games to celebrate. Joe didn't feel much like celebrating if Mary wasn't there. He had taken a little teasing about being whipped when he had declined. Joe had just smiled and kept going toward his car. So Joe knew that Allen was trying to keep him busy. He smiled to himself, got dressed for sledding and headed downstairs to breakfast. Allen would be here in 20 minutes.

Mary hung up the phone almost half mad at Joe. It wasn't her fault that Gary had called. He was just a friend and nothing was going on. 'Oh well, I guess it means he cares about me,' she said to herself. 'No matter how ridiculous it seems to me.' She glanced at the clock on the nightstand; 7:15. She had 45 minutes to get ready. No time to worry about Joe right now; she had a big day ahead. She could fix this later with Joe. He just needed a little assurance. No big deal. She headed for the shower.

Mary walked into the restaurant about 8:15. "You had better get to the buffet," Karen interrupted. Mary glanced at her cell phone; 8:30. "Good idea," Mary agreed. She got up and headed for the buffet. She reached for a tray but before she could get it someone bumped into her from behind. Mary turned around to see who it was and was greeted with, "I'm sorry, I wasn't paying attention to where I was going." It was that guy who had asked her if she could give him a few minutes.

"Remember me?" Brad quizzed. "I'm Brad; I'm one of the guys you danced with last night. Do you still have time to talk after lunch?" "Sure," Mary replied with a smile. "I'll look for you in the lobby." She was glad that he mentioned his name. She made a note to remember it this time. "Great!" Brad said. Mary took the opportunity to quiz Brad about the reporter. "Say Brad," handing him the spoon for the eggs. "I saw you talking to that reporter before he got thrown out of the lobby last night. What was he saying to you?" The question had obviously caught Brad off-guard because he immediately started stuttering and stammering. His eyes were looking at everything in the room except Mary. "Uh nothing much; he was just asking me some questions about where I'm from, what I am doing here, you know, stuff like that." His answer didn't convince Mary that he was telling the truth. His body language said that he was holding something back. Brad changed the subject. "Pass me a biscuit, please." "No problem," she said placing one on his plate with the tongs. Mary wasn't going to let him off the hook that easy. "You know that guy is a sleazy reporter who works for one of those gossip tabloids that tells everything but the truth. He's trouble." "Is that right?" Brad tried to sound as if he wasn't concerned. "I don't read that stuff. I have enough trouble reading my homework. Well, my plate's full. I'd better get to eating. I don't want to miss Gary's session." Brad didn't wait for a reply before heading to his table.

Fifteen minutes later, Mary took her place at the podium in the front of the room as the rest of the girls came in and got settled. She knew that Gary was next door in the Garden Room doing the same thing. She had an idea of what Gary was going to say to the guys because she and Gary had talked on the phone for hours discussing their presentations. They had collected a lot of data and pictures in order to produce an effective and informative presentation. Both of their presentations were similar in nature, each were just slightly modified for the boys or for the girls. The whole point of both presentations was to drive home the fact that pre-marital sex is wrong, period. Sex is not needed in order to have fun. Rationalization that sex is OK based on modern ways of thinking is unacceptable. It was not about birth control or how to avoid getting caught. Gary and Mary had put together facts regarding the effectiveness of birth control and how none of them are 100% effective. Startling pictures of aborted children were to be shown. They had also collected information regarding sexually transmitted diseases and had included some fairly graphic and frankly disgusting pictures of people who were in some severely advanced stages of the diseases. Finally, they had included some information regarding teenage pregnancy. The data proved that the children born under such conditions had a more difficult time adjusting to life and the mother and father of the children had to alter their lives because of what happened. Promising dreams and careers were shattered when the responsibility of parenthood took precedence. It was quite an effective presentation. Mary was anxious to get started. Karen would be bouncing from room to room, checking on equipment, troubleshooting, and making sure that things ran smoothly in general. She had a big job. Suddenly, the lights dimmed and the room got quiet. Mary could hear Gary's muffled voice in the next room; he had already started. Mary looked out at her audience and said, "Welcome, I'm so glad you came this morning...."

Exactly one hour later, Mary saw Karen standing in the back of the room pointing to her wrist. That was Mary's clue that it was time for a break. Mary nodded slightly to acknowledge that she had seen the sign. She paused the Power Point slide and told the girls to stretch and get a snack in the hall. She heard Gary telling the guys something similar and she could visualize Karen in the back of his room pointing to her wrist. She started down the stage to the door to retrieve a bottle of water because her throat was dry. Several of the girls in the crowd came up to her and told her how interesting the presentation had been. Some of them had no clue about the facts that Mary had presented regarding birth control. Other girls talked about how the pressure to have sex they received from their boyfriends was unbelievable. Mary listened to the conversations going on around her and felt as if she was really making a difference. She was somewhat surprised about how little these girls knew about sex. Hadn't their mothers talked to them? She made a mental note to thank her mother when she got home.

Mary was just wrapping up the Power Point presentation and was beginning to open up the floor for questions. There was ten minutes left in the session and the second half had gone better than the first half. The girls sat in stunned silence as pictures of aborted babies and disease-riddled teens scrolled across the screen. Mary pointed to a hand raised in the middle of the room when an uproar of laughter and hooting could be heard coming from the Garden Room. Before it quieted down Karen slipped in the door and Mary thought she looked as if she had seen a ghost.

Mary wanted to ask what was wrong but thought better of it. Karen slid into a seat in the back row and Mary motioned for the girl to proceed with her question.

After the session ended, Mary stayed on the stage until the room cleared. She walked up to Karen who had her head in her hands and was crying. She sat down and put her arm around her shoulder. "What's wrong?" Karen looked up at Mary with red eyes and said, "You won't believe what happened next door. Gary was taking questions and everything seemed to be going alright when all of a sudden this jerk stood up and asked Gary what it was like to be sleeping with you! Gary handled it well and told him very nicely that you two were just friends and that there was no way he would do that with anyone. That's why he was representing this organization. Then the jerk produced a copy of that picture of you and Gary from the tabloid. He had this fiendish grin on his face and the guy next to him yelled, 'I would like to be a friend to Karen!' If I could tag that I would be king of the world! They didn't know that I was in the back of the room then someone from the back row noticed me and yelled, 'There she is! Why don't you ask her now?' That's when all the hooting and howling began and I got out of there."

Mary's jaw hit her chest as she listened to the story. She grew angrier as she sat there. She didn't know what to say to Karen. "Boys can be such jerks!" she said emphatically. Gary had slipped in behind them unnoticed. "Not all boys, he said. They looked up and saw him standing over their chairs. "I'm sorry Karen, those guys were way out of line. You OK?" "I guess so. I just can't believe that some people are so mean. I'd like to give those guys a piece of my mind." "Way ahead of you," Gary said as he walked out the door. "Don't do it!" Mary pleaded. But it was too late. Gary was already gone. By the time they caught up with Gary he had already caught up with the two losers. They couldn't hear what he was saying but he had their backs against the wall and was up in their faces yelling something. Mary could tell that a scene was developing because kids were all around them waiting for a fight to break out. Several of them had cameras and cell phones taking pictures. The two losers looked more and more scared as Gary's voice got louder. Karen and Mary were walking as fast as they could. When they got within earshot of Gary they heard him screaming, "You've got two choices, go home or apologize!" He wasn't more than two inches from their faces and screaming at the top of his lungs. There was an awkward silence for what seemed like hours. Gary stood there glaring at them seeming not to even blink. "Easy dude," the first guy almost pleaded. "Yeah man, be cool," the second one's voice cracked. "We didn't mean anything, just a little harmless locker room talk." "HARMLESS?" Gary growled. "Look at her!" he said pointing to Karen. "Does she look like she hasn't been harmed?" The boys both looked at Karen who had obviously been crying. "Sorry Karen," they both said in unison. Karen nodded and Gary backed just far enough away from the boys so that they could slide away. They slipped into the crowd like rats on a shipyard dock. Gary turned to Karen, "Feeling better?" "Yeah, thanks, you didn't have to do that." He leaned over and whispered into her ear, "Nobody talks to my fiancée that way." She looked him in the eyes and he flashed that big California smile. Suddenly, Gary yelled, "Anybody hungry? I'm starved." Cheers erupted from the crowd. Karen pointed to Gary, "He's ALWAYS hungry." The crowd headed for the restaurant.

Mary finished her lunch and headed for the sports complex. George had set up eight volleyball courts in the gym so the kids could burn off a little steam before the next session. Mary thought it would be fun to get some exercise and meet some more of the kids. As she entered the lobby on her way to the sports complex, she saw Brad sitting on one of the couches. It was a good thing that she had noticed him because she had forgotten about their meeting. She walked up to him and said, "Hey Brad, what's up?" Brad nearly jumped out of his skin. He had been lost in his thoughts and hadn't noticed Mary come up to him. "Oh, um, hi Mary; I was uh...just thinking, I mean wondering if uh...." "Sorry I startled you; I guess you were off in Brad land." Mary laughed. Brad blushed and admitted that he had been deep in thought. "Still want to talk?" Mary questioned. "Yes I do," Brad said almost embarrassed. "Have a seat." Mary sat down on the couch next to him. "I really don't know where to start. I can't believe that I am in such a mess. You see, I've made a series of poor choices and I need someone to talk to. I need help. I hate to put this on you, but I have no one else." Slow down," Mary soothed, "Why don't you start at the beginning." Mary realized that her plan to play volleyball this afternoon had just been changed. Brad seemed terribly upset and she needed to listen, and maybe even help.

"I'm a second semester freshman at the University of Utah. My girlfriend was supposed to go to school with me this year but...." "But what?" Mary interjected. "Well she got pregnant and just gave birth to our daughter one month ago. My parents disowned me and my girlfriend broke up with me and lives at home with her parents. I have spent my entire savings on my tuition and hospital bills so I have been working at a grocery store in the evenings. However, that still wasn't enough money to pay the bills. I'm paying child support and was getting desperate for money. Then I noticed a job posted on the bulletin board near one of my classes. You see, I want to major in journalism and this job was working for a newspaper. I applied for the job and that's when I met Gus. He seemed a little weird but offered to pay me $20 per hour cash if I would just help him with some photo opportunities. I really didn't know what I was getting into but the money was great. I never really understood why he needed me to help him but he said he needed a "good-looking young man" to help him with obtaining candid pictures of ordinary people for his articles." Brad paused a moment and stared at the floor. "I'm sorry you have had such a rough time," Mary said sympathetically. "I'm still not sure what you want me to do." "Wait a second, there's more. Gus called me last Thursday and asked if I could help him this weekend. He asked me if I could come to this conference and meet you. He told me that you were a celebrity and he needed some pictures of me with you for the article about the conference. It seemed a little quirky but I needed the money so I said sure. The plan was for me to get close to you so he could take pictures of us. That's why I made my way up to you at the dance last night." Mary's face turned white. "Is Gus that slime ball that George threw out of the lobby last night? The guy I saw you talking to?" "Yes, that's Gus. The plan was to arrange this meeting today. That's when he was going to take the pictures. However, he grabbed me in the lobby last night and said that he had gotten all he needed at the dance and told me that I was finished for the weekend. He handed me a hundred right before George threw him out." "Why are you telling me this?" Mary asked. "I really didn't think much about it until today," Brad answered. "I wasn't even planning to come back this morning but your speech last night really hit home with me. I wanted to hear more. So I went to Gary's session this morning. That's when I found out which paper Gus works for. I was sitting next to the guy who made up that story about you and Gary." "You mean the guy who flashed that awful tabloid and made accusations about Gary and I?" Mary's eyes started to show anger. "Yeah, that guy. Anyway, when he left for the break, I picked up the tabloid and put together who Gus was and what he was doing, first with Gary, and now with me. He's trying to sell papers by creating lies about your organization. I'm so sorry."

Mary didn't know what to say. Her emotions were running wild. She didn't know how to respond. Brad had just given her a huge amount of information. What could Gus have "gotten" during the dance for his awful tabloid? She just sat there staring into the wall for several minutes mulling everything over in her mind. Her thoughts were interrupted by Brad. "Are you OK, Mary?" "I, I just don't know what to do," she replied in a quiet voice. "I should not have come here at all." Brad growled at himself. "This is all my fault." "Brad, listen to me. It is not your fault," Mary assured. "Gus would have found another innocent person to do his dirty work. God has put you here for a reason. All things work together for His good. We may not understand it at the time, but we must have faith in Him." "Do you really believe that?" Brad asked with tear-filled eyes. "Of course I do!" Mary stated firmly. "Then tell me what good is it for me to be here? I obviously didn't practice abstinence. I don't belong here. I don't belong anywhere! I am just another loser who knocked up a girl and ruined his life," Brad bemoaned while sobbing into his hands.

Mary placed her hand on his back and said, "Please don't talk like that. God made you in His image and He has a very specific plan for your life. You are very special to Him." Mary had forgotten about Gus and was now focusing her energy on Brad. "Maybe you are here to help me." Brad laughed through his tears. "How could I possibly help you? I am such a mess. I can't even help myself, let alone anyone else." Mary was quiet for a moment. She prayed, 'Father please give me the right words to speak to Brad, Amen.' All of a sudden Mary felt someone brush by her hair. It was the same feeling she had when she was alone on the stage the night before. She looked around and there was no one in the lobby except for the hostess behind the desk. A peace fell over her immediately and then an idea came to her. "Brad, look at me." He pulled his head out of his hands and looked at her. His eyes were red and pathetic.

He looked as if he had been whipped. Mary returned his look with a sympathetic, warm smile. "I think I know why you are here. You know, you can start all over again. You can commit to God. Turn your life over to Him right now. Follow Him. He will lead you where you need to go. You can start on a new life of abstinence. You can become a child of God. All you have to do is ask." "Really?" Brad questioned almost as if it were too good to be true. "God would forgive me?" "All you have to do is pray with me," Mary soothed. "Let's do it!" Brad exclaimed.

Mary reached for both of Brad's hands and bowed her head. Brad placed his hands around Mary's and bowed his head. Mary led a simple prayer in which Brad gave his life to God. Brad asked God to use him in His service and to help him in his current situation. After the prayer was over Mary looked at Brad with a sparkle in her eye and said, "I've got an idea. Would you be willing to share your story with the rest of the kids in the afternoon session? I'm sure that there are a lot of other kids in similar situations who are feeling hopeless. If they hear words of encouragement from someone who is going through the same thing, it would mean so much more to them." Brad sat back in the couch. "Wow, when I asked God to use me, I didn't know it would be so quick! Sure, I'll share my story if you think it would help." "Great!" Mary jumped to her feet. Brad stood up and gave her a big hug. That's when it hit Mary. She remembered the big bear hug Brad had given her at the dance last night. Gus probably took a picture of the hug and was most likely going to use it to create some screwed up lie about her. No matter, Gus wasn't going to stop the momentum of this organization. Gus meant this for evil, but God turned it around for something good. Much like how He had performed miracles for Joseph in the Book of Genesis, she recalled.

Mary looked at her watch. She wanted to call Joe before the afternoon session and tell him the good news. Brad looked as excited as a kid on his birthday and asked, "What time is the next session?" "Starts in 15 minutes," Mary replied. "Just enough time to collect my thoughts," Brad laughed. "I thought I'd be rushed." "You'll be fine, just speak from the heart. God will give you the words," Mary assured him. "Guess I'll be trying out this faith stuff sooner than I had expected," Brad quipped as he disappeared down the hall.

Mary grabbed her cell phone from her purse and hit speed dial #1. Five rings later Joe's voice picked up, "Hey, it's Joe, leave a message, I'll get back to you." Mary spoke into the phone, "Hi Joe, it's me; the worst and best things are happening to me. I can't wait to tell you about it. I met this guy who was involved with that tabloid and we talked. He is really a nice guy down deep, he is sorry for what he did to me and he is going to help with the rest of the conference. Oh, I'm rambling. I'm sorry I missed you. I'll call you tonight. I love you."

CHAPTER TEN

Joe pulled his head out of a pile of snow at the bottom of the hill where they had been sledding. He had attempted to ramp over the pile but didn't quite make it. All of the guys were laughing hysterically at Joe's 'snow beard'. As Joe got up, he heard his phone ring. It was that ring that told him he had missed a call. He fumbled for a few seconds in his coveralls for his phone and finally pulled it out and flipped it open. "Is the little woman checking on you?" Allen teased. Joe turned red which signaled to the rest of the guys that Allen was correct. This laid the ground-work for a host of good-natured ribbing from the guys as they trudged back up the hill. Joe listened to Mary's message as they walked. The reception was poor because they were in the middle of nowhere and he could only make out a few words; 'best thing happened', 'met this guy', 'really nice', and 'sorry' were all he could make out. Joe laughed to himself. These phrases add up to some bad news if taken at face value. But he had learned his lesson about doubting Mary. He decided to wait until he got home and listen to the message again. The reception was better there.

"Alright, you won, you cheated, but you won. I'm wet and cold. Anybody want to call it a day and head for the diner down the road for a cup of hot cocoa?" one of the guys asked. "What time is it?" Joe reached for his cell phone and said, "It was a little after 3:00 when I looked at my phone before this last run; it is now...." Joe looked at his phone and the screen was dark. He hit the start button to see if it had somehow gotten turned off during his 'face slide' down the hill. Nothing, the battery must be low. By now the other guys had pulled out their phones and one of them said, "It's 3:30." "Perfect." Joe responded, "Just enough time to stop at the diner and head for my house. Mom said she would make a big pot of chili for us. She said it would be ready about 5." Everyone knew that Eve Goldstein was a great cook; and she was especially known for her great chili. All the boys knew it because they had eaten it several times over the years. "Mama Eve's special chili?!" I'm in!" "Me too!" "Not without me!" They headed for the car.

When the boys piled out of Joe's car in front of the diner, Allen noticed a familiar car in the parking lot. "Hey, isn't that Angie's car?" A hint of excitement was in his voice. Angie was on the cheerleading squad with Mary. Allen had been trying to muster up enough courage to ask her on a date for a couple of months and the rest of the guys knew it. "Yeah, that's her car." One of the boys answered. "Bet you a dollar that you won't ask her out tonight." "I'm not going to throw away a good dollar," Allen replied. "There's no way Angie would go out with me." "How do you know if you don't ask?" Joe snorted as they opened the door to the diner. The boys walked in and notice that Angie was there with three other girls from school. The girls waved at the boys to come and join them. After some awkward moments, table and chair shuffling, everyone sat down. Unbeknownst to Allen, the guys had silently decided through a series of head nods and slight gestures that Allen was going to wind up next to Angie. Allen, who was obviously nervous, didn't see the scheme unfold until it was too late. He shot a horrified glance at his buddies who were snickering silently. "Aren't you going to sit down?" Angie asked Allen innocently. "I promise I won't bite." Allen quickly pulled out the chair and sat down. He could feel sweat beginning to run down the back of his neck. Joe broke the ice. "What are you all up to this afternoon?" "We've been shopping at the new outlet mail down the road by the interstate. We got some great deals." Melissa answered. Melissa was on the girls' basketball team, very outgoing and attractive. She loved to flirt, especially with Joe who she had had a crush on since 7th grade. She had managed to arrange it so she was sitting next to Joe. "You should come over sometime and I'll model some of the clothes I bought for you," she said to Joe looking at him dreamily. Joe rolled his eyes and just smiled at the group. Angie sensed the awkward moment and asked, "What have you guys been doing? You are all wet. I'll bet you haven't been shopping." She had directed the question toward Allen but one of the other guys answered, "Sledding, and boy was it a hoot!" That was all it took and the guys began retelling the sledding stories.

The hot chocolate arrived and the kids continued talking about the events of the day, school subjects, music, and who was in trouble with their parents. Allen had started to calm down and even carried on a couple of direct conversations with Angie. The kids finished their hot chocolate and the waitress brought the bill. The guys slid it to Joe and explained why the hot chocolate was on him. Melissa squeezed Joe's arm and said, "Thanks for the hot chocolate; next time, I'll buy." Joe ignored the comment.

As they were walking out to their cars, Allen raced over to Angie's door and opened it for her. He had decided that it was now or never. He was going to ask her out before they left the parking lot. He had rehearsed his speech over and over in his mind while they were in the diner. As Angie slid into the driver's seat, she said, "Thank you, Allen." Allen held the door open for a few seconds, leaned into the car and said, "I'd like to do it again tonight when I take you to the movies." There, he had done it. His heart was racing; he felt the sweat running down the back of his neck. His stomach was churning and for a moment he felt as if the hot chocolate might 'reappear'. The girls in the car giggled and Allen turned red. Allen looked directly at Angie; his eyes pleading with hers. Angie returned the look and shifted awkwardly. "I'm sorry Allen, I would love to go but I have plans. The girls are spending the night at my house. I'll take a rain-check." Allen's face fell. He wished the earth would open up and he could drop into a hole. The girls in the car giggled again and Allen slowly closed the door. The guys had heard the conversation and felt for their buddy. They had all, except for Joe, been there. The humiliation of rejection was awful, especially in front of a bunch of people. They got into the car and waited for Allen to climb in.

It had begun to snow and Allen just looked up at the flakes coming down. He didn't want to get in the car because he knew that one of two things would happen. Either the guys would tease him or they would attempt to console him. Either choice was distasteful. Angie felt horrible. She had always thought Allen was nice and would have accepted if she hadn't already committed to her friends. If only he had asked earlier in the week. Angie started the car and slowly backed out of the parking space. Allen headed for Joe's car, opened the door, and slid in. "I don't want to hear it," he grumbled. "Sorry dude," "Her loss," "Shake it off," "Bus runs every five minutes," were all the comments the guys could offer.

Joe started the car and took off back to town. The guys rode in silence following the girls. They could see them talking and laughing as they drove along. 'Great,' Allen thought to himself 'They're probably having a good laugh at my expense. It will be all over school by Monday. I can't wait to walk down the halls. Maybe I'll get sick if I'm lucky.' 'I'll take a rain check,' yeah right. That's the oldest dodge in the book. I don't blame her; she is way out of my league.' Joe reached for the radio. He thought some music might change the mood. Just as he turned it on, Allen's cell phone rang. He checked the caller ID but didn't recognize the number. "Hello?" "Hi Allen its Angie." Allen's heart stopped. Was this a pity call? Angie would be the type to call and apologize; she's just that sweet. "Allen? Are you there?" Angie questioned into the phone. "Uh... yeah; hi Angie, what's up?" Joe turned down the radio and the guys got quiet. "The girls and I were just talking; maybe you guys would like to come over to my house tonight. We could play some games, watch a movie or hang out. I thought you and I could discuss that rain check you just gave me. I hear it's supposed to rain this Friday," Angie teased into the phone. Allen's heart hit his throat so hard that he almost choked. "Sounds like fun, we'll be there. In the meantime, I'll be doing a rain dance for Friday." Angie giggled into the phone. "See you guys around 7:00, bye." "Bye Angie." Allen closed his phone, put his hands behind his head and leaned into the headrest. Joe could see a big grin on Allen's face. "What's going on?" "Yeah man, don't leave us hanging." The guys in the back were leaning up in their seats. "Congratulations boys, you all just became wingmen for tonight!"

Mary had just finished her presentation for the afternoon session. She had focused on abstinence and how it was the only true way to insure no unwanted pregnancy. She also emphasized the beauty of having a monogamous sexual relationship within the confines of marriage. She told the kids that waiting to have sex until marriage was God's wonderful blessing because you would share this one and only experience with your spouse. It had gone well. She could see in the some of the kids' faces that they had gotten the message and that some deep thoughts were running through their minds. However, she could also see how some of the kids looked bewildered and dejected. She guessed to herself that these kids had most likely had sex and were feeling hopeless. She sensed that now it was time for Brad.

"Some of you out there might be thinking, 'it's too late for me, that ship has sailed,' but it isn't too late. You can make a commitment to start all over. Forget the past, and renew you mind. Start your abstinence commitment today. If you don't think it's possible, think again. I would like to introduce to you someone who has just made this commitment. He has graciously agreed to share his story with us. Please welcome Brad!" Mary started the applause and glanced in the back of the room at Karen. She had a weird look on her face as if to say, 'this isn't on the schedule' but Mary smiled and nodded to Karen that it would be OK.

Brad walked to the podium and began telling his story. As he got deeper into it, the room got quiet. The kids were leaning forward in their chairs and were hanging on every word. Brad didn't leave out one detail right up to his prayer with Mary in the lobby a few minutes ago. Brad concluded his story by saying, "So you see, you can change, you can start over, just make up your mind to do it. I know I have responsibilities because of my actions. But I have decided to take control of my life and give it direction. If I can do it, so can you. Thanks for letting me share my story with you." Brad walked off the stage in total silence...no whispering, no shuffling, nothing but the sound of silence from the audience.

Mary waited a few seconds before walking to the podium. The kids, still in silence, seemed not to notice her. After a few seconds, Mary spoke into the microphone, "Thank you Brad for sharing with us; you are an inspiration to many people." That was all it took, the kids broke out in a thunder of applause and cheers that lasted for a couple of minutes. Mary glanced at Brad who was standing offstage with Gary. Brad had a couple of tears in his eyes and Gary had him in a huge bear hug. As the cheers died down, Mary glanced at Karen in the back who was pointing to her wrist as if to say, 'we're late'. Mary looked at the clock on the wall and Karen was right; 5:15. They were supposed to be finished at 5:00. "Looks like we've run into our dinner hour; is anybody hungry?" Mary asked. The crowd erupted again. Gary ran out to the podium and grabbed the mike, "Well let's eat! See you back here in two hours. We are going to show Salt Lake City how to party!"

Joe and the guys walked through the back door into the kitchen at Joe's house. Eve was stirring a huge pot of chili on the stove. "Smells good mom," Joe complimented as he headed for the wall outlet to plug in his cell phone. The guys chimed in, "Sure does! A little slice of heaven; I'm starved!" "You boys are soaked! Get out of those coveralls and quit tracking mud all over my kitchen!" Eve tried to sound angry but the boys knew she was teasing. The boys looked at each other and mentally communicated a plan. They began circling Eve who was now standing near the table. Eve began to suspect foul play and warned the boys, "Don't you dare!" "Aw Miss Eve, we're sorry. We just want a hug." "Stay away from me, you are all wet!" Eve squealed in fake resentment. The boys were closing in and just like a cat would attack a mouse, they all grabbed her in a huge, wet group hug. Eve attempted to get loose but failed miserably. The boys were all laughing when all of a sudden a big deep voice from the doorway boomed, "What's going on here? Get away from her!" There was Abraham standing in the doorway to the living room, arms folded across his chest with a scowl on his face. Joe was taken back. He had never seen his dad so worked up. The boys backed up and stared at the floor. "Just teasing mom a little dad," Joe offered apologetically. "Well she doesn't like being teased like that!" Abraham growled. Then he flashed a fiendish smile. "She would rather be teased like this." He grabbed an aerosol can of whipped cream and started toward his wife. "Help," Eve pleaded as she took off around the table. "Sorry Miss Eve," Allen stated. "Mr. Goldstein told us to stay away from you." "Abraham, I'm warning you, don't even think about it!" "Too late sweetie, I've already thought about it and guess what; it's funny. In fact, it is downright hilarious!" Abraham replied as he started to chase her around the table. After only two laps, Abraham caught her by the wrist. He quickly pulled her tight up to him trapping one of her arms against his body and the other with his hand. He had one hand free...the one with the whipped cream. Eve was helpless; half screaming, half laughing. The boys were yelling, "Go, go, go, go...." Eve began laughing so hard that she couldn't fight any longer. Abraham raised the can to her eyebrows and carefully outlined each one. He then added a moustache and finally, a beard. Allen grabbed his phone and began taking pictures as rapidly as possible. Two of the guys were lying on the floor, holding their sides laughing.

When the commotion settled down, Eve, looking like a very thin old man, bowed gracefully to the boys who started clapping and hooting. She then turned to Abraham who asked, "You're not angry are you?" "Of course not honey, I love you." As Eve said this she quickly grabbed Abraham by the collar and planted a kiss right on his lips. At least half of the whipped cream had transferred to Abraham which caused another eruption of laughter from the boys. Eve grabbed a kitchen towel and began wiping her face. When the laughter subsided she said, "Alright boys, get cleaned up for dinner." The boys took off for the laundry room and Abraham spun around and headed for the bathroom. Just as he turned around to leave, Eve cracked him on the butt with a towel flick. "Ow!" Abraham faked pain. "Don't mess with me." Eve smiled and kissed him again.

Allen glanced at the clock on the wall; 6 p.m. They had an hour before they were to be at Angie's. "Wow, time flies when you're eating in Miss Eve's kitchen. We need to get moving!" Allen tried to act calm but his voice, being elevated about an octave, gave him away. "What's up?" Eve asked trying not to meddle. "We're going over to Angie's house to hang out for a little while if that's OK Mom?" Joe inquired. Angie and Mary had been friends for quite awhile. Eve knew her parents from school activities and also had sensed that Allen had a crush on her for quite some time. "It's OK with me, Abraham?" Eve looked at her husband for approval. "It's OK with me. Who all is going to be there?" Joe named off the girls. When he got to Melissa's name, Eve bristled slightly. She had witnessed how Melissa flirted with Joe and she didn't like it. "Be good," Eve looked directly at Joe; her tone had gotten serious. "Don't worry mom, I'll be home by midnight." "Guys, we need to get going!" Allen pleaded. Abraham tilted his head up in the air and sniffed. "I don't know how things go in the teenage world these days, but if I were to have gone to see Eve smelling the way you boys do right now, well let's just say, she would have run me off." "Good idea!" Allen came to his senses. "Is it alright, if we get showers here, Miss Eve?" Eve had already disappeared into the laundry room and was emerging with towels and wash clothes. "Do you think I would let you boys out of this house smelling like a bunch of pigs!? Go get cleaned up." Eve pushed the towels into Joe's arms and pointed them out of the kitchen.

Thirty minutes later the boys thundered down the stairs looking and smelling much better. "You boys look nice," Eve complimented. Abraham was sitting in his chair reading a magazine. He looked up over his glasses and said, "See you at midnight or before. Call if you are going to be late...." It was the same old speech that Joe had heard a thousand times. "Be good." Eve warned again. Joe knew she was talking about Melissa. "I will mom." Joe promised. "Guys, we have got to go!" Allen was in panic mode now. "Thanks for dinner, Miss Eve." All of the boys echoed each other as they headed out through the kitchen. Joe reached for his cell phone; it should have some charge in it by now; nothing. The screen was black. "Mom? Dad? I think my phone is broken; if you need me, call Allen. Bye, I love you." The back door closed and the house became quiet again. "Angie is a very nice girl," Eve said to Abraham. "But that Melissa, she is so flirty, especially with Joe. She can't keep her hands off of Joe." "Now Eve, it's OK. Joe can handle himself. He is a good boy." Abraham tried to calm her. "Besides, you can't blame her, Joe looks just like me!" Eve chuckled and flipped on the television.

Mary was finishing up dinner with a bunch of kids from Colorado who had come over for the conference. She had enjoyed visiting with them. They had told her how much they were enjoying the conference and how they had made a commitment to abstain from sex. They were even forming an accountability group so they could support each other when they got back to school. Mary had thought that accountability groups were a good idea and planned to discuss it with Gary and Karen. Maybe they could incorporate it into the next conference. She was so happy that the conference was a success. She knew that God had put her in that position for a purpose. She felt so blessed.

Mary glanced at her cell phone; 6:30. She had a half hour before the evening event started. She excused herself, disposed of her tray, and headed for a secluded area backstage. She wanted to call Joe before the final session. Five rings later she heard Joe's recorded voice. 'Hi Joe, me again, sure would like to talk to you tonight. I can't imagine where you are but give me a call. The last session will be over at 10:00. Call me after that. Love you, bye.' Mary closed her phone and just stared at it for a few seconds. It wasn't like Joe not to return her call. She started to worry just a little. "It works better if you actually dial it," a voice behind her interrupted her thoughts. It was the lead singer of the band. "Are you OK? You don't look so good." "I'm fine," Mary said unconvincingly. "I was just deep in thought." "Well, from the look on your face, it wasn't a very pleasant thought." "I just can't get in touch with my boyfriend. When we talked this morning, it didn't end well. I'm afraid his feelings are hurt." He put his arm around her shoulder. "It'll be OK, he would be a fool to let you go; and if he does, give me a call. I'll be your boyfriend." Mary looked up at him and smiled, "Thanks, I'll keep that in mind." "I'm not kidding. I've got to go do a quick sound check before the party starts," he said as he walked away toward the curtain. Mary smiled at her new friend. She felt all alone in a big crowd. As she stood there she felt a chill down her back. It was a slight motion of some kind. She looked around to see if someone had brushed by; no one around. 'Must be a draft back here,' she analyzed.

The party at Angie's was going great. The kids had played games for a couple of hours and had just settled down to watch a movie. Angie and Allen were having a great time and the guys were doing a good job as wingmen. They all had decided that pizza sounded good so Joe offered to go pick them up. "I'll go with you." Melissa volunteered. Joe rolled his eyes and said, "Don't you want to see the movie?" "I'll catch up; I could use a little fresh air." She smiled dreamily at him. Joe and Melissa grabbed their coats and headed for the door. The rest of the kids started the movie and Angie settled in next to Allen. She had gotten an afghan because she was cold. She threw it over both of them and curled her feet under her. Allen just sat there, frozen; happy, scared, elated, and terrified. He didn't know what to do. Things had been going so well, he didn't want to screw it up. "This isn't comfortable," Angie wiggled against his shoulder, hoping he would take the hint. Allen slowly raised his arm and put it gently around her shoulder. His heart was pounding and his mind was racing. He waited for her to yell, 'What are you doing?' Nothing; total silence. She snuggled into his chest and said without looking at him, "'Bout time." Allen grinned from ear to ear.

Just then Allen's cell phone rang. He looked at the caller ID and it was Mary. "Hi Mary, what's up?" "Hi Allen, is Joe with you? I've left him a couple of messages but he hasn't called back." "Well, yes and no. We are all over at Angie's hanging out, but Joe and Melissa went to get pizza. He should be back soon." "Melissa?" Mary sounded alarmed. "Would you please tell Joe to give me a call when he gets back?" "Sure Mary." "Thanks, bye." Mary closed her cell phone. 'That's weird,' she thought. 'What's he doing riding around with Melissa?' Allen put his phone down and returned to his daydreaming about Angie.

The advertisements on the radio in Joe's car ended and a new song began to play, "If you can't be with the one you love, love the one you're with...." Melissa giggled and said, "It must be fate" and began singing it to Joe. Joe was concentrating on driving. He was glad that the roads were snow covered. It gave him an excuse to ignore Melissa. "Come on Joe," Melissa got bolder. "What's wrong with a little harmless fun? Mary will never know. Besides, she is probably doing the same thing with that Gary guy." Joe's blood ran cold and his face turned white. He composed himself and asked, "How did you know about him?" "It's a small town Joe. Everyone knows about Gary. I saw a picture, he's cute. I wouldn't blame her if she...." "Don't go any further," Joe interrupted. "I don't want to hear it." Joe stared straight ahead and didn't notice Melissa open up her cell phone and start recording. "I'm sorry Joe, I know the truth hurts. Maybe this will help you feel better." She held the phone out with her right hand while turning toward Joe. Unbeknownst to Joe, she leaned up close and kissed him. "I would do ANYTHING to help you feel better." Joe was caught off-guard. He turned red and quickly glanced in Melissa's direction. She hit the stop button on her phone and slid it under her leg. "Melissa! Please don't do that! I don't need that right now." "OK Joe, anything you say. But, like the saying goes, what's good for the goose is good for the gander; the offer stands, anytime, anyplace, just give me a call. Mary will never know." Joe pulled up in front of Angie's house. Thank goodness. He couldn't wait to get out of that car. He jumped out of the car and grabbed the pizzas from the back seat. Melissa didn't get out. Joe rolled his eyes and went around to the other side and opened the door for her. "Thanks sweetie." Joe was holding the pizzas with both hands so Melissa took advantage of the situation. She grabbed his arm and walked closely next to him up the sidewalk.

Joe juggled the pizzas as he opened the door for Melissa. "Where have you all been?" One of the guys asked. "I'm starving!" "There was a line at the pizza place and the roads are getting bad," Joe said in an apologetic tone. "That AND our little detour," Melissa chimed in. "What detour?" One of the girls was now interested. "Oh nothing really, we just had a little fun." Joe changed the subject. "You two look cozy," nodding at Allen and Angie. Allen blushed and Angie smiled.

Allen stopped the movie and changed the subject himself, "I'm hungry too. Let's eat." He removed his arm from Angie's shoulder and she reluctantly squirmed out of the couch. "Anything new?" Joe looked at Angie and Allen with an innocent grin. Allen ignored the tease and said, "seems like I wanted to tell you something, but I can't remember what it was." He had forgotten about Mary's call. "I guess you were just too engrossed in the movie." Angie offered. "Yeah, something like that," Allen said as he looked at her for the first time since they had sat down on the couch. They both blushed and smiled at each other. "Oh brother!" One of the guys injected with a mouthful of pizza. "You two had better quit it unless you want to see this pizza again!" Everyone laughed and dove into the pizza.

CHAPTER ELEVEN

"**T**hank you and good night! Have a safe trip home," the band leader spoke into the microphone after they had played their second encore. The final concert had been an overwhelming success. The kids had been dancing and partying the entire two hours. Many of the kids had gotten acquainted with kids from other schools and towns and were busy exchanging phone numbers and e-mail addresses. Mary had handed her number out to more people than she could remember. She wondered how many of them would call. She had had an OK time at the dance. There was no pressure on her because she didn't have to give a speech. All she had to do was mingle with the kids. However, she couldn't get her mind off of Joe. She had put her phone on vibrate and held it in her hand all night. She had been afraid that she wouldn't hear it over the band and the crowd. She even checked it frequently to see if Joe had called.

Just then it vibrated in her hand. Her heart jumped. She was so sure that it was Joe that she didn't even look at the caller ID. "Hi Joe!" she said in her most excited voice. "Uh Mary, it's Gary. Where are you? Karen found me and told me that George wants to see us in the lobby. He isn't going to be here in the morning so he needs us to wrap things up with him this evening. Can you meet us there?" "Sure," Mary replied; disappointment overshadowing the few seconds of excitement. She closed her phone and headed for the lobby.

Joe glanced at the alarm clock as he fell into bed; 12:30. All of the guys left Angie's about 11:30. He was happy for Allen. He and Angie had planned to get together tomorrow for lunch. It seemed as if they were going to get together. Joe had to be at the airport to pick up Mary by 1 p.m. He would set the alarm for 10 a.m. in just a minute. His mind raced about the days events. He hadn't liked the way that he and Mary had ended their conversation this morning. He had fun sledding with the guys and hanging out at Angie's was a good thing. However, the whole Melissa thing ate at him. Maybe she was right. He and Mary had even had discussions about wondering what it would be like to date other people just to be sure that they were meant for each other. They would always come to the conclusion that neither one of them was interested in dating someone else and the subject was dropped. But, Mary had been acting funny lately. She was slightly more distant and distracted than normal. Joe had assumed that it was because she was so busy with the 'Teens for Abstinence' activities. Maybe she was reconsidering dating others since she had become a "world traveler." Melissa was cute and she could be fun, but...Joe's mind wandered as he drifted off to sleep.

Mary, Gary and Karen stepped onto the elevator after their meeting with George. Although they were excited about the success of the conference, they were beat. Gary wasn't even hungry. Their flights were scheduled to leave around 11 a.m. They agreed to meet for breakfast at 8:00 before heading to the airport. Mary shut the door of her room. The clock read 12:45. It had taken longer than expected to wrap things up with George. In addition, there were a few reporters in the hotel that wanted interviews with the three of them. Mary was relieved that Gus wasn't there. She wasn't sure how she would have handled an interview with him. She picked up the phone and left a wake-up call for 7 a.m. The adrenaline rush was definitely over. She was drained. As she eased into bed, she thought of Joe. Why hadn't he called back? Well, she was sure that he'd be home and close to his phone by now. He always plugged it in by his nightstand. He had always told her that he wanted to be available to her 24/7. She hit speed dial #1. Five rings later, Joe's message picked. Mary didn't even leave a message this time. 'Yeah right, 24/7,' she thought. 'He's probably busy kissing Melissa good night.' She cried herself to sleep.

Joe awoke to the sound of his mother's voice, "Joe, it's 11 o'clock. What time are you supposed to pick up Mary?" Joe opened his eyes and looked at the clock. He had fallen asleep and didn't set his alarm. He threw back the covers and attempted to get up. Wow! His head was spinning and his knees went soft. He was so dizzy that he had to sit back down. He was soaking wet and his head pounded. "You OK?" Eve asked. Joe tried to swallow but his throat felt like sandpaper. "I may have a touch of something, but I'm OK." Joe tried to put on his best macho voice. "I'm not buying it." Eve said with authority as she put her hand on his forehead. "You're burning up." "Mom, I'm fine." Joe protested and began to stand up to head for the bathroom. "All I need is a shower and a chance to wake up." After three steps into his journey to the bathroom, Joe had to grab the desk chair to keep his balance. "Sure, you're just fine; back to bed for you. Here's a dry T-shirt." Joe allowed his Mom to lead him back to the bed. As she covered him up, she brushed the hair out of his eyes and said, "You are just as stubborn as your father. I'll go get you something to help with the pain. Does anything sound good to you?" "No thanks, Mom. I don't think I can pick Mary up. Can you call her, Mom?" "No problem, I've already planned on it."

Eve hung up the phone after talking to Ruth for a couple of minutes. "Jake is picking Mary up," Eve announced to the house in general. Abraham responded, "OK, I'm on standby general sir." Eve gave Abraham a sarcastic smile, grabbed the bottle of aspirin and headed for Joe's room. She slowly opened the door and discovered that Joe had already fallen back to sleep. She laid the aspirin next to his alarm clock and tiptoed out of the room. She knew that he would find it and take it when he woke up.

Mary showed her ticket to the gate agent and started down the walkway to the plane. The line was backed up and she waited patiently for the people to continue moving. Just then she saw something flash in the corner of her eye and she felt that 'movement' on the back of her hair that she had felt several times that weekend. She turned quickly to see what it was. Nothing; no one was that near to her and there was no breeze in the hall. There was a man in line behind her, but he had his back to her talking to a woman; presumably is wife. Mary was beginning to believe that this 'feeling' or 'experience' was more than just the wind. It was happening in different places but in the same way. If she didn't feel such a sense of peace come over her when it happened it would be creepy. She stood there contemplating what was happening and forgot where she was. Suddenly, she snapped out of it when the man behind her tapped her on the shoulder. "Miss, you can go ahead now." Mary looked up and saw that the line was moving. "Sorry, I was daydreaming." "It must have been a good one." The man smiled.

Mary stumbled down the aisle of the airplane and found her seat. She, Karen and Gary had had breakfast together and shared a cab to the airport. After hugs in the terminal they had gone to their respective gates. Mary plopped down in the window seat. She already missed those two. She had gotten to know them a lot better over the weekend. She really liked them. Karen was a good friend. She was the type of person who would always be loyal, no matter what. Gary wasn't so bad. He was kind of flirty, but it was harmless. Besides, he always made her laugh. Mary looked at the people who kept walking by her. She wondered who would be sitting next to her. The crew eventually began closing up the plane and Mary realized that no one would be sharing the seats next to her. "Good, I'll have all three seats to myself," she said silently. However, she did remember the trip to Salt Lake City Friday evening. She had enjoyed chatting with Gabby. She looked around to see if by some miracle that Gabby was flying on the same plane. No luck. Mary was disappointed but remembered she had Gabby's business card in her purse. 'I guess I'll call her this week sometime.' As she pondered this idea, she searched her purse for Gabby's card. She couldn't find it. She tore her purse apart several times but it was nowhere to be found. She KNEW that she had kept it with her plane tickets and itinerary. She specifically remembered putting it in the envelope with the ticket. She started to panic because she wanted to talk to Gabby again. Besides, Gabby had known her parents. They would be happy to know that she had run into Gabby. Mary began retracing her steps after Gabby had given her the card. Then it hit her, she had dropped the papers near the baggage claim when Gary and Karen had startled her. She must have lost it then. It upset her at first and that feeling gave way to a little sadness. She had been looking forward to contacting Gabby. Gabby would probably think that Mary was blowing her off. A tear ran down her cheek. Mary leaned back in the seat and closed her eyes. 'Oh well, I'll just spread out and take a nap.' Just before she drifted off, she felt that brush on her hair again. She smiled and drifted off. She knew that something was going on that couldn't be explained. However, she didn't care; it made her feel good.

The next thing Mary knew was that the plane was landing. She had slept for the entire two-hour flight. She had been dreaming one of those kinds of dreams that you wished you could finish and almost become angry when you are awakened. She couldn't quite remember the specifics of the dream which annoyed her further, but the general idea was that she was totally at peace and in a wonderful place. She tried very hard to remember the details as the plane taxied to the terminal. However, she was unsuccessful. Oh well, reality was setting in as the passengers began filing off of the plane. Her thoughts turned to Joe and she became anxious to see him. She could just see him standing at the metal detectors waiting for her. It wouldn't be unusual for him to have a surprise for her, flowers, perhaps a balloon. She quickened her pace down the terminal in anticipation of a big reunion. As she passed by security, she scanned the crowd but couldn't find Joe. She slowed down a bit and looked behind her but didn't see Joe anywhere. "Hi honey!" a familiar voice echoed in her ear. She recognized the voice and spun around. "Hi Daddy!" She threw her arms around him and he returned the hug.

They headed down the escalator toward baggage claim. After exchanging a few pleasantries about the trip and things back home, Mary asked somewhat shyly, "Where is Joe? I thought he was going to pick me up." "Eve called your Mom and said that Joe woke up with the flu and was feeling rotten. I guess you're stuck with me instead." Jake grinned at his little girl. She was his precious little gem. Jake couldn't say no to Mary and everyone knew it. She could have taken advantage of that but Mary was too kind. Jake would do anything for Mary. "Oh Daddy, you know better than that. I was just wondering." She slapped him playfully on the arm. "Look, there's my bag." Jake grabbed the suitcase from the carousel and they took off for the car.

After they got out of the parking lot and onto the highway, Mary looked at her father and asked, "Daddy, do you remember a pharmaceutical rep that used to call on you? Her first name was

Gabby." "Sure do, I remember little ol' Gabby. She was as sweet as the day is long; loved to talk and always had something nice to say about you and Joe. She always seemed to take a special interest in you two." Jake paused and Mary grinned at him. "That's funny Dad because...." Jake's tone lowered as he interrupted Mary. "Too bad about Gabby; you know she was killed in a car accident about ten years ago. I think she was hit by a drunk driver. Your Mom and I went to the funeral over in Billings. She had a lot of friends but no family. There sure were a lot of people at the funeral. Her church family really loved her. They went on and on about how much she had done for the community and the church." Jake's voice trailed off. Mary's blood ran cold. She couldn't believe what she was hearing! It didn't make sense! It had to be someone else; but it couldn't; after all how many pharmaceutical reps named Gabby came to her dad's store. Mary felt that familiar brush against the back of her neck and the air around her swirled slightly. "Mary...Mary? Are you in there?" Mary snapped out if it. "I'm sorry daddy, what did you say?" "I asked you what made you think of Gabby." "Oh, I was just reminiscing about the good old days while I was in the airplane." Mary leaned back against the headrest and closed her eyes. Jake knew the tone of her voice. It meant that she didn't want to talk about it anymore. He wanted to hear more but figured that she was probably tired and didn't want to deal with bad news right now. They drove the rest of the way home in silence.

Mary threw open the front door and yelled, "Hi mom, I'm home!" There was the smell of dinner cooking in the air and the radio was playing in the background. Mary immediately knew the smell; spaghetti, her favorite. Ruth walked in from the kitchen. "Hi honey, how was your trip? We really missed you around here." "I didn't even know she was gone." Jake teased as he walked through the door carrying Mary's bag. Mary laughed at her dad's fake apathy. "It was great. There were a lot of kids there and I met so many nice people. I'll tell you all about it over dinner. Do I have time to get a shower before we eat?" "Sure honey." Ruth replied. "Take your time; we'll eat when you're ready." Hurry up, I'm starved!" Mary heard her dad say teasing her even more. "Oh daddy, you are always hungry."

Jake followed Ruth as she returned to the kitchen. "Did Mary have anything to say on the ride home?" Ruth asked Jake. "Not much, just that it was successful and that she had a lot of fun," Jake replied. "She did mention something that was really random. Do you remember that pharmaceutical rep that used to call on us— Gabby White? Mary asked about her on the way home." "Sure I remember Gabriella. She was such a nice person. That car accident was such a terrible thing. I remember her funeral. Why was Mary asking about her?" "She really didn't say, it was kind of weird. As soon as I mentioned the accident, Mary acted like she didn't want to discuss it; so I let it drop." "That is weird," Ruth observed. "Mary would have had to be seven or eight years old when she last saw Gabby." Both Jake and Ruth let the topic drop as they heard Mary come into the room.

They sat down to eat and Mary began recounting the events of the weekend. She told her parents about the band, the dances, and the sessions. She even told them about the meeting with Brad and how he had come to know Gus. When Jake heard the story about Gus, his eyes narrowed and he sort of grumbled under his breath. Both Ruth and Mary knew that Jake was still upset about that guy and that he wanted to 'do something' about it. However, Ruth had convinced him that it would only make things worse. Mary continued telling them about how she, Karen, and Gary had become closer over the weekend. Mary especially sang the praises of Gary as she related that he had defended Karen when those two guys had made inappropriate comments about her during the morning session. "It sounds like he is one great guy," Ruth observed. "Yeah," Jake chimed in. "Has my little girl got a crush on the California surfer dude?" "Oh daddy, stop it. I get enough of that from Joe."

After dinner, Mary was helping her mom and dad clear the table. "Daddy tells me Joe is sick. Have you seen him? I haven't talked to him since Saturday morning. I've tried to call several times but he doesn't pick up or return my messages." "That doesn't sound like Joe at all." Ruth responded. "We haven't seen him since the game Friday night. The cheer squad did OK without you but you could tell they missed you. Anyway, Joe had a great game and Eve said when she called this morning that Joe had felt fine yesterday but woke up sick today." "So I've heard," Mary quipped. "He was running around with Melissa last night. I guess he was too busy with her to give me a call." "I thought you hadn't talked to him?" Jake questioned the logic. "I haven't. I called Allen last night to check on Joe because I was worried about him. Allen told me he had gone out for pizza with Melissa. I asked Allen to tell Joe to call me when he got back. Well, no call from Joe. Apparently he was lipped locked with Melissa!" Ruth was well aware of how Mary felt about Melissa. Mary had made it clear over the years that she didn't like the fact that Melissa flirted constantly with Joe. Oh yeah, a lot of girls flirted with Joe, but not like Melissa. She was relentless. Joe had never given her any reason whatsoever to think he was interested in Melissa or any other girl for that matter. But, Joe had been acting funny lately. Mary's thoughts were interrupted by her mom's voice, "Now Mary, you know Joe better than that. I'm sure there is a perfectly good explanation for what was going on. You need to calm down." "Yeah honey," Jake agreed. "Joe would never do anything to hurt you or he knows I'd kick him all over town. Why don't you go over and talk to him? I'm sure he will be glad to see you." "Maybe you're right, daddy. I think I'll go over right now."

Mary walked up to the Goldstein's house and rang the bell. "Why Mary, since when do you ring the bell?" Eve exclaimed as she open the door. "Come on in, it's freezing out there. How was the conference?" Before she could answer Abraham came around the corner. "Is that my little Mary? It sure was lonely around here without you." He reached out and gave her a big hug. "I missed you guys too. What a whirlwind trip. It was a big success...." Mary gave Abraham and Eve the short version of the weekend. "Wow," Eve said in amazement. "We sure are proud of you." "Thank you, but it wasn't me. The glory goes to God." "Mary, that's just one of the many reasons we love you so much. Your heart is in the right place." Abraham complimented. "How's Joe?" Mary asked innocently. "Not too well; he woke up this morning feeling dizzy. He has a temperature and doesn't feel like eating anything. I think he has a touch of the flu," Ruth stated in a concerned tone. "Do you think it would be OK if I went up to see him for a little while?" "Well, I guess so," Ruth said hesitantly. She thought Joe needed his rest. "Sure it would!" Abraham stated. "I know Joe will feel much better if he gets to see you." "I just took some chocolate muffins out of the oven. Maybe you could take some up to him. He might eat for you." Ruth agreed.

Mary knocked softly on Joe's door; no answer. She gently pushed open the door being careful not to drop the muffins and hot tea that Eve had made. Joe was sleeping. She carried the tray to the night table and pulled a chair up next to the bed and sat down. She watched him sleep for a few moments. She didn't know if she should wake him, be angry with him, feel sorry for him or what. He looked so peaceful, but she could tell that he was hot. There were beads of sweat on his forehead. She looked for his phone on the nightstand, the cord was there but the phone was missing. 'That's odd,' she thought. After a few moments, he stirred and said with his eyes still closed, "Hi sweetie." "I'm sorry to wake you; I just wanted to see you. How did you know it was me?" "I'd recognize that perfume anywhere," he said smiling with his eyes still closed. "That is the perfume of a goddess." Mary blushed at the compliment. A tear began to emerge from her eye as she wrestled with the conflict going on inside her. On the one hand, she was angry with Joe over the Melissa thing and not returning her call; but on the other hand, she loved him and felt sorry for him because she could tell by looking at him that he didn't feel well at all.

"Mary, what's wrong? Why are you crying?" Joe was looking at her now. "I just hate to see you feeling so bad." Mary decided not to confront Joe about Melissa. "Your mom made some hot tea and muffins for you. Would you like some?" "No thanks. I'm not hungry, maybe later." Mary knew he was sick now.

Joe had thought about bringing up the Melissa thing to Mary but didn't see it as a big deal. Besides, talking wore him out and he wanted to save his strength talking to Mary about important things. Melissa had been flirting with him for years; this was just one more time. Mary began to fume inside. Why wouldn't Joe explain his 'date' with Melissa? If it was so innocent, why was he hiding it? "Why didn't you answer my calls? The last time we talked was Saturday morning. I left several messages but you didn't call back." There, she said it. Maybe that would jog his memory. Joe remembered the call. He hadn't liked the 'wake-up call' from Gary. It sounded a little too friendly for his taste. "My phone broke while we were sledding. I didn't get any messages," Joe offered as an explanation. "Well, I called Allen Saturday night and asked him to tell you to call me. He said you weren't around but he would have you call me when you got back," Mary's voice raised a little. Joe tried to remember the events of Saturday night. His head was swimming with fever and he couldn't think clearly. He rubbed his brow and said, "Well, I didn't get the message. Maybe he forgot to tell me. He was pretty busy snuggled up with Angie." "Yeah, maybe, that's probably what happened." Mary wasn't buying it but she decided to drop it. She knew Joe felt terrible. "I had better get going and let you rest." Mary got up and headed for the door. "OK Mary," Joe said reluctantly. "I love you." "I love you too, feel better. Do you think you'll be at school tomorrow?" "I wouldn't miss a chance to be with you if I could at all help it." Joe tried to smile as big as possible. "See you tomorrow Joe."

CHAPTER
TWELVE

Joe opened his eyes to the sound of his alarm. He felt rotten. He had been up several times during the night and had made mad dashes to the bathroom for a round of the dry heaves. His stomach ached from the spasms last night and his head pounded. Eve was passing by his door and had heard the alarm go off. She opened the door and peeked in. "Good morning Joe, how do you feel?" Joe was sitting on the side of his bed staring at the floor. "I'm OK," he lied. "Sure you are," she said in her sarcastic voice. "I heard you praying to the porcelain throne last night on more than one occasion. How are you really?" "Not so good, I feel like I've been beaten with a baseball bat." "You still have a fever," Eve announced as she felt his forehead. "I think I'll stay home from school today," Joe announced. "Good idea. I wouldn't have let you go anyway." Joe flopped back down in bed. He reached for his cell phone on the nightstand to call Mary and tell her that he wasn't going but the phone wasn't there. 'Oh yeah, it's broke,' he remembered. "Mom, would you call Mary and tell her that I'm not going." "Sure honey. Are you hungry? Does anything sound good?" "No thanks mom, I could use an aspirin please." "I'll be right back." "One more thing mom, could you have dad stop by the store and get me a new phone today?" "Sure thing, Joe." The door closed and Joe fell back to sleep.

Mary walked into school all by herself. It felt weird without Joe. She felt bad about questioning him so much last night. She didn't realize how bad he had felt. She caught sight of Angie at her locker as she walked down the hall. "I heard you had an interesting weekend, Angie." Angie blushed. "Allen and I connected and we're going out this weekend. He really is sweet. We had lunch and then talked on the phone for over an hour yesterday. How was your weekend? Did it go well? Where's Joe?" "Whoa! Slow down Angie. One question at a time. I'm really glad you and Allen finally got together. I knew that you two would hit it off. The conference was great and very successful. Joe is sick and won't be here today. Now, tell me more about Allen." Just as Angie was starting to fill Mary in on the details, the bell rang. "Rats," Mary shook her head. "Don't worry, I'll tell you all about it at lunch. See you later."

Mary carried her lunch tray out into the cafeteria and spotted Angie sitting at a table with a bunch of other girls. Melissa was among them. 'Oh well, you have to take the good with the bad,' Mary thought, and sat down at the table. "Hi Mary," Angie said. "Hello everyone. Now tell me all about you and Allen Saturday." "Oh it was so cute!" One of the girls at the table said. "They were snuggled up on the couch; Allen had his arm around Angie and she was grinning from ear to ear. I don't think you could have slipped a piece of paper between them." All of the girls giggled while Angie recounted the events of the afternoon and evening.

After she had finished, Melissa spoke up, "Angie isn't the only one who got a little action Saturday night." Angie looked around at all of the puzzled looks on the girls' faces. "Who?" Angie questioned. "Me!" Melissa said with a fiendish smile. "With whom?" "Why, don't you remember when Joe and I went to get pizza?" All of the girls immediately looked at Mary. She felt the stares but kept her composure and didn't say anything. After a few seconds that seemed like hours Angie came to the rescue. "Yeah right Melissa. You forgot we were there. You practically forced yourself into Joe's car. He acted like he didn't even want you to go." "Is that so," Melissa quipped. "Well we had a pretty good time; if you don't believe it take a look at this!" She pulled her cell phone out of her purse and brought up the video that she took when she kissed Joe. She played it for the girls on each side of her. "I don't believe it!" One of the girls gasped. "Let me see that." Angie grabbed the phone. Mary looked over Angie's shoulder as the video started. It only took a few seconds. Mary's face flushed and she looked as if she had been hit by a truck. The other girls just sat there in silence. Melissa broke the silence. "He was so sweet. He swept me off my feet. I felt just like a princess." "Shut up Melissa!" Angie ordered. "You can be so mean sometimes!" "What did I say?" Melissa faked innocence while looking at Mary. "I was just telling you what happened." Mary sat there stunned not knowing what to say. She could hear the other girls whispering but couldn't make out what they were saying.

The bell rang and broke the silence. The girls grabbed their trays and started off to class. Mary sat there in a daze. She hadn't even heard the bell. Her mind was a million miles away. Angie touched her shoulder and snapped her out of it. "Mary, are you coming? The bell rang." Um yeah, sorry, I was somewhere else." "Forget about her. I'm sure there is a simple explanation for what happened." "I know. I just wish Joe had said something about it so I wouldn't have been caught off-guard. Believe me, he's going to get an earful tonight!"

Joe plopped down in front of the soup and grilled cheese sandwich his mom had made him for lunch. After he finished about half of it, he decided to take a shower and finish the rest of it while he checked his e-mail. The shower made him feel much better. As he was getting out, he heard the door to his room close so he peaked out of the bathroom to see who it was; nobody. However, there was a new smell in the room; chocolate chip cookies. He slipped on his favorite pair of gym shorts and headed for the desk. There was a note: "Just took these out of the oven; don't eat any until you finish your lunch." Joe grinned and grabbed a cookie.

There was nothing on his e-mail except a few messages from college coaches so Joe decided to surf the internet while he finished his lunch. He decided to see if Mary's conference had gotten any coverage from the press over the weekend. There were several articles from local and national newspapers talking about how successful the rally had been and how it was refreshing to see kids who were willing to step up and take a stand for something good. There were even some photos of Mary and the other kids. Joe was very proud of her. Then he ran across the article from the tabloid. He almost skipped it because he knew that it was some kind of lie but the picture caught his eye. There was a bunch of kids dancing and having fun. He could see Gary in the background with a somber look on his face. Gary appeared to be watching Mary in a very tight and warm embrace with this guy. Both the guy and Mary had huge smiles on their faces. In addition, the picture that had ran the time before showing Mary and Gary with their heads together was right next to it. The caption below the pictures read, "Teens for Abstinence president plays the field, dumps previous fling for new one while boyfriend stays home."

Joe just sat there for a moment. He knew that there had to be a reasonable explanation for this but he couldn't help but let it bother him. After all, pictures don't lie. This didn't look like a conference, it looked like a party; and boy did Mary seem to be enjoying herself. Not that he cared if she hugged people, Mary did that all of the time. It's just that she didn't mention this at all last night. You would have thought that she would mention the fact that she met a new friend and had given him a hug in front of a photographer. He hit the print button on the computer, closed out the internet connection and lay back down on his bed. Suddenly, he didn't feel so well any longer.

Mary sat in class the rest of the afternoon stewing about the video on Melissa's phone. She just couldn't believe it. So that's why Joe didn't want to mention the pizza run Saturday night. He didn't want to admit that he had been making out with Melissa. She wondered how long this had been going on. She wondered if Joe had changed his mind about dating other girls or maybe he just wanted a little something on the side. She grew angrier as the day went on. The final bell rang and Mary shot out of her seat. She was going straight to Joe's to confront him about it. She didn't care if he was sick or not.

As she was leaving the school, she ran into Melissa. "Say Melissa, can I have a copy of that video?" She choked on her words and it pained her to ask because she knew Melissa would be gloating over it. "Sure." Melissa grinned slyly. "But, I've got to go right now; you can catch it on YouTube if you want." Melissa walked away not looking back. 'YouTube! Great! It would be all over school by morning.' Melissa was one sinister person. She wanted Joe and would stop at nothing to get him. Mary took off for her car.

"I'm home," Mary announced flatly as she came in through the door. No answer. There was a note on the counter, "We are at the store; call if you need anything. We'll be home around 6:15; love mom." Mary scratched a note below her mom's, "Gone to Joe's."

She looked around the kitchen as if to find answers on the walls. She couldn't decide if she was hurt, angry, confused or some combination of all of them. No matter, she needed to clear this up right now.

Mary knocked on the door at Joe's house. "Hi Mary!" Eve was startled because Mary was part of the family; she never knocked. "Hi Mom." Mary returned in an emotionless tone. She always called her mom, that's how close she and Eve were. There had been times through the years that Mary had gone to Eve for some of that "female advice" when her mom wasn't available. Because they were so close, Eve could tell there was something bothering Mary. "How was school today?" Eve probed hoping Mary would open up. "It was the same old junk. I hate school." Eve was speechless! Mary had always loved school! She loved learning, reading, the social aspect of it, everything about it. Now she knew something was wrong. "Could it be that you just missed a certain someone?" Eve tried to cheer Mary up. Mary ignored the question. "How is Joe? Is it OK if I go up to give him his homework?" Ever since grade school, whenever one of them had missed school, the other would always collect the assignments and bring them home for the other. "He's feeling better. Sure, go on up. I'm sure he would love to see you." "I'll bet he won't," Mary muttered under her breath as she headed up the stairs. Eve just stood there and watched Mary climb the stairs. Something was up and it wasn't good.

Mary opened the door to Joe's room without knocking. He was sleeping on top of the covers where he had laid down after printing the picture of Mary and Brad. Mary just stood there a moment looking at Joe. He was still in his gym shorts and wasn't wearing a shirt. He looked so innocent lying there. No wonder Melissa, and for that matter half of the girls in school, were after him. He was gorgeous; and so sweet and kind. She threw his books on the floor next to the bed which caused a thud loud enough that Eve could hear it downstairs. Joe sat up so quickly that it made his head spin. He looked around and saw Mary standing over him with her arms folded over her chest. "Didn't see that coming." Joe half questioned not understanding the abrupt wake-up call. "There seems to be a lot of that going around," Mary snarled. Now Joe was really confused. He had only heard that tone from Mary a few times and it was never good. It usually meant that she was angry with someone who had been mean to her. Joe shook his head in an attempt to wake up and clear his mind. His head pounded. He silently blamed Mary for the way she woke him.

"Are you OK? You aren't making any sense. What's wrong?" Joe tried to be sympathetic but he felt terrible. "You're what's wrong, Joe!" Mary snapped. Joe looked at her through bloodshot eyes. He had a mixture of feelings varying from disorientation to anger. "What have I done?" Joe gave Mary that innocent look. "It seems like you have forgotten some pretty interesting events that occurred this weekend," Mary snarled as she walked to Joe's computer and sat down. "What are you talking about?" Joe was beginning to get miffed. Mary didn't respond to Joe's question. She was busy at Joe's computer. Joe just sat there staring at Mary's back and occasionally tried to see what she was doing on the computer. After a couple of minutes, Mary hit the enter key on the computer. "Maybe this will jog your memory a little." In a few seconds the YouTube video of Melissa's kiss began to play. Joe stood up and walked over to the computer to get a better look. Joe leaned over Mary and she rolled the chair away from him. Joe couldn't believe what he was seeing. How did Melissa pull this off without him knowing what was going on. He watched it twice. "Reliving a pleasant memory?" Mary had a sarcastic tone in her voice. "Mary, I don't know how this happened." "What do you mean you don't know how it happened? It seems clear to me you and Melissa were out riding around having what appears to be a pretty good time!" "That's not what I mean." Joe was getting disgusted. "I mean, I don't know how it got recorded and why it's on YouTube." "You mean you don't know how you got caught!" Mary was on her feet with fire in her eyes. "How many other times has this gone on that I didn't know about?!" "Now Mary, calm down, this has never happened before. You know Melissa. She flirts with everyone. It was no big deal. We just went to get pizza; I mean, I went to get pizza the other night and she insisted on going along. On the way home, I was concentrating on driving because it was snowing. That's when she kissed me. I guess she recorded it with her cell phone. It was not a big deal. How did you find out about it?" "If it wasn't a big deal why didn't you tell me about it yesterday? I was humiliated at the lunch table when Melissa showed it to all of the girls." Tears began to run down Mary's cheeks.

Joe was getting really angry now. He didn't like being accused of things he didn't do. He felt like he had been betrayed by Mary. She was assuming the worst of him and he didn't like it. His eyes darted around the room, occasionally glancing at Mary who was staring a hole in him. All of a sudden, his eyes fell on the printer and the picture of Mary and Brad in a big embrace. Mary's eyes followed his to the picture. Her heart skipped and she held her breath. Joe, in his anger, decided to retaliate. After all, he had some questions of his own. He leaned down and slowly picked up the picture. He held it up so Mary could see it. The confused look on his face turned to a sly smile. "Looks like I'm not the only one who had a good time this weekend! Maybe I should call Gary. We could form a support group for guys you have cheated on!" The words cut Mary like a knife. Her tears turned to sobs as she yelled at Joe, "Don't you dare try to turn this around and put it on me! There is a perfectly good explanation for that and you know it. How could you jump to conclusions like that?" "Apparently, we both have some secrets," Joe snarled. "I guess it's OK for you to jump to conclusions, but when the shoe is on the other foot, it is a different story!" "So you ADMIT that you were trying to keep it from me!" Mary returned the attack. "I'm not admitting anything because I didn't do anything wrong!" Joe was getting red in the face. All rational thinking was now gone for both he and Mary. "Well I guess if you didn't do anything wrong, neither did I!" Mary was now beside herself with anger. "Maybe I'll call Jimmy and go out for a little make-out session of my own!" Joe had never liked Jimmy and Mary knew it. Jimmy was always causing trouble for Joe. After he had shown Joe the article about Mary and Gary, Joe had always glared him down in the hallways. The thought of Mary going out with Jimmy made Joe feel sick inside. However, he wasn't going to show it. His anger was out of control. "Whatever trips your trigger!" he snapped. "Oh by the way, what's the number of the guy in the picture? Maybe he would like to join our support group!" "Joe, you are a total jerk!" Mary snapped half sobbing and half screaming. "I'm out of here!" "Suits me! I've got to call Melissa to see if she can come over and help me with my homework!"

Mary ran out of Joe's room and headed down the stairs. Joe walked to the door and slammed it so hard that the whole house shook. Eve had heard the yelling but couldn't understand the words. She met Mary at the bottom of the stairs. "What's wrong honey?" Eve asked as Mary continued toward the door. "Nothing, mom; I just need to go home." Eve grabbed Mary's arm and spun her around. Eve saw that Mary was crying. "What happened? Eve was sterner now. "I just don't understand him anymore," Mary said through her tears. "I just want to go home." Eve hugged Mary and said, "OK honey. Everything will be fine." "I don't know," Mary questioned as she opened the door to leave. "Do you want me to talk to him?" Eve was trying to help. "No thanks. There's nothing to say," Mary said as she closed the door behind her.

Mary could hear Ruth talking on the phone when she walked through the door. "OK, thanks; I'll talk to you later. Bye." Mary knew that Eve, her second mom, would most likely have been the one on the other end of that call. She knew that Eve loved her and wanted Ruth to know that she was hurting. Ruth hung up the phone and looked at Mary with concern written all over her face. "I guess that was my other mom on the phone," Mary questioned while knowing the answer. "She's just concerned about you and Joe and now I am too." Ruth walked to Mary with open arms. Mary accepted the hug and broke down into sobbing. After a couple of minutes of soothing talk from her mom, Ruth asked, "Do you want to talk about it?" "No," Mary said as her sobs began to slow down. "It might make you feel better." Ruth prodded. That was all it took. "Joe and I had a big fight. He was messing around with Melissa Saturday and then he accused me of cheating on him in Salt Lake City!" "Hold on just a minute." Ruth was trying to catch up. "Slow down and start from the beginning." They sat down at the kitchen table and Mary began to tell the story.

Joe walked over and sat down on the edge of the bed cradling his head in his hands. His mind was going 100 miles an hour. His anger hadn't subsided as he was still furious with Mary. How could she jump to such conclusions? Especially since it looked like she was cheating on him. He hadn't considered it seriously until now. Maybe she WAS cheating on him. That's why she didn't bother to consider the other possible explanations for the video of him and Melissa. Sometimes the guilty assume that everyone else is guilty of the same action in order to justify their actions. No matter, she had made it clear; they had broken up; or had they? His head pounded from the fever which caused him to think irrationally.

There was a knock on the door, "Joe?" The door opened and it was Eve. "Are you OK?" "I couldn't be better; after all, I'm so sick that I'm going to have to die to feel better; I think the one and only girl I have ever cared about just accused me of cheating on her and I'm pretty sure we just broke up! Man, I'm on top of the world!" The sarcasm oozed from Joe. "Do you want to talk about it?" Eve was concerned not only for Joe and Mary as a couple, but also for Joe's health. She knew that stress was not good for someone who was sick. "I think I just did!" Joe snapped at his mother. "Eve raised her eyebrows in astonishment. Joe had never talked to her like that. She briefly considered a harsh rebuke, but thought better of it. Joe was beside himself and she knew it.

CHAPTER THIRTEEN

Mary walked into the school the next day with dark circles under her eyes. Her mind wouldn't allow her to get much sleep because she kept recounting the fight with Joe over and over. She couldn't believe that Joe had accused her of cheating on him. Especially after it was so obvious that he had been cheating on her! Had they broken up? She wasn't quite sure. They had both said things to the other that neither one had ever said before. The warm air inside the school hit her as she walked through the doors. She put on a fake smile just in case Melissa had spread the news. There was no way she was going to let anyone think it bothered her. At least she wouldn't have to face Joe today. She had learned from her mother that he was still sick. She couldn't believe that she was actually glad that Joe was sick! Not that she wanted him to be ill; she wouldn't wish that on anyone. She just didn't want to face him. That was a new feeling for her. She had ALWAYS wanted to see Joe.

Mary didn't want to speak to anyone so she tried to avoid eye contact as she walked briskly to her locker. She did glance in the direction of several kids as she breezed past them to determine how widespread the knowledge of Melissa's video had become. The guys seemed OK but she thought that some of the girls had given her some sad looks as she passed by. Great, Melissa was doing as Mary had suspected. It wouldn't be long before it would spread all over school. She arrived at her locker and began the process of piling books in along with her coat. Just as she closed the door to her locker Allen startled her as he came up behind her and said, "Hi Mary! What's up? Where's Joe?" "Oh, hi Allen." She could tell by the tone in his voice that he hadn't heard. "I guess he's still sick. I haven't talked with him today." Allen thought to himself that something was up. Joe and Mary had always ridden to school together; and on the days that they hadn't, they had always communicated. Just as he was about to question Mary, Angie walked up to them. "Hi guys! Is everyone ready for that English quiz today?" Angie knew that Mary was hurting. She could tell it by looking into her eyes. She also knew that Allen hadn't seen the video. She was there to rescue Mary and Mary knew it. "I'm as ready as I'll ever be." Allen chirped. He was glad to see Angie. Tears welled up in Mary's eyes as she looked at Angie. They were tears of thankfulness for being a good friend. Allen noticed the tears. "What's wrong Mary? Surely you can't miss him that much." He was trying to tease Mary out of whatever was bothering her. Angie intervened, "She's just happy to see us together. Hey Allen, would you mind getting my sweater from my locker? My first period class is cold and I'm sure I'm going to need it." Allen wasn't stupid. He knew he was being dismissed and he was OK with that. If there was something that he could do to help, Angie would let him know. Right now, he knew that Mary needed to talk to Angie. "Sure Angie, I'll see you in class." He gave her arm a gentle squeeze, winked at Mary, and started down the hall.

Angie glanced at the clock in the hall; one minute until the bell rang. "OK, here is what I know. Melissa sent a broadcast text message to at least 25 people last night telling them about the video and where to find it. She implied that you and Joe were breaking up and that Joe was interested in her. There were a lot of text messages, e-mails, and phone calls after that. I tried to do my best to tell everyone I talked to that it wasn't true, but people love a good story. It doesn't help that Joe isn't here so everyone could see you two together. I'm sure it will blow over. Just hang in there." The bell rang. "I'm not so sure Melissa isn't right," Mary said through her tears and started off to class. Angie just stood there; paralyzed in disbelief and watched her best friend walk down the hall. By then Allen had returned with her sweater and gently put it around her shoulders. "We had better get to class." Allen said. Angie turned around and looked at Allen. She had a bewildered look in her eyes. "What's wrong?" "I'll tell you later."

The bell rang signaling the end of fourth period. Mary had mixed feelings. She was glad that the day was half over, but was dreading lunch. She headed for the cafeteria. She glanced nervously around the room as she finished loading her tray. She spotted Melissa talking and laughing with a bunch of girls as they ate. She scanned the room for Angie but couldn't find her or Allen. She looked for a way to avoid the table where Melissa sat but there was no way. Mary decided to hold her head high and hope for the best. She caught Melissa's eye as she passed and forced a smile. The other girls got quiet and waited for an altercation. The smile caught Melissa off-guard for a second but she composed herself quickly. "Hi Mary, want to eat with us?" Melissa sneered. Mary's mind raced. A chill ran down her spine as she caught a glimpse of a dark object move quickly behind Melissa. She thought of a thousand terse replies but decided not to stoop to Melissa's level. Suddenly, she caught sight of a hand waving. It was Allen and Angie. They were motioning her to come over. "No thanks Melissa. Thanks for asking but I'm going to sit with Angie. It looks like she and Allen have been saving a seat for me." Mary's response made Melissa look terrible in the eyes of everyone who had heard the conversation. It was one thing for a couple to break up, but quite another thing to rub it in. Everyone rolled their eyes at Melissa and gave Mary a look of approval. "Thank you, Lord, for helping me through that just now," Mary whispered under her breath.

Mary sat down at the table with Allen and Angie. By now, Angie had told Allen about the video. The three of them sat there in silence for a few minutes. Finally, Allen broke the ice. "Mary, you know Joe. There has got to be a better explanation than the one the Melissa is spreading around. You know how she is. Have you talked to Joe about it?" Mary laid her fork down and swallowed hard. "As a matter-of-fact we did discuss it last night." "Well, how did it go?" Angie questioned. "Not well, we ended up in a big fight. We both accused the other of cheating. He dug up another newspaper article from the tabloid that implied that I was partying with this guy in Salt Lake City. I confronted him about Melissa and he denied it. I think we broke up." Tears were streaming down her face by now.

Angie and Allen sat there dumbfounded. They didn't know what to say. There was a terrible silence for what seemed like hours. Angie finally decided to jump in. "I don't believe it. Mary, you are my best friend and I've known Joe all of my life. Something doesn't add up. You need to talk to him. I know that you guys have got it messed up somehow." "Yeah Mary," Allen added. "Joe is no idiot. He knows that he has a good thing going with you. He wouldn't do anything to jeopardize that!" "I just don't know anymore," Mary lamented. "He was so irrational last night. I just couldn't believe how he spoke to me. He has never treated me like that before." "No offense Mary, but how did you treat him?" Angie always tried to cut through the fog. The bell rang before Mary could answer. "Just think about it Mary, before you make any hasty decisions." Allen pleaded as they headed for their afternoon classes.

Eve knocked on Joe's door. He hadn't wanted any breakfast when she had checked with him earlier but she was determined to get some food in him now. It was 1:30 p.m. and he hadn't emerged from his room all day. "Come in Mom." Eve rubbed his shoulders. "It was nice of Mary to drop your homework off yesterday, wasn't it?" Eve was fishing for details about the fight but Joe didn't bite. "Yeah, I guess." Joe's words trailed off. Eve tried again. "Maybe she'll bring you today's assignments after school." The words from Eve sparked a glimmer of hope in Joe. He had thought about their fight over and over in his mind all night last night. He hated how it had unfolded. He wished that he had held his tongue and handled it differently. The only reason that he was working on his homework was to get his mind off of the fight. The idea of Mary stopping by excited him. Maybe he could fix it. He smiled for the first time that day. However, she had left extremely angry. He just didn't know if she would stop by or not. "Yeah, maybe," he said hopefully. "I'm getting tired mom, I think I'll take a nap." Joe had finished the sandwich and had eaten a few carrots. "OK sweetie, let me know if there is anything I can do for you." "Thanks Mom, I love you." "I love you too." Eve paused, "It will be OK Joe." Joe knew what his mom was talking about. She always knew more than what anybody had told her. She had a gift. She could read a person and figure things out even before the person did. It always amazed Joe. "I hope so," Joe replied. "Don't forget to pray about it," Eve advised as she closed the door. Joe flopped down on his bed and began to plan how to fix it with Mary.

Mary was startled out of her daydream by the sound of the bell. Finally, school was over. She hadn't heard much of the lecture. She had been replaying the fight in her mind. She had decided to take Joe his homework and try to talk it out. She at least needed to know if they really had broken up. As she headed out the door, she noticed Jimmy trying to get his car started. He had parked next to Mary so she couldn't ignore him. "Having trouble Jimmy?" Mary asked hoping the answer would be no." "I can't get it started." Jimmy was frustrated but decided to make lemonade out of lemons. "Could you give me a ride home?" Mary dreaded the question because Jimmy knew that she couldn't say no. "Sure Jimmy, hop in," Mary said as enthusiastically as possible without being too obvious. Jimmy jumped in the car. "Thanks Mary, you're just about the sweetest girl I know." Mary smiled at Jimmy and started the car and headed for Jimmy's house. Unbeknownst to Mary, Melissa had been walking across the parking lot and had witnessed the whole scene. She grinned and got in her car. She saw an opportunity.

Jimmy lived about 15 minutes out of the way so it was no big deal for Mary to take him home. Normally, it wouldn't have bothered her. Jimmy was OK. He could be annoying at times and everyone knew he was a player but, contrary to Joe, she could put up with him. Jimmy had heard about the video and decided to see if Mary and Joe were fighting. He silently hoped so. He wanted to go out with Mary so bad he couldn't stand it. He wanted to see how far he could get with her. It was a challenge to him. "I saw an interesting video on YouTube today in the library," Jimmy stated nonchalantly. Mary bristled. She couldn't believe that Jimmy would be so bold as to bring it up. She decided to play innocent. "Really, what was it about?" Jimmy decided to go for it. "It seems as if Joe was getting busy with Melissa this past weekend. I'm surprised you haven't seen it." "Oh that," Mary tried to play it off. "Yeah that!" Jimmy knew he had her attention now. "I wouldn't stand by and put up with that kind of carousing from my girlfriend." Mary tried to change the subject. "I didn't know you had a girlfriend Jimmy. I did hear that you went out with Katie last weekend. How did that go?" Jimmy couldn't refuse a chance to brag. "It was great! She did everything I wanted and more. But I'm finished with her. I'm looking for a lasting relationship with a real keeper. Someone like you, Mary." Mary became indignant. "I really don't like being compared with a fish, Jimmy. I'm a keeper?! Really!! Does, that mean that Katie isn't?! I like Katie and I don't care for the way you talk about her! Besides, you know that I'm dating Joe." "Relax, Mary, calm down. I didn't mean anything. I heard that you and Joe broke up. I have always had a crush on you. You can't blame a guy for trying. I was just wondering if you would like to go out sometime." Jimmy was back-peddling now. "I'll let you know if I want to go out with you Jimmy. Just don't try to play me. If you want to be friends, that's great. But if you want more...." Her voice trailed off. She reached for the radio and turned it up. They rode the rest of the way to Jimmy's house in silence.

Mary pulled up to Jimmy's house and waited for him to get out. Jimmy decided to try another approach. He grabbed the door handle and said, "I'm sorry Mary. I was out of line. I want to be your friend. I know that video had to hurt. If I can do anything for you or if you just need to talk, give me a call." "Thanks Jimmy. That's a true friend. I might just take you up on it sometime." "Anytime at all, thanks for the ride." "Bye Jimmy." He got out of the car and shut the door. Mary backed out of the driveway and waved at Jimmy as she drove away. 'Maybe he's not so bad after all,' Mary thought. Jimmy returned the wave and maintained the concerned look on his face. Once Mary was out of sight, Jimmy's concerned look turned to a fiendish grin as he skipped up the steps. 'It's just a matter of time,' he thought to himself.

Melissa pulled up in front of Joe's house and walked up to the door. The doorbell woke Joe up and he glanced at the clock; 3:40. School let out at 3:15, maybe it was Mary. He was ready to apologize for everything he had done and anything he hadn't done. All he wanted was to get things back to normal. He headed for the bathroom to wash his face and splash on a little cologne.

Eve opened the door ready to chastise Mary for ringing and not just coming in. "Oh, hi Melissa. I, um, I wasn't expecting you, I mean anyone...come in." "Thanks, Mrs. Goldstein, I was just in the neighborhood and decided to drop in and see how Joe was doing. After all, we are going to need him Friday night for the game. We have a tough one coming up. It is for the conference championship and it will be brutal. Besides, I brought his homework. I don't want him to fall behind in school." "That's very nice of you, Melissa. Joe is doing much better. I'm sure that he will be able to play Friday."

"That's great news Mrs. Goldstein. Do you think it would be OK if I went up and gave him his homework?" "Well I guess so, he was resting but you can check." Melissa was halfway up the stairs. "Thanks, I won't keep him long."

Joe heard the knock on his door and his heart leaped. As he opened it expecting Mary he said, "Hi sweetie! I'm so glad you came over...." His voice trailed off as he realized that it wasn't Mary. "Well hello yourself, cutie." Melissa gushed as she walked in to the room. "I'm sorry Melissa, I wasn't expecting you." "Are you disappointed, honey?" Melissa moved in close to Joe. "Um, no, uh, just surprised. Is there something I can do for you? Why are you here?" Joe glanced out the window. He wanted to see if Mary was home. Not yet, however, after last weekend, if she saw Melissa's car at his house she would be furious. She wouldn't have a right to be, but.... Melissa saw him look out the window and decided to divert his attention. "I was just worried about you. After all, you haven't been at school for two days. Besides, we haven't had a chance to discuss our relationship. Obviously, things have changed since Saturday night." She moved in close and put her head on his chest. Joe backed off as if he had been bitten by a snake. "Whoa, what relationship? Nothing happened Saturday night. What did you think happened?" "I had a wonderful time with you and I know you had fun. I think it's time we quite dancing around our feelings and take our relationship to the next level. Joe, I have always wanted to be your girlfriend and I would do ANYTHING for you. All you have to do is just say the word." Joe looked around the room. He couldn't believe what he was hearing. How could this mess have happened? He looked out the window again. Still no Mary.

Melissa saw her chance. "Mary is probably going to be late. I saw Jimmy get into her car after school. You know Jimmy, he moves fast. Face it Joe, you and Mary are finished. It's you and me now. I can make you feel better. Just give me a chance." She touched his arm which made a cold chill run down his back. He thought he saw a dark flash in the corner of his eye. He turned to see what it was, but it was gone. Whatever it was caused him to shiver just a little; goose bumps rose on his arms. He looked out the window again and saw Mary standing there in the driveway. She was staring at Melissa's car. Joe looked at Melissa who had also seen Mary. "I guess she is realizing that you two are over. The only one who doesn't see it is you Joe." Joe sat down on the bed and rubbed his head. "I'm not feeling well, Melissa, maybe you should go." "Sure thing, honey. I'll call you later." She leaned down and kissed him on the cheek. Joe pulled away. Melissa headed down the stairs and made eye contact with Eve. "Thanks Mrs. Goldstein. I'll be seeing you." "Goodbye Melissa. Be careful going home." Melissa opened the door and saw Mary still standing in her driveway. She waved to Mary as if to say, 'I belong here now.' Mary spun around and walked into the house. Melissa smiled to herself and got into her car. 'This is going great.'

Joe watched Mary storm into her house. How could things get so screwed up? He knew that she would be furious. But he hadn't done anything wrong. It was just circumstances. How could he explain it to her? Besides, she was the one playing around in Salt Lake City. He was the innocent one, not her. He walked to his stereo and turned it up. He needed to think.

Mary slammed the door and walked up the stairs. Ruth was in the kitchen and heard the commotion. "Are you OK, Mary?" "Couldn't be better." Mary tried to be convincing but Ruth knew better. She decided to give Mary a little space. Eve didn't know exactly what was bothering Mary, but she could tell that Mary needed to cool off. Mary threw her books on the desk and flopped down on her bed. She looked at the picture of her and Joe on the nightstand. It was taken on New Year's Eve at a party they had gone to. He had told her that night that she was the only girl for him. He said that he would love her forever. 'Yeah right, forever until Melissa gets to him.' She laid the picture face down. How could he do this to her! She was in Salt Lake City doing God's work. How could he cheat on her while she was away! Well if that's the way he wanted it, fine. Let's see how he likes it. She grabbed the phone. "Hello Jimmy, this is Mary, I could use a little help on my English paper. Would you mind coming over and giving it a once over?" "Sure Mary, when?" Jimmy was excited. "How about 6:30?" "Great Mary, I'll see you then." He rubbed his hands together after he hung up the phone. 'Take that Joe.'

The Goldsteins were just finishing dinner. Joe hadn't said much as he picked at his food. He had eaten a little but not near as much as usual. "You need to eat if you plan to get better," Abraham observed. "I'm not very hungry. I guess it will take awhile to get my appetite back. I think I'll go back upstairs." Joe got up and headed for his room. "I guess you need to get started on today's assignments," Eve said. "It sure was nice of Melissa to drop them off for you." "What?" Joe questioned. "She didn't give me any assignments." "Melissa?" Abraham was trying to catch up. Isn't she on the basketball team? I read in the paper where she had a triple double last week. Thirty-three points, 12 rebounds, and 11 assists." Silence fell across the room as the three of them realized that they were all on a different page. "Am I missing something? Abraham questioned. "Yeah, that's her. She stopped by earlier. I'm going upstairs." Joe headed through the living room and glanced out of the picture window. Jimmy was getting out of his car. Joe watched him skip up the driveway and knock on the door to Mary's house. Mary met him with a big smile and glanced over at Joe's house. The door closed and Joe felt as if he would explode. He ran up the stairs and fired up the stereo.

CHAPTER FOURTEEN

Joe woke up the next day feeling better. He was tired but felt good enough to go to school. However, he sure didn't want to go. Facing Mary and the rest of the kids at school was the last thing he wanted to do. He sat back down on the bed and tried to come up with an excuse not to go. Eve knocked on the door and went in. "Good morning sweetie. How are you feeling today?" Joe thought about lying to his mom but reconsidered. "I'm OK. I just don't want to go to school for some reason." Joe hoped that his mom would agree and let him stay home. Eve put her hand on his forehead. "The fever is gone. Is your stomach upset?" "No." Eve began to figure out why Joe didn't want to go. "Joe, I know you and Mary are in the middle of a disagreement. But you have to face it. It isn't like you to ignore a problem. You have always attacked a situation and figured it out." "I know mom, it's just that this time it's Mary. We have never had an argument. I just don't know how to handle it." Joe was expecting some sympathy from Eve. He didn't get it. "Joseph Goldstein! How dare you run from a problem! The Lord will help you through it but you have to take the first step. Now you get dressed and get to school. You need to talk to Mary and figure this out. Maybe you two should pray together. Now get going!" Joe knew his mom was right. He had to go, but boy was he dreading it. "Get away from me Satan," Joe said under his breath as he went to the shower.

Across the street, Mary was getting ready for school as well. She wondered if Joe felt good enough to go. She had even asked her mother to call Eve to check. "Are you kidding me?!" Ruth had responded. "I know that you and Joe are having a little spat and I want you two to work it out but I'm not going to get in the middle of it like I was in junior high." Mary knew Ruth was right and she was embarrassed for asking. She just wanted to know if she was going to have to face Joe or not. Mary wondered if Joe had seen Jimmy at her house last night. She hoped so. Two could play at that game. She hadn't enjoyed Jimmy being there at all. He kept making wise cracks and innuendos about how he and Mary should make out. After about an hour she had asked Jimmy to leave. She just couldn't stand it any longer.

Mary finished getting ready and looked at the clock on the kitchen wall; 7:30. She and Joe had always left the house at 7:40; she had ten minutes. She decided to wait and see if Joe was gone. She looked out the front window and saw that Joe's car was still there. Maybe he wasn't going. "Good morning, pumpkin!" Jacob had snuck up behind Mary and picked her up from behind and swung her around. "Good morning Daddy." Mary replied after he had set her down. "Are you driving to school or riding with Joe?" Jacob didn't know about the fight. "I'm going to drive today." "OK, I'll start your car and scrap the windows so you can get going. See you tonight. I love you." "Thanks daddy. I love you too." "Bye Ruth, see you at the store. I love you too." Jacob yelled at the kitchen. "Be careful Jacob, I love you too."

Joe walked into the school with one thing on his mind; to talk to as few people as possible and get to his seat in class as quickly as possible. Joe arrived at his locker and began organizing his books for the day. Just as he closed his locker, Jimmy walked by with a few of the guys. Joe glared at him as he passed by, but Jimmy just sneered at Joe.

Joe had his back to Jimmy by now but he could here him bragging to the guys about being at Mary's house last night. Then he heard him say, "Hi Mary! You are looking good today!" Apparently Mary had arrived and was heading to her locker which was right next to Joe's. He wasn't ready to see Mary so he spun around to head to class and bumped into Melissa. "Hi, cutie!" Melissa grinned at Joe. "I'm glad you're feeling better. Care to walk me to class?" Joe could hear Mary talking to Jimmy less than ten feet away from him. "Sure, let's go!" Joe grinned at Melissa. He held out his arm and she slipped hers through it and they headed down the hall. Mary had witnessed the whole thing and resisted the urge to run down the hall and tackle Melissa. 'Oh well, it's not her fault. I guess he's available now.' She thought to herself. Jimmy was talking to her but she wasn't listening. She just wanted to get away from him. She heard someone say her name; it was Angie. She had sensed Mary's dilemma and decided to come to her rescue. "Excuse me, Jimmy, I need to talk to Angie." The bell rang and Angie fell in step with Mary as they walked to class.

"I need for you to sit with me in class. I don't want to be alone and I sure can't sit with Joe." Mary pleaded with her friend. "I already planned on it." Angie assured her. "It's a good thing we don't have assigned seats." When the girls got to class, Joe was already sitting in the far back corner. Allen was sitting next to him and waved at the girls as they came in. They both waved back. Joe hadn't seen them because he was staring into the opened text book. The girls grabbed a seat in the front. Several of the kids noticed that Mary and Joe weren't sitting together and shot confused looks at each other because they had never seen them sitting apart. Mary assumed that these were the ones who hadn't seen the video or hadn't had the chance to pick up on the gossip in the halls. Even the teacher took a double take when she came in. Although there weren't assigned seats, the kids usually sat in the same places. After all, we are all creatures of habit.

Both Mary and Joe successfully avoided each other all morning. It was a little difficult because they have all of their classes together and their lockers are right next to each other. Angie and Allen keep urging them to talk. After all, Joe and Mary weren't sure that they had in fact broken up, even through Melissa and Jimmy were going around school saying that they had. Joe and Mary both refused to be the first one to speak to the other. They both secretly didn't want to know how the other felt. Neither one of them wanted to break up. It hurt Mary terribly when she saw Melissa with Joe. She wanted to smack that grin off of her face every time she saw Melissa. Joe felt the same way about Jimmy who was all over Mary and Joe hated it. He wanted to knock him through the wall. He missed Mary. All day long he wondered how he could fix it or even if it could be fixed. They were both miserable but were too stubborn to admit it. The only other ones who knew were Angie and Allen who were getting tired of babysitting them.

Angie and Allen were discussing it as they headed for lunch. "Angie, Joe is my best friend and I love Mary to death, but, aw... never mind." "No, go ahead. Tell me what's on your mind." Angie pleaded. "Well it's kind of selfish, but, I, um, I would like to sit with you at lunch." Allen blushed and looked at the floor. "Why Allen, you are turning as red as a cherry." Angie teased as she squeezed his arm. This observation didn't help his color but he appreciated the touch on his arm. "I feel the same way. I have an idea. Let's sit together and save them a seat. Maybe that will force them to talk. I know they can work it out. They are just so stubborn." "Good idea, we had better hurry and beat them to the cafeteria."

Mary finished filling her tray and scanned the lunch room for a place to sit. She spotted Allen and Angie sitting at a table with two empty chairs. She knew what they were up to and didn't like it at all. She quickly glanced around the room. She didn't see Joe anywhere. There was a spot open next to Melissa at a table with a bunch of other kids. She was friends with them but she couldn't bear to eat with Melissa. Besides, she was probably saving it for Joe. Jimmy waved at her to come over and sit by him but that made her want to throw up. She stood there frozen.

Joe had watched Mary go through the line and kept a safe distance behind her. As he emerged with his tray, he quickly observed what was going on. Jimmy was waving to Mary, Melissa was waving to him, Allen and Angie were trying to ignore them, and Mary standing there not knowing what to do. He was slightly encouraged that Mary hadn't immediately headed for Jimmy. He sensed her fear and instinct took over. He had always come to her rescue and he automatically took charge. He walked right by her and whispered, "You can sit with Allen and Angie, and I'll go someplace else." She could have said, 'I don't care where you sit,' or 'Don't you tell me what to do' but neither of those words came out of her mouth. All she whispered was, "Thank you." Joe kept walking because he felt the eyes of a lot of kids staring at him. He didn't wait to hear Mary's response. He walked up to a bunch of freshman girls, flashed a smile, and said. "Is anyone sitting here?" The girls giggled and quickly made room for him. He glanced at

Mary who was just sitting down next to Angie. Mary looked up and thought she caught a smile from Joe but wasn't sure. She returned the smile but by then one of the starry-eyed freshman girls was trying to get his attention.

Abraham walked into Witz's Drug Store after lunch and waved at Ruth who was working at the register. "Where's Jake?" "He's in the back. He's supposed to be filling prescriptions, but is probably taking a nap." Ruth teased and pointed to the rear of the store. "I'll wake him up for you!" Abraham was out running errands that day. He had given the construction crews the day off because it was just too cold to be outside. He needed a few things to restock his safety kits so he decided to use it as an excuse to stop in. He grabbed a box of bandages as he walked back to where Jake was working. "Hi Jake, how's it going?" "Hello Abe!" Jake was the only one who could get away with calling him Abe. He had called him that ever since they had been roommates in college. "I'm as happy as a fox in a hen house when the farmer is gone on vacation!" Abraham laughed at Jake's analogy. Jake never ceased to amaze him with his humor. "How's my buddy Abe?" "Well to tell you the truth, I need to talk to you; do you have a minute?" Jake knew that from Abraham's tone that something was bothering him. He glanced at the bandages in Abraham's hand and decided to make a joke in order to get him excused from the pharmacy. "Now Abe, I've shown you several times how to use a band-aid. I'll show you just one more time. Come on back to the office." He signaled to his helper to cover for him and led Abraham back to his office; both of them laughing all the way.

"Have a seat Abe." Jake offered as he closed the door. "How's Joe?" "Joe's fine Jake." "He was pretty sick Sunday and yesterday but he's on the mend. I think he'll be able to play Friday. Actually, he drove to school this morning." "Really?" Jake was surprised. "I wonder why he and Mary didn't ride together. Maybe one has to stay later than the other." "Never has been a problem before, they always seemed to work around practices, meetings, events...things just don't add up Jake." "You're right Abe. I suppose that they are having a spat. Mary mentioned that she was upset with Joe. It was something about Joe and Melissa at some party this weekend. I didn't pay much attention to it. Sounded like teenage stuff to me." "Could be, Jake. I know Joe has been acting strange lately. He's been real edgy. He doesn't like it much when Mary is gone for the weekends." "Yeah, I know that Joe doesn't like that Gary guy that works with Mary on the project. Now that you mention it, Mary has been a little grouchy for the past couple of days." "You know Jake, those two have never been apart for very long; and they have never been apart since they hit puberty. Do you suppose that Mary's responsibilities have put a strain on things?" They both sat there in silence for a few seconds and then Jake hit the intercom button, "Miss Ruth, would you please come to the office?" Jake released the button. "I bet the women know something about this."

In a few seconds Ruth came in. "What are you two up to now?" "I don't know Ruth but it had better be good," Eve's voice called out of the speaker phone. "I was in the middle of some book work." "I've got Eve on the line," Jake informed Ruth. "Are either of you two aware of any problems between Mary and Joe?" After a few seconds Eve spoke up. "I know they had a pretty big argument Sunday night. Mary came over to see Joe and I heard some pretty loud voices coming from Joe's room. I couldn't make out what they said but Mary was pretty upset when she left." Ruth chimed in, "I thought it was pretty unusual that Mary would ask Jimmy over to help with her English last night. She never has problems with English." "That explains why Melissa came over yesterday," Abraham observed. "Sounds like Joe and Mary have had an argument and are playing games with each other." "You know, if they want to break up, they should do it like adults. They can still be friends. I would hate it, personally; I think they are great together, but…." Jake's words trailed off. "There's just so much tension right now," Abraham said into the air. He looked at Jake who was already grinning. That phrase went all the way back to their college days. Whenever it was used, it only meant one thing: both men stood up and yelled, "Luau!"

Ruth and Eve knew immediately what the 'boys' had on their mind. They had known Abraham and Jake in college. In fact, one of the things that attracted them to the guys was their famous luaus. Whenever the kids at college got stressed, usually during finals, the guys would throw an impromptu luau on the campus commons. It wasn't unusual for 100 kids to end up joining the party. "Now boys, it's 20 degrees outside," Ruth warned trying to stave off the idea. "You had better put on long underwear under your grass skirt, sweet thing." Jake smiled at Ruth. "Abraham, we haven't done that since college. The neighbors will think we are crazy," Eve protested over the speaker phone. "Honey, they already think we are crazy. It's time we prove it to them. Jake, your place or mine?" "How about yours, you have a better grill than mine," Jake admitted. "Great! I'll get the steaks and you cook them." Abraham was on his feet and headed out the door. Jake was right behind him. "Could you girls take care of the rest? You know, potatoes, salad, dessert?" Jake said over his shoulder as he followed Abraham out the door. He didn't wait for an answer. He and Abraham were already gone.

Joe got into his car about 6:45. He had been the last one to leave the locker room after practice. He had stayed late to do some individual conditioning because he was afraid that the two-day layoff may have caused him to get slightly out of shape. At least, that was his excuse. The truth was that he really enjoyed the solace of the gym after practice. He felt like it was just he and God alone in the gym. He prayed as he ran the stairs, shot free throws, and just sat at his favorite spot on the top row. He thought a lot about Mary. He had been glad that she didn't sit with Jimmy at lunch. Maybe that was a good sign. He finally admitted to himself that he didn't want to break up with her and hoped that she felt the same way. He needed to get that message across to her. If they were going to break up, it would have to be her decision, not his. However, he couldn't just lay his feelings out there for her to step on; if in fact, she did want to break up. He couldn't take that. He needed to be a little more subtle.

It occurred to Joe that Mary had cheerleading practice and on Wednesdays they stayed later to make posters to put up on the walls of the gym. Still in his workout shorts, he walked out of the gym and through the lobby where he could see the parking lot. It had snowed during the day and the cars were covered. The only cars that remained in the lot were his and the cheerleaders'. Joe had an idea. He looked around to make sure no one was watching and sprinted to his car and grabbed the snow scraper. Joe nearly turned his ankle because he slipped on the ice running toward Mary's car. 'Apparently, tennis shoes aren't too good in the snow,' he thought. He worked furiously on Mary's car cleaning the windows. He knew she hated scraping windows. By the time he finished, he couldn't feel his hands and his legs were turning blue.

Mary came out of the school relieved that the day was over. It had been tense all day. Both she and Joe avoided each other all day. She had tried to get his attention in class. She wanted to give him a smile for what he had done at lunch, but she could never catch his eye. It encouraged her that he had cared enough for her to come to her rescue. Maybe he didn't want to break up. She knew she sure didn't. She hadn't gotten over her anger and had realized that maybe Angie and Allen were right. They just needed to talk it out. However, she wasn't sure how Joe felt. She hoped he felt the same way but what if he didn't. She would be embarrassed beyond belief if she opened her heart to him and he wasn't interested. How could she be sure?

She arrived at her car and was dreading scraping her windows. The rest of the cheerleaders were working on their windows as fast as they could in order to get out of the cold as soon as possible. Angie was parked next to Mary and noticed that her windows were clean. "Looks like someone has a guardian angel," Angie observed. Mary looked at her windows. All of them were clean. Not a bit of snow or ice on any of them. Mary also knew what Angie was referring to with the guardian angel comment. That was Mary's pet name for Joe. "What makes you so sure it was my guardian angel?" Mary asked hopefully. "Maybe it was Jimmy or some secret admirer." "First of all, those windows would have had to have been scraped within the last 15 minutes or they would have frosted over again by now. Secondly, Jimmy left right after school with Katie; and although you have plenty of admirers, look around." Mary scanned the parking lot. The only other car around was Joe's. Everyone else was gone. Mary suppressed a giggle but couldn't hold back a big grin. Still, she had second thoughts. She hoped it was Joe, but....

Mary walked in the back door and was surprised that her mother wasn't in the kitchen cooking supper. "Is anyone here?" "Hi honey, I'm upstairs getting ready," Ruth's voice echoed down the stairs. "Getting ready for what?" "We're going out for dinner tonight." Mary started to get excited. Whenever they went out to eat during the week, it was usually some sort of celebration. She could use the diversion. "What's the occasion?" Mary was curious. "It's just a little surprise, honey; a little something to relieve the tension of the winter blues." "OK fine, don't tell me. What should

I wear?" "Don't worry about it, honey. I'll lay something out for you while you get a shower." "Mom, I don't mind telling you that you are acting a little strange. How much time do I have?" Ruth looked at the clock. "We have about 20 minutes. We are meeting your dad there; now scoot!" Mary laughed and ran down the hall to the bathroom.

Joe pulled up in front of his house and looked over at the Reubenowitz's; Mary was home. He could tell that she had just gotten there because heat was still coming out of the exhaust pipe. He mused to himself that he would be a pretty good detective. He was glad that she was home and not out with Jimmy somewhere. Joe walked into the house and hung up his coat. Delicious aromas were coming from the kitchen. For the first time since Saturday he was really hungry. "Smells good mom, what's for dinner?" "Hi Joe! How are you feeling? We are having steak." "Steak!? That sounds wonderful. I'm feeling better and I'm starved." Joe made a beeline to the stove. He assumed that Eve was cooking them in the oven. He flipped the door open and was surprised to see rolls cooking where the steaks should be. "Where are the steaks?" Joe wanted to make sure that his was cooked medium rare. Eve had a tendency to overcook the steaks. She liked hers well done. "The steaks are on the grill," Eve announced proudly. Suddenly Joe noticed that his mom was wearing a Hawaiian shirt and shorts. The kitchen was decorated with strings of lighted lanterns and there was Jimmy Buffet music playing on the stereo. "Is dad grilling the steaks in this weather?!" "Of course not dear," Eve assured him. "Jacob is grilling the steaks; you're dad is just helping him." Joe walked to the patio door and looked out at his dad and Jake standing near the grill. They were wearing straw hats, Hawaiian shirts and grass skirts over their sweatpants. Jake saw Joe and waved the cooking fork at him. Abraham looked up, smiled at Joe and waved him to come out. Joe slid the door open and said, "You guys are nuts! You're going to freeze to death!" "Now Joe, we are wearing sweats pants," Abraham teased. Jake spoke up. "You know the only good steak is a grilled steak; medium rare, right?" Joe laughed, nodded slowly and closed the door in disbelief. "Mom, what's going on?" "We're having a luau with the Reubenowitzs tonight dear. Doesn't that sound like fun?" "Um, I guess, are we eating outside too? Are ALL of the Reubenowitzs coming?" "Yes Joe, they are ALL coming.

I know that you and Mary have been arguing but can't you at least be civil? Your dad and Jake cooked this thing up this afternoon. You've heard the stories about their famous luaus in college. They just thought it might be a good idea to have one tonight. Jake has been working a lot in the store doing inventory and your dad has been working on income taxes for about a month." Joe knew that his dad disliked doing paperwork. He would rather be out on the job working with his hands. He had also been regaled with the memories of the luaus. In fact, Joe thought it had been a good idea and he planned to have a few of his own once he got to college. "OK mom, but it may be awkward. Mary is pretty mad at me. I'll try, but I'm not going to predict how she will react. What time are they coming?" "They should be here in about five minutes." "FIVE MINUTES? I NEED A SHOWER!" Joe took off up the stairs taking them three at a time. 'I guess he still cares for her,' Eve smiled to herself.

Mary got out of the shower and walked into her room. There on the bed was a Hawaiian shirt, grass shirt, a lay of flowers, and a flower for her hair. Mary looked at what her mom had laid out and thought that her mother had lost her mind. She walked into her mother's room and saw that her mother was wearing a similar outfit. "Oh honey, you might want to put on some shorts under the grass skirt, it's kind of chilly outside," Ruth stated nonchalantly. "KIND OF CHILLY? IT'S DOWNRIGHT FREEZING OUTSIDE! The guy on the radio said it was ten degrees with a wind chill factor of zero!" "Well then, maybe you should take a sweater too." Ruth smiled impishly at Mary. "Mom, what's going on? I'm not going any- where until I get some answers." Mary was extremely confused by now. "Alright dear, calm down. We are going to a party. Specifically, it is a luau. OK?" Mary's eyes narrowed. "Is this one of those luaus like daddy used to have in college?" "Yes dear." "Are the Goldsteins involved?" "Come to think of it, they are. Is that a problem?" Eve was trying to be coy. "Mom, you know that Joe and I have been fighting. I can't go over there. It would be weird. He wouldn't even speak to me at school today." "Did you try to speak to him?" "Well, not exactly," Mary admitted. "Look Mary, your dad and Abraham have had a rough couple of weeks. They need a diversion and like it or not, the Goldsteins are our best friends. If you and Joe can't suck it up and at least be civil I will be very disappointed in both of you." "I'm sorry mom, of course I'll go." Mary headed down the hall to her room.

A few minutes later Mary and Ruth walked into the Goldstein's house. Ruth walked in first and yelled, "Aloha!" Mary walked in behind her mom and looked around nervously. Joe was no-where in sight, thank goodness. "Aloha." Eve's voice came from the kitchen. Ruth and Mary headed for the kitchen. When Ruth saw Eve she started laughing and both of them broke into a hula dance right there in the kitchen. "Come on Mary, join the fun," Eve urged. The ladies danced over to Mary and started dancing all around her. Mary started laughing and joined in. "Where's daddy?" Mary said between giggles. "He's on the deck grilling steaks with Abraham." The girls danced their way over to the patio door and peered at the guys huddled over the grill. They both noticed the girls dancing in the door so both of them immediately started dancing around the grill. The site of Big Jake doing the hula was hilarious and all three girls laughed so loud that the guys heard them through the glass.

When things settled down Ruth sensed that Mary was nervous. Joe hadn't appeared from anywhere. Both Ruth and Mary assumed that he was on the deck with the guys but he wasn't anywhere outside. "Where's Joe?" Ruth asked on Mary's behalf. "Is he feeling OK?" Mary secretly hoped that Joe was tired and wouldn't be joining them. "He's in the shower," Eve replied. By now the women were busy in the kitchen. "Is there anything I can do?" Mary offered. "Would you mind going down to the basement and getting a jar of homemade strawberry jam from the shelf?" Eve asked. "I know that Jake loves my jam." "He loves anybody's jam," Ruth teased. Mary headed for the basement door. She was glad to have some-thing to do. She didn't want to be in the kitchen when Joe showed up. Maybe she could eat in the basement.

After a couple of minutes, Joe slipped around the corner and dropped his gym clothes by the basement door. He didn't know where Mary was or if she even came. "Hi Moms," Joe said as cheerfully as possible. He grinned at their outfits. They returned the look and both immediately disapproved. "You are not dressed for a luau young man!" Eve said in her fake, stern voice. He was wearing shorts and a T-shirt. "I don't have any luau stuff, mom. Thank goodness." "Well, you don't eat here tonight unless you are dressed for a luau. Why don't you go downstairs and look in the box marked 'luau stuff' maybe you can find something." Ruth shot Eve a knowing glance and Eve replied with a wink. "Aw mom, I'll look stupid. Do I have to?" "Absolutely not, that is unless you want to eat, now get! And take those dirty clothes down with you and throw them in the washer." "Yes mom." As Joe headed for the door, he wondered where Mary was. He doubted that she was outside with the guys. Maybe she was in the bathroom or didn't come at all. He wasn't sure which option he wanted. He sure would like to make up, but the thought of facing her scared him to death.

He opened the door and noticed that the lights were on. 'Mom forgot to turn them off again' he thought. When Joe hit the bottom step he heard the door to the kitchen close. 'Must be the wind from the patio door.' Mary was in the laundry room taking her sweet time looking for the jam. She really didn't care if she ever found it. The thought of facing Joe upset her. The door was closed and she didn't hear him walk across the TV room toward her. Joe hit the door with his free hand and flung it open. Mary screamed and knocked an empty glass jar off the shelf which hit the floor and broke into a hundred pieces. Joe was so startled that he tripped over the laundry basket that was in the middle of the floor and fell to the concrete floor with a loud thud. The clothes he was carrying went all over the room. Eve and Ruth were listening at the door and heard the commotion. "I guess they found each other," Eve smiled at Ruth and whispered.

Joe looked up at Mary. She was standing on a stool with her back to Joe reaching for the jam, her arms frozen above her head. The light in the laundry room made Mary's long dark hair look as if it were laced in gold. She was looking at Joe over her shoulder and the orchid in her hair offset her big beautiful eyes. He felt like she was looking right through him. Joe thought she looked like a Hawaiian goddess. He laid there in the middle of the dirty laundry, speechless. They just looked at each other for a long time. Neither knew what to say. Finally, Mary lowered her arms and stepped off the stool and faced Joe. "Are you OK?" Her voice cracked as she spoke. The sound of Mary's voice snapped him out of his trance. He missed hearing her talk. He thought she had the sweetest voice he had ever heard and had told her so on more than one occasion. He looked up at Mary. 'Please say something, please say something, Joe, anything' she begged him over and over in her mind. "I'm sorry

I startled you," he mumbled as got to his feet. "I didn't know you were down here." He turned to leave and Mary's heart sank. She watched him disappear through the door and go up the stairs. When he got to the door to the kitchen he tried to turn the handle, but it was locked. Joe beat on the door. "Hey mom, open up; the door is locked." "Is Mary with you?" Eve spoke through the door. "No." "I won't open the door until you talk and come up together. You two are FRIENDS FIRST! Now start acting like it." "Joe beat on the door louder, "Come on mom, open up!" Eve replied sternly, "NO!" "Not you, my other mom!" Ruth had been listening and said, "I'm with Eve; and don't bother calling for either of your dads. They are sitting here nodding in agreement with us." Joe didn't believe it. "Dad?" "Listen to your moms, Joe." Abraham said with finality. Jake spoke up, "By the way Joe, your steak is just about ready. If it goes much longer, it's liable to be medium-well!" Abraham snorted holding back the laughter. "You all are really enjoying this aren't you?" Joe spoke into the door. "You have no idea," Ruth said through her laughter.

Joe trudged down the stairs and sat down on the couch facing the TV. Mary had been listening to the whole conversation from the laundry room door. He looked at her but didn't say anything. She moved slowly in his direction and sat down in the recliner across the room from Joe. They sat there in silence for a long while each looking around the room trying to avoid making eye contact. Mary tried to break the ice. "Thanks for scraping my windows." She used her best shy voice. Joe brightened up a little. "No problem; I know how much you hate doing that." Things got awkward again. Joe fidgeted a little. Mary tried again. "Thanks for saving me at lunch. That was nice of you." "I just didn't want you sitting with that creep Jimmy." Joe played it down. More silence. Finally, Mary said, "Joe, we can't sit here all night. We have to get this out in the open. I would like to know what's going on in that mind of yours. Besides, they are not going to let us out of here until we do." Joe remained quiet still looking around the room. His eyes landed on a picture of Mary and him right after he set the pole vault record in junior high school. He was handing the trophy to Mary. He remembered how she tried to refuse it but he had insisted since she had coached him through the training. She was holding the trophy with one hand and had her arm around his waist with the other. "Do you remember that day?" Joe nodded at the picture. Mary followed Joe's eyes to the picture. She blushed, "How could I forget? We had a lot of fun doing that." "There are a lot of memories down here, Mary. Do you remember the time we built that fort down here? There were tunnels, trap doors, and all kinds of stuff. We spent days down here." "Oh yeah," Mary recalled. "We weren't even in school yet. I bet we were only four or five years old!" They both laughed thinking of the fun they had down there over the years. When the laughter died down, the awkward silence crept back in. Joe put his head in his hands. Mary knew that was a sign of frustration for Joe. He always did that when he was upset. She took that opportunity to look him over. Suddenly she noticed that blood was running down his leg. "Joe, you're bleeding!" Joe lifted his head and looked at Mary. "Where?" He didn't feel anything. By now she had jumped out of her chair and was quickly walking toward Joe.

Joe glanced at his knee and saw that the blood had run down into his sock. "Aw man! These are my favorite socks!" Mary was on her knees by now and was inspecting the wound. "Joe, there is a piece of glass sticking out of your knee. You must have fallen on it after I dropped the jar in the laundry room. I'm sorry." Joe looked at his knee and saw the glass. It was about the size of a quarter. It looked like about half of it was buried just below the kneecap. "Sorry for what? I'm the clumsy oaf who can't walk on level ground." He wondered why he didn't feel it. "We need to get that cleaned up and get you to the emergency room. It looks like you need a couple of stitches. I'll go see if I can find some bandages." Mary raced up the stairs and banged on the door. "Mom! Joe cut his knee and is bleeding. Open the door; I need to get some bandages." "Nice try, honey," her mom replied from the other side of the door. "I'm not buying it for a minute." "Really Mom, Joe is hurt and I think he needs some stitches." "That's some real good acting, Mary." Ruth laughed through the door. "I think you are ready for Broadway." Mary stomped down the stairs and hurried past Joe into the laundry room. Joe had heard the whole thing and snickered as Mary walked by. "It's not funny, Joe." Mary corrected him and disappeared into the laundry room. "It's kind of funny," Joe shouted as he snickered loud enough for Mary to hear. The fact that Joe was teasing her calmed her down a little "Well, maybe it's a little funny." Mary admitted and laughed loud enough for Joe to hear.

In just a few seconds, Mary appeared with two washcloths and a bottle of rubbing alcohol; one she had dampened in the sink and the other was dry. She knelt down in front of Joe and started for his leg. "Wait a minute," Joe protested. "Those are mom's good washcloths; we can't get blood on those." "Well, first of all these are the only clean cloths I could find and secondly, it will serve her right for that Broadway crack." Mary gave Joe a sly smile. "I like the way you think, Mary." Joe smiled back at her. "We need something to get that glass out," Mary observed. "I looked around for tweezers or something, but I couldn't find anything. Besides, I hate to pull it out. I'm afraid that I might break it off under the skin. I don't want to make it worse." "Let me give it a try." Before Mary could protest, Joe grabbed the piece of glass and yanked it out. Now, he could feel it. He wished he had left it in. He wanted to yell but suppressed it. His male ego wanted to let Mary know that he was tough. He winced through the pain. "Joe! What's wrong with you! You could have hurt yourself even worse! To be so smart, sometimes you do the most stupid things!" Mary scolded. "Hey, you're the one who wanted it out; and I know you always get what you want." Mary looked up at Joe who had a big smile on his face. She returned the smile and said nothing.

Mary started cleaning up the injury as Joe sat back and watched. "We need something to put pressure on it until we get you to the emergency room. I can't stop the bleeding," Mary stated in a concerned voice. "I've got an idea," Joe straightened up. "There is some duct tape on the top shelf in the laundry room. Would you go get it, please?" "Joe, I am not going to put duct tape on your wound. It will get infected." "Just trust me Mary. Besides, if you won't get it for me I'll get it myself." Joe started to get up. Mary shoved him back down. "Oh, alright; but you hold pressure on that until I get back." She gave in. By the time she returned, Joe had taken off his other sock and was holding it to his knee. She gave him the tape and he quickly wrapped it around the sock and his knee. When he finished, he looked at her and said, "What do you think of that?" "Mary smiled and inspected the makeshift bandage. "Not bad, it seems to be holding OK and I'm sure the sock is clean." Sarcasm oozed from Mary. "Now Mary, are you suggesting that my feet aren't clean?" Joe teased back. Mary laughed and pinched her nose as if to suggest that Joe's feet stunk.

Mary sat back down in her chair. The 'crisis' which had temporarily covered the awkwardness was over and tension began to fill the room again. After a few minutes, Mary spoke up. "Joe, did you mean it when you said that I always get what I want?" The question caught Joe off-guard so he paused for a few seconds before he answered. "Look at it this way; can you ever remember a time when you didn't get what you wanted?" He was proud of himself by the way he had turned the question around. "Well, there have been a few birthdays when I had wanted a pony...." Mary was teasing Joe now. "OK fine," Joe admitted. "But seriously, Mary, when you really want something, you ALWAYS get it, don't you?" Mary sat back in the chair and pondered the question. A thought came to her but she was afraid to say it for fear of how Joe would respond. It meant putting her feelings out in the open. It frightened her but she decided that it was time. "Joe, I can think of one time that I didn't get what I wanted." "Oh yeah, when?" Joe had been thinking of how persuasive Mary could be. "Now Joe, right now." Mary had seriousness in her voice. Joe was really confused. "What are you talking about? Getting upstairs?" "No Joe, I want YOU! I don't have you, Melissa does!" Tears welled up in her eyes.

Mary's words cut Joe like a knife. "Melissa doesn't HAVE me! I don't even like her that much. You know that, Mary. Besides, I was getting the feeling that you DIDN'T want me. What about Gary, Brad, and Jimmy? I thought that you wanted to play the field or something." "Joe, it has always been you. Gary is just a friend and co-worker on this project; Brad is a guy who needed help, and Jimmy! Really! I was just trying to get under your skin by flirting with him! Joe, it has always been you, only you and it always will be." "Mary, I want you to know that Melissa means absolutely nothing to me. I was just flirting with her to get back at you. I love you. I have been miserable these past few days without you. I'm sorry." He held out his arms. Tears ran down her cheeks as she jumped into his arms. She hugged him so tight that Joe had trouble breathing but he didn't care. "I'm sorry, too, Joe. I love you more than anything." Joe's heart melted as he looked into Mary's eyes. He leaned down and kissed her. Warmth ran through them and they held the embrace for a long time. Finally, Joe picked Mary up in his arms and sat down on the couch with Mary on his lap. "I guess things aren't always the way they seem. I'm sorry for the confusion," Joe confessed. "I guess they aren't," Mary admitted. "I'm as much to blame as you. I'm sorry, too." Mary laid her head on Joe's shoulder. They sat there in silence soaking up the moment for a few minutes. Relief washed over them like waves on the ocean.

All of a sudden Mary sat up. "Joe, I forgot about your knee! We need to get you to the emergency room!" She jumped up and faced him. "Knee? What knee?" Joe faked amnesia. "Come on Joe, we have to get that stitched up." "Now wait a minute, Mary. Let's think this over. The bleeding has stopped and there is a party waiting for us upstairs. You heard the moms say that the dads needed a tension reliever. Let's not ruin the party. We can go later. Besides, I'm starved." "Mary wanted to protest but decided that it would be futile. "OK Mr. Brainiac. But there are just two things. First, how are you going to explain the duct tape on your knee?" Joe glanced at his knee and then he remembered the box marked 'luau'. He walked over to it and pulled out a grass skirt. "Easy," he said triumphantly as he held it up to his waist. The grass skirt covered the tape perfectly. "Now, what was the second thing, Sugar Plum?" Joe was feeling cocky now. Mary blushed at the pet name. She loved it when he called her Sugar Plum. She walked over to him and took his hand and led him to the stairs. She climbed two steps so she could look him in the eyes. She turned around, put her hands on his cheeks, and kissed him lightly. "The second thing is that you have to admit that I don't always get my way. I want to go to the emergency room now, but I am giving in to your need to party. I am just saying." Mary grinned at Joe with that look like 'I got you'. Joe grinned back and teased, "Well maybe this one time."

When they got to the top of the stairs they tried the door; it was still locked. "Mom?" Mary questioned if Ruth could hear her. "Yes honey." "Please open the door, "Jake responded in his fake gruff voice. "Are you two friends yet?" "Yes daddy," Mary pleaded back. "Where's Joe?" Eve questioned. "Right here mom." Joe replied. "Do you agree with Mary? Are you friends again?" Abraham injected into the conversation. "Well, not exactly dad," Joe said into the door. Mary glanced at Joe who returned the look with a wink. "She's my Sugar Plum." Mary slapped Joe playfully on the arm and giggled. Abraham rolled his eyes and Jake just shook his head. Eve jumped up and opened the door. The kids walked in hand-in-hand;

both wearing the grass skirts. Abraham busted out laughing when he saw them. "Mary, you look absolutely beautiful; but you Joe, on the other hand, would not make a good Hawaiian." "Have you looked in the mirror, dad?" Joe teased back. "What took you two so long? I'm starved." Jake spoke up. "I had to check and see if those pretty little lips still worked." Joe replied as he smiled at Mary. Jake bellowed in laughter, Ruth smiled at Mary who was blushing and hiding behind Joe. Eve said, "Joseph Goldstein!" and tried to fake aggravation at the innuendo. Abraham spoke up and said, "And?" Joe took the hint. "Those lips are working better than ever! Ow!" Mary dug her fingernails into Joe's ribs. Everyone laughed as they all took their seats at the table.

Everyone got up to help clear the table before dessert. Joe grabbed his plate and headed for the counter where Ruth and Eve were piling dishes into the dishwasher. Eve glanced at Joe and noticed that his grass skirt was stuck to his knee. Upon closer inspection she noticed the duct tape and what appeared to be dried blood on his leg. "Joe, what happened to your leg?!" Joe looked down at his leg and observed that the grass skirt had stuck to the blood that was seeping out from under the duct tape. He glanced at Mary who was giving him the look which told him that it was time to confess. "It's just a scratch, mom. It's no big deal." "So what's with the duct tape…and is that a sock?!" Ruth, remembering the conversation in which she had accused Mary of acting earlier, was interested now and looked at her daughter for clarification. "I TOLD you that Joe had cut his knee earlier, but you wouldn't let us in so we had to do the best we could. I'm pretty sure he needs stitches," Mary affirmed to her mom. Eve had led Joe to a chair and was on her knees inspecting the wound. "Why didn't you tell us when you came into the kitchen from the basement?" Jake questioned Mary. Mary looked at Joe for help. "I decided that I would prefer a luau over the emergency room," Joe said with a grin on his face.

Joe was happy to see that the parking lot at the hospital was almost deserted. He had been sure that the waiting room would be full of people who would be more than willing to exploit the embarrassment of coming into the hospital with an entourage of people who were so strangely dressed. There was no one in the waiting room and the lady at the front desk didn't even look up as they entered through the automatic doors. All six of them marched up to the desk and waited for the lady to acknowledge their presence. After a few seconds, she finished what she had been doing and began to apologize for the delay as she raised her head to look at them. She had barely gotten half of the apology out of her mouth when she took in the whole scene. Her mouth dropped open in astonishment, which soon gave way to a snicker as she recognized Big Jake from the drugstore. "Hi Sally!" Jake grinned. "Hi Jake." Sally's snicker broke into a giggle. "What can I do for you?" "Nothing for me, thanks. But you can fix up Joe. He banged up his knee and needs a little needlework." Sally looked down at Joe's knee still giggling at the sight of everyone dressed up in Hawaiian attire. Sally saw the blood running down Joe's leg but couldn't see where it was coming from. Still giggling, Sally asked Joe, "Could you raise your skirt up a little so I can get a better look?" That was all it took. Everyone, except Joe, burst out in laughter. Sally was laughing so hard that tears were running down her cheeks. Joe turned beet red and parted the grass on the skirt so that Sally could see.

By now the commotion had drawn the attention of the staff on duty and they came out into the reception area. As they took in the scene, first the nurse, then the technician, and finally the doctor began laughing. Joe just stood there looking for some sympathy from someone; but it wasn't to be had. The doctor stumbled over to Joe and looked at his knee. "Looks like a horrible pineapple accident occurred at this luau. I can't tell you how many of these we see this time of year!" This caused everyone to gasp for air because they were laughing so hard. Mary was holding her sides, Jake was bellowing huge laughs, and Abraham couldn't tell if the moms were laughing or crying because of the tears running down their cheeks. Joe just stood there in the middle of all of them nodding and grinning.

After the commotion died down, the doctor said, "Come on Joe; let's get you patched up before you bleed all over the floor." "Thanks Doc," Joe replied. "Your concern for the floor is touching. Anybody coming along?" Mary volunteered to accompany Joe, but the adults decided to stay in the waiting room. "You'll be fine, son," Abraham spoke to the room in general. "Besides, someone has to stay out here with the cake!"

Twenty minutes later, Joe and Mary emerged from the doors into the waiting room. Everyone, including Sally and the technician, was eating cake and ice cream while watching a basketball game on TV. "How many stitches did you get, honey?" Eve asked. "Five." "Want some cake?" Ruth asked. "Sure," Mary and Joe said in unison. They all stayed until the cake was gone.

CHAPTER FIFTEEN

The next couple of weeks went smoothly for Joe and Mary. They were always together and had gone out on several double dates with Allen and Angie. Things were going great. Jimmy and Melissa had retreated as soon as they found out that the argument between Joe and Mary was over. Mary found great pleasure in grabbing Joe's hand or squeezing his arm when they passed Melissa in the halls. Mary would always make it a point to say hi to Melissa, just to make sure that Melissa had seen them, but Melissa would only return a curt smile. Jimmy avoided Joe like the plague. However, when they did cross paths, Joe wasn't as 'pleasant' to Jimmy as Mary was to Melissa. Joe would stare Jimmy down which caused him to either quicken his pace or take another path. Joe rather enjoyed intimidating Jimmy, but a small part of him felt a little guilty about it. He knew it was wrong to carry a grudge.

It was Monday night before Mary was scheduled to fly to Chicago for the rally there. Abraham, Jake, and Joe were in the Reubenowitz's living room watching Monday night football. The moms were in the kitchen whipping up snacks and talking about the upcoming trip that Jake and Ruth had planned. They had decided to fly to Chicago with Mary for the weekend to get away for awhile and to see what their little girl was doing at these rallies. Joe was glad that Jake and Ruth were going; they could keep an eye on Gary. Not that he didn't trust Mary, he just didn't trust Gary.

Mary was in the den on the phone with Karen and Gary discussing plans for the weekend. She had them on speaker so she could have her hands free to make notes. Joe was half listening to the game and half listening to the conversation. He heard Karen say, "What time is your flight? Maybe we can share a ride to the hotel." "You guys go ahead, my parents are flying out with me and I'll just ride with them," Mary said while still scribbling notes. Gary piped up not knowing he could be heard by Joe and the dads. "I guess we won't be able to party like we did in Salt Lake City since the 'rents' are tagging along!" Mary grabbed the receiver in an effort to get Gary off of the speaker and started talking softly into it. She hoped that Joe and the dads hadn't heard Gary's comment, but it was too little, too late.

Joe looked at his dad who shook his head as if to say, 'shake it off'. Joe then looked at Jake who was frowning while staring a hole in the television. After a couple of minutes of awkward silence, Jake growled, "I'm looking forward to meeting this California dude. I think he needs to meet a real Montana dad who loves his little girl." Abraham snickered a little and Joe slapped Jake on the back and said, "I can't think of a better man for the job." "I'll keep you posted," Jake assured them and they went back to watching the game.

The week flew by and before Joe knew it, it was Sunday afternoon. He was up in his room studying for an English test that was scheduled for Monday. He knew the material extremely well and really didn't need to study. He was just doing it to keep his mind off of Mary. She was scheduled to land with her mom and dad at 4:30. He glanced at the clock on his nightstand; 4:20. They should be home around 5:30. He was anxious to see how the weekend went in Chicago. He had prayed that it would be as successful as the one had been in Salt Lake City. He really was proud of Mary and all of her accomplishments with the 'Teens for Abstinence' program. He was convinced that God had called her to do it. In addition, he was also looking forward to talking with Jake. Joe really wanted his impression of Gary. Every time Joe thought about Gary he felt a type of negative feeling that was new to him. He couldn't quite explain it. Something just didn't feel right about this guy.

Mary sat in her seat on the plane between her mom and dad. Jake was asleep and her mom was looking through a magazine.

Mary was about to settle back for a nap when something white flashed by her in the aisle. She looked around, but no one was in the aisle. She half stood up to look in the back of the plane and thought for a moment she had noticed Gabby look in her direction, smile, and go into the bathroom. Her blood ran cold. How could that be? It must be someone who looked like her. However, she felt compelled to investigate. She crawled over her dad barely waking him and headed for the bathroom. She looked at the sign and it said, 'Vacant'. Whoever, went in forgot to lock the door. Mary decided to wait. After a few minutes, a flight attendant came up to her. "Can I help you?" "I'm just waiting for the bathroom." "It doesn't seem to be occupied," the flight attendant replied. "I thought I saw someone go in a couple of minutes ago." Mary offered. The flight attendant knocked on the door and no one answered. She eased the door open and said, "Is there anyone here?" No answer. She opened the door and said, "There you go honey." Mary had a confused look on her face but went in. "Thanks." She locked the door and the lights came on. She decided to take a quick look in the mirror to check her hair. As she caught her reflection she thought she saw Gabby standing behind her smiling! Mary gasped and spun around; nothing. She turned back around and looked in the mirror; nothing! Mary didn't know what to think. It must be some sort of subconscious response to her last plane trip when she thought she had spoken with Gabby. But Gabby was dead according to her dad. Maybe she had been dreaming and was speaking to Gabby in her dream somehow. It was all so confusing. She opened the door and walked quickly to her seat.

Joe decided it was time for a break. He flopped down on his bed, grabbed the remote for his stereo and turned on some soft music. His thoughts turned to Mary. He pictured her sitting between Jake and Ruth on the airplane. Jake was probably asleep while Mary and Ruth chatted about girls things and the events of the weekend. As he attempted to consider what Mary and her mother were discussing he drifted off to sleep.

The thoughts of Mary and her family on the plane turned into a dream as Joe slept. He envisioned the people sitting around Mary. There was Karen, Brad, Gary and a bunch of other kids who had been at the rally. Brad and Gary were sitting across the aisle from Mary. Mary was turned around in her seat talking to some of the kids. Music was playing and the kids were having a great time. All of a sudden, the kids were out of their seats and dancing in the aisle. Mary was dancing with Brad on one side and Gary on the other. They were dancing way too close which caused Joe to get upset. He wasn't in the dream so he couldn't do anything about it. He felt helpless. As he watched this scene in his dream, a cold, dark feeling came over him. It was distasteful and sinister. All of a sudden, Joe noticed a black figure hovering over Mary, Brad, and Gary. It wasn't really in the form of a man but it had some recognizable human type features. Joe sensed that it was evil and wanted to warn Mary so he yelled as loud as he could but Mary couldn't hear him.

Just as he yelled in his dream he woke to a shout from downstairs. "Hi honey, I'm home!" Jake announced as he walked through the doors. Joe sat up in bed with a start and looked at the clock; 5:45. His shirt was soaking wet and he was panting like a dog in August. Joe collected his thoughts, sorted out the dream from reality and realized that the Reubenowitz's were home. He leaped out of bed and ran down the stairs taking them two at a time.

Joe's parents were hugging the Reubenowitz's and welcoming them home. Joe made a beeline for Mary and gave her a big hug as he lifted her off the ground. "Hi Joe, I missed you. Hey, you're soaked with sweat. Turn me loose you big lug. What have you been doing?" Mary observed. "Oh, I was just working out a little. Sorry." Joe didn't want to explain the dream just then. "Anybody else want a hug?" he teased. "No thanks, maybe later," "I'll take a rain check," "After your shower." All of the parents had a smart remark.

The alarm on the stove went off and Eve announced, "Dinner's ready; is anyone hungry?" "What are you having?" Jake asked. Ruth slapped him playfully on the shoulder. "As if it mattered to you." "Roast beef, your highness," Eve replied as she bowed before him. "I guess that will have to do." Jake said in a stately tone. "Good." Abraham said as he headed for the kitchen. "You can tell us all about the weekend during dinner."

Jake and Ruth spent the first ten minutes talking about how great Mary was at the rally. Had it been under any other circumstances, Mary would have been totally embarrassed. However, the Goldsteins were family. They understood how her parents were. In fact, Abraham and Eve would brag on Mary as much or more than Jake and Ruth. "Alright daddy, they get the picture," Mary interrupted. "I get manna from heaven." "Ha! Ha! Very funny," Jake replied. "Let's have your take on the weekend. Mary began by telling them that there were approximately 1,000 kids at the rally and that over 200 had made commitments to abstain from sex until marriage. They had a great time and the band in Chicago was fantastic. As she recounted some of the details of the weekend, every time Gary's name came up Joe looked in Jake's direction. They would make quick eye contact and both would glance away. Jake's eyes told Joe that they could talk about it later.

After dinner, the guys offered to help clean up but were excused by the ladies. "I know the Cowboys are playing, go watch the game." Eve knew what the men were thinking. They were out of the kitchen before she finished her sentenced. Abraham grabbed his recliner while Jake and Joe plopped down on the couch. "Well?" Joe questioned into the air.

Jake knew what Joe was asking. He had met Gary and Joe wanted some feedback. Jake looked over his shoulder into the kitchen to insure that the women weren't listening. "Well Joe, Gary is one of those guys that are very likeable. He is funny, outgoing and charming; and frankly, I don't like him much. I don't know why, he just rubs me the wrong way." "Why not, is he disrespectful to Mary?" Abraham asked as he leaned forward on his knees. "No, not at all. He's a charmer. He is real sweet to Mary, and all of the girls for that matter. He seems to have a way with the ladies. He kind of comes off like a player to put it in today's terms." "I KNEW IT!" Joe exclaimed. "Shhh!" Jake warned him as he looked at the kitchen door. "Even though he's that kind of guy, I don't think you have anything to worry about." "Why not?" Joe still sounded worried. "Because it's Mary, Joe. She may be a little naïve about the world but she is still smart and I am pretty sure that she is dedicated to you." "I just don't want her to be taken in by his smooth talk," Joe snarled. "Joe, look at me." Abraham was staring at Joe. "You have a decision to make. You don't have to trust Gary. There are a million Gary's out there who would love to be with Mary. The decision is if you trust Mary or not." "I trust Mary," Joe admitted. "She is just so darn sweet and innocent. She thinks everyone is nice and doesn't think that anyone would think of taking advantage of her." "You had better let it go, Joe," Jake advised. "Let God handle it." Just then the girls came in the living room, "Who wants a brownie?" Mary's chipper voice rose above the conversation. "I do!" The guys said in unison. The conversation was over.

CHAPTER SIXTEEN

February came to a close and by the middle of March spring was attempting to push winter into the past. Basketball season had come to a close and Mary was finished with cheerleading until next year. She was glad because she had so much planning and preparation to do for the big 'Teens for Abstinence' rally at Fort Myers Beach. It was to begin on a Saturday and run through the following Friday. She had put the planning for this event on the back burner after she had returned from the Chicago rally. She had been so busy with basketball tournaments, mid-term exams, and some community service projects for National Honor Society that working on the rally in Florida had to wait. However, in two weeks she would be at the rally and there was much work to do before she left. She had been on the phone with Gary and Karen almost every night preparing for the event.

Joe had been busy himself with many of the same events. He had been named to the all-tournament team in basketball and had broken the record for most points scored in a single game. He had aced all of his mid-terms but he also had spent a large amount of time studying for them. Baseball practice had already started. It had been too cold and wet to practice outside so the team had been working out in the gym. The team had a good chance at the state championship this year so the coach was working the boys pretty hard each night. Practice started at 3:30 and he usually didn't let them leave until 6:30 or 7:00. Joe routinely walked into the house, greeted his parents, and went straight to his room. There was a quick shower and then he hit the books until about 10:00. His mom would bring him a plate of food so that he could eat while he studied.

But now mid terms were over and there was light at the end of the tunnel. It seemed like the teachers were beginning to lighten up a little as spring break got closer. A hint of nice weather on an occasional afternoon made the anticipation of a vacation even more exciting. Joe was excited about it because he had planned to go with Mary to the rally in Fort Myers Beach. The coach had promised the boys to give them the week off if they worked hard. He had spent some time helping her with some of the planning and preparation. He had even been involved with Gary and Karen a few times when Mary had schedule conference calls. He liked Karen. She was nice and very energetic. Gary, on the other hand, was just as Jake had described. Joe had learned to deal with it for Mary's sake. Besides, he would be with her this time.

It was Wednesday evening and Joe was at Mary's house helping with the final touches on several presentations that Mary was to make at the rally next week. Spring break was two days away and Mary was starting to get into panic mode. Karen had gotten a cold and was struggling to keep up. Gary was doing the best he could to help Karen but it had been a real hassle. Notwithstanding, the four of them had managed to get things accomplished. All that remained were the last minute details. Joe and Mary were in the den and the house phone rang. Mary looked at the caller ID and saw that it was Gary. "Hi Gary, what's up?" "Hang on a minute, Mary I've got Karen on the other line." Mary hit the speaker button on the phone and laid the receiver down. Joe had been so involved in the preparation that he would most likely need to hear what was going to be said. In just a few seconds Gary's voice came on the line, "Mary?" "Yes, I've got Joe here too." Gary continued, "Can you hear me Karen?" A voice that was unfamiliar answered, "Yeah Gary, I'm here." Mary looked at Joe. Karen sounded awful. "Are you OK?" Mary asked knowing the answer. "I've been better." Her voice cracked. She sounded like a frog. "I'm afraid I've got some bad news. I've got mono which caused my immune system to weaken. That resulted in pneumonia." Mary forgot about the rally. She was concerned about her friend. "Are you going to be OK?" "Yeah, the doc says I need a lot of rest and he has me on some antibiotics. However, he says that I can't go to the rally this weekend. I'm sorry."

Mary looked at Joe with panic in her eyes. Joe held his finger up to his lips to keep Mary from reacting out loud before she had a minute to process the information. After a few seconds Gary broke the silence, "I thought you should hear it from her." Mary took a deep breath and said, "That's OK Karen. We'll get by. We'll miss you terribly, but we'll make it happen. The important thing is that you get better." Joe gave Mary a 'thumbs up'. Joe spoke up, "Besides Karen, I'll be there to help. I know I can't replace you, but if you could be available by phone to coach me along, I think I can handle it." Gary jumped in. "Besides cutie, I've got your back. You just take it easy and let ol' Gary and Joe cover this one for you." Joe winced at the thought of working with Gary for a week. However, he would do anything for Mary: AND he STILL liked the idea of being there with Mary; just to make sure that ol' Gary behaved himself around her.

"OK then, we have a lot to discuss and duties to redistribute," Mary said with authority. "Karen, do you feel well enough to stay on the line a few minutes so that we can get through some of this?" "Sure Mary, I'll do the best I can." "Well if you get to felling poorly, just let us know and we'll pick it up tomorrow." Mary had a soothing tone in her voice that relaxed everyone. "Let's get started." The kids began discussing the details of the changes that needed to be made. After a few minutes, Joe's cell phone rang. He looked at the caller ID and said, "I've got to get this." Mary nodded, continued the discussion with Gary and Karen and Joe walked out of the room.

After a few minutes Joe came back into the room. Mary was just finishing up the call with Gary and Karen. "I guess that's about all for now," Mary was saying into the speaker as she finished jotting down the last of her notes. "Oh, Joe's back. I'll fill him in later. Thanks for everything Gary and Karen, don't worry, we'll take care of everything. You just take care of yourself. Bye." Gary and Karen said goodbye at the same time. Mary pressed the speaker phone button on the phone and the line went dead. She sat down in the chair behind the desk and put her feet up on the desk in grand style. She leaned back in the chair, put her hands behind her head and said, "Well, it isn't going to be easy, but with your help, I think we can pull it off. I'm so glad you're going to be there...."

Mary's voice trailed off as she made eye contact with Joe. She sat up in the chair. "Joe, what's wrong? You look like you just lost your best friend. Who was that on the phone?" Joe looked down at his feet. This wasn't a good sign. Mary knew that whenever Joe had bad news, he always looked down. "That was the baseball coach at Harvard." Joe hesitated and Mary interrupted. "Aw, I'm sorry Joe; you didn't get the scholarship did you? Don't worry, it's their loss, they don't know what they are missing. Something better will come along...." "That's not it, Mary." Joe was still speaking to the floor. "Well, what is it?" Mary was now on her feet in front of Joe. Since he was a head taller than Mary, she could look up at him, effectively block his look at the floor, and force him to look at her. "He said that the scholarship is 99% in the bag." Mary grinned. "However, they want me to go work out with the team, just to make sure the team chemistry is right and all of that stuff. He said it's just a formality but it is a requirement; something about school policy." Mary threw her arms around his neck. "That's great news, Joe! What's the problem? You know I'm already going on an academic scholarship! We'll still be together!" "Mary, they want me to go next week. I told him that next week was really bad for me. We tried to work something else out, but there was just no other good time for both of us. He said that I could still go to Harvard on an academic scholarship, but the baseball scholarship would most likely be given to someone else. I really want to go with you on the Florida trip, but I still want to play baseball for Harvard. I don't know what to do."

Mary's face fell. Her grin turned into a look of despair. She released her hold on Joe's neck and stepped back. Now Mary was looking at the floor. She had been looking forward to Joe going along with her. She knew that she would have so much more fun AND feel confident knowing that Joe would have her back; especially since Karen wasn't going to be there. However, she knew that Joe wanted to play baseball for Harvard ever since they had shown an interest in him last year. Whenever college came up in conversation, his eyes always lit up when Harvard was mentioned. Besides, he wanted to major in business so that he could return home to work with his dad at Dream Builders and everyone knew that Harvard's school of business was one of the best in the country. He had worked very hard athletically and scholastically to get accepted into Harvard. Now his dream was about to come true.

Mary looked up and peered deep into his coal black eyes. "Joe, you have to go to Harvard next week." "But Mary, what about...?" "No 'buts' Joe, you know I'm right. You have been working for this almost all of your life. You can't pass this up for a vacation in Florida." Joe knew she was right but decided to protest because he was feeling so guilty. "But what about Karen, you know how much you depended on her in Salt Lake City and in Chicago, and those were just weekend events! Florida is for a week! I promised you I would help you out and that what I'm going to do. I can still go to Harvard on a scholastic scholarship; I don't have to play baseball. "Joe, if you did that, I would feel guilty for the rest of my life. It would make me feel so selfish. Besides, it's just a week." "Mary, what you are doing is important work, who knows how many lives you have touched and how many people have come to God because of your work. I don't want to be responsible for inhibiting God's work."

Mary thought for a moment and then hit the speaker button on the telephone and pushed redial. After two rings Gary's voice came on, "Hello hot stuff, can't stay away from ol' Gary too long huh?" Joe cringed. He had forgotten about the 'Gary factor'. If he didn't go, Mary would be alone with him for a week. He felt sick to his stomach. "Gary, you're on speaker and Joe is here. I've got one question for you. Can you and I handle the Florida event without Joe?" There was a long pause on the other end of the line. Finally, Gary said, "You mean just the two of us? No one else?" "That's right, just us." Mary's tone was matter-of-fact. "Sure we can!" Gary's voice picked up. "We'll have to spend tomorrow evening figuring out the details and we'll probably be joined at the hip next week doing things on the fly, but I think we can do it. Is Joe OK?" "Yes, he's fine. Something just came up that he HAS to do." "Don't worry Joe." Joe could picture Gary smiling on the other end of the line, "Ol' Gary will take good care of Miss Mary." Joe's face turned red and he thought to himself, 'I bet you will.' "Thanks Gary, I'll talk to you tomorrow. Bye." Mary hung up the phone without waiting for a reply.

Mary turned to face Joe who was looking at her in astonishment. "There, it's settled," Mary announced with finality. "You are officially uninvited." "I don't like this at all," Joe muttered. "It just isn't fair." "Look Joe, I know you don't like Gary, but really, he's harmless. Besides, you do trust me, don't you?" "Of course I trust you, Mary. It's just that Gary is so smooth. He gives me the creeps. Besides, do you really think you can do your job and Karen's job for a week?!" "Yes Joe, I do. Gary's going to help. It won't be easy, but I can do it. Look Joe, this isn't easy for me either. I would like nothing more than to have you with me down there, but it isn't right. God has a plan for both of us and you know as well as I do that you being in Florida isn't it. I'll be fine."

"I know," Joe relented. "Just promise me that you'll keep ol' Gary at arms length next week." "You know better than that, Joe. You're the only guy for me."

Their conversation was interrupted by Jake. "Good night kids!" Joe looked at the clock on the desk; 10:30. "Good night daddy," Mary responded in her chipper voice. "Sleep well," Joe added. "I didn't realize that it was so late. I'd better get going. I suspect we are going to have a tough practice tomorrow since it will be the last one for a week. Are you sure you're OK with everything?" "I'll be fine, Joe," Mary smiled. Joe walked over and kissed her on the cheek. "Good night Sugar Plum."

Joe awoke the next morning to the sound of his mother's voice. "Joe? It's time to get up. Your alarm has been going off for ten minutes." Joe opened his eyes and saw his mother standing in the doorway. "What happened in here last night? It looks like a tornado went through here." Joe looked around the room. His sheet and covers were in a pile next to the bed. His pillow was across the room. Textbooks were lying around everywhere and several magazines were strewn all over. "I guess I had a rough night." "I guess you could say that." Eve laughed as she exited. "Hurry up, breakfast is almost ready."

Joe tried to recall last night. He had had trouble getting to sleep. He tried reading, playing computer games, and even studying for awhile. Finally, he remembered lying down around 2 a.m. He had rolled and tossed for at least an hour before drifting off to sleep. However, the sleep hadn't been sound. His mind wouldn't allow him to rest and caused nightmares. There had been flashes of sinister, evil, black images swooping and flying around his room. In addition, they had been all around Mary but she didn't know it. Joe was trying to get to her to protect her from them but there was a huge bottomless, black pit between Joe and Mary. He felt helpless as he yelled to her but she couldn't hear him. All she did was wave at him across the pit. She didn't seem to know that she was in danger.

The dream changed suddenly and Joe could see Mary and Gary in Florida. They were at dinner with a bunch of other kids that Joe didn't recognize. Everyone was having fun and Gary seemed to be the life of the party. He kept flirting with Mary by leaning over to her, making references about how close they were, putting his arm around the back of her chair, and even offering her a bite of his dessert. Joe was livid as he watched this helplessly in his dream. Mary seemed oblivious to what Gary was doing which angered Joe even further. As the kids finished dinner, Gary said to the group, "Mary and I have a lot of 'work' to do before tomorrow so we had better get at it." Gary winked and grinned at the guy next to him as he said 'work' who returned an evil smile. Joe watched as Gary led Mary to the elevator. He stood close to her as they went up and even held her arm as they walked down the hall to their rooms. "Let's work in my room," Gary offered. "I've got everything all spread out." "Suits me," Mary replied to Gary and they slipped into Gary's room.

Joe had awakened at that minute to the sound of his alarm. He had been thrashing around in his bed so violently that he had thrown all of the covers off of the bed. His mind raced as he came to terms that it had just been a dream. He decided to lay there for a few minutes while he collected his thoughts. What a weird dream. He wondered what it all meant. The fact that he dreamt that Gary was hitting on Mary was not a new thought. That could be explained. But the presence of those horrible black images and the pit made him wonder. Joe was a firm believer that God spoke to people in dreams so he laid there trying to figure it out. He must have fallen back asleep and that's when his mother had come in. Joe sat up and decided to try and shake it off. He headed for the shower.

Abraham was sitting at the table waiting on Joe to eat breakfast. Abraham loved eating as a family and attempted to make sure that it happened whenever possible. "Good morning mom, it smells good. What are we having?" He kissed his mom on the cheek and tried to be as chipper as possible even though he was sleep deprived. "Pancakes and sausage," Abraham answered as he put down the newspaper. "Good morning dad. Let's eat, I'm starved." After the blessing, Abraham noticed that Joe had dark circles under his eyes. "You look like you should be going to bed instead of just getting up. Are you OK?" "I had some trouble sleeping last night, I had this weird dream." "Something on your mind, son?" Abraham asked the question already knowing the answer. He and Eve had been up when Joe got home from Mary's last night. They had helped him make travel arrangements to Harvard before they went to bed. They knew he was upset about not going to Florida with Mary. "I guess I just don't like how next week is shaping up." Joe had his head down. It appeared as if he were speaking to his pancakes. "Joe, I know this is hard for you, but you have to press forward. You have made a decision and now you have to trust God. He works in very mysterious ways. For some reason, you are not supposed to be in Florida. I don't know why. Maybe you are supposed to be in a position to witness to some of the guys on the team at Harvard. After all, you have always said that your athletic abilities were a gift from God. Maybe it's time to use them. Besides, you have to allow Mary to use her gifts for God's glory. Don't forget, you are NOT her protector; God is." "I know dad, believe me, I've tried to let it go; and I'll get the job done. It's just that Gary is such a weasel. Even Jake doesn't like him." Eve had been listening to all of this and interrupted, "Jake doesn't care for Gary, either?!" "Now honey, it's OK." Abraham scowled at Joe for letting that little secret out. "Jake met him in Chicago and said he wasn't our type of person. He's just from a different culture, that's all. Besides, WE ALL TRUST MARY, and that's what matters. Now Joe, don't let Satan allow you to get off track. You stay focused on what God is leading you to do and get it done. Satan wants you distracted next week and he is using this little detour to try and do it. Joe, you are a winner and a child of God. DO NOT LET SATAN DEFEAT YOU!" "You're right, dad." Joe sat up a little straighter and dug into his breakfast. Unbeknownst to Joe, Eve looked at Abraham who winked at her. She mouthed the words, 'I love you' and gave him a huge smile.

It was Friday afternoon before Joe knew it. He had gotten home late Thursday because baseball practice had gone on until 8 p.m. He had wanted to go see Mary but she had been VERY busy finishing up the final adjustments with Gary. Besides, he had been extremely tired because of how he had slept Wednesday night.

Joe and Mary pulled up in front of his house and he shut off the car. He looked at his cell phone. "We've got one hour before we leave." Eve and Ruth were going to take them to the airport. Their flights were scheduled to depart 45 minutes apart so everyone had decided to ride together. "I'll see you in a little while." Joe leaned over and kissed Mary. "OK sweetie, I love you." "I love you too."

After a quick dinner, everyone was in the car. Joe and Mary climbed in the back and sat close enough so that their shoulders touched as they held hands. Eve and Ruth were giving them motherly advice about being careful...but the kids weren't listening. They just looked at each other and occasionally squeezed the hand of the other. Neither one was looking forward to being apart for a week, but both of them knew they were doing the right thing. It wasn't what they wanted, but they knew it was God's will.

Eve pulled the car up in front of the airport and turned around to the kids, "Are you sure you don't want us to help you inside?" "Mary's flight takes off in 90 minutes and mine leaves just a little while later. By the time we check in and go through security, you won't be able to be with us very long anyway. Besides, we can take care of ourselves." Joe smiled at his moms. They all got out and unloaded the luggage. After hugs goodbye the moms got back into the car and drove off while Joe and Mary waved until the car was out of site. The moms drove home in silence. Eve pulled into the driveway and turned the car off. "What is on your agenda today?" Eve asked. "I suppose I should get back to the store and make sure Jake is working." Ruth tried to joke but was unsuccessful. "Want to come in for a cup of coffee and a good cry?" Eve offered. "I feel so silly," Ruth replied. "Why am I so emotional? They will only be gone for a week." "I don't know, but I feel the same way," Eve replied as tears ran down her cheeks. Ruth walked around the car to her best friend and hugged her tight. Both ladies giggled through their tears as they walked into the house.

Joe grabbed Mary's suitcase and they walked into the terminal. Their flights were taking off at opposite ends of the terminal but Joe stood in line with Mary while she checked her luggage. "I check in way down at the other end so I guess this is it," Joe lamented. Mary hugged him tightly and gave him a quick kiss. "I'll see you in a week. I love you." "I love you, too." Mary turned to walk through security. "Be good Sugar Plum!" Joe said as tears filled his eyes. Mary saw what was happening to Joe and immediately grabbed his arm. "Joe, don't get me started." Tears began to run down her cheeks. "I don't want my mascara to run." She was joking. Joe laughed and hugged her again. "You better get going." Mary started to walk away, got about ten feet from Joe and turned around. He was still watching her. "You watch out for those college women. I don't want to have to come out there and kick the butt of some Ivy League girl who tries to steal my guy!" Mary held up her tiny fists in preparation for a fight. Joe laughed and said, "Don't worry Sugar Plum. I would hate to see any of those girls get hurt." Mary smiled and wagged her finger at Joe. "That's more like it. As long as you know who's in charge." "I've known that since you told me we had to build Cinderella's castle instead of a racecar out of Lego's when we were four years old!" "Good! I was afraid you had forgotten!" Mary grinned in that special way that always made Joe feel good. She moved into the line for the metal detector. Joe watched as she went through and picked up her carry-on. She waved and blew him a kiss as the crowd pushed her in the direction of her gate. Joe watched until he couldn't see her any longer. "Dear God, please watch over Mary this week and keep her safe." As Joe took off to the other end of the terminal, a warm 'breeze' came over him. It was so distinct that he stopped and looked around to see where it was coming from. Nothing, there were just people moving all around him in both directions. 'Man, that's weird,' he thought to himself. However, he suddenly felt better. He walked on, a little quicker, and a little happier.

Mary plopped down in her seat and sighed. It always wore her out getting through all of the airport madness. In addition, her flight was full. It seemed like everyone in Montana was going to Florida for spring break. She closed her eyes as the rest of the passengers filed onto the plane and settled in. Her thoughts began to run through the upcoming events. She was anxious about doing this without Karen. It would be a big job to do it over a normal weekend event. But this was the big one. It was for a week and preliminary numbers estimated up to 3,000 kids! She began to panic as she thought about all that she had to do. She said a quick prayer and a peace came over her almost immediately. Just then someone passed by her and inadvertently bumped her head with a purse. "I'm so sorry." The lady's voice sounded familiar but Mary couldn't place it. She opened her eyes to see who it was but the person had moved on down the aisle. Mary unbuckled her seat belt and turned around on her knees in the seat so that she could get a glimpse of the person associated with the voice. There was a lady about ten feet down the aisle carrying a purse over her shoulder that was most likely the candidate. There were no other women in the area. She looked familiar but Mary couldn't place her. The flight attendant interrupted her thoughts as she came up behind her. "Miss, please take your seat, we are preparing to take off." Mary turned and nodded to the flight attendant. However, as she sat down, she glanced over her shoulder in an effort to see who had bumped her. Too late, she was gone.

Joe's plane was less crowded. He assumed that most people were not going to New England for spring break. He found his seat, thank goodness it was an aisle seat; at least he could stretch his legs out in the aisle. There was a girl sitting next to the window, eyes closed, headphones on. She appeared to be about 14 years old. Joe thought she looked familiar and after some careful thought, he realized that she attended his high school. He had seen her in the halls occasionally and had said hi to her on occasion but she had only responded with a blush and a smile. As Joe sat down his big frame shook the seat but the girl didn't even flinch. She seemed lost in another world. Her eyes were still closed. She had a frown on her face. 'Probably sleeping', Joe thought to himself. The flight attendant came through for a final check before take-off. She leaned over Joe and touched the girl's arm. "Miss, you need to turn off your headphones during take-off, thanks." She opened her eyes and nodded in submission. She caught Joe's eye as she pulled the headphones off. He flashed his famous smile. "Oh, uh, hi," she stammered and blushed as she recognized Joe. "Hi yourself, that must be some pretty good music or you were asleep. You were really out there." "I was just dreading this flight." She was trying to regain her composure. "How come?" Joe questioned. "Are you afraid to fly?" "No, I just don't want to go. My parents are getting a divorce and they are sending me out to spend spring break with my uncle while they figure things out. They are probably arguing about who has to take me." Joe sensed pain in her voice. "I'm sorry; I bet it's not that way. They probably need to take care of some stuff. Maybe they'll get back together or something. By the way, we haven't been formally introduced, I'm...." "Joe Goldstein," the girl interrupted. "Everyone knows you." She smiled just a little. "I've seen you around school but I don't know your name." Joe hoped to turn the conversation to a lighter subject. "I'm Cindy. You sat at our lunch table last week when you and Mary were arguing about Melissa and Jimmy." "Wow! We do live in a small town don't we?" Joe exclaimed as he sat back in his seat. "Is there anything else you'd like to tell me about me?" "Well, I would like to remind you about a promise you made me," Cindy smiled shyly at Joe. Promise? Joe didn't even remember talking to her, ever. "By all means, refresh my memory." Well, when you ate with us, the other girls were chatting away with you about anything, you know, anything to get your attention, and I was just sitting there listening when out of the blue you said...." Joe interrupted, "I see you are taking algebra, cutie.' "I remember now. You told me that you were struggling and I offered to help you sometime. I think I even gave you my cell number. But you never called. Did you get things figured out?" "Actually, no; I'm more lost now than I ever was. I didn't think you really meant it. Besides, the rest of the girls told me that you were just being nice." "Well thanks for the compliment, I think, but I really did mean it. I'd be glad to help you any time. I know what it's like not knowing what is going on in class. It is really frustrating." Joe sounded sincere. "Well, I have my book with me now...." Cindy's voice trailed off waiting for Joe to accept the implied invitation. "YOU HAVE YOUR BOOK WITH YOU FOR SPRING BREAK?!" Joe couldn't believe what she had said. Cindy blushed. "I guess I'm kind of a nerd. You see, I want to be an architect and I need to understand algebra." "So you like construction?" Joe questioned. "I've always been fascinated with how buildings are built, the design, infrastructure, everything about it." Cindy's eyes sparkled as she spoke. Joe could tell that she was excited about it. "I know what you mean," Joe replied. "I want to be a civil engineer and do the same thing. I just love buildings; especially the old ones. I would love to build an old style structure and fill it with modern conveniences." "Me too!" Cindy almost yelled with enthusiasm. "I've dreamed about building a castle that would be used as a shopping mall." "Interesting." Joe was getting excited. "Would you have a moat?" "Sure would, that is what would separate the shops from the parking lot. I have sketches in my backpack; would you like to see them?" "Sure! This is a wild concept. I love talking about this stuff but I don't know anyone beside my dad who likes it," Joe lamented. "I know what you mean," Cindy replied reaching for her backpack. "All my friends think I'm weird." "Well, if cute and smart is weird, you are one of the weirdest girls I know." Joe flashed his signature smile. Cindy blushed and opened her backpack.

Mary was awakened by the flight attendant asking the passengers across the aisle if they wanted a beverage. She must have drifted off shortly after take-off. Feeling a little disoriented, she ordered an orange juice. As the flight attendant moved up the aisle she heard a lady laugh a few seats behind her. It was a familiar laugh. 'Gabby?' Mary was sure that the laugh was Gabby's. But how? Her mind whirled as she remembered the conversation that she had with her dad after her flight from Salt Lake City; and what about the flight from Chicago when she was in the restroom and saw Gabby standing behind her in the mirror?! This was getting weird. Mary leaned out in the aisle and looked back. There was the same lady that had bumped her. She was walking toward the back of the plane. Mary was sure that it was Gabby. She spun around to take her seat belt off. She was determined to get to the bottom of this. She fumbled just a second getting out of her seat but did manage to catch a glimpse of Gabby going into the restroom. Mary headed down the aisle. She decided to wait outside the door until Gabby came out. After a few minutes, the flight attendant came by. "Can I help you with something?" "No thank you, "Mary replied. " I'm just waiting for the restroom." "You can go on in, it's not occupied." Mary followed the flight attendant's eyes to the sign on the door. It read, 'Vacant'. "I'm sure that I saw someone go in there a couple of minutes ago." Mary replied with a confused look on her face. "Maybe she forgot to lock the door." The flight attendant nodded at Mary but didn't believe her. She knocked on the door. There was no answer. She waited a couple of seconds and slowly cracked open the door. There was no one in there. Mary blushed with embarrassment as well as amazement. "I'm sorry. I could have sworn that someone was in there." Mary looked at the floor. "Don't you worry about it honey, it happens all the time."

Mary smiled and entered the restroom. She needed the alone time to clear her head. She locked the door and looked in the mirror. She examined her make up and reviewed the last few minutes. She was absolutely sure that she had seen Gabby go into the restroom. She knew her laugh, she knew her walk, she was positive, and yet, no one had come out. But still, here she was. Standing in the room where she was sure that she had seen a person enter who had died several years ago! Was she losing her mind? As her mind raced, she glanced around the tiny room when something caught her eye that made her heart stop. A business card was lying by the edge of the sink. The name on the card read, 'Gabriella White, Sales Associate'. Mary started to tremble. She slowly reached for the card and picked it up. She read it slowly and then turned the card over. She gasped as she read the handwriting on the back. In black it read, 'call anytime, love Gabby'; then, right below that in red ink was written, 'I think you lost this at the airport. See you soon.'

Mary's hand trembled as she read the card over and over. Her breathing became rapid and shallow. What was going on? How could this be!? Something strange was happening that couldn't be explained rationally. She felt faint and the room started to spin. She opened the door and the flight attendant happened to catch sight of her. "You look terrible honey, are you OK?" She grabbed Mary's arm to steady her. "I just need to sit down. I don't feel well." An elderly gentlemen sitting close by overheard the conversation and spoke up, "Here, take my seat." He got up and grabbed Mary's other hand and the two of them helped Mary into his seat. "Thank you," Mary's weak voice acknowledged the kindness. "Miss, you are shaking like a leaf in a 40-mile-an-hour wind. Can I get you anything?" The gentleman's eyes were kind and concerned. The flight attendant was checking her pulse while signaling to another flight attendant for help. "Your pulse is rapid and you look pale. Are you taking any medications?" "No." "When did you eat last?" "I had supper with my family before I came to the airport." The other flight attendant arrived with a bottle of water. "Here sweetie, would you like some water?" "Thanks." Mary took the water and had a small drink. She closed her eyes and tried to collect her thoughts. After a couple of minutes she began to feel better. When she opened her eyes, the man was gone but the flight attendant was still there. "I should get back to my seat, and let that nice man have his seat back. Where did he go?" Mary started to get up but the dizziness caused her to lose her balance and the flight attendant helped her sit back down. "He took your seat, maybe you should stay right here," the flight attendant said kindly but firmly. "That's right honey, you just stay put. I'll take care of you. That old guy doesn't care where he sits." The voice came from a smiling lady sitting next to Mary. She looked about the same age as the man who had given Mary his seat. "Do you know him?" Mary asked. "I've been married to that old coot for 40 years." She replied with a gleam in her eyes. "I need a little time away from him." She laughed and patted Mary's hand. Mary giggled a little and blushed a lot. She was feeling much better and was starting to get embarrassed about causing the commotion. The lady winked at the flight attendant who smiled and walked down the aisle. "I'm Maggie," the lady introduced herself. "Hi, I'm Mary. Thank you for the help." Glad to be able to help. Now you just sit back and rest while you get your color back. If you need anything, you just let me know." Mary eased her seat back, closed her eyes and was soon fast asleep.

Joe and Cindy were having a lot of fun going over Cindy's sketches. He was very impressed with her creativity and knowledge of structural requirements. Joe had pulled out his computer and was showing Cindy how to apply her sketches to a CAD program. They were working on the castle shopping mall. They had added towers for bridal boutiques, a dungeon for movie theaters. The king's personal residence was a five-star restaurant complete with waiters dressed in period attire. It was complete with a fountain and a stage for entertainment in the middle of the mall. Joe and Cindy were quite pleased with themselves. Just then Joe's computer started beeping, 'low battery'. He quickly hit the save button and said, "I guess I'm about out of juice." "Do you think we could copy the file to my computer before it dies?" Cindy's eyes pleaded with Joe. "Well, we could, but you don't have the software to support it." "Aw shoot," Cindy was disappointed. Joe perked up. "I have an idea. My dad has multiple copies of the software at work. I can check to see if he has one left that hasn't been licensed. If he does, I'm sure he would let you have it."

Their conversation was interrupted by a voice over the intercom. "Ladies and gentlemen, we are beginning our descent into Boston;

please turn off all electrical devices...." "Boy, that trip went fast." Joe observed to Cindy. "It sure did," Cindy agreed. "I sure had a great time, Joe. Thanks for everything. You sure have helped me get some perspective on things." Joe reached over and patted Cindy's hand "Are you kidding? I had a great time. You're going to be OK. I'm looking forward to seeing that mall in real life someday. Then I can say, 'I know the architect.'" "Yeah right," Cindy blushed. "I'll need to get through algebra first." "Like I said, I'll be glad to help you anytime. Do you still have my phone number?" "Yes." Cindy smiled. Joe didn't know it but Cindy had written it down in several different locations as well as putting it in her phone. That was one number that she did not want to lose. After all, it was possible that Joe and Mary could break up someday. She had witnessed the fight they had earlier, and Joe did call her 'cutie' and they did have some things in common. She began to daydream about the possibility. "Good!" Joe interrupted her thoughts. "You call me next week and we'll get the algebra figured out." Joe squeezed her hand in reassurance. He wasn't flirting and Cindy knew it. Still, she could fantasize about the possibility. She gave Joe the biggest smile that she could muster up.

The plane hit some turbulence and woke Mary up. "This is just like riding in a wagon on a country road," Maggie mused to Mary. "Mary giggle and agreed. "You look much better now honey. You looked like you saw a ghost when you came out of that restroom. How are you feeling?" Mary smiled. She wanted to say that she had seen a ghost but thought better of it. "I'm feeling better now. How long was I asleep?" "I'd say about 30 minutes," Maggie guessed. "Oh no!" Mary gasped. "What's wrong dear?" Maggie asked. "I was planning to review my speech before we landed. Do you suppose your husband would trade seats back so that I could get to my computer?" "Sure he would, honey. You just tell him what you want. He's a sucker for a pretty face." Mary didn't miss a beat. "I can see that. I suppose that's why he married you." "Maggie laughed and patted her shoulder. "Thanks, Maggie." "No problem honey. Now get up there and tell that ol' coot to get out of your seat."

Mary thanked Maggie's husband as he got out of her seat. She sat down and collected herself. She was still reeling about the whole Gabby thing but she needed to review her speech for the opening rally tonight. She looked forward to the diversion of working on the speech so that she could stop thinking about Gabby. Mary opened her computer and waited for it to boot up. Her head pounded. The combination of cabin pressure and the whole Gabby thing made her feel as if her head were going to explode. She leaned back in the seat, closed her eyes, and waited for the familiar seven musical notes that would come from the computer when it was ready for use.

Mary decided that she needed to attempt some relaxation techniques that she had read about in a magazine. She focused on removing the tension in each part of her body beginning with her face and working her way down to her toes. Her headache eased and she drifted off into a daydream. She was in that state between sleep and consciousness; the place where a person can go to hide from the world and just let their mind wander. You are still aware of your surroundings but your mind goes wherever it chooses. She found herself sitting on a deserted beach. The sun was shining and the air was warm. Her hair blew gently in the wind. As she admired the wonders of God's creation, an object appeared on the horizon. It was a dot at first; but as it came closer, she could see that it was a small boat. There was one person in the boat and the person was waving at Mary. She couldn't tell who it was at first, but in a few minutes Mary recognized that it was Gabby.

"Hi Gabby!" Mary yelled at the top of her lungs. "Hello yourself!" Gabby replied. Mary motioned for Gabby to come over to the shore. "I can't right now, Mary. But I'll see you soon." The boat began to drift away. "But Gabby, I'm so confused. I need to talk to you." "I know dear, but it isn't the right time now. Trust me; I'll be back soon. Just be patient and let God lead you. I'll see you soon." Mary held her breath as the boat disappeared around the end of the island.

Mary stood there gazing at the water for a few minutes until she was interrupted by the sound of music. It was her computer booting up. She snapped back to reality and realized that she was still on the plane. Her entire daydream had only lasted a few seconds! The daydream had seemed so real that she briefly considered the possibility that it was reality and that the airplane was a daydream. After all, neither circumstance really made sense. After a couple minutes of evaluation, Mary decided to store the whole

Gabby ordeal away in the back of her mind. It had to be some sort of repressed childhood memory that was coming back to her for some psychological reason. She mused that she would look forward to taking a psych class in college. Maybe she could figure it out then. Besides, if she kept thinking about this, she would go nuts. She pulled up her speech and began reviewing it.

Joe walked with Cindy to baggage claim. Cindy fantasized that she and Joe were on their honeymoon. She knew it wasn't true, but with all the negative things going on in her life, she needed a little diversion. Joe's bags had arrived and they were waiting on Cindy's. A voice behind them interrupted their concentration on the carousel. "Hi Joe!" It was the baseball coach from Harvard. "Are you ready to go?" "Hi Coach. Well, I have my bags but," he stammered just a bit and looked at Cindy. "This is my friend, Cindy from back home. If it's OK, I'd like to make sure she has a ride before I leave her." "Sure!" Coach slapped him on the back. "Never leave a lady alone. It's nice to see that there are still gentlemen around. It's nice to meet you Cindy." Cindy smiled and started to reply when she heard her uncle's voice from the other side of the carousel. "Cindy!" He started toward her and she met him halfway with a great big hug. They shared greetings and she looked across the crowd at Joe. He smiled and gave her a 'thumbs up' and then held his hand up to his ear to signal for her to call him. She smiled and returned the 'thumbs up'. Jo and Coach disappeared into the crowd.

Mary's plane landed without incident and she immediately felt the warmth of the Florida air as she walked through the airport. It felt good to get out of the Montana winter. She loved snow but by March every year, she was always ready for spring. She got her luggage, climbed into a cab, and headed for the hotel. As the cab pulled up to the lobby, Mary couldn't believe what she saw; there were kids everywhere! It seemed as if a party was going on. There was music playing, tables of food and drinks, and some of the kids were dancing in the lobby. This was going to be fun. Mary checked the time on her cell phone; she had plenty of time before the rally. She decided to check in, freshen up, and head back down to the lobby for a snack before the rally.

Mary was at one of the buffet tables filling her plate and chatting with some girls she had met in the lobby when her cell phone rang; it was Gary. "Hi Gary." Hi Mary, have you arrived yet?"

"Yes, I'm in the lobby. Where are you? I thought your plane was to land an hour ago?" "I'm here, in the lobby too. Where exactly are you?" "I'm by the buffet table." Mary spun around so that she could scan the crowd. As she turned, she bumped into someone. "Excuse mmm..." The phrase was interrupted when she realized that she had bumped into a smiling Gary. "Oh, there you are," he teased. "You are so short that I was looking over your head." "Very funny you big goof." Mary slapped his shoulder playfully and gave him a big hug. "Is everything ready for tonight?" Mary looked at Gary with hope in her eyes. "We are definitely ready. The manager here is great! There are a few things we need to go over before the rally. It should just take ten or 15 minutes." The girls that Mary was talking to before Gary walked up were standing there taking it all in. One of them said, "Are you guys in charge of all this?" Mary blushed, "Well, we have a lot of help. I'm sorry, I didn't introduce myself; I'm Mary."

After the girls introduced each other, they looked at Gary who was flashing his best California smile. "This is my friend, Gary." Mary looked at him. "Not, BOYFRIEND?" One of the girls wanted clarification. Gary spoke up, "No, I'm single, still looking for that right girl." Gary tried to act shy but Mary called his bluff and teased. "Don't trust him, girls, he is as flirty as they come." "Don't pay any attention to her ladies. We can discuss this while Mary stuffs her face a little." The girls laughed as Gary shuttled them to the couch in the lobby. "We'll talk after you have a snack, Mary." Gary smiled over his shoulder. Mary waved her fork at him as they walked away.

CHAPTER SEVENTEEN

Joe stumbled into his room Saturday afternoon feeling as if he had been beaten. He fell into his bed hoping to get a little nap. He had never been through a workout like this before. There had been a three-hour practice this morning. That was followed with a two hour weight room session and a quick lunch before finishing with another two-hour practice. Coach had put him in a suite with three other guys who were upperclassmen. Joe asked the guys how they managed to get through practices like that. One of the guys teased. "This was an easy day, Joe, just wait until we have a tough one." The other guys laughed and then admitted that this day had been really tough. "Coach was just seeing what you are made of, Joe. I think you did well. In fact, Coach mentioned that he was impressed. By the way, you have a wicked curve. When you threw that at me with that 2-2 count you froze me in my tracks." The other guys agreed. "You hit the ball well. I heard the batting coach arguing with the pitching coach about how they plan to utilize you. The batting coach doesn't want you to be a pitcher because he doesn't want your bat out of the line-up when you're not pitching." Joe blushed. "I guess I got lucky today, thanks for the pep talk guys." "Hey, don't fall asleep, we go to dinner in a half hour and then there is this big party at a sorority later. There will be plenty of girls and beer! We'll show you how college guys party." Joe looked at Tom who was looking out the window. Joe had noticed that Tom had a Bible on his desk and seemed a little less crazy than the other two guys. "Are you going Tom?" "Naw, he never goes," one of the other guys piped up. "It just isn't my thing," Tom replied. "Besides, if I go, you guys won't have a chance with the girls; they'll be all over me!" Everyone laughed. "I'm pretty tired," Joe interjected. "Maybe I'll just hang with Tom tonight. I don't want to get into trouble with Coach." Joe wasn't sure it would be his thing either. "Suit yourself, more beer for me! Let's get a quick shower and go eat. We're having steak tonight." "Steak?!" Joe couldn't believe what he had heard. "They serve steak in the dining hall?" "Just the athletic dining hall," Tom clarified. "Only the athletes are allowed to eat there. Of course, we can take a guest if we choose." "Wow!" Joe exclaimed. "I think I am going to like it here!"

After dinner Tom showed Joe the campus. Joe was very impressed with the college, as well as the traditions and history that had been established there over the years. As they walked back toward the dorm, Joe spoke up, "I hope I'm not keeping you from anything. I'm sure that the last thing you wanted to do tonight was babysit a high school guy on Saturday." "No worries Joe. The only thing I had going was that my girlfriend and I were going to hang out later. You're welcome to join us." "I don't know man; I don't want to be a third wheel." "Don't be crazy, Joe. Colleen would love to meet you. We'll talk about it later. Besides, it may not even happen. She has a part-time job at the hospital and she gets a lot of overtime."

Tom discussing Colleen made Joe think of Mary. He hadn't talked to her since the airport on Friday. They had been playing phone tag ever since then and hadn't been able to connect. He really missed her, but Coach had kept him so busy that he didn't have time to dwell on it much. "Hey Joe, do you play pool?" Tom interrupted his thoughts. "Yeah, but I'm not very good." "Great!" Tom snickered. "I'll play you for an ice cream cone. The rec hall is right over there."

Joe and Tom were having a great time playing pool. They had talked about everything from girls to cars. After Tom beat Joe two out of three games, they headed to the ice cream bar so that Joe could 'pay up.' Tom's cell phone rang. "I'm at the rec hall playing pool with Joe. OK. See you soon." Tom hung up. "That was Colleen, we're going over to her place to watch a movie. She just got off work and invited us over." "Oh great." Joe lamented. You, me and Colleen; that's awkward." "Relax tiger," Tom slapped him on the back. "Her roommates are there. It's just a bunch of kids getting together."

Colleen and her roommates lived off campus in a cute little Victorian house. After Tom and Joe arrived and introductions were made, the kids piled into the living room to watch the movie. Joe sat down on the couch while two of Colleen's roommates sat on either side of him. The movie hadn't been going for more than 15 minutes before Joe fell asleep. "He's a lightweight," Tom whispered. One of the girls replied, "At least he's a cute one." The rest of the girls giggled and agreed. Joe was so sound asleep that he actually slumped to the left and wound up with his head on the shoulder of Colleen's roommate, Ginger. Just then, someone's cell phone rang. No one recognized the ringtone and Tom concluded that it must be Joe's. He decided to look at it to see if it was from someone important. All it said was 'Sugar Plum'. "I'm not sure who 'Sugar Plum' is but let's have a little fun with 'em." Tom's eyes lit up. After the phone stopped ringing, Tom flipped open the phone and took a picture of Joe asleep on Ginger's shoulder. Then he sent 'Sugar Plum' the picture along with the following text message: 'too busy to answer the phone, call back later.'

Mary hung up the phone without leaving a message. She had slipped out of the dance after Saturday night's rally to try and get Joe. No luck, she had missed him again. Ever since she arrived last night she had been going non-stop. There were planning sessions, last minute details, and of course, there were a number of snafus that had to be addressed on the fly. She and Gary had stayed up until 2 a.m. finishing up the details for Saturday. Everything was going well and she had heard nothing but praise from everyone that she talked to. It would have been perfect if Joe had been there, but it wasn't meant to be. She headed back to the dance. As she started to open the door, her phone rang. It read, 'Text from Joe'. She opened the phone and read the message that Tom had sent and then looked at the picture. Mary stood there in astonishment. She didn't know what to think. Obviously, Joe hadn't taken the picture and he probably hadn't sent the message; but, there he was, asleep on some girl's shoulder. She tried to rationally think it through. All of a sudden, Gary appeared. "There you are. Everyone is asking for you. Your speech was a home run. You've got to get in here!" Mary looked distracted. "Are you OK, Mary? You look like you just saw a ghost." "I'm fine. What were you saying?" "Come back in here, you are being summoned by your fans your highness." Gary bowed and opened the door to the auditorium. Mary smiled at him and walked through the door. She decided to figure this out later.

"Time to go back to the dorm there Sleeping Beauty." Joe woke up to the sound of Tom's voice as he playfully slapped Joe on the arm. Joe looked up at Ginger and realized he had fallen asleep during the movie and quickly came to the realization that he was quite comfortable on Ginger's shoulder. "Oh, uh, sorry about that. I guess I dozed off." "No problem cutie, you can fall asleep on my shoulder anytime." Ginger giggled.

As Joe and Tom walked to the dorm it began to snow lightly. It was about 11:30 and Joe couldn't believe how many kids were still out and about. "Is this normal?" Joe questioned as he looked around at all of the activity. "Things are just getting started. This is when all of the drunks come out and make fools of themselves. It really is quite entertaining." "I'm not into that personally," Joe offered. "Me neither. It was a good call not to go with the guys to that party tonight. It would have been crazy." After a long pause Tom changed the subject. "Say, what are you doing tomorrow for lunch? I know we have to be at Coach's house for supper and a chalk talk but what are you doing until then?" Joe forgot that there was no practice on Sunday. "Nothing, I guess." "Well my history professor has invited a few kids over for Sunday brunch. Do you want to go?" "Well, yeah, sure but I'm not invited." "He won't care, he's really cool. Hang on a second." Tom whipped out his phone and hit speed dial. "Hello, Dr. Rogers? This is Tom. Yeah, I'm coming. We have a recruit visiting this weekend. Is it OK if he comes along? OK thanks, see you tomorrow." Joe's eyes were wide open. "I can't believe you called your professor at 11:45 p.m.! Are you nuts?!" "Relax Joe, it's not a big deal. You've been stuck in little ol' Pleasantville, Montana all of your life. Things are different here. You'll like Dr. Rogers. He has some really cool little kids that have a basement full of games. Besides, Colleen and Ginger will be there. If you get bored, you can take another nap on Ginger's shoulder." Tom grinned. Joe turned red and looked down at the accumulating snow. "Ever been nailed by a snowball from a Montana kid?" Joe said fiendishly as he bent down. "No, and I don't intend to." Tom took off down the sidewalk with Joe in hot pursuit.

Mary fell across the bed. She was completely exhausted. She looked at the clock; 1:30. She wondered if Joe was up or still asleep on that girl's arm. She fumed a little but decided to wait for an explanation. She and Joe had been through their share of miscommunications recently and she refused to jump to conclusions. However, she couldn't help but be a little upset. She hit speed dial and let it ring. Joe's phone rang six times before it went to voicemail and Mary knew it. On the sixth ring she closed her phone. She was too tired to leave a message. It was a good thing that the conference wasn't scheduled to resume until after lunch. The kids were getting the morning off to have a little free time on the beach. Mary decided to sleep in. She had to meet Gary at 11 a.m. to clarify things for Sunday and Monday. She laid there for a moment and collected her thoughts.

Mary woke up with a start. She had fallen asleep in her clothes. It was 9:45. She had just enough time to get cleaned up, grab some breakfast and head off to meet Gary. Mary tried calling Joe while she was riding in the elevator on the way down to breakfast.

"Hello?" Joe grabbed the phone after five rings. He had just come back to the room after getting a shower. He and Tom were getting ready to go to Dr. Rogers' house for brunch. "Hello, Hello?" Joe was almost yelling into the phone. He knew it was Mary but couldn't hear her. "Joe? Joe? You're breaking up, I'm in the elevator, hang on a minute and I'll get to the lobby. Joe? Can you hear me?" All Joe could hear was garble. "Mary? Can you hear me?" It was one of those frustrating moments that everyone with a cell phone has experienced. Both Mary and Joe wanted desperately to talk to each other, but.... Joe's phone began to beep rapidly, low battery. He had forgotten to plug it in last night. "Mary, if you can hear me my phone is dying. I'll call you later. I love you." His phone went dead. The elevator hit the 1st floor and Mary ran toward the door. She couldn't hear a word that Joe had said. "Joe, are you there?" Her phone read, 'call ended'. She quickly hit redial. Six rings later Joe's voicemail picked up. Mary, dejected, slowly closed her phone and headed for the restaurant.

Mrs. Rogers answered the door and ushered Tom and Joe into the living room. There were about a dozen kids milling around. Joe spotted Ginger and Colleen at the buffet table. Joe's eyes met Ginger's and she smiled and waved. Joe turned red and returned the greeting. "Help yourself to the food, boys. Glad you could come along Joe." "Thanks for having me," Joe replied. "Where's Dr. Rogers?" Tom was anxious to introduce Joe. "I believe there is quite a competitive game of Ping-Pong going on in the basement. You know how he loves to play. My guess is that he is down there." Mrs. Rogers nodded in the direction of the basement door. "Let's get some food and head down," Tom suggested. "I would like a little revenge for the beat down he gave me last weekend."

The boys got their food and headed downstairs. When they got to the bottom of the steps a little boy and girl about seven years old came running over to Tom and gave him a big hug. "Hi, Uncle Tom!" "Hi guys! How was your week in school?" "It was great," the girl said. "We began learning Spanish," the boy added. They both looked at Joe. "This is my friend, Joe. Joe, this is Andy and Annie, they are twins." "Yeah but I'm older," Annie announced proudly. "Yeah, by two whole minutes," Andy lamented. "Hey, Joe, do you want to play 'Go Fish'?" "I would love to," Joe said grinning at the invitation. The kids led Joe over to a small table next to a wall. Joe caught a glimpse of the heated Ping-Pong game that Mrs. Rogers had alluded to. Joe immediately picked out Dr. Rogers. He was slender, about six feet tall, had a goatee, and appeared to be in his mid thirties. Joe sat down and began playing with the twins.

After purposely losing a couple of games to the delight of the twins, Joe caught Dr. Rogers out of the corner of his eye walking over to them. "Be careful, they have been known to cheat," Dr. Rogers teased his children. "We both have won a game, daddy," Andy announce proudly. "And we didn't cheat!" "Hi, I'm Don Rogers." He stuck out his hand in Joe's direction. Joe stood up and returned the handshake. "Hi, I'm Joe Goldstein. Thanks for the invite. You have a couple of great kids here." The handshake was warm and firm. Their eyes met and Joe immediately felt drawn to the man. "How do you like our school, Joe?" "I've never experienced anything like it before. It is great." Joe got excited. Dr. Rogers sparkled. "I'm glad you like it. Do you have a major picked out?" "Architectural Engineering; I want to go into the family business back in Montana." "That's great, Joe. I guess I'll be seeing you first semester. I teach a core course in Architectural History." "Sounds great, Dr. Rogers; I'm looking forward to it." Dr. Rogers' voice softened and he peered deep into Joe's eyes. "You know Joe, they say that the measure of a man can be judged by how he treats children. I've never seen my kids warm up to anyone as quickly as they did to you. I know you are a fierce competitor or you wouldn't be coming here to play baseball. However, I know that you let them win. My wife says that I have a gift for reading people. If my gift is correct, there is something very special about you. I feel as if your destiny, if fulfilled, will be of great significance. Even if you don't come here for some reason, I feel like we'll see each other again." Joe didn't know how to respond. He was embarrassed, complimented, and confused all at the same time. All he could do was smile.

Just then, Ginger walked by, "Hi Joe, feeling a little tired?" She giggled and continued walking. Joe blushed and Dr. Rogers laughed and Joe felt like he owed him an explanation. "I heard about the nap." He offered before Joe could speak. "That's just great." Joe looked down. "It really is kind of great, Joe." Dr. Rogers laughed. "Ginger is pretty popular around campus and I can tell she likes you. You haven't even started going here and you are already a legend. I doubt if Ginger would let just anyone nap on her shoulder!" "Thanks, Dr. Rogers. You really know how to handle an awkward situation." "No problem, Joe. Now you will have to excuse me. Tom needs another lesson in Ping-Pong." Joe nodded and watched him return to the table. Andy and Annie had moved on to their next victim at cards so Joe decided to just fade into the background for awhile. He was going to like it just fine here.

CHAPTER EIGHTEEN

Mary and Joe tried unsuccessfully to call each other for the next 24 hours. Mary was either in a meeting, leading a session, speaking at a rally or participating in some of the activities. In her spare time, which was rare, she and Gary would get together and finalized plans for the next few hours. Joe was equally busy. Sunday was chalk talk at Coach's house where they went over game situations in great detail. Joe spent Monday attending various classes with some of the players and then it was off to a three-hour practice in the evening.

Four other kids joined Mary and Gary in the elevator. They had just finished a game of beach volleyball and had decided that it would be fun to order pizza from room service. They decided to meet in Mary's room and she had decided to take a shower while they waited for the pizza.

It was 10 p.m. Monday night and Joe was walking back to the dorm from practice. He thought he would try Mary again. Four rings later a guy's voice answered. Joe recognized it immediately. "Hi Gary, is Mary around?" "Well, uh yeah, she's here. But she can't come to the phone, she's in the shower." Joe's blood ran cold. What was Gary doing in Mary's room while she was in the shower!? A long silence ensured. "Joe, you still there?" "Yeah." "Do you want me to have Mary call you?" "No thanks." Joe hung up.

In a few minutes Mary came out of the shower. "Did I hear my phone ring?" "Yeah, Joe called. No message. He sounded kind of strange." "What did you say?" "I told him you were in the shower." "Did you bother to tell him that there are other people in the room besides you? "He didn't give me a chance. Besides, what's the big deal? We are just hanging out." Mary looked at the other girls in the room and rolled her eyes. They nodded in agreement and exchanged the look that says, 'Boys are so stupid'. Mary grabbed the phone and called Joe.

Joe had made it back to the room and was in the shower. The hot water felt good. It had been another rough practice. He had hit well in batting practice and had worked out at shortstop for awhile. He had been pleased with his performance. However, that seemed like a long time ago. He couldn't get his mind off the fact that Gary was in Mary's room while she was showering! His mind raced. He finished his shower and headed back to the room. "Hurry up Joe, the dining hall closes in 20 minutes." One of the guys reminded him. "By the way, your phone rang. You just missed it." Joe picked up the phone and saw that Mary had called. He tossed it back onto the bed. "I'm not hungry; I think I'll go for a walk. You guys go on. Maybe I'll grab a burger at the rec hall." "You OK man?" Tom sensed something. "Yeah, I'm good." Joe lied and Tom knew it but realized Joe wanted to be alone.

Mary walked out onto the balcony and sat in the chair. She had a great view of the ocean and the crashing of the waves coupled with the warm night air had a soothing affect on her. Still, she was upset because she knew Joe would be hurt. It was unfortunate that Gary was being so insensitive about the whole thing. But, California was a different culture than Montana. He still didn't understand what the fuss was all about. He and the rest of the kids were in the room eating the pizza and watching TV. She needed to be alone. Perhaps Joe would call and she could explain.

Joe wandered around the campus in no particular direction. He happened to pass the library and decided it might be a nice quiet place to get in out of the cold. He walked through the doors and spotted some leather chairs over in the section by the magazines. He grabbed a copy of *Sports Illustrated* and flopped down in the chair. He started to flip through the pages trying to get his mind off of Gary and Mary. It wasn't long before the warmth of the library, along with the stress of the day overtook him and he nodded off to sleep. After a few minutes he woke up when someone walked by and sat down in the chair next to him. He sat up and looked over and saw that it was Ginger who had sat down. "Looks like you need another nap." She smiled. Joe returned the smile and fumbled for some words but couldn't find any. "Joe, I was on my way back to my place and I don't want to walk by myself. Would you mind walking me home?" Always the gentleman, Joe was taught from a very early age to NEVER turn down a lady's request for help. Joe shook the sleep out of his mind. "That is the least I could do for someone who has literally lent me her shoulder." Joe flashed his signature smile.

Joe and Ginger opened the door from the library and the cold air hit them like a ton of bricks. "Wow! It's cold out here!" Ginger immediately zipped her coat all the way to the top. "It is kind of breezy," Joe replied. As they headed down the steps Ginger slipped on the ice and out of reaction, reached for Joe's arm. He grabbed her and prevented what could have been a rather nasty fall. "Thanks Joe." Ginger looked up and grinned. "Mind if I hang on to you? These shoes are slick and I could use the body heat." "No problem." Joe stuck out his arm and they headed in the direction of Ginger's house.

"Do you like it here?" Ginger questioned. "It's great." Joe replied. "Everyone has been so kind to me. I have to admit that this country boy from Montana was a little bit apprehensive about coming to the big city, but..." "I know what you mean, Joe. I live in Pennsylvania now, but I was raised in a small town in Vermont and I was scared to come here, but I soon found out that it is a pretty cool place." Just then a gust of wind blew past them which caused Ginger to instinctively squeeze closer to Joe. "I see what you mean," Joe quipped. "This IS a pretty COOL place." Ginger laughed but didn't release her grip on Joe's arm. As they continued to walk along, they discussed sports, family, hobbies.... It was the first time since he had gotten to Harvard that he really relaxed. Ginger was easy to talk to and the more they talked, the more he realized how much he and Ginger had in common.

Joe's phone rang. He could tell from the ring that it was a text from Mary. He had temporarily forgotten about the Gary/Mary ordeal. He had been enjoying walking and talking with Ginger. His mind returned to the thoughts of Mary and Gary together. "Are you going to answer that?" Ginger interrupted. "No, it's just a text from my girlfriend." Joe looked at the message, it read, 'Call me'. "From the sound of your voice, it seems like something's wrong," Ginger observed. "Do you want to talk about it?" "No, it's complicated. Suffice it to say that there have been a lot of misunderstandings lately and we seem to be growing apart." "I know what you mean," Ginger replied. "My boyfriend and I both came here as freshmen last year. We both thought that we would eventually get married but…I guess we kind of went in different directions. We broke up at the end of our first semester." "I'm sorry." Joe was sincere. "It's OK. We are still friends. Sometimes, life throws you a curve." "Sounds like you got it all figured out. I wish I could say the same thing." Joe sounded depressed. "You're a smart guy, Joe. You'll figure it out." Ginger tried to encourage him.

The conversation fell silent as they came up to a busy street. As they stood there waiting for the light to change, a taxicab raced by and hit a huge puddle directly in front of them. A wall of water, snow and ice rose up from the tires and proceeded to cover both of them. They were soaked. It was so cold that it immediately took their breath away. Ginger gasped and Joe grabbed her with both arms to make sure she wouldn't fall down. She buried her head in his chest and tried to regain her composure. Joe wrapped his arms around her in an attempt to warm her up. Her shoulders started shaking and Joe thought she was beginning to cry. "Are you OK, Ginger?" She slowly raised her head and looked up at Joe. To his surprise, she wasn't crying; she was giggling! Her hair was dripping wet and mud covered her face! Joe began to giggle along with Ginger which caused them both to burst out in uncontrollable laughter. The light changed and they both jumped into the puddle and splashed around for about ten seconds before heading toward the other side of the street. The cars waiting at the light honked their horns and flashed their headlights at the 'crazy college kids'.

A block later they arrived at Ginger's house. "Well, here you are," Joe said politely and started down the sidewalk. "Oh no you don't!" Ginger caught his hand and pulled him toward the door. "I'm freezing and I know you are too. It's a 25-minute walk back to the dorm; you'll freeze to death. Now get in the house and warm up." Joe protested a little but he gave in quickly. He wasn't looking forward to the walk back.

Ginger's roommates laughed hysterically at Joe and Ginger and even decided to take a few pictures. Ginger excused herself to get changed and Joe headed to the bathroom to clean up as best he could. In a few seconds Colleen knocked on the door. "Joe, I've got a pair of Tom's sweatpants and a T-shirt. Put them on and I'll throw your clothes in the washer." Joe thought about protesting but he was freezing. He opened the door. "Are you sure it's no trouble?" He hoped the answer was no. "I wouldn't have it any other way," Colleen assured Joe. He grabbed the clothes. "Thanks." In just a few seconds he emerged from the bathroom carrying his soaked clothes. Ginger met him at the door. "I'll take those." Before Joe could protest, Ginger had put them in the washer and turned it on. "Now, how about some hot chocolate?" "Sounds good," Joe replied.

Joe sat at the kitchen table and chatted with Ginger as she moved around the kitchen. "It sure is nice of you to wash my clothes," Joe offered. "It's the least I can do. After all, you were walking me home when you got splashed. Say, it will be about an hour before your clothes are dry. Would you like to play backgammon?" "I love backgammon," Joe replied. "Good." Ginger slid the game across the table to Joe. "You set it up while I finish making the hot chocolate."

Halfway through the game Joe's phone rang again. Ginger recognized the tone from before and said, "It sounds like she really wants to talk to you." Joe looked at the message, 'are you there?' He laid the phone down and said, "Whose turn is it?" Ginger grabbed his hand and said, "It's YOUR TURN, JOE. Your turn to call her back. You seem like such a nice guy. Don't treat her like that. You can't just ignore her. If you are angry with her, just tell her. It's none of my business, but if you truly care about her, you will at least acknowledge her text." Joe looked at Ginger. "You're right." He picked up his phone and sent a brief message and turned the phone off. "Now can we finish the game?" He smiled at Ginger and handed the dice to her.

Mary grabbed her phone after the first ring. She knew Joe's ringtone for a text. The message read, 'Got soaked walking Ginger home—she's washing my clothes; how was your shower with Gary?' Mary's blood boiled. She couldn't believe what she was reading! What was he up to out there in the big city? How could he say such a thing to her? She quickly responded to his nasty comment with one of her own. 'I suppose this is Ginger.' She attached the picture of Joe sleeping on Ginger's shoulder. Mary hit 'send', fell back on her pillow, closed her eyes and waited. What was going on with Joe? She thought she knew him like the back of her hand; but he was acting so strange. She knew deep down that there had to be a perfectly good explanation about the picture with Ginger, but that text was just mean! He had promised her that he would never doubt her again. Her world seemed to be spinning out of control. As she contemplated all that was going on, her mind returned to the conference. She began to review all that had to be done this week. Her mind bounced between Joe and the tasks at hand. She drifted off to sleep.

The dryer buzzed and Ginger jumped up to check on Joe's clothes. In just a few seconds she returned with the clothes and handed them to Joe. "Thanks." Joe headed for the bathroom to change. When he returned Joe looked at the clock on the wall; 12:45. "Wow, where did the time go? I guess I'd better get going. I really appreciate everything." "No problem, Joe. I had a good time; and thanks for walking me home." Joe bowed low in grand gesture as he opened the door to leave: "At your service, Miss Ginger, good night." By now Ginger's roommates had gathered in the kitchen to say goodbye to Joe and had witnessed the performance. Joe headed through the door into the screened in porch toward the swinging door. Colleen looked at Ginger and teased, "Why Miss Ginger, I do believe you are blushing just a little!" Another one of the girls giggled and said, "Why not? He is so cute!" "Relax ladies," Ginger assured them. "He's taken. However, there is trouble in Paradise and IF it doesn't work out, I'll be close by to pick up the pieces." "You may have some competition from us!" The other girls agreed. Colleen rolled her eyes as she started to close the door. However, before she could close it there was a knock. It was Joe! "Sorry, I forgot my phone." Afraid that he had overheard their conversation about him, the girls scurried out of the room leaving Ginger alone with Joe. She was doing some serious blushing and was extremely nervous. She did manage to collect her thoughts quickly enough to grab Joe's phone and hand it to him. "Thanks." The coldness of Joe's hand against hers made a shiver go up her arm. "Is something wrong, Ginger?" "Uh, Joe, how long had you been standing on the other side of the door?" She had to know what he had heard. "Not long at all, why?" "No reason, just curious." "OK then, good night!" Joe backed out of the door and stopped. "Oh, by the way, I think you are pretty cute when you blush and you wouldn't have to worry about any competition." Joe smiled his biggest smiled and winked. Ginger gasped, then laughed, and playfully smacked Joe on the shoulder. "Good night, Joe!"

Joe skipped down the steps and headed for the street. He reached into his pocket to check the time and realized that he had turned the phone off earlier. After it powered up, it beeped indicating that there was a message waiting. He read Mary's message and saw the picture of him asleep on Ginger's shoulder. Well that explains the nasty text that he had received from Mary. I guess she had a right to be upset over such a picture. Too bad she didn't know the whole story. It was very innocent, but how could Mary have known that? Suddenly, Joe felt guilty. His mind rewound to the past several weeks in which he and Mary had had a series of misunderstandings because situations had not always been the way they seemed. This had to be another one. He decided to let the shower incident go. There had to be an explanation; just like there was an explanation for the picture of Ginger and him. He needed to talk to Mary, but he didn't want to wake her. He flipped open his phone and sent 'Sugar Plum' a text; 'R U awake?'

Mary was startled out of her sleep by Joe's ring tone. She shook the sleep out of her brain and read the text. At first she hesitated to reply. She was still angry with Joe and it probably wasn't the best time to talk but she desperately wanted to talk to him. They had never gone this long without talking. She NEEDED an explanation. Not only for the picture, but she had to know what was going on with Joe. She replied, 'Yes.'

It was cold as Joe walked back to the dorm. There were a few kids here and there but, for the most part campus was deserted. The wind seemed to blow through him as he walked. Being from Montana, he was used to cold weather. But this 'cold' was different somehow. He had a weird feeling. It was if something evil was lurking around him. He stepped up the pace as he hoped to hear from Mary. His phone rang and he nearly dropped it trying to answer so quickly. He read Mary's text and immediately hit speed dial.

"Hello?" Mary's sweet voice answered. Joe could tell she was apprehensive. His heart melted. "Hi Sugar Plum, I'm sorry. I love you." There was a short pause and Joe held his breath. Mary sighed with relief. "Hi yourself you big goof, I love you too and I'm sorry." Joe's stomach leaped inside. "I miss you so much. I don't know what is going on. It seems like Satan is trying to get between us for some reason. But I'm not going to let that happen. NEVER!" Mary got excited. "I know what you mean. It is crazy down here. I am constantly on the run and am always trying to play catch-up. I agree, Satan is in full swing trying to get between us, but why?" "I don't know, sweetie, but I will not let it happen. I am nothing without you and I intend to be with you for the rest of my life!" Joe was emphatic and Mary liked it. "Why Joe, is that a proposal?" Mary teased. Joe laughed and replied, "Absolutely!" Joe and Mary both laughed at the promise. Although they had always known deep down that they would be married someday, it had never been formalized. "Joe, I want to explain about the shower. There were a bunch of kids in the room and...." "Don't say another word," Joe interrupted. "You don't need to explain a thing to me. I just got jealous when Gary answered your phone. However, I would like to explain the picture to you." "You really don't need to, Joe. I trust you. Gary is nice, but sometimes he can be so stupid. You should have seen how the girls reacted to his conversation with you after I got out of the shower. He is simply clueless." "I know, Mary, the picture of Ginger and I is innocent too. I had just gotten out of a really tough practice and my roommate took me over to his girlfriend's house to watch movies. I guess between the jet lag and the practice, I just fell asleep. That's all. But something puzzles me, how did you get the picture of me and Ginger?" "Mary laughed. "I bet they think you are some kind of lightweight. The picture came from your phone right after I tried to call you." Joe thought for a minute, then, it came to him. Someone at Ginger's must have taken the picture and replied to Mary's call. Joe laughed out loud into the phone. "What's so funny?" Mary was trying to catch up. Joe explained his theory to Mary who concurred. "It really is kind of funny when you think about it." "Yeah, I guess so," Joe admitted. "As long as you and I are OK, that's what's important to me. I'll get even with whoever took that picture." "Joe, we're great! Let it go. It sounds like you have started out on the right foot out there. Don't forget, we are both going there next year. It would be nice to have a few friends when we get there." "No worries, Sugar Plum. I'll just have a little harmless fun with the guilty party. Now, tell me about your week, how's it going?" Mary launched into a detailed account about the conference. Things were back to normal. Joe felt a real peace and confidence again. The 'weird' feeling about the cold weather disappeared. 'That's right, Satan. You lose, again,' Joe thought to himself as he listened to Mary fill him in on her week.

CHAPTER NINETEEN

It was Wednesday night and the past couple of days had been great. Mary and Joe had been talking on the phone and Mary had told him that 500 kids had made commitments to abstain from sex until they got married. Mary gushed with excitement as she went into great detail about how successful the conference had been. Joe was equally excited. He had been doing very well at the baseball workouts and all of the guys assured him that he was sure to make the team. Several of the guys had even asked Joe for some batting tips. Joe had found out that Tom was the culprit behind the picture incident so Joe had borrowed a pink bunny from Colleen, placed it next to Tom while he was taking a nap and took his own picture. That picture wound up on the bulletin board in the locker room. All of the guys got lots of laughs at Tom's expense. Mary was proud of Joe and he felt the same about her. After about twenty minutes they said good night and Joe went to bed.

Mary was too excited to sleep so she decided to go for a walk on the beach. The warm air and the crashing waves created a very pleasant evening. There were a few people milling around but the beach was amazingly quiet for 9:30. Mary spotted a lounge chair by the ocean and decided to sit down and enjoy God's creation. As she laid there and absorbed the sounds and smells of the ocean, she realized how bright the stars sparkled. It was a perfect evening. She wished that Joe could be here to enjoy it with her. All of a sudden she saw a star shooting across the sky! She had seen shooting stars before; after all, Montana is 'Big Sky' country. But this star was the brightest one she had ever seen; and it lasted longer than any other! She held her breath as she absorbed the wonders of God's world.

A woman's voice behind her interrupted her thoughts, "Beautiful, isn't it?" Mary turned around to see who it was but the woman was standing between Mary and a spotlight from the hotel. She shielded her eyes in order to attempt to make out who it was but all Mary could see was a shadow. "Did you see that shooting star, Mary?" the voice continued. It was somewhat familiar but Mary had met hundreds of people in the past few days. However, this person knew her name so they must have met sometime or she had remembered it from a program or something. Mary decided to be polite. "Why yes, I did see the star. It was beautiful." "You know, if that star could think, I'll bet it didn't have any idea that God intended to change its course tonight." The woman's voice still sounded familiar, but Mary couldn't place it. Mary smiled at the shadow. "I suppose it didn't have a clue about its destiny. I guess no one knows what God has in store for us." That's right, Mary." The woman stepped out of the shadows. "Do you mind if I sit down?" Mary sat up and swung her legs around so the woman could share her seat. "Sure, be my guest." Mary decided to confess. "I'm sorry; I don't remember your name. Have we met?" The woman sat down and turned toward Mary. For the first time Mary could see her face. Mary froze. The woman smiled and said, "Now Mary, after all we've been through; you can't remember my name?"

After a few seconds, Mary whispered as if she couldn't believe her eyes. "Gabby?" "Yes Mary, it's me. Take a minute and gather yourself. I assume you have some questions." Mary just stared at her for a minute. "But, but, daddy says you, uh...." Mary looked for the words. "Died?" Gabby finished her sentence. "Mary, you of all people should know that things are not always the way they seem. After all, look what you and Joe have been going through lately." "How do you know about that?" Mary was really confused. "Mary, this may be difficult for you to understand, but you need to have faith. I am an angel. God sent me to watch over you." Mary gasped and felt as if she was going to faint. "Deep breaths honey. Let it settle in. If you think about it for a moment, you will realize that it makes sense; all of our encounters; all of the mystery; everything."

Mary looked deep into Gabby's eyes. She could see nothing but kindness and honesty. Her mind raced back to all of her experiences with Gabby. It did fit, but, an angel? That was stuff you read about in the Bible. It didn't happen in real life. But yet, it was the only explanation for Gabby's existence, unless she was dreaming or hallucinating. She and Joe had had several long discussions about the existence of angels and both agreed that they are scriptural. But, that seemed so abstract compared to the here and now. "This is so hard Gabby. I believe you, but it doesn't make sense. Can I touch you?" Gabby laughed out loud. "Sure honey, I won't bite." Mary slowly reached out and took Gabby's hand. Immediately, she felt a warmth in Gabby's touch. Mary smiled. "Feel better?" Gabby questioned. "Yes. But I have a question. Have long have you been 'with' me?" Gabby smiled and squeezed her hand. "Mary, God is ALWAYS with you. Every time you 'feel' something but can't explain it, it's God. That brush behind you, the cool breeze from nowhere, that peace that comes over you in difficult times; those are times when God is revealing Himself to you. But He is always there." Mary remembered all the times she had experienced the things that Gabby had just mentioned. It all came together. She came to the realization that there really is more to this life. There really is another dimension out there. Her faith returned. She sighed and relaxed. All was well. She had never felt a peace like this in her life.

Neither one of them spoke for a few minutes. Gabby knew that Mary needed some time to allow all of this to sink in. Finally, Gabby broke the silence. "Mary, there's something I have to tell you. You know how God suddenly changed the course of that star. God needs to change your course much like he did the star. It is time for the Messiah to come to the world. You have found favor with the Lord. He has selected you to be the mother of the Savior, the King of Kings, and the Lord of Lords. In just a little while, you will become pregnant with the Savior and when He is born you will name Him Jesus." Mary's jaw hit her chest. She felt as if she were going to pass out. "But how can this be? I am a virgin." Gabby smiled and touched Mary's face. "Relax my child. The Holy Spirit will come over you and cause this to happen. The power of God is unlimited. You are truly blessed to be given this mission from God." Gabby's warm touch soothed Mary which caused her to smile. "I am a servant of

God. I am willing to do anything that He asks me." "That's my girl, Mary." Gabby said as she stood up. "Wait!" Mary started to panic as she thought about the ramifications. "I have so many questions. What am I supposed to do? What will my parents say? What about Joe?" "Mary, trust in the Lord. Listen to the Holy Spirit. God doesn't just give someone a task and then leave them to flounder on their own. He will be with you. Just follow your heart." Gabby walked toward the beach and disappeared into the shadows. "I will, Gabby; I will. I promise."

Mary leaned back in the chair and looked at the stars. They were as bright and vibrant as she had ever seen. The view was amazing. Her mind whirled as she thought about everything that had just happened or did it? Maybe she was imagining it. After all, Gabby had been in her 'daydreams' a lot lately. But it seemed so real. Then again, what are the odds that God had chosen her to be the mother of the Messiah? Why her? 'There is nothing special about me.' She thought to herself. Just then something brushed against her leg. There was a piece of paper stuck between the straps of the chair. Mary reached down and grabbed it before the wind blew it away. It was a business card, Gabby's business card. Mary turned the card over and read the handwritten note; 'Believe me, Mary, it's real; love Gabby.' Mary smiled and tucked the card in her pocket. She laid there pondering everything that Gabby had said. She wondered about the future, school, 'Teens for Abstinence', her parents, Joe, her friends. What would she do? How was she supposed to go about this? However, with all of the questions swirling around in her head, Mary remained strangely peaceful. She knew everything would work out. She had been called for a mission by God. Her job was to answer the call. He would handle the obstacles. She leaned back in her chair, looked at the stars, listened to the ocean, felt the warm air flow over her body and fell asleep.

Mary dreamt that she was being flown on a cloud around the world. She saw the majesty of mountains, the beauty of rainforests, the massive expanse of the desert, and the awesome power of volcanoes. She witnessed oceans and rivers as they churned their way through valleys. The thrill of the journey made her giggle like a school girl. Suddenly, the cloud turned straight up and headed toward the sun. As it raced closer, she was blinded by the brilliance of the colors. The cloud slowed down and as she opened her eyes, she marveled at what was in front of her. It was a city made of gold and precious jewels. Buildings were made of the whitest ivory that she ever saw. The streets were outlined with diamonds. Bricks were gold and silver. The gates were made of pearl and outlined with emeralds. In the center of the city was the most spectacular temple that she had ever imagined. It was made of clear chrysolite and flashes of lightning and fire emitted from it in all directions. It was magnificent. All of a sudden, Mary found herself dozing in a meadow filled with flowers. It was sunny and warm and the flowers were as lovely as any garden that she had ever seen. The warmth of the sun on her face caused Mary to open her eyes.

"Beautiful morning isn't it?" A man's voice came from a chair next to her. Somewhat startled, Mary looked around. The sun was coming up over the ocean, there was a blanket on her, and a man that she had never seen before was commenting on the sunrise. She could have sworn that Gabby had just left and that she had just closed her eyes. However, he was exactly where she had been when Gabby had left. She turned and looked at the man, "It is a beautiful sunrise." He was wearing a security guard uniform and looked to be about 40 years old, a little on the pudgy side, and was looking at her with a big silly grin. "I must have slept here all night," Mary stated in a questioning tone. "Well I spotted you just before my shift ended at 11 p.m. and you were sound asleep then. I didn't have the heart to wake you up, you looked so peaceful and you were grinning like a kid on his birthday. I hope you don't mind, but I got a blanket for you, pulled up this chair and took a little nap myself. I didn't want anyone to steal a pretty little thing like you!" "Why thank you very much. That was very kind of you. There aren't too many people who would go out of their way like that to help a sleepy teenager through the night. I don't believe we've met, my name is...." "Mary," he interrupted. "I know who you are. You're the one in charge of all of the kids around here. Everyone knows who you are. My name is Lester." Mary shook his hand. "It's nice to meet you Lester." It was awfully nice of you to spend the night out here protecting me." "Glad to do it, Mary. By the look on your face, you were having one great dream! I didn't have the heart to interrupt. Maybe you can tell me about it sometime. Right now, I've got to get home." He jumped up, headed across the beach, and disappeared around the corner of the hotel. She wanted to lie there and fall back to sleep. Lester was right, it was a great dream and she wanted to finish it. In addition, she didn't want to leave that spot. After all, it was here that her life changed forever. She glowed in the moment wondering what the future had in store for her. However, after a minute Mary decided that she had better go in and get ready for the day's activities.

As she walked through the lobby she passed the security guard office and decided to return the blanket and tell the chief how nicely Lester had treated her. She opened the door and the chief happened to be in the room. "Hi, my name is...." "Mary." He finished her sentence. Mary looked surprised. "You are quite popular around here, Mary. I don't mind telling you that when the manager told me about all of the teenagers that were going to be around here this week, I was prepared for the worst. But, these kids have been the most polite and respectful kids that I have ever seen. We think you have a lot to do with it. Thanks. Now what can I do for you?" "Well, I'm glad that we aren't causing any trouble but I can hardly take the credit. They are just a bunch of great kids. I just wanted to return this blanket. I fell asleep in a lounge chair out by the beach last night and Lester was kind enough to get this blanket for me and even stayed with me all night on his own time. He is a wonderful employee and you should be proud of him." "You spent the night on the beach! Wow! You're lucky. It can get dangerous out there at night. There are some gangs that roam the beach at night looking for trouble." The chief looked puzzled and glanced at the secretary. "Well Mary, I would be proud of him if he worked here. But we don't have a guy named Lester working here." "Are you sure? He's about six foot tall, stocky, and about 40 years old?" "Nope no one here that fits that description." The chief looked at the secretary who shook her head in agreement. "Are you OK Mary?" "But what about the blanket?" Mary protested. Doesn't it belong to the hotel?" The chief took the blanket and said, "No, it's the wrong color." He looked it over and noticed some writing on the corner. "Who is 'G. White?" Mary felt something brush by her hair. It was a whisk of warmth that felt like a dove cooing on her neck. Then it dawned on Mary; G. White was Gabby. Mary smiled. "Do you know G. White, Mary?" "Yes, a friend of mine. She must have seen me and put it on me last night." But what about this Lester? I don't want some weirdo roaming around here impersonating a security officer. Do you want me to look into it?" "That won't be necessary," Mary assured the chief. "I'm sure I was dreaming or something. I'll let you know if I see him around again." "You do that, Mary. I don't want anything to happen to you." The chief handed the blanket back to Mary and she smiled, "Don't worry, chief, nothing's going to happen to me. I have a bunch of guardian angels protecting me." She walked down the hall toward the elevators smiling to herself. 'Thanks Gabby and tell Lester that I said hi.' She laughed out loud as she hit the button for the elevator.

CHAPTER TWENTY

Joe walked through the airport Saturday morning on top of the world. Coach had just dropped him off and had assured him that his scholarship 'was in the bag'. The guys on the team had thrown a small party for him at Colleen and Ginger's Friday night. Joe had really hit it off with them and had a great time at the party. Ginger had asked how he and Mary were getting along. Joe knew that Ginger was a good friend but, he sensed that she would be interested in more than friendship IF Mary was history. Joe assured Ginger that things were fine. She had responded honestly when she had said, "I'm glad for you, Joe, I can't say that I'm not disappointed, but I am glad for you. Please stay in touch. I would love to be friends with you and Mary when you get here." Joe was deeply grateful to Ginger. He felt like for the first time in his life, he had developed a true friendship with a girl.

As Joe came to his gate he glanced around to find a seat. It was then he heard a familiar voice behind him. "Hi Joe! How was your week?" Joe spun around. "Well hello yourself, Cindy. My week was great. How did you get along?" "It was good to spend some time with my uncle. He is a great guy. We went sightseeing, ate at some really cool restaurants, and generally enjoyed some relaxation time. It is good to see someone from back home. I am kind of homesick." "Me too. I miss our little ol' town. Say, where are you sitting?" "27B." Cindy replied, hoping it was next to Joe. "Rats, I'm in 13C. Come on, let's see if they can make some changes." Joe took off toward the agent at the counter dragging Cindy by the hand. After a few seconds of Joe's charm, the lady at the counter hit the computer keyboard a few times and handed them both new boarding passes. They were in 20A and B. "I don't know how you pulled that off," Cindy mused slightly amazed. "You never know unless you ask," Joe laughed. "Plus, it doesn't hurt to have God on your side." Joe had said it like everyone had God on their side. Cindy felt uncomfortable. She had never really been interested in the 'God thing.' Up to this point, it seemed like the God folks were just sort of weird people who were out of touch with reality. But here was a really cool guy who just assumed that God was looking out for him. Cindy made a mental note to find out more about this God stuff. After all, if it were good enough for Joe, maybe there was something to it.

Ever since the encounter with Gabby, Mary had floated through the rest of the week. The conference had been an overwhelming success. Over 1,000 kids had made abstinence commitments. There had been nothing but positive feedback from everyone. Mary had made many new friends with whom she had exchanged phone numbers and e-mail addresses. She and Gary had stayed in touch with Karen during the planning sessions and she was very happy about how things had worked out. Karen had been a real trouper throughout the week. Even though she hadn't felt good, she had been a big help to Mary and Gary in the planning sessions. It was strange to Mary though, this was the week for which she had been preparing for months and she was happy about the outcome, but it had been overshadowed by the visit with Gabby. The week had been surreal. There were times when she briefly wondered if the whole Gabby thing was a dream, but she quickly dismissed that thought as being a temptation from Satan. Still, could it be possible that Mary Reubenowitz from Pleasantville, Montana had been chosen to be the mother of the Savior!? She had pondered these things for the rest of the week.

It was Saturday afternoon, and Mary had said her goodbyes to many of her new friends. She headed down the terminal toward her gate. Her phone rang and it was a number she didn't recognize. "Hello?" "Is this Mary Reubenowitz?" A man's voice was on the other end of the call. "Yes," Mary answered cautiously. A cold shiver went down her spine. "This is Jim; I am an aide to the president. We met in Washington a few months ago. Do you remember me?" "Why yes! I do now! How are you?" Mary tried to sound enthusiastic but there was something about this guy that rubbed her the wrong way. "I'm fine Mary. I'm just calling to congratulate you on the conference this past week. I hear it was a big success." "Thank you very much, Jim. It was a success. But how did you know?" Jim laughed. "Honey, it's the government, we know everything." Mary didn't know how to respond to that so she just returned the laugh. "All jokes aside, Mary. We have been tracking the progress and the president wanted me to tell you that he is very proud of the job you're doing. Keep it up." "Thanks, I will; but you know there are a lot of people who have contributed to this effort. It isn't all me." "Always humble, that's the sign of a good leader. Anyway, any organization is only as good as its leadership. I'll let you go Mary. If you need anything, please give me a call." "Thanks Jim, I will." The phone went dead. Mary closed her phone, somewhat disturbed, but still on top of the world.

Joe and Cindy's plane took off and they waited for it to reach the cruising altitude. The seat belt sign went off and the flight attendant gave the passengers permission to move around the cabin. Cindy and Joe talked about the past week. Cindy was happy that Joe had done well working out with the team. Joe was impressed with all of the places that her uncle had taken her. "He sounds like a real cool guy," Joe observed. "He really is a great guy." Cindy smiled. The conversation fell silent and both kids felt awkward. Joe broke the silence. "Have you heard from your folks?" Cindy looked down. "Mom called a couple of times to check on me and I talked to dad once." Joe hesitated; he didn't know if he should ask if they were splitting up or not. He didn't want to pry but he did want to be a friend. He decided to be cryptic. "Any news about the future?" Cindy looked up at Joe with tears in her eyes. "They didn't say anything. My guess is that if it was good news, they would have told me over the phone. I assume that they are getting a divorce." Joe put his arm around Cindy and she leaned into his chest and cried.

After a couple of minutes, Joe patted her on the back and said, "Look Cindy, you don't know it for a fact, you never know. One thing I do know, God has a plan for your life. Sometimes we don't understand what it is or why things are happening to us. But, know this, if you rest in His will, everything will work out." Cindy looked up at

Joe and wiped her eyes. "I don't know anything about God, Joe. I've never even thought much about it." Joe grinned, "Well how do you think all of this got here?" He waved his hand around the plane. "The earth, the sun, moon, stars, universe; it's all God's creation. Why you've seen the beauty of Montana! That's not coincidence! That's God's handiwork. I could go on forever. YOU are God's creation! You are a unique individual with a special personality. God has never made anyone like you and He'll never make another one! You are it for all eternity!" Cindy brightened up just a little. "Do you really think God has a plan for me?" She acted as if she thought that she wasn't worth it. "Of course He does. Cindy, God loves you. After all, He made you." "Joe, how do I find out more about this?" "Well first of all, you need to pray. Just tell God that you want to be a part of His family. Tell Him that you want Him to be the Lord of your life and that you want to know His will for your life. Then you just need to trust Him. Read the Bible, pray often, and fellowship with other believers." "It sounds too simple, Joe. Will you help me?" "Sure!" Joe almost shouted. "Do you want to pray right now?" Cindy thought for a minute and then looked deep into Joe's eyes. "Yes." Both kids bowed their heads, held hands, and Joe prayed loud enough for both of them to hear; "Dear God, thank You for Your unfailing love. Thank You for blessing us and for watching over us. Cindy wants to have a relationship with You. Please reveal Yourself to her and show her the way to You. She trusts You and commits her life to You. Amen. And, oh, by the way God, if it is OK with You, please make it so that Cindy's parents stay together. Amen." Immediately, Cindy felt better. She had never felt like this before. She was excited, peaceful, and anxious all at the same time. "Thanks, Joe. I hope it sticks." She couldn't believe it was that easy. "There isn't any hoping to it, Cindy. You have to KNOW that it 'will stick'. Now, do you still need help with that algebra?" Cindy grinned and reached for her backpack.

Joe and Cindy worked on her algebra during the entire flight. The only time they took a break was to change planes in Chicago. They decided to try a famous Chicago hotdog during the layover. They laughed that although it was really good, they could get a Montana steak back home for the same price as that airport hotdog! They continued working on the algebra on the second leg of the flight and were just finishing as the plane started its final descent. Cindy closed her book and put her stuff in her backpack at the request of the flight attendant. "Thanks Joe, I think I really understand it now. You're the best." "No problem. You are really smart. You make it easy to explain. I think you were making it more difficult than necessary. Intelligent people do that sometimes. They overthink too much." "No one has ever said that to me before, thanks. You are going to make my head swell." Don't let that happen," Joe warned. "After all, you didn't have anything to do with your intelligence; it is a gift from God. All you have to do is use it." Cindy grinned.

The plane hit the ground and turned off the runway and began to taxi to the terminal. Cindy's grin quickly turned into a concerned look. Joe noticed. "What's wrong?" "I was just thinking about my parents. I wonder which one will pick me up?" Joe grabbed her hand and squeezed, "maybe they will both pick you up?" "No way," Cindy rolled her eyes as if Joe didn't have a clue. "They haven't been in the same room for two months." Joe smiled at her. "Don't forget, you have God on your side now. But whatever happens, trust in Him to lead you in the right direction." "OK Joe, but is it alright if I'm scared?" "I sure hope so, I'm scared half of the time and frightened the rest of the time!" Joe squeezed her hand a little tighter. Cindy smiled, "That's hard to believe."

Joe and Cindy walked down the terminal in silence. Joe was worried about how Cindy would react to whoever was there to greet her and Cindy was worried about being embarrassed in front of Joe. As they reached the security checkpoint, Joe heard his mother, "Joe! Over here!" Joe looked in the direction of the voice and spotted not only his mother and father, but Jake and Ruth as well. Joe's instinct was to rush over to his parents but he didn't want to leave Cindy all by herself. Cindy looked up at Joe with pleading eyes as if to say 'please don't leave me alone' which Joe read loud and clear. Both of the kids scanned the crowd for someone to meet Cindy but neither one spotted anyone. "I guess no one came to pick me up." Cindy sounded dejected. Joe grabbed her hand, "Come on, I want you to meet my parents." "That's OK Joe, you go ahead. I don't want to be a bother." "Cindy, you're no bother. Besides, dad would love to meet another architectural nut." Joe wouldn't let go of Cindy's hand and drug her along.

Joe hugged his parents as well as Jake and Ruth. After a few pats on the back and initial greetings, Joe turned to Cindy who was watching the entire proceedings. "Hey everybody, this is my friend, Cindy; Cindy this is my mom Eve, my dad Abraham, Mary's mom Ruth, and Mary's dad Jake. Cindy is a freshman at the high school and just happened to be going to Boston for spring break. We got to spend time together both going and coming." "Hi Cindy!" Both Ruth and Eve said in unison and, much to Cindy's surprise, they gave her a hug. Abraham and Jake said hello to Cindy and she shook their hands. "Dad, Cindy is interested in civil engineering. She has some amazing sketches and unique ideas. You should see them sometime." Cindy blushed. "I'd love to." Abraham smiled at Cindy. "If you're interested, we are looking for an intern to work at Dream Builders this summer. You could stop by after school and we could go over your ideas. "Cindy beamed. "I'd love to, Mr. Goldstein." "Well maybe Joe can bring you over sometime this week. There's just one thing. Please call me Abraham. That Mr. Goldstein stuff makes me feel old." "Anything you say, Abraham." Cindy was ecstatic. "There she is!" Cindy heard her mother's voice in the crowd. Cindy whirled around and spotted her mother waving while she made her way through the crowd. It was then that her heart stopped. She couldn't believe what she was seeing. Cindy's dad (who was having trouble getting through the crowd behind her mom) was following right behind her mom; and they were holding hands with big, huge, stupid grins on their faces! "Friends of yours?" Joe inquired. "Yes, it's my parents!" Cindy pushed her way through the crowd and fell into the waiting arms of her mom and dad. Joe watched for a few seconds as they exchanged some words and smiles. Cindy leaped into the air and hugged them again. She turned around, caught Joe's eye, and gave him the two 'thumbs up'. Joe just pointed heavenward and smiled at Cindy. She waved and disappeared down the hall holding her mom's hand with her left and her dad's hand with her right. Joe wasn't sure but he thought he saw her skip just a little.

Joe turned back to his family who also had witnessed everything. "What's going on, Joe?" Ruth asked. "Are there tears in your eyes, honey?" Eve questioned. "I'll tell you all later. It's a great story. And if you tell anybody about the tears, I'll deny it," he grinned. "Why you ol' softy," Jake teased. "When does Mary's plane get here?" Joe changed the subject. "It hits the ground in half an hour," Abraham announced with authority. Then he added, "You wouldn't want to wait, would you?" Abraham knew what the answer would be. "Well, I guess if we have to." Joe tried to act cool and smiled at his 'family'. "Yeah right." Eve called his bluff. "I'll bet we couldn't get you out of here with a bulldozer!" "Alright, you got me; I miss her a lot. Where do we pick her up?" "It's at the other end of the terminal," Jake said. "You can tell us about your week as we walk along."

Joe continued telling the parents about his week as they stood near security waiting for Mary's plane. "Sounds like you're in." Jake slapped him on the back. "I'm real proud of you, son." Abraham beamed. "I never had any doubts," Ruth added. Joe looked at his mom who had tears running down her cheeks. "Aw mom." Joe hugged her. Just then the announcement came over the speakers. Mary's flight had landed. Joe flipped open his cell phone to check the time and began anxiously looking down the terminal toward the gate where Mary would emerge. "And, we've lost him." Ruth nodded to Eve who smiled as if to say, 'That's OK with me.'

"There she is!" Joe almost yelled as if he were getting an award for being the first one to spot her. He began jumping and waving, "Hey Mary!" Joe looked quite silly but he didn't realize it and probably wouldn't care if he had. The moms looked at each other and grinned at the spectacle while the dads rolled their eyes at each other. "The boy's got it bad," Jake casually observed. "You think?!" Abraham agreed. Pretty soon Mary came into view of everyone and waved. Joe could see her real well now. She was as pretty as an angel. He had never seen her look so beautiful. When she finally got to them, he picked her up in a big bear hug and squeezed her for a long time. Finally, Mary whispered, "Can't breathe, Joe." "Oh, sorry." He turned red as he put her down and came to his senses. After hugs all around they headed for baggage claim. "Honey, you got some sun," Ruth observed. "Yeah, looking good, sweetie. Better watch out, Joe, the guys will be after her," Jake teased. "That's nothing new," Joe lamented. "I spend half of my time fighting off the guys." Mary blushed. "You all wait here. Jake and I will get the bags." Abraham signaled to Jake.

Joe just stood there looking at Mary. "I've never seen you look so good, Sugar Plum. There is something different. What is it?" Ruth and Eve chimed in. "Maybe it's the tan." Or, "Is your hair just a little lighter?" "I don't know what it is," Joe confessed. "But you

have an aura about you that I've never seen before and I like it."
"Oh, you have just forgotten what I look like." Mary tried to play it
off. "You are probably suffering from whiplash from looking at all
of those college girls." The dads walked up carrying the suitcases.
"Let's go, I'm starved." "Oh daddy, you're ALWAYS starved," Mary
teased.

CHAPTER TWENTY-ONE

The next few days flew by. Joe had been busy with baseball practices until 7:00 every night so he and Mary had driven separately to school. They really hadn't had much time to talk about their experiences last week but when they did, they just had time to cover the highlights. Mary wanted to tell Joe about Gabby, but she wanted to do it when they really had time to think it through. It still seemed like a dream to Mary, but somehow, she knew it was real. It was one of those times that everyone goes through in life in which reality doesn't mesh with common sense. In addition, she had begun to wrestle with the thoughts of being pregnant. How would she tell her parents? What would her friends think? What would become of her status as 'Teens for Abstinence' Chairperson? She was still a virgin, but would they believe her? 'Oh, you are carrying the Savior. Then everything's OK; no worries.' Even she had a difficult time with the argument when it was stated that way. But, she had been sure that the 'Teens for Abstinence' responsibility was her calling from God. Now she's pregnant? Maybe it wouldn't be a normal pregnancy. Maybe it was going to be some kind of divine intervention that wouldn't really show in the normal way. Maybe the Savior would just appear somehow. Her mind whirled constantly, but yet, she was at peace with it. She wasn't sure why. In reality, she should have been going crazy with this situation. She just knew that God was working it out. She was His servant. He would lead her in due time.

Friday finally arrived and Joe was ready for the weekend. Coach had promised to let the boys out of practice by 6 p.m. and he was looking forward to going out with Mary. He called between the end of school and the beginning of practice to make arrangements. "Hey Sugar Plum! I don't have much time before practice but what do you say we go out with Angie and Allen tonight? Maybe we could go bowling or catch a movie?" "Hi Joe, that sounds like fun but I'm feeling a little tired right now for some reason. I'll go home and take a nap. Call me on your way home, maybe I'll feel better by then. We can call Angie and Allen then, OK?" "Anything you say, sweetie. Are you OK? You haven't felt really good for a couple of days now." "I think all of the activities and lack of sleep last week are catching up with me. No big deal. I'll see you in a couple of hours." "OK Sugar Plum, I love you." Before Mary could reply she heard an outburst of guys in the background who were laughing and teasing Joe. One of them shouted, "I love you too, Sugar Plum!" Another said, "Come on lover boy, Coach is waiting!" Still another, "How about a little kissy big fella!" Mary giggled. "Apparently, you have company." Joe was as red as a sunburned cherry. "I didn't know they snuck up behind me. It's going to take a little while to live this one down. I'd better get going. See you later." "Bye Joe." Mary laughed into the phone as she hung up. She could only imagine the teasing that Joe was going to get for that one.

Mary was startled out of sleep by the sound of her phone. It was 6:10 and Joe was calling. "Hi Joe." "Hey Mary, how are you feeling?" Mary tried to shake the sleep out of her brain and attempted to focus. Everything was a blur. Ruth had heard Mary's phone ring and had quietly opened the door to see if she could turn it off before it woke her. Mary waved her mom in and motioned for her to sit down on the bed. "Well, right now, I seem to be having a difficult time waking up. I'm just so tired. Would you be too disappointed if we just stayed here tonight? We could watch a movie or something." Mary gave her mom a 'thumbs up' to see if that was OK. Ruth waved her off and smiled as if to say she was insulted at the question. Joe was family. "Too disappointed?!" Joe was feeling spunky. "Let me see. I've just been invited to spend a quiet evening with the most beautiful girl in the world who also happens to be the sweetest person I've ever met. This is a tough question. Is there anything to eat over there?" Joe teased like he would need a bribe to agree to Mary's suggestion. Ruth grinned because she could hear the entire conversation. Before Mary could respond Ruth spoke loud enough so that Joe could hear, "You tell that weasel that I just took a chocolate cake out of the oven and if he can be here by 7:00, I might let him have a piece. After 7:00, I'll turn Big Jake loose on it." Joe picked up on the tease. "That's the second time today that someone has overheard our conversation. I'm starting to get a little spooked. Anyway, I guess I can put up with you for an evening if there's cake involved. I'll be there by 6:59." Mary laughed and teased right back. "Well I'm sorry to burden you by having to hang out with me. But I assure you, the cake is great!" Someone beeped into Joe's phone. Joe laughed. "Hey Mary, mom is calling so I gotta go. Tell momma Ruth that I like extra icing! See you in a few." "I'll tell her; bye Joe." Joe switched lines, "Hi mom, I'm glad you called. I'm going straight to Mary's if that's OK. We're going to hang out over there tonight." "That's fine honey, but don't you need a shower?" "I took one at school." Eve was always looking out for Joe. He was still her baby. "Good, where are you right now?" "I'm passing by Witz's, why?" "Good, would you please stop by Mamma's Pizza Den? We're getting together with the Reubenowitz's tonight. We are bringing pizza and Ruth is making...." "A chocolate cake." Joe finished the sentence. "How did you know that?" Eve inquired. "Mom, you know I can smell chocolate cake for miles." Joe laughed into the phone. "I'll see you at Mary's in a few minutes. Bye mom." "Bye honey, be careful." Joe grinned to himself. There was that mom thing again. He wondered if she would ever see him as a man.

Joe walked into Mary's house at 6:45 carrying three pizzas. "Hi honey! I'm home!" "'Bout time," Jake growled in fake anger. "I was just about to have cake for supper." Joe set the pizzas down on the kitchen table and kissed his 'moms' and then Mary. "Hi dad; how was work today?" "Good news." Abraham perked up. "We won the bid on the new strip mall out by the highway. We plan to break ground as soon as the weather breaks. It's going to be a big job. I'll need some help in the field office this summer. Are you interested?" "Of course I'm interested!" Joe replied. "In fact, I'm going to need to hire all kinds of part-time help. Do you think any of your friends would like to work on the project this summer?" "I'm sure the answer is yes. I'll ask around and tell them to give you a call." "Can we talk about this over dinner?" Mary interrupted. "I'm hungry."

After everyone sat down, Jake offered the blessing. Mary immediately grabbed three slices of pizza and devoured them quickly. "I
guess you are hungry, honey." Ruth was surprised at Mary's appetite.
"You are eating faster than Jake." "That's my girl. Jake winked at
Mary. Mary just smiled, selected two more pieces and said, "It just
tastes so good." When everyone had finished, Ruth brought the cake
over to the table. "Does anyone have room left for dessert?" Mary
was the first to respond. "I do! Cut me a big piece, please." Joe
looked at her in amazement. "Where are you putting all of that
food?!" "I didn't eat much lunch today." Mary, a little embarrassed,
offered an explanation. "Joe recalled that the lunch at school wasn't
the best. "Oh yeah, it did leave a little to be desired, didn't it." "Hey
Joe, let's eat cake in the living room and start the movie." The kids
headed for the door with cake in hand. Mary looked over her shoulder,
"You old folks can join us if you like." "No thanks honey," Abraham
teased. "I'm afraid that's an awful long walk for this old man."
"Who you calling old?" Jake grunted. The ladies laughed and waved
the kids on.

The kids started the movie and finished about half of their cake.
"I'm stuffed," Joe said and slid his cake onto the coffee table. "Me
too, let's finished it later." Mary put her cake next to Joe's and
settled back against his chest with her head on his shoulder. Joe
smiled. He liked it when they snuggled like this. He enjoyed the
fragrance of her perfume and the softness of her hair on his chin.
He didn't care that Mary had picked out a 'chick flick' to watch. It
just didn't get any better than this.

After about 20 minutes, he noticed that Mary's breathing became deeper and slower. He looked down and noticed that her eyes
were closed and concluded that she had fallen asleep. Ruth walked
through the room and said, "We're going to play cards, how's the
movie?" Joe put his finger up to his lips in a shushing motion. He
pointed to Mary and indicated that she was asleep by signaling like
a baseball umpire with his thumb in the air that she was "out."
Ruth came over to inspect her daughter and confirm Joe's assumption.
"I can't believe she's asleep. She slept for two hours after school. I
wonder if she's coming down with something," Ruth whispered into
the air. Joe shrugged his shoulders. "I think maybe I'll get out of
here. She would rest better if she went to bed." Ruth nodded in
approval. "I hate to wake her up." Joe had second thoughts. "It's

OK Joe, you're right. She would do better in bed." Joe gently stroked her hair in an attempt to wake her. Nothing doing, she was out. He slid his arm out from under her head and slipped out from under her. He gently laid her down on the couch. "Maybe we'll leave her here for awhile," Ruth said as she covered Mary with an afghan. Joe followed Ruth into the kitchen. "I think I'll head for the house. Mary is out like a light. Good night everyone. Thanks for the cake." Joe kissed his moms and slapped Jake and Abraham on the back. "Good night son."

"Hello?" "Hi Joe, it's Cindy. You know, from the airplane; you helped me with my algebra and looked at my sketches...." "I know who you are Cindy. How could I forget you?" There was a brief pause while Cindy blushed and accepted the 'compliment' from Joe. "What's up?" "I was wondering if I could take you up on your offer to meet your dad sometime. I would like to learn more about that CAD program." "Sure Cindy! What are you doing tomorrow? I know dad will be in the office in the morning. Besides, this is great timing. He is looking for some help this summer on a big project. He just asked me tonight if I knew of anyone who might like a job. Are you interested?" "Are you kidding? I'd love to work for your dad this summer. What time tomorrow?" "I'll pick you up at 9:00 and we can head over to the office. Is that good for you?"

Joe held the door open for Cindy as they left Abraham's office the next morning. "See you later, dad." "Thanks Mr. Goldstein, I mean, Abraham. I appreciate your time," Cindy added. "It was nice to see you again, Cindy. I'm looking forward to having you on board this summer." After they got into the car Joe looked at Cindy. "I think that went well," Joe observed casually. "YOU THINK!?" Cindy almost couldn't contain herself. "Your dad is the sweetest man. I can't believe that he gave me a copy of that CAD program AND he gave me a job for the summer! I'm so excited. I can't wait to tell mom and dad!" "I could tell he liked you. I'm glad it worked out for you. So since you brought it up; how are your mom and dad?" "Things are great, Joe. They are working things out and it's going well. I couldn't be happier. I want to thank you for helping me. You know, I have been watching you and Mary for a long time. You know how you look up to the kids who are a couple of years older than you." Joe nodded and smiled. He remembered similar experiences in which he had admired some of the seniors when he was a freshman.

"Well, I know you and Mary don't go for all of that crazy stuff like sex and drugs and I want you to know that I want to be like you guys. You seem to have something that other people don't have and I want it too. I just wish I could meet someone like you. It's hard to resist when you are all alone. Anyway, I want you and Mary to know that you are setting a good example for a lot of other people." Joe blushed. He didn't know what to say. He figured that some of the younger guys might look up to him because of sports, but he had never realized that this situation might exist. He was in unchartered waters here. "Well, I, uh, I'm sure that you'll meet someone who shares your beliefs. Just hang in there. You know Mary is the national chairman for 'Teens for Abstinence' and I know she has some literature about this stuff. I'm sure she would share it with you sometime." "Thanks Joe, but do you think Mary would want to take the time to mess around with me?" "Cindy, you are a child of God. Don't put yourself down. You are especially made with an amazing purpose for your life. Of course Mary would love to spend time with you."

Joe pulled up in front of Cindy's house and she jumped out. "Thanks again Joe, you're the best. See you Monday." Joe flashed his smile and waved as he drove away. He hit speed dial #1 on his cell and it read 'Calling Sugar Plum'. He was excited and flattered about his conversation with Cindy. Six rings later he got her voicemail. He didn't leave a message. He would tell her about Cindy later.

A few minutes later he swung into his driveway and noticed that Mary's car was in the driveway along with Ruth's. He knew Jake was at the store so he decided to see if Mary was home. The door was locked so he rang the bell. Ruth answered, "Hey Joe, come on in." "Is Mary home? I tried her cell but there was no answer." "She has been throwing up this morning." There was sympathy and concern in Ruth's voice. "Wow, is she sick or is it something she ate?" Joe wondered out loud. "I don't know, she finally stopped about a half hour ago. I think she is resting." "Can I see her?" "If you want to take a chance of catching whatever she may have, go right ahead." "I'll take my chances. I won't wake her if she's asleep."

Joe tiptoed up the stairs and down the hall to Mary's room. He slowly opened the door and spotted Mary sitting at her desk, working on the computer. "Hey Joe!" She sounded chipper. "Hey,

Sugar Plum. How ya doin'?" "I'm great, sweetie. What have you been up to this morning?" Joe was confused. Mary looked great; radiant as usual. But Ruth had said that she was sick. "Uh, your mom said that you had been throwing up. Are you OK?" "Oh yeah, I'm fine. I guess I ate too much pizza last night. I threw up a couple of times, but I'm great now. So where have you been?" "That's good," Joe was relieved but still confused. "I took Cindy to meet dad at the office. She's the girl I told you about who is interested in construction. Dad offered her a job this summer." "That's great, Joe. It was nice of you to help her out. It sounds like she's been through a tough time." "You don't know the half of it." Joe sat down on the edge of the bed. "I think you can help her as well." "Oh yeah, how's that?" Joe recounted his conversation with Cindy. "Of course, I'll help her if I can." Mary was excited. "This is a God thing, Joe. Think about it; we had an argument, you sat at her table at lunch, wound up sitting next to her on a plane trip, I am chairman of 'Teens for Abstinence'...it all fits. This is what I'm supposed to do." Joe got up, walked over to Mary and gave her a hug while she sat in her chair. "I'm so proud of you, Mary."

It was then that he looked at her computer. "Is someone having a baby?" Joe asked innocently. Mary's blood ran cold and she got visibly nervous. "Why? What makes you ask that?" She half muttered under her breath. Joe pointed at the computer. The bold-faced title of the website read 'Suggestions for Expectant Mothers'. Mary held her breath for a second. She decided it was time to share her experiences with Gabby. "Well, speaking of a God thing, I have wanted share something with you for awhile now. It is difficult to comprehend and I don't understand it fully. But it is miraculous, scary, and exciting. I don't know where to start, but I need for you to hear me out. It is going to sound crazy...." "Mary," Joe spun her around in her chair, got on his knees in front of her and held her hands. "Tell me what's going on." "OK, but I need you to trust me, please?" "Mary, I love you more than life. I trust you." He looked deep into her eyes. They were shining more than usual. She was glowing. There was also a sense of fear and excitement in her eyes. "Joe, I'm pregnant."

The seconds ticked by as if they were hours. Joe was frozen. Mary's gaze of contentment was returned by Joe with a look of astonishment. He didn't even blink. After a little while, Mary smiled and squeezed Joe's hands. "Breathe Joe; I need you now more than ever." Joe snapped out of his trance and fell back against the bed. He just sat there on the floor looking at Mary. He didn't know what to say. Finally, he stammered, "But, what, how, when, WHO?"

"Joe, a lot of very strange things have been happening to me over the past several months and I didn't know what they meant until last week in Florida. I know this is overwhelming news and it doesn't make sense. But one thing I've learned over the past few months is that things are not always what they seem. You and I have talked about that when we've had our misunderstandings lately. This is another one of those circumstances. You have to trust me." "Trust you with what?!" Joe was beginning to get upset. "If you think you're pregnant, then that must mean you have been having sex. I KNOW FOR A FACT THAT IT ISN'T ME!" "Please Joe, just listen. This is TOO BIG for you not to hear my whole story. Besides, you PROMISED that you would never doubt me again. All I ask is that you listen to my whole story before you jump to conclusions; please?" Joe buried his face in his hands. Mary got up from the chair and went over and sat down on the bed next to where Joe was leaning. She gently stroked the back of his head and ran her fingers through his hair. "Joe, I love you more than anything on this earth. I would never do anything to hurt you. Please sit up here next to me while I tell you what's going on." Joe slowly got up and sat down on the edge of the bed next to Mary. He looked like a lost puppy. Mary hated to see him that way, but she knew that he would understand, somehow. Joe looked deep into Mary's eyes. He expected to see remorse, regret, and agony. Instead he saw peace, happiness, and joy. He was extremely confused. He had known Mary all of his life! This was not like her at all. Pregnant?! The national chairman of 'Teens for Abstinence'... pregnant? He and Mary had talked many times about their convictions regarding this. Both agreed that God had meant sex for married people only. What had changed and why was she so happy about it? Joe started to get angry.

"Before you start, I just want to know one thing—who is the father?" Joe's tone demanded an answer. He expected her to say, 'Gary'. Mary looked at Joe and smiled. It was that kind of comforting smile that someone gives you when they are trying to console you. "God," Mary said with confidence. "OK, yeah, I get it.

We are all God's children. But who is the earthly father?" Joe snapped. He wasn't happy about the smart answer. "Joe, I'm still a virgin. There is no earthly father. I believe that God has called you to be the earthly father." "WHAT?! Mary, have you lost your mind?! I'm pretty sure that you can't be both pregnant AND a virgin. That is of course, if you are pregnant with the Messiah like it says in Isaiah, chapter seven I think." Joe was being sarcastic and a little self-righteous for remembering where the virgin birth was referred to in the Bible. Mary didn't respond. She just continued her peaceful gaze into Joe's eyes. He felt like she was looking into his soul. They both sat there for a minute in dead silence. All of a sudden, Joe's expression changed from confusion to astonishment. "Are you telling me that you think that you are carrying the Messiah?" "I don't think so, Joe. I KNOW so."

"Mary, this is crazy, and most likely blasphemy. Are you taking drugs? Do you feel OK? Do you know where you are? Do you know who I am?" Joe was starting to think that Mary was in some kind of denial or had flipped out. Mary laughed. "Joe, I'm fine. In fact, I'm great! I'm on top of the world! Now, I answered your question. I want to tell you the entire story." "This ought to be good." Joe decided to humor Mary. He wasn't sure how to handle someone who had lost touch with reality. Mary started at the beginning and went into great detail about the entire Gabby encounter. She recounted all of the details beginning with the first time she met her on the way to Salt Lake City all the way through the visit on the beach. Mary even mentioned that Gabby had seen her and Joe playing in the store as kids. When Mary described Gabby's appearance, Joe gasped slightly. He had a vague memory of her somehow. When Mary finished, she leaned over and hugged Joe. "It feels good to get that off my shoulders. I have wanted to tell you that for some time." "That's quite a tall tale, Mary. It sounds crazy." Joe's mind was racing. This just didn't make sense. "Don't you believe me, Joe?" Mary wasn't ready for anyone to doubt her story. "I WANT to Mary, but, it's, it's just so much. It's difficult. I need some time." Joe got up and headed for the door. "Joe, wait." Mary got up and fell into Joe's arms. "I know it's a lot to com-prehend. But, it's all true. Joe, I love you. I need you to help me through all of this. I'm scared." "I believe that you believe it, Mary. I just need some time. You just laid a lot on me. I promise that I'll help you through this, somehow." He hugged her and gave her a kiss on the cheek.

Ruth caught Joe as he headed down the stairs. "How's Mary?" Joe didn't stop but said as he walked out the door. "You may want to check on her now and then. She seems out of sorts." 'That's odd,' Ruth thought to herself as she closed the door behind Joe. 'I wonder what's bothering him.' She started up the stairs to check on her daughter, but Mary was standing at the top of the stairs. "Are you feeling OK, honey?" "I'm much better now, mom. I still feel a little weak so I'm going to lie down for awhile." Mary turned around and headed for her room. For the first time since her encounter with Gabby, she felt scared. Ruth started to ask some questions but thought better of it and remained silent. Her intuition told her that something was wrong, but Mary needed rest. She knew that she would find out later; she always did.

Joe felt sick to his stomach. He felt disoriented and unsure of each step he took. His feet felt like there were ten pounds of extra weight in his shoes. It was 35 degrees outside, but he was sweating profusely. He made his way across the street to his front door. He paused for a minute to collect his thoughts before going in. He eased the door open and tried to go unnoticed to his room. "Is that you, Joe?" His mom's voice almost sang from the kitchen. "Yes mom." Joe mustered up his normal voice. "Would you like some lunch, dear?" "No thanks, mom; I'm not hungry." That was the wrong thing to say and he knew it before he finished saying it. Joe was ALWAYS hungry. As Joe tried to slip up to his room, Eve zipped around the corner. "You wait right there mister. What do you mean, 'not hungry'? What's wrong?" It was a question that Joe knew would require an answer. He knew his mother's tone. He was halfway up the stairs when she caught him. "Why Joe, you are sweating like you are playing ball and you look terrible. What have you been doing?" "Nothing mom; I just got back from taking Cindy down to meet dad and I stopped by to see Mary for a minute. I just don't feel good. I'd like to go to my room." "Ruth said Mary was sick this morning; do you think you might have what she has?" It was then that it hit Joe: 'sick this morning' were his mother's words; 'morning sickness'; she WAS pregnant! "I doubt it, mom." Joe turned and continued up the stairs. "I'm OK. I just need to rest. It's been a long week." "OK dear. I'll check on you later."

Joe walked into his room and felt like it was the first time that he had ever seen it. He stood there looking around at all of the memories. All of them included Mary. There were pictures, plaques, awards, souvenirs...it seemed like his entire life had been shared with Mary! They were fond memories. Even the struggles had turned out well because they had endured them together. He couldn't remember his life without her. He loved her. He planned to marry her, someday. They had talked about it numerous times. He flopped down on the bed and recalled his life with Mary. Playing as kids, riding bikes, baseball and soccer games, studying, family vacations, watching her lead cheers as he played football, dates, parties; they all came rushing back as he scanned the pictures on his walls. But now she was pregnant!

Joe closed his eyes; he couldn't concentrate on the here and now if he kept thinking about the past. Things had changed. He had to adjust and quickly. There were decisions to make; decisions that no teenager should have to face. 'Is Mary having some kind of mental breakdown? Maybe she's not really pregnant. But, why would she say that she was? Gary probably seduced her, now Mary is ashamed and in denial, and conjured up this whole Messiah business. But she seemed so calm. It didn't make sense.' The anguish of the situation was awful. Anger began to well up inside Joe. This wasn't fair! How could Mary do this to him, and herself? Joe started to hyperventilate. He felt like the walls were closing in on him and broke out in a cold sweat.

'I've got to get it together' he thought to himself. Then he remembered what Abraham had told him about difficult situations. "Sort out the things you can't change and set them aside. Then, determine what you can do about the things you can change, analyze the options, make a decision, and attack the task with everything you have. Then let God handle the rest." "Dear God," Joe prayed, "please take control of this situation. I don't know what you want me to do so please guide me. Make Your will clear to me." Amen.

Joe breathed a little easier. 'OK, I can't change the fact that Mary thinks she's pregnant. It really doesn't matter if she is or isn't. The fact that she thinks she is changes things. If she isn't, she has either had sex or she needs psychological help. If she needs help, I need to stand by her while she gets better. If she has been unfaithful but isn't pregnant, I can't leave her to deal with the consequences alone. I may not want to marry her, but I have to help her through the guilt. Who knows, maybe I can get over it, in time; or maybe not. If she is pregnant, she is in big trouble. Again, I can't leave her to face it alone. She needs my help. Our relationship will be probably end, but I do love her. I'll help. She is still my best friend. Now, about her story: the Messiah!? Really? But, this was Mary. She had never lied to him and always claimed that God was number one in her life and I believe it. WHAT IF...?' Joe pondered his options. Maybe she could get away for awhile...go visit a relative or something. He wouldn't break up with her right away. Maybe he could just back out of the relationship quietly over time while helping her through whatever she is facing.

Joe's mind wandered and he drifted off to sleep. It wasn't a deep sleep, it was one of those "naps" in which you are somewhere in between sleep and consciousness. The state of mind in which you are aware of the physical world but remain, as if by choice, in a type of spiritual trance. One in which your mind flows from place to place with no direction whatsoever. It is a wonderfully relaxing place where you are carefree.

Joe found himself sitting on top of a mountain looking out over the landscape. This was not unusual as Joe loved to hike in the mountains by himself, especially when he needed to think. It seemed like he was closer to God when he was in the mountains. It was a beautiful sunny day and the view was magnificent. He was sitting on a rock wearing hiking shorts and a T-shirt. Although there was snow on the ground all around him, he wasn't cold. The warmth of the sun was just perfect. As he sat there admiring God's creation, he noticed a figure walking along the ridge in his direction. He watched as the person got closer. He appeared to be a man about 6' 5" and 60 years old. He was ruggedly handsome and had a hug grin on his bearded face as he approached. He wasn't strolling, like most backpackers do, he seemed to be walking with a purpose.

He walked straight up to Joe and stuck out his hand. "Hi Joe! It's good to see you. I've been waiting for you." Joe stood up and returned the handshake. "Hi, do I know you?" The gentleman laughed heartily. "Well, Joe, I've known you all of your life. I've watched you grow up. I know everything about you. I even know what you're going through right now." Joe peered at the man and toyed with the thought that he was crazy, but there was something about him; he wanted to know more. "Who, exactly, are you?" "I go by many names, Joe, but you can call me Guardian. You see, I'm an angel sent to you by God to help." This was weird. Joe thought about snapping himself out of this dream. But he was curious and felt no fear.

Joe patronized Guardian. "OK, so if you say you know what I'm going through. What is it and how can you help?" "First of all, Joe, you called me. You asked God for help, guidance, and His will with this Mary situation. You remember, don't you, your prayer a few minutes ago?"

'Wow!' Joe thought to himself. Now the dream is crossing over into reality. Or, is reality crossing over to his dream? Maybe he should wake up. He was getting anxious. OK, just a little longer.

"Yes, sir, I do remember my prayer," Joe responded cautiously. "Good." Guardian laughed and slapped him on the back. "You are too young to be losing your memory." Joe smiled but was still terribly confused. "Listen to me, Joe. This is extremely important." Guardian's mood turned serious. "Mary is telling you the truth. God has found favor with her, AND you. She is to be the mother of the Messiah! It is time for Him to come into the world as human flesh. The prophecy in the Bible is to be fulfilled. You are to be His earthly father. You and Mary are to get married and raise the Savior. You will not have sex with her until after the Messiah is born. This is going to be difficult, Joe. You have many challenges ahead of you, but, God will never leave you. Stay steadfast in your faith. You are to love, protect, and care for the Messiah and his virgin mother. Joe, this is your calling; your purpose; your destiny. It may seem impossible at times; Satan will make it rough on you, but know this: God is the final victor. Trust in Him."

Joe started to fall to his knees in reverence but Guardian picked him up to his feet and faced Joe. Joe was amazed at Guardian's strength. "You must never kneel before anyone but God." Guardian's expression assured Joe that he had the fortitude to fulfill his destiny. Joe looked Guardian squarely in the eyes, "I am God's servant. May His will be done. I will do as you say. Thank you, Guardian." Joe extended his hand to Guardian who grabbed it and pulled Joe in for a hug. "Bless you, Joe. Tell Mary that Gabby says, 'hi!'" They released the embrace, Joe smiled at him, slightly astonished that he knew about Gabby, but then again, it should be expected, and Guardian vanished.

Joe snapped out of his trance and leaped out of the bed so quickly that he experienced a 'head rush'. "Wow, that's cool!" Joe said out loud to no one at all. When he got his bearings, he couldn't believe how happy he was. He actually, jumped up and down while skipping around the room. He had always known that there was another dimension out there where one could experience God on a different realm, but he never really thought that he would get to experience it. EVERYTHING IS POSSIBLE WITH GOD! He glanced at the clock; 5:30. He grabbed his cell phone, speed dial, 'Sugar Plum'. "Hello?" Mary had seen the caller ID and didn't know what to expect from Joe. "Mary, have you had supper yet?" "Uh, no. It should be ready soon. Are you coming over to eat?" "No, let's go out to dinner. I've come to a decision and I've got to share it with you. How long will it take you to get ready?" "I don't know Joe, I'm kind of tired. Besides, you're acting kind of weird. I know that what I told you earlier created a lot to think about...." "Please Mary!? I can't tell you how important it is!" "OK Joe." Mary was dejected. She feared that Joe had decided to break up with her." I'll be ready in 30 minutes." "Great!" Joe replied. "Oh, yeah, Mary? Are you still there?" "Yes, Joe, I'm here," the soft voice replied. "Wear something nice, maybe a dress. Let's do it up right tonight. I love you, so much!" Mary sighed with relief. "In that case, I'll need 45 minutes. I love you, too." Mary hung up the phone, 'what's he up to?'

Joe hung up the phone and grabbed the phone book. He was glad to have the extra 15 minutes. He needed to make some plans. "This is Keith's. May I help you?" "This is Joe Goldstein, I need to make reservations for two at 7:00." The voice on the other end of the line laughed. "This must be your lucky day, Mr. Goldstein. I just received a call from a gentleman who cancelled his reservation at 7:00. Tonight has been booked for over a month." "Thanks, I'll see you at 7:00," Joe replied as he hung up the phone. 'Lucky day'; that wasn't luck, that was God; you da man, Guardian.' Joe laughed as he dialed another number. "Hello, is this the florist? How late are you open tonight?...."

Forty minutes later Joe came bounding down the stairs two at a time. "Whoa there, son. What's the hurry?" Abraham's voice came from behind a newspaper that he was reading in his easy chair. "Gotta pick Mary up in five minutes." Joe sounded out of breath. Abraham put down his paper and noticed how Joe was dressed. "Kind of dressed up for burgers, aren't you?" Just then Eve appeared from the kitchen. "Why look at you Joe, all dressed up in a suit. You do look handsome. Where are you off to?" "I'm taking Mary to Keith's for dinner." Joe stood there grinning like a kid in a candy store. "Keith's!?" Abraham exclaimed. "How did you get in there? They are booked up for weeks in advance." Joe broadened his smile. "It's not so hard when you have connections." He pointed upwards. "I've got to go, I don't want to keep the lady waiting, my dad wouldn't like that." Abraham grinned. "I've taught you well, son. Have a good time." Joe kissed his mom as she adjusted his tie. There's that 'mom thing' again. "I love you mom. We might be late. If it's going to be after 12, I'll give you a call. Bye."

Joe jogged across the street up the walk to Mary's front door. He rang the bell and let himself in. "Hello everyone!" He entered in grand gesture, bowed low to Ruth and Jake and flashed his smile. "Well, hello yourself handsome." Ruth got out of the chair and walked over to Joe. "Don't you look nice." She adjusted his tie and turned her cheek to him for the kiss she always received. Joe obliged and said, "You know, you're the second lady that has adjusted my tie in the last five minutes. I'm beginning to wonder if I am doing something wrong." "The only thing you're doing wrong, son, is questioning a female." Jake laughed from behind his magazine. "Ruthy, he looks fine. Leave the boy alone." "Oh be quiet, you big lug." Jake looked at Joe and winked, "See what I mean?" I'll go help Mary finish up. She has been running around here like crazy. You didn't give her much time to get ready." Sorry about that. I'm just excited." Ruth disappeared upstairs. "So what's all the excitement about?" Jake asked. "You guys go out all the time. However, I must admit, you usually aren't dressed like that; special occasion?" "Well, as a matter-of-fact, it is a VERY special occasion." You know, pop, I REALLY love Mary. I have loved her for as long as I can remember; and I uh...." Joe began to stammer a little. "Why, for heaven's sake, boy spit it out. You are as nervous as a long tailed cat in a room full of rocking chairs." Well, you see, sir...." "SIR?!! What in the world is going on, Joe? You never call me sir." "Well, uh, pop...." "That's more like it," Jake snorted and grinned. "Well, a lot of things have changed in the last few months and I was thinking...."

"Hi Joe. What have you been thinking?" "Mary's voice sounded like a songbird behind him. Joe responded, "Oh nothing, really...," as he spun around and looked at her. As he focused on her he forgot what he was saying. She was absolutely stunning. She looked like an angel. He immediately laughed at the irony of the thought. She SHOULD look like an angel. After all, she must have a few hundred around looking after her. He noticed things about her that he had never seen before. Her hair was shining. Her face was radiant. Her eyes were brighter than ever. He couldn't take his eyes off of her. She was wearing a white dress and had a white coat trimmed with white fur. The contrast between her outfit and her coal black hair was amazing. After about 30 seconds of awkward silence, Mary stepped up to him, pulled him down and kissed him on the cheek. "You are looking at me as if you have never seen me before; are you OK?" Joe just smiled. Jake answered for him. "Honey, you look absolutely beautiful. My guess is that you have taken the boy's breath away." Joe continued looking deep into Mary's eyes and nodded. "Where are we going, Joe?" "I thought we would go to Keith's." Joe continued gazing at Mary.""KEITH'S!" Mary squealed. "You two better get going, if you are going to make it to Keith's by 7:00." Ruth patted Joe's shoulder to wake him from the trance. Joe snapped out of it and gently helped Mary on with her coat. "We can finish our conversation later." Jake smacked Joe on the shoulder. "Drive safe and have a good time." Mary kissed her mom and dad goodbye as Joe filled them in on the plans for the evening. "We'll call if we're going to be late." "Thanks, good night." Ruth closed the door behind them. "Mary was sure acting strange, tonight." Ruth observed. "So was Joe! He called me sir; for crying out loud!" Jake laughed a deep belly laugh. "I wonder what they're up to?" Ruth asked into the air. "Who knows, honey. They ARE teenagers."

Keith's was an upscale lodge up in the mountains. It overlooked a lake and was known for great service and fantastic steaks. The ride there took the kids up a winding road through the mountains. It was quite scenic because the sun was shining brightly on the new fallen snow. They didn't talk a lot during the 40 minute ride up the mountain. They merely held hands and occasionally commented on a particular view or some deer that they noticed en route. There was a feeling of peace and calmness in the car. Joe couldn't stop smiling and Mary was just happy to be with Joe. She did notice that he was being extra attentive tonight and she liked it. She decided that it was probably the fact that they had dressed up. She made a mental note to dress up more often.

After taking advantage of valet parking, Joe stuck out his arm for Mary as he escorted her up the stairs into the lodge. Joe checked the coats and the kids followed the maitre d' to their table. Mary held onto Joe's arm as they walked and couldn't help notice that many of the guests were looking at them and smiling. It made her a little self-conscious. "Joe, why are all of these people looking at us? Is there something on my dress?" "Mary, you look great. However, these people are NOT looking at US; they are looking at YOU. They are wondering how a plain ol' guy like me, could be with the most beautiful girl in the world!" "Oh Joe, stop it. You're going to make me blush." "Too late," Joe looked down at Mary who was trying to hide her face behind his shoulder. "No matter, though. Your red face matches your white dress and your black hair. You still look gorgeous!" The tone of his voice rose as he spoke the last sentence so that patrons around them could hear. They had arrived at their table and Joe held the chair for Mary. As she sat down, she smiled, giggled, and whispered sheepishly. "Joe, I'm going to get even with you for that." He kissed her on the cheek and whispered back, "I know, but I still love you." Then he took his seat.

Their table was right next to the window that overlooked the lake. The sun was setting over the mountains and the colors were as vibrant as a rainbow. It looked like a Thomas Kinkade painting. On the opposite side of the window there was a fireplace in the round that had a roaring fire going. It was about 15 feet away from Mary and Joe. There were couches all around the fireplace where patrons were seated, talking, and enjoying the fire. It was a perfect setting. "Joe! Look! There's an American Eagle flying over the lake!" Joe responded, "How could a person see something like this and NOT believe in God. We are so blessed to be able to enjoy something like this that He has made." The kids just sat there in silence and watched God's wonderful creations.

After a couple of minutes, the coat check girl walked up to them carrying a vase full of red roses. "Ms. Reubenowitz?" "Yes?" Mary said cautiously. "These are for you." She set them down on the table and disappeared. Mary's eyebrows raised and Joe flashed his smile. Again embarrassed as the flowers had caught the attention of the guests in their area, Mary reached for the card. 'The splendor of these flowers pale in comparison to your gentleness and beauty. I love you, Joe." A tear ran down Mary's cheek as she reached across the table for Joe's hand. He cradled her dainty hand in his as if he were holding a precious jewel. "Thank you Joe, I love you too." After a few seconds, they remembered where they were and looked around. Several couples seated around them were looking at them and smiling. The ladies were saying, "Aw" and a few of the men were giving Joe a 'thumbs up'. Now both Mary and Joe were blushing.

The waitress arrived to take their order. Joe ordered an appetizer for them to share and both kids asked for sweet tea. "What are you going to have, Sugar Plum?" Joe asked through a huge grin. Mary returned the smile. "I don't know, I might just have a salad. I'm sure that the appetizer will fill me up." "Don't be silly," Joe replied. Then he lowered his voice to a whisper, "After all, you have to keep your strength up since you are eating for two." He winked at her and reached for her hand again. Mary looked down and then into Joe's eyes. She looked radiant. Her smile oozed with peace and satisfaction. Joe broke the silence. "Let's have steak!" "OK sweetie, as long as I can have a doggy bag."

The appetizer came, Mary ordered a fillet and Joe ordered a T-bone. After Joe blessed the food they snacked on a variety of munchies on the plate and watched the sun set over the mountains. In a few minutes, just as the sun was just about gone, the main course arrived. The colors of the sun reflected off of the snow with a brilliance that only God could have created. Both of the kids sat there and watched as the gleaming streams of orange, yellow and red melted into evening. It was breathtaking.

"Is there something wrong with the food?" The waitress had come by and had noticed that Mary and Joe weren't eating. Joe came back to reality first. "Aw, no, it's fine. We were just caught up in the sunset. It sure is amazing." "Yeah!" Mary chimed in. "It must be great to work here and enjoy this view all the time!" "I guess so. I really don't notice it like I used to." The apathetic tone in her voice shocked Mary. She didn't know what to say. After a moment, the waitress said, "Well, I'll check on you two in a little while. Enjoy your dinner." After she walked away, Mary looked at Joe, "How could anyone not be amazed at getting to see something like this all of the time?" "I guess we all get used to things and tend to take God's miracles for granted. I suppose God is up there saying to himself, 'what do I have to do to get their attention?!'" Mary laughed and started to cut her steak. "I suppose you're right, Joe. Let's decide to embrace life and enjoy all of God's miracles; big and small." Joe shoved a piece of steak in his mouth and said, "You've got a deal, Sugar Plum; as long as we do it together for a very, very, long time." Mary smiled and her eyes sparkled as she took her first bite.

After a couple minutes of silent eating Mary spoke first, "Joe, I have a question for you. When you mentioned that I was 'eating for two' a little while ago you seemed extremely comfortable with that fact. You are a lot different than you were when I first told you. I'd really like to know what's going on inside your head. Don't get me wrong. I love being treated this way, but, I want to know what you're thinking." Joe finished chewing what was left in his mouth and washed it down with a long drink of tea. He lit up as he gazed at Mary. He smiled so big that Mary thought he was going to crack his face. He just stared at her for the longest time, admiring her inner and outer beauty. Finally, he leaned in and spoke ever so softly. "Mary, I had a vision after I left your house this morning. I was visited by an angel!" Mary gasped and leaned closer. She was so excited that she could hardly breathe. "What did he say?" Mary barely got the words out. "He told me that what you said is true! He told me that you are going to be the mother of the Messiah! I am going to be his earthly father! Mary, I believe you. I believe IN you; and I believe in God. I know that we are destined to fulfill this mission. I don't know why He selected us, but he did. Mary, I'm so proud of you. And I'm humbled that He wants me to be a small part of this. Talk about miracles! Wow! We are living the greatest miracle of all! I love you, I love God, I love life, I love everything! I'm so excited about all of this that I am about to burst!"

Mary was giggling with excitement as she watched Joe express his giddiness. Relief washed over her because Joe believed her. She had been afraid that she was going to go through it alone. But now, watching Joe, acting like someone had just given him a million dollars, she felt safe, happy, and no longer alone. He had always been her rock, and now he always would be. Joe was still yammering like a magpie. "We have so much to do. We have to tell our parents, get you under a doctor's care, figure out where we are going to live next year, after all, we can't have the Messiah living in a shack!…Oh by the way, Guardian said to tell you that Gabby said hi." "Joe, slow down, you are going to hyperventilate. We need to think very seriously about each and every move we make. For example, think about telling our parents. Do you have any idea how they are going to react? After all, do you think they are going to believe that I am carrying the Messiah?! Look how you reacted when I told you. How do you think daddy is going to look at you when I tell him that I'm pregnant?" Joe got quiet and his smile turned into a look of concern. Mary could see the wheels turning in his brain. "Good point, Sugar Plum. Maybe we had better keep our mouth shut for awhile until we think this through." "I agree, Joe. This is huge. We have to handle it right and not rush into things. After all, this IS the Messiah!" She winked at her boyfriend.

"Did you two save room for dessert?" The waitress had slipped up on them. Joe looked at his empty plate and then at Mary. "I'm ready, how about you Sugar Plum?" "Well, I'd like to take the rest of my steak home so he," Mary pointed to Joe, "can eat it later." "I understand sweetie," the waitress nodded knowingly. "My husband eats all of my leftovers too." Joe laughed "That's why we take you girls to dinner. We know that we are going to get to enjoy it twice!" He looked in Mary's direction. "What sounds good to you, Mary?" "I'll have a scoop of vanilla ice cream." "Me too," Joe joined in. "Only, would you mind slipping a piece of chocolate cake under mine?" Mary rolled her eyes and the waitress quipped, "Funny, you sound just like my husband, but you don't look like him. I'll be right back."

"Joe, I need to go freshen up." Mary started to get up and Joe was out of his seat like a shot to help her with her chair. As he watched her walk down the aisle, he caught the eye of the coat check girl. He nodded in her direction and she gave him the 'thumbs up'. Mary returned shortly and as Joe helped her with her chair the desserts arrived.

They had barely begun to take their second bite when the coat check girl arrived with another dozen roses; this time they were white. Mary's look of shock was almost matched by those of the guests who had witnessed the event. "Joe! You must be out of your mind! They are beautiful! You are so sweet. I feel like a princess." Joe got out of his seat and came over to Mary. He got down on one knee and held both of her hands. He looked deep into her eyes and said, "Sugar Plum, you ARE a princess. You are MY princess. I know we have to consider all of the options and not rush into any decisions. And I want you to know that I have thought this through and there is one thing that I know in my heart is the right decision. I want EVERYONE to know that you are my princess." Mary was so embarrassed by Joe's actions and words. He wasn't whispering and all of the people around them had stopped whatever they were doing and were listening to what Joe had said. "Well, Joe, I think everyone within earshot knows how we feel, so why don't you get up and finish you cake before I die of embarrassment." "I will in just a minute. There's just one more thing. These folks don't know EXACTLY how I feel; and I'm not sure that you do either." Mary looked at him quizzically. Joe reached into his pocket and produced an old ring box. He opened it and showed Mary an antique ring that she recognized immediately. She gasped and held her hands to her face. "Mary, this is the engagement ring that my grandfather gave my grandmother. She gave it to me before she died two years ago and told me that she wanted you to have it. She said that she knew that we were destined to be married and that something wonderful was in store for us. I guess she was right. The red roses are symbolic of my heart and my undying love for you and the white roses represent your purity and honesty. Mary, I've loved you for as long as I can remember. I can't imagine life without you. Will you marry me?" He took the ring out of the box and held it up waiting for her to extend her hand so that he could slip it on.

It only took a couple of seconds for it to sink in. Mary giggled and said, "Joe, I have waited all of my life to hear those words from you. Of course I'll marry you!" She held out her left hand and Joe slipped the ring on her finger. It fit perfectly. He stood up and Mary jumped into his arms. Half of the restaurant erupted in cheers and applause. Even the kitchen staff had been alerted by the coat check girl and they had slipped out into the dining room to watch the event. Joe picked Mary up off of the ground and gave her a brief kiss on the lips. The cheering continued as he put her down and Joe raised his arm over his head to symbolize victory. Mary was as red as the roses and clung onto Joe's arm as he received 'high fives' and congratulations from several of the guys.

Joe noticed that no one was sitting on a couch near their table next to the fire. "Why don't we have coffee by the fire?" Good idea, sweetie." Joe helped her out of the chair and they sat down on the couch. The warmth of the fire soon engulfed them and Mary slipped comfortably under Joe's arm. The waitress walked by and said, "Can I get you two, anything?" "Two decafs, please; one with cream and sugar and one black." Joe and Mary smiled at her but didn't move. They were extremely comfortable and weren't moving unless they had to. "OK kids, I need to put on a fresh pot, it may take a little while." "No problem," Joe waved his hand. "Take your time; if it's OK we like to stay awhile." "You kids stay as long as you want. You two have been great for business tonight. Everyone is celebrating because of you." Mary smiled and said, "Thanks," while she snuggled closer under Joe's arm. Joe put his feet up on the hearth and settled back into the couch and said, "This must be what heaven is like." "I never expected an evening like this." Mary cooed. "This is perfect." In a few minutes, the waitress returned with the coffee. Before she could say anything, an older gentlemen who was sitting with his wife on the next couch held his finger to his lips in a 'shushing' sign and pointed to Mary and Joe. They were sound asleep. Mary curled up with her head on Joe's chest and Joe had his arm around her tiny shoulders. They were so cute. Several people took pictures of them with their phones. The waitress placed the coffee on the hearth and slipped away.

Someone was gently tapping Joe on the shoulder. "Sir? Sir? We are closing in a few minutes." Joe woke up to see the waitress's smile. "What do you mean closing? We've only been sitting here a few minutes." He pulled out his cell phone; 11:30. "Oh my goodness!" He looked at Mary who was still asleep. He stroked her face gently. "Honey? Sugar Plum? Are you in there?" Mary opened her eyes and looked at Joe dreamily. "Please tell me that it wasn't all a dream. Please tell me that you proposed to me tonight." Joe couldn't help himself. "What in the world are you talking about; proposed, me, are you kidding?" Mary sat up with a start. "But it seemed so real, you sat right over there and…." She pointed to the table where they sat with her left hand. It was then that she noticed the ring on her finger. "Oh, Joe! That's just plain ornery. If I didn't love you so much I'd just give it back." She reached up and kissed him on the cheek and then looked around. She noticed a change of scenery in the restaurant. The people who had been there when she sat down on the couch had been replaced with new people. She was slightly confused. "What time is it, Joe?" "11:30." "You mean to tell me that we have been sleeping here for over two hours?!" "That's right honey." The voice of the waitress was right behind them. "You two looked so comfortable that I couldn't bear to wake you up. In fact the manager took your picture. I wouldn't be surprised if it didn't show up on the wall in the hallway." Mary blushed. "We need to get out of here, Joe." "You're right, Sugar Plum. May I have the check please?" "It's already been paid by your friends, sweetie. Boy is he a good tipper. Tell him thanks a lot." "Friends? What friends? I didn't see anyone here that I know, did you Mary?" "No. I didn't. What did they look like?" Mary said with a confused look on her face. "The man was about 60 years old; he had kind of a handsome rugged look. The lady was about 40, maybe 45, very pretty, and had that sophisticated look about her. Oh yeah. I almost forgot. They left a note." She handed Joe a folded napkin. He opened it and Mary leaned in so that she could read it as well. Both kids read it silently, 'We sure enjoyed watching you kids get engaged. The nap was cute too. Dinner is on the Big Guy tonight. We'll being seeing you soon. Love, Guardian and Gabby.'

Both Joe and Mary read the letter twice in order to make sure that they got it right. They didn't know how to react. Should they be shocked or appear nonchalant? After all, it's not like they hadn't been exposed to that dimension before, especially Mary. She had seen Gabby on several different occasions. They finally glanced at each other and their confused looks faded into smiles. They didn't need to speak. They could read each other's minds. "Oh yeah, Guardian and Gabby. You remember them don't you sweetie?" Mary found words first. "Sure do." Joe picked up on the game quickly. "That sure was nice of them. They are always pulling surprises like this." The waitress spoke up. "It sure WAS a nice surprise. I wish I had friends like that. You two must have an angel watching out for you or something." Mary looked at Joe and giggled. Joe looked back and busted out laughing. "Thanks for a great evening. We'd better get going." "You kids come back anytime, and bring your friends!" Both Mary and Joe laughed all the way to the car.

As they drove down the mountain, Joe looked at Mary and said, "How's it feel to have God buy dinner for you?" Mary thought for a minute. "Well, in a way, He buys ALL of our dinners. He just bought this one in a little different way. I think this may be one of those situations that makes us remember that God performs miracles every day. Remember, we aren't going to take anything for granted?" Joe thought for a minute. "You're right, Mary. God is pretty cool. Not to change the subject but we need to call our parents so they won't worry. I'll call yours and you call mine, OK?" "Sounds good, sweetie. Should I tell them that I have a fiancé?" Mary snickered. "Maybe we should wait for awhile and plan this out. We don't want to give them a heart attack on Saturday night." Joe played along with the sarcasm. Both of them laughed and hit speed dial on their phones.

As Joe pulled into the driveway, both kids noticed that the lights were out in both houses. "Looks like they went to bed already," Joe observed. "Well it IS 12:45," Mary mused. Joe walked her to the door. "I can't believe we are engaged." Mary looked up at Joe. "I am the luckiest guy in the world," Joe replied. "Don't you mean bless-ed?" Mary corrected him. "That's why I love you so much. I plan to spend the rest of my life trying to make you happy." Joe kissed her good night, watched her go in the door and yelled, "YES!" at the top of his lungs as he ran across the street to his house. Mary heard him and giggled as she walked up the stairs.

CHAPTER TWENTY-TWO

Ruth woke up Sunday morning to the sound of Mary throwing up. She looked at the clock; 6:15. Now she knew Mary was sick; this was the second day in a row. She quietly got out of bed so as not to wake Jacob and headed down the hall toward the bathroom. She knocked gently on the door, "Are you OK, honey?" "Yes, mom, I'm fine." Mary's voice was weak and unconvincing. Ruth tried the door and found it to be unlocked. "Can I come in?" Mary opened the door and smiled at her mom. "Good morning, mom. Sorry I woke you up. Did you sleep well?" Mary attempted to sound chipper. Ruth wasn't buying it. "I slept well, thank you. But I'm more interested in you right now. Are you sick? This is the second day in a row that you have been throwing up." "Uh, I feel fine right now, mom; really. I just wake up feeling a little queezy. Maybe it was something I ate at Keith's last night. We had a big dinner." "OK, but what about yesterday morning? You were sick then too." "I don't know, mom. I just know that I feel fine now." Ruth sensed aggravation from Mary and decided to drop the subject. She felt her head and decided that she didn't have a fever. Ruth looked closely at Mary's face; 'her color seems fine' she thought to herself. "Are you hungry, dear?" Ruth asked thinking that maybe Mary would like a little yogurt or toast, something. "I'm starved! Let's make pancakes!" Ruth looked at Mary as if she had seen a ghost. "What?" Mary noticed the shocked look on Ruth's face. "Can't a teenage girl have a big breakfast once in awhile?" Ruth smiled and hugged her daughter. "Of course, sweetie." As they

217

hugged, Ruth had a feeling that she had never experienced before. It was a warm, calm, comforting feeling. The type of feeling that one gets during a pleasant dream. It is a sense of total bliss in which you never want to wake or leave. After the embrace, Ruth held Mary by her shoulders and looked her over. Something was different. She couldn't tell what; but something had changed. Her motherly instinct told her so. Mary broke the silence, "Could we have some kosher sausage, too?" Ruth laughed. "Sure honey, but I didn't think you liked sausage." "I usually don't," Mary conceded. "I'm just kind of craving it for some reason." Mary almost choked on her words: 'craving'? She had always heard that pregnant women had unusual cravings, but she hadn't thought about it affecting her. She didn't want to start her mom thinking about her being pregnant, not yet. She and Joe had to figure that out later. She decided to divert the thinking. "You always said that people's taste in food changes as they get older. Maybe mine is beginning to change. Who knows? I might begin to like Brussels sprouts someday." Ruth laughed out loud. "If that happens, let me know. I still don't like Brussels sprouts." They headed down the stairs toward the kitchen. 'That was close,' Mary thought to herself. She didn't like misleading her mother, but the time wasn't right. She was going to come clean; just not now. Joe had to be there as well. She resolved to be more careful.

Later that afternoon, Joe came over for a study date with Mary. "She's up in her room." Ruth nodded in the direction of the stairs as she let Joe in the door. "Thanks!" Joe kissed Ruth on the cheek and took the stairs two at a time. They had a chemistry test tomorrow and they both wanted to quiz each other to prepare. This was not unusual for them. They had developed a system over the years and had come to know each others' strengths and weaknesses so one could help the other in specific areas. They had been quite successful with their methods and both sets of parents encouraged it. Besides it was another excuse for them to be together. Joe knocked on the door. "Hey Sugar Plum, it's your future hubby." "Shhh!" Mary shushed. "What if they hear you? Get in here you big goofball." Joe walked over to Mary who was sitting on the edge of the bed. He noticed that she was wearing the engagement ring as he bent down to give her a quick peck on the lips. "That ring looks good on you." He smiled. "Thanks," Mary beamed. "I love it. I hate that I have to take it off so my parents don't see it." "Yeah, I know.

It bothers me too. We'll get to tell them soon. We just need to figure things out first. How are you feeling?" "Well, I threw up again this morning, but I'm OK now; just a little tired." "Feel like reviewing for the test?" "Sure, we can't let a little thing like being pregnant with the Savior stop the educational process." Mary smiled at her own sarcasm. Joe laughed and opened his book. He knew what she was saying. Sometimes God allows or causes something to happen that makes us re-evaluate our priorities. If this wasn't one of those situations, Joe had no idea what one could be. Notwithstanding, Mary and Joe also realized that their responsibilities as children of God did not mean they were to ignore the less important things such as chemistry. It merely meant that they were to keep things in perspective.

After about an hour of intense questions and answers, Joe closed his book, "I need a break." He leaned back in Mary's desk chair and put his feet up on her desk. Mary had been sitting against the headboard of her bed. "Me too." She shoved her book and folder away and curled up in the fetal position.

A few minutes passed before either of them spoke. Joe looked at Mary who appeared to be sleeping. He got up from the chair and started for the door. "Where are you going?" Mary sensed Joe's movement. "I didn't mean to wake you. I thought you were asleep." "I was just resting my eyes. You're not going, are you?" Mary almost pleaded. "Nooo." Joe sensed Mary's desire for him to stay. "Good." Mary laid her head back down on the pillow and closed her eyes. "Sit here on the edge of the bed, Joe." She patted the area next to her. "I want to make sure that you don't slip out on me. After all, you promised to marry me. No fair changing your mind." Joe picked up on the tease and decided to give Mary some in return. "Well, Mary, funny you should bring it up because I've been thinking that maybe I rushed into this decision too quickly." He gazed up at the ceiling to pretend contemplation of the idea. WHAM! Mary smacked Joe with a pillow that almost knocked him off the bed. He giggled and covered his head because he knew another blow was coming. He slid down onto the floor as Mary, who was now on her knees at the edge of the bed, pummeled him with several more blows. Both kids were laughing uncontrollably. Mary finally relented, mostly because she was tired, and fell back on the bed. Joe remained sitting on the floor leaning back against the bed.

After they calmed down and had collected themselves, Mary spoke at the ceiling in her serious tone. "Joe, have you thought about what we're supposed to do? I'm getting a little nervous." Joe stared out the window. "That's ALL I've been thinking about, Mary. Do you have any suggestions?" "Well, we need to tell our folks, first; and soon. I think my mom is beginning to worry about me throwing up all the time. Besides, they just need to know." "Do you think they'll believe us, Mary?" Joe had hope in his voice. "Of course they'll believe us. They love us. However, I'm not sure how the community will accept the news." Mary hadn't thought of her image in the community until now. Joe hadn't thought about that aspect of it either. "Wow, there are A LOT of things that are going to change aren't there?" Joe's mind was running 100 mph. He had been thinking about how to care for the baby AFTER he was born; not the ramifications of being pregnant. "Maybe we should get you to see Dr. Reynolds. You know, prenatal vitamins, sonograms, all that stuff we learned about in health class?" "I guess we should, Mary agreed, but before or after we tell our parents?" "I don't know." Joe was feeling overwhelmed. "When do you think the baby is due? Have you figured it up?" "The best I can guess is sometime in the middle of December." Mary sensed Joe's concern and began to panic. "Joe, I'm scared." Tears began to run down her cheeks. Joe got up and sat on the bed next to Mary. He put his arm around her and she leaned into his chest. "Don't worry, it will be OK. I'll take care of us. I promise. We can do this. After all, we've got God on our side." "I know," Mary sighed with some relief. "This just isn't how I envisioned my life turning out. I don't regret it, mind you. I'm just shaken up a bit. I just have to know that you're OK. I need you, Joe. If you fall apart, we're sunk." "I'm great, Mary!" Joe's tone changed. "I think we should pray about it. Every time we get into a tough spot, God has always gotten us through it." Good idea!" Mary perked up.

Mary bowed her head and Joe prayed. "Our Father in heaven; we thank you for blessing us with this task. Thank you for fulfilling your promise to send the Savior to us. We are your servants and are humbled that you have chosen us for this mission. Please give us guidance, strength, and perseverance so that we may implement Your plan for Your honor and glory. Amen."

It was like a light went off in Joe's head. "I've got an idea." Excitement was in his voice as he grabbed Mary's hands. "The first thing we have to do is make sure that we do our best to take care of the Savior. That means getting to Doc Reynolds ASAP. I'll bet if you continue with morning sickness, your mom will make you go see him. You can tell him that you're pregnant and get started on all of the prenatal stuff." "What if he tells my parents?! They MUST hear it from us FIRST!" "Now calm down, Mary. He won't tell; he can't. It's the law. I know he's an old friend of the family. But he won't tell. I just know it. We have to trust God." "OK, Joe, what's next?" "Next, we have to plan on how and when we will tell our parents. We should wait until you go to the Dr. so that we have all of the information from him; maybe in a couple of weeks. Next, we need to think about the 'Teens for Abstinence' stuff. Do you have any more rallies planned?" "Not until July; we are scheduled to have one in Washington DC on the 4th." "Good, that will give us plenty of time. We will need to tell the head folks about the situation. There again, we just tell the truth. It's up to them if they believe it or not. We will deal with their reaction later." Mary started to panic again. "Joe, I love being involved in 'Teens for Abstinence'. What if they don't believe me? Do you think they will make me quit? I was sure that God had called me into that position for a reason." "I don't know how they will react, Mary. We'll take this one step at a time. I just know that we have a direction from God and we need to do it; no matter what." "You're right, Joe. As long as we continue to do God's will, we can handle whatever comes our way." "That's my girl." Joe smiled and squeezed her hand. "Then, as soon as we tell the folks at 'Teens for Abstinence', it will get out into the community. You know there will be talk, we'll just have to deal with it. I'm sure we'll have support from our syna-gogue, but the kids at school will be mean; except for Allen and Angie. They will be supportive."

Mary's face turned sour. Thinking about the kids at school and how they would be mean to her and Joe made her feel sick. Melissa would be in the height of her glory. Mary knew that Melissa had been jealous of her and that she would make a huge deal out of this. Her thoughts turned to Angie. Would she really believe her? It was a stretch, for anyone. But Angie had been a close friend for years. They had cheered together ever since they had been in 5th grade. Then it hit her. "What about cheerleading next year?! Joe, I can't cheer my senior year! There's no way I can do flips, hand springs, and pyramids when I'm...." she hesitated to count the months: "Six months pregnant!" She burst into tears. Joe held her tightly in his arms. "I'm sorry, Mary. I know there's a lot coming at you. I know that this was not in the plan. But it was in God's plan and that's what matters. It will be OK. At least we will have our parents on our side; not to mention the church. AND, most importantly," Joe stood up and bowed low in front of Mary. "You have ME!" Joe rose up and looked at Mary with his eyes crossed, hair messed up, and his tongue sticking out of the side of his mouth. He looked absolutely goofy. Mary jumped up and hugged Joe tightly. "Aw, Joe; you always know how to make me feel better. I love you." "I love you, too, Sugar Plum. Now how about a little kissy for your fiancée?" He stuck his cheek out to her still holding his tongue out of the corner of his mouth. "How could I refuse such a handsome face?" Just as she got close to his cheek, he turned and licked her on the nose! She backed away quickly. "Gross!" She slapped him on the shoulder. Joe yelped in fake pain and ran down the stairs with Mary in hot pursuit.

Jake looked up from the basketball game that he was watching on TV and laughed as he observed the kids running down the stairs. "Is she picking on you, Joe?" Jake mustered up his best fake gruff voice. Joe ran behind Jake's chair as if to hide from Mary. "Yeah, pop, she's been beating on me. I think she's crazy!" Mary approached the chair like a lion on the hunt. "Well, it wouldn't surprise me," Jake snorted. "After all, she IS just like her mother." "I heard that!" Ruth's emerged from the den. "See what I mean, son. I'd love to help you but I've got my hands full with that one. I'm afraid that you're on your own." Jake pointed at Ruth. "And don't you forget it." Ruth shook her finger at Jake. Mary put her hands on her hips and glared at Joe in fake anger; "Don't you forget it either, mister." It was then Joe noticed that Mary had forgotten to take the ring off. He nodded, ever so slightly in the direction of her left hand which was still on her hip. Mary read Joe's glance and began to panic. She quickly collected herself and, with her hand still on her hip, discreetly spun the diamond around so that it would face her palm. Both kids sighed with relief.

"Guess what?!!" There was excitement in Ruth's voice. "I just hung up the phone with Liz." "My sister, Liz?" Jake inquired. "Yes, your sister." "What's new with her?" "Well, she's three months pregnant!" "WHAT?!" Jake jumped out of his chair. Ruth hadn't seen him move that quick since he had caught Mary falling off of a slide when she was two years old. "Are you teasing me?" Jake walked over to Ruth who had her arms open waiting for a hug. Jake picked her up and swung her around like a rag doll. "Nope," Ruth squealed with glee as Jake put her down. "She's due in September. It's a miracle, Jake. I'm so happy for her and Zac. They have wanted a baby for so long. Isn't that great kids?" Ruth and Jake turned toward Mary and Joe. Both of them looked like statues: frozen in place, mouths open, they didn't even blink. The mere mention of the word 'pregnant' had definitely caught them off-guard.

Mary came to her senses. "That it so great, mom! Isn't it, Joe?" She squeezed Joe's arm. "Yeah," Joe came out of his stupor. "Is Aunt Liz doing OK?" Ruth responded to the question by going into great detail about the pregnancy, doctor visits, how they came to find out; the whole ordeal. Joe's mind wandered to the times he had been with Liz and Zac. They were wonderful people; kind, gentle, honest, hard-working people. Joe didn't get to see them often because they lived on a farm up near the Canadian border. Joe guessed they had been married for at least 30 years because they were in their mid-fifties. They had always wanted children and Joe thought it was a shame that they hadn't been able to, because he had observed them interact with kids over the years and could tell they loved children. He was glad that they were finally going to get their wish. "...and Liz told Zac right in the middle of the supermarket that she was pregnant!" Ruth's story came to a close. "You guys are going to be Aunt Ruth and Uncle Jake!" Mary was giddy. "And, you, Missy," Jake put his big arm around Mary, "are finally going to have a cousin! I'm going to call them." Jake headed for the den. Put them on speaker daddy." Mary, Joe and Ruth followed him. "Hello?" "Liz, it's Jake, congratulations!" Hi Aunt Liz, it's Mary, we are so happy for you guys." "Mary? Mary, who?" Liz loved teasing Mary. "Very funny; it's your favorite niece." "You mean my only niece," Liz replied quickly. Mary thought she heard the line click on the other end indicating it was on speaker phone as well. She could hear her Aunt Liz tell Zac, "I am not going to say that." "Say what Aunt Liz?" He is just being his old ornery self." "Put the phone on speaker, Aunt Liz, I want to talk to Uncle Zac." "Well you are on speaker, but you can't talk to Zac. It seems like he has lost his voice. He hasn't been able to speak since we found out that I was pregnant. How are you, Mary?" "I'm fine Aunt Liz, but the bigger question is 'How are you?'" "Why I'm as happy as a fox in a hen house when the old dog is chained up!" Jake howled with laughter. He loved his sister's down home country sayings. She had graduated Magna Cum Laude from Yale with a degree in Journalism and had an excellent command of the English language. However, she never was one to impose her intelligence on anyone and tried to remain humble in everything she did. Whenever she was confronted about it, she would say, "I don't want to ever be accused of 'puttin' on the dog." Mary could never really figure out that saying, but she always assumed that it had something to do with showing off.

Joe and Mary traded glances as Jake and Ruth spoke with Liz and Zac. There was relief in Mary's eyes at times and Joe knew that she was glad that the good news might overshadow her morning sickness symptoms in her mother's mind. However, at other times, Joe could tell that Mary flinched each time the word 'pregnant' or 'baby' came up in the conversation. Mary didn't want her mother thinking along those lines until the kids had a chance to tell them. After a few minutes, everyone said their goodbyes and Jake hung up the phone. Both kids sighed as if they had just finished the S.A.T. test.

"Are you going to have dinner with us, Joe?" Ruth asked. "We are going run out for some fast food but you know you can come along with us." "No thanks, mom." He always called her mom. "I think I heard my mom say that we are having spaghetti." Now spaghetti was one of Eve's specialties and everyone knew it. "Spaghetti!" Jake got excited. "What time?" "Around 6:00, I guess." Joe grinned. "Now Jake," Ruth reasoned. "We haven't been invited." "INVITED?" Jake repeated. "Since when do we invite or wait to be invited by the Goldsteins? We are practically family. After all, these two will most likely get married in a few years and we'll be grandparents along with Abe and Eve a couple years after that! Right Joe?" Jake winked at Joe who had turned white. Mary jumped in for the save. "It will happen before you know it daddy." Mary clutched Joe's arm. "Mom, spaghetti does sound good." Joe came to his senses. "Are you kidding? Dad would slap me in the back of the head if I didn't make sure you all knew that mom was making spaghetti." "There, it's settled," Jake said with finality. He looked at the clock; 4:45. "Tell your mom and dad we'll be there in an hour." He rubbed his hands together with excitement. It was always fun to break bread with Jake. He made it an event. He ate with gusto and made everyone feel like it was a blessing to be at the table. Joe headed for the door and Mary grabbed his hand. "Care if I go along?" Mary really wanted to be with Joe right now and he could tell. "I wouldn't have it any other way." He flashed his signature smile. "See you all in a little while." Mary almost sang with happiness as she closed the door. Ruth looked at Jake. "They are so cute together. I hope they get married someday. We are blessed to have the Goldsteins in our lives." "You can say that again, Ruthy. Joe is a good boy from a fine family. But don't plan a wedding just yet. They have a long way to go before they are ready for that. Harvard is a tough school and being married would only make it tougher. Besides, they aren't even 18 years old yet!" "I know, Jake. I wouldn't want them to get married until they graduate, either. I'm just saying...."

The aroma of rich spaghetti sauce met Joe and Mary as they walked in the front door of the Goldstein's house. Abraham was asleep on the couch with the newspaper over his faced. The kids could hear Eve busy in the kitchen. They didn't want to wake Abraham so they decided to slip upstairs to do a bit more studying. Eve caught them halfway up the stairs. "Hi kids," she whispered. Both kids waved and Joe pointed at his chemistry book and then at Mary to signal Eve that they were planning to study. Eve gave them a 'thumbs up' and headed back to the kitchen. Joe and Mary tiptoed into his room and sat down to review chemistry, again.

In what seemed like minutes, the doorbell rang and the kids heard Jake bellow, "Smells good in here! I'm not too late am I?" Abraham sat up with a start and almost knocked over the lamp on the end table. Mary looked at Joe as they read each other's minds, 'we forgot to tell Eve about Mary's parents coming over for dinner.' Joe laughed out loud and Mary giggled as they ran down the stairs. Eve was just coming out of the kitchen and Abraham was still trying to shake off the nap. Jake and Ruth were standing in the living room watching Abraham. "Hey mom! The Reubenowitz's are coming over for dinner, tonight." "You don't say, honey." Eve headed straight for Ruth who rolled her eyes as they embraced. "What time are they coming?" Eve was sarcastic as she received a kiss on the cheek from Jake. "Right about now," Mary said innocently with a fiendish look on her face. By now Abraham had made his way over to Jake and Ruth. After the routine embraces, Ruth said, "They forgot to tell you, didn't they?" "No matter," Eve waved her hand. "I figured that Jake would sniff out my spaghetti and show up here anyway!" "Abraham, you married a smart lady!" Jake announced. "Let's eat!" They all laughed as they headed for the kitchen.

CHAPTER TWENTY-THREE

Mary and Joe ran to the doors of the school and walked in just in time to hear the first period bell go off. They had left the house on time but were late because Mary had to stop three times to throw up. Joe felt bad for Mary but both kids were glad that she had made it out of the house without incident. Mary headed for the girls restroom as soon as they entered the school and said over her shoulder, "See you in class." Joe looked at her helplessly and headed down the hall.

Joe sat down in his seat just as the second bell rang. The teacher scanned the room and looked at Joe, "Where's Mary?" "Running a little late. She should be here in just a minute." Joe was slightly embarrassed. In a couple of minutes Mary came into the room smiling and apologized to the teacher for being tardy. "Have a seat, Mary." She pointed to her chair next to Joe. "We'll let it go this time." Mary headed toward her seat and looked at Joe as she sat down. She could tell that he wanted to know how she felt by the look in his eyes. Mary winked and gave him the 'OK' sign as she sat down. Joe grinned and nodded as the teacher began to lecture.

The teacher stopped her lecture about ten minutes before the bell was to ring and gave the class an assignment. Most of the kids began working on the assignment or studying for another class. Joe decided to take a quick look at the chemistry notes and pulled out his book. He noticed Mary slip out of her seat and approach the teacher who was erasing the blackboard. Joe watched Mary whisper something to the teacher who nodded as Mary walked out of the room. Joe figured that Mary was returning to the restroom.

Mary hadn't returned when the bell rang so he grabbed her books and headed for his locker. Mary was nowhere in sight so he threw Mary's books into his locker, grabbed his chemistry book, and headed off to study hall. Mary got to study hall about five minutes after the bell. She walked up to the study hall monitor and said, "Sorry, I'm late. The restroom was busy." "No problem, Mary." Ms. Jones was pretty laid back. Mary scanned the room and didn't see Joe. "Where's Joe?" "He went to the library. I don't suppose you want to go too?!" Ms. Jones knew that Mary and Joe were joined at the hip. Mary smiled and turned a little red as Ms. Jones handed her a library pass. "Thanks, Ms Jones; you're the best." Don't tell anybody honey. They'll never believe you." Ms. Jones laughed and returned to reading her newspaper.

Mary found Joe working on a computer in the library. He seemed awfully intent at whatever he was doing. She touched him on the shoulder as she sat down. "I figured you would be studying chemistry," she whispered in his ear. Joe was noticeably startled at Mary's touch as he flinched and snapped back to reality. "Oh, hi Sugar Plum. You kind of caught me off-guard." "So I noticed," Mary replied. "What's so intriguing?" Mary moved the screen so that she could see. "Well, the thought occurred to me last period that the Bible says the Savior will come from the line of King David. So I thought I would check out our ancestry to see if we are related to him. I've looked on several websites but they don't go back that far. I'm kind of stumped." "Have you tried the synagogue's website? Maybe there is a link or something," Mary offered. "Good idea, sweetie! Now I know why I'm marrying you. You are pretty and smart!" Joe acted proud of himself. "Well, that and the fact that God told me that I had to," Joe teased. Mary rolled her eyes and slapped him on the shoulder.

The website came up and there was a link to Jewish genealogy. Joe got excited as he clicked his way through a series of links. After about 15 minutes, he sat back in his chair and confirmed it. "Well, I guess I'm doing OK." He put his feet up on the desk as he folded his hands behind his head. "I am, in fact, engaged to a princess! You are a direct descendant of King David." Mary gasped with excitement as she looked over Joe's shoulder at the screen. There was her family name, 'Reubenowitz'. "Type in Goldstein, Joe. I want to see if you are royalty or if I'm settling for a peasant!" "What if I'm not?" He thought out loud. "Would that mean I'm NOT supposed to marry you?" There was concern in his voice. Mary slid Joe out of the way. "That's nonsense you big goofball. I'll check." She typed furiously on the keyboard. Joe stared out of the window as Mary searched. After about 30 seconds, Mary sighed and said, "Oh no!" "What's wrong Mary?" Joe looked at her waiting to hear the bad news. "She looked at him sadly. "I'm afraid we got a problem...." "What Mary?" Joe just knew that Goldstein wasn't on the list. "Well," Mary hesitated. "It looks as if I am marrying my cousin!" Mary beamed with happiness. Joe flipped the screen so he could see it. Mary had highlighted 'Goldstein'. "See Joe, right there. You are in the line of David, too!" We are 123rd cousins." Joe smiled and squeezed Mary's hand. "This is truly the work of God," Joe whispered.

Their thoughts were interrupted by the bell. "Well I guess it's time to see how much chemistry we've learned." Joe quipped as he collected his stuff and logged off of the computer. "I'll bet I get a better score than you," Mary said with confidence. "Oh yeah, I'll take that bet." Joe grinned. "OK, what shall we bet?" Mary put her finger up to her chin as if she were contemplating the possibilities. "How about loser washes the winner's car?" Joe suggested. "Oh Joe, it is still a little chilly outside. I'd hate to see you catch a cold washing my car!" "No worries," Joe teased right back. "You'll be the one outside freezing." "We'll see about that." Mary smirked as they headed down the hall.

Mary finished her test before Joe so she decided to see if the teacher could grade it right away. She was determined to see Joe wash her car. She slid out of her seat and took two steps down the aisle before she felt faint and wobbled just enough that it caught Joe's attention who was sitting in front of her. She caught herself on his desk and he jumped up to steady her. Just as he grabbed her by the arms she passed out. Joe caught her as she slid into his arms. He scooped her up and started for the door. By now the teacher was up and heading for the door to open it for Joe. "Take her to the nurse. I'll call her and tell her what's going on," he ordered Joe. "Way ahead of you sir, thanks," Joe replied as he kept going.

The nurse's office was at the other end of the hall and Joe walked as quickly as possible. Mary was as light as a feather so carrying her was no problem. Halfway down the hall Mary started to come around. She opened her eyes and looked at Joe. "Where are we?" "You passed out in chemistry a couple of minutes ago. I'm taking you to the nurse." The cloud was beginning to lift in Mary's mind. "Oh brother," Mary lamented. "Did I cause a scene?" Joe looked down and smiled at her. "Well, you did manage to get everyone's mind off of the test for awhile." Mary closed her eyes in embarrassment. "You must be OK if you are feeling good enough to be embarrassed about it." Joe tried to comfort Mary. He knew she was scared.

Joe looked up and saw the nurse come flying out of her office in his direction. She jogged toward them as she started asking questions. "What happened? Is she OK? Did she hit her head? Is she awake?" By then she had gotten to the kids and was looking Mary over like a lion inspecting her cub. Mary opened her eyes and said, "I'm fine. Just a little weak, that's all." They walked in the door of her office and Joe gently laid her down on the couch. He looked on as the nurse began to check her over and ask her questions. Mary began feeling better in just a few minutes and sat up. "I feel fine now. Can I go back to class?" "Let's just hold on a minute," the nurse ordered. I need to find out what's going on. I don't want you to pass out again. We need to figure out what caused this to begin with." Mary met Joe's glance and they read each other's minds. They both knew what had caused it; she was pregnant. "Joe, you can go on back to class." Joe shuddered as he heard the nurse. "I would like to stay if I could?" Joe pleaded. "Sorry Joe, I think I can handle this." She smirked a little. "I'll let you know if I need your help. Now get!" She flipped a towel in Joe's direction. "OK, OK," Joe relented. "I'll see you later, Sugar Plum." "I'm fine Joe," Mary assured him. I'll see you in English." "IF she feels OK," the nurse interjected.

Joe looked at the clock while he was sitting in English class. The class would be over in 15 minutes and still no sign of Mary. Joe had returned to chemistry class to finish his test after the nurse had shooed him out of the office before the bell rang last period and now he was half listening to the English lecture. Five minutes later Mary entered the room, handed the teacher an excuse note and headed for her seat in front of Joe. Just as she sat down she glanced in his direction and saw concern in his eyes. She smiled and nodded slightly which told Joe that she was alright.

A few minutes later they were in the line at the cafeteria. "I'm so hungry, I could eat a horse!" Mary spoke with enthusiasm. Joe laughed as he watched her select almost twice as much as she usually did. Even the cafeteria workers were surprised at the amount of food on her plate. The kids finally headed out to the eating area where they were met with waves from Angie and Allen who had saved them a couple of chairs.

"What happened?!" Angie exclaimed before Mary could sit down. "What are you talking about?" Mary hoped that it wasn't about the incident in chemistry. "I'm talking about you passing out! It's all over school! Are you OK?" Mary looked around the room and noticed that almost everyone was looking at her. She put her face in her hands in a futile effort to act like an ostrich and hope that it would all go away. "I didn't eat much breakfast and I guess my blood sugar got a little low," Mary mumbled into her hands. "It's no big deal." Angie opened her mouth to question her further but was halted by Allen's squeeze on her elbow. Angie looked at Allen who was looking at Joe. Joe was shaking his head slightly back and forth as if to say, 'Let it go.' Angie nodded in Joe's direction signaling that she understood. Allen broke the ice. "Well it looks like you're making up for it now, Mary. You've got enough on your plate for all of us." Everyone chuckled as Joe looked at his friend with a 'thank you' in his eyes. "I'll bet you a dollar she can't finish it all!" Allen said as he leaned back in his chair. Angie picked up on the diversion. "I'm in! I know my girl, she can do it!" All of the kids relaxed and began eating.

After a couple of minutes, an announcement came over the intercom. "Mary Reubenowitz, please come to the office." Mary shoved her plate back and said as she got up to leave, "Well, it looks like we'll never know if I could finish or not. But leave my plate here for a little while; just in case this doesn't take long." Joe, Allen and Angie laughed as Mary headed out the door.

About ten minutes later, Joe felt his phone vibrate inside his pants pocket. The kids weren't allowed to have cell phones in school but none of the teachers cared as long as they stayed out of sight during class and didn't ring. Joe looked at his phone. It was a text from Mary. 'Nurse called parents. Mom here to take me to Doc Reynolds. Please pray.' Joe closed his phone and stuffed it back into his pocket. Allen saw the concern on Joe's face and said, "What's up Joe?" "Aw nothing really, it looks like Mary isn't feeling as well as she thought. She's going home." "I KNEW she wasn't doing well," Angie announced. "I could tell by her expression."

As soon as Joe got into his car after baseball practice he called Mary. "Hi Joe." Mary's voice was somber. "Hi sweetie, how did it go?" "Oh just fine, Joe. Just a minute. Mom, should I take the casserole out of the oven yet?" Joe heard Ruth in the background. "Let's give it five more minutes." "Can't talk huh?" Joe said knowing the answer. "That's right," Mary chirped into the phone. "I can't wait to hear how the doctor appointment went." "Did you bring my homework home?" Changing the subject meant that Mary was nervous. "Sure did, Sugar Plum." Joe was enjoying the game they were playing. "How about if I bring it over after dinner?" "That would be great, Joe. I'll see you then, bye." Joe smiled as he hung up the phone. He knew what Mary had been going through on the other end of the line.

Joe shoveled down his dinner and announced to his parents that he was going to take Mary's homework over to her. "That's fine honey," Eve said as Joe walked out the door. "Tell Mary to get better soon." "I will, I'll be back in a little while." Joe closed the door behind him.

The air was chilly and Joe pulled the collar of his letter jacket up over his neck. 'It may be Spring officially but the April air in Montana is still chilly,' Joe thought to himself. He walked quickly across the street and started up the sidewalk to Mary's front door. Just as he passed the mailbox he caught a glimpse of something out of the corner of his eye. He turned his head to see what it was, but it had vanished. He assumed it was a cat or something and turned up the sidewalk. A rush of wind came up suddenly and blew his cap off. 'That's weird,' Joe thought as he ran after his hat. He had worn that hat in windstorms before and it had never blown off. It fit his head perfectly. As he picked up his cap and returned it to its proper position, it struck him. That breeze was WARM! Even though it was cold out, the breeze that had blown his cap off was definitely warm. He looked around quickly in both directions. He saw a figure walking up the street in his direction.

Joe stood there and watched as the figure came closer to him. The darkness prevented him from seeing who it was; but he did notice that the warm breeze picked up again. He just stood there watching. His feet felt like they were stuck in the concrete. Chills began to run down his spine as the stranger came closer. Joe felt as if he was in a trance. The person stopped about 20 feet from Joe and remained just far enough away that Joe couldn't see his face. The breeze stopped as suddenly as it had started. "Hi Joe! How are you doing?" The voice was familiar but Joe couldn't place it. "Aw, I'm fine. Do I know you?" "Why Joe, of course you know me. I bought your dinner just the other night." Joe was puzzled for just a second and then it hit him. "Keith's! Guardian? Is that you?" Guardian stepped into the light. "In the flesh! Kind of." Guardian smiled at Joe. Joe stepped up and hugged him. "Things have been happening pretty fast for you lately," Guardian stated knowingly. "Are you holding up OK?" "I think so. Mary and I are making plans to get ready. I feel a little overwhelmed. But I know God is going to get us through." "Good attitude." Guardian patted Joe on the back. "I want you to know that God is always with you, always. Don't ever forget that. I will always be here. You may not see me, but you must know that you are never alone." Joe was excited and apprehensive at the same time. "There's just one thing I came to tell you tonight," Guardian continued. "It's time you and Mary told your folks what is going on." "Yeah, I know." Joe felt good about himself because he and Mary had made a plan to tell them. "Mary and I...." "You need to tell them tonight," Guardian interrupted. "TONIGHT!?" Joe couldn't believe his ears. "Yes, tonight." Guardian was calm. "But, uh, I'm not, umm, I mean, we haven't...." "Joe, you are stammering." Guardian was smiling. "I just don't think we're ready!" Joe finally blurted out. "Joe, history is filled with people who weren't ready for God's call. But when they heard it, they responded. It doesn't matter if you are ready, what matters is that God IS ready. I'm sure it seems surreal to you right now; that's normal. But you need to get it out beyond you two. That's when reality will set in. You need to know exactly how everyone is going to react to this; even your parents." Guardian was kind but firm. Joe knew he was right. "OK Guardian. I am God's servant. I will do as He says." "I know you will, Joe." Guardian hesitated a little and then continued. "I need to get going. The next few months are going to be busy." Guardian headed down the street. After about 15 seconds, Joe called out.

"Hey Guardian! Did you blow my hat off?" Joe was smiling into the shadows. Guardian turned around waved. "I thought you could use a little warm air after a long cold winter. Ha! I'll see you soon." He pivoted in the opposite direction and disappeared into the shadows. Joe laughed as he jogged up to Mary's house.

Joe rang the doorbell and let himself in. "Hi honey! I'm home!" Joe yelled as he entered the room. "In here Joe." Ruth's voice came from the kitchen. We're just finishing up supper. Are you hungry?" No thanks, Mom. I'm full." Joe kissed Ruth on the cheek and gave Mary a brief hug. Abraham was sitting at the table. "How about some of Ruthy's cherry pie?" he offered between bites; purposely chewing with his mouth open. "Jake, that's disgusting." Ruth snapped Jake with the dish towel. "As appetizing as it looks, I think I'll have to pass," Joe laughed. "Mary, I've got your homework assignments. Do you feel like going over them?" "Sure Joe, I feel fine. Let's go up to my room." "Take it easy dear," Ruth cautioned after her. "You know that Doc Reynolds said that you have to take it easy."

Mary sat down on the bed as Joe closed the door. "What did the doctor say?" "Well, it's confirmed. I'm pregnant!" Mary had a scared smile on her face. "He was quite shocked." Mary had know Doc Reynolds all of her life. "He assumes you are the father. I didn't bother with the real story. I figured he would think I was crazy if I told him the truth. The way he looked at me made me feel horrible. He just seemed so disappointed in me." "Did you tell him not to tell your parents?" Joe asked. "He said he wouldn't tell them. But he did say that we should as soon as possible. He wants to talk to you." "Me? What on earth for?" Joe couldn't imagine why he needed to see the doctor. "He mentioned something about making sure that you understand your responsibility in all of this. He wants to make sure you are going to take care of me." "What kind of a guy does he think I am?!" Joe got indignant. "I've known him all of my life! He wrote me a letter of recommendation to Harvard for heaven's sakes. Does he think I'm going to run out on you or something!?" "Joe, think about it for a minute," Mary soothed. "Doc Reynolds and his wife have known our parents for 30 years. They all are friends, go out together, and the Reynolds' even claim us as their own since they don't have children. He thinks we've let him down." "Well, I guess I can see how he might feel. But we didn't do anything wrong." Joe scratched his head as he contemplated Mary's words. "No matter Our parents will straighten him out after we tell them. They will know how to get the truth across without sounding crazy." Joe felt confident again. "Good point, Joe. When ARE we going to tell our parents?"

"Why I'm glad you asked." Joe walked over to Mary and sat down next to her. He gently placed his arm around her shoulder and whispered, "Tonight." "Very funny, Joe. No really. We need to have a plan." Mary looked up at Joe who just silently sat there, smiling. Mary read his mind; he was serious. "Tonight! Really! Have you lost your mind! We aren't ready for this! THEY aren't ready for this! We can't do it tonight. There's just no way…." Mary rambled on for a few seconds while Joe sat there quietly listening to her. After she slowed down for a breath, Joe squeezed her and gave her a peck on the cheek. "I need to tell you something, Mary."

Mary's facial expressions changed from pure joy to intense excitement and extreme contentment, mixed with a little fear as Joe told her about his encounter with Guardian a few minutes ago. "And that's why we have to tell our parents…tonight," Joe concluded. Mary fell back on the bed and stared at the stucco ceiling. She had become lost in thought while looking at the ceiling many times before. She had imagined seeing horses, cats, sunsets, castles, faces…all kinds of things as she had allowed the images in the ceiling carry her away from reality. It was one of her happy places.

Joe leaned back next to her and brushed the hair from her eyes. Her eyes sparkled and her hair glistened. It was as if Joe was looking at her for the first time. "Mary," Joe snapped her out of her trance. "Have I told you that you are the most beautiful girl that I have ever seen?" Mary looked at Joe and smiled. "Not today." Both kids chuckled a little as Joe fell back on the bed to join Mary's escape into the ceiling. After a few minutes, Joe said, "You KNOW we need to do this, right?" "I know, Joe," Mary relented. "I'm just a little scared. I know our parents will understand, but I guess the reality is just setting in. We might as well get it done, though. Call you parents and ask them to come over." Joe sat up and flipped open his phone. "Hi mom. Can you and dad come over to Mary's house? We have some good news and we want to share it with everyone at the same time. OK, see you in five minutes." Joe hung up the phone. "There's no turning back now, Sugar Plum." "Joe, let's pray about this." "Good idea!" Mary prayed, "Father God; we are your servants and are committed to doing Your will. Please give us the right words to share this wonderful information with our parents. Amen."

Mary opened her eyes and said, "I've got an idea." She jumped up and rummaged through some papers on her desk. "Here it is!" She held a piece of paper up at Joe. "It's a prescription that Doctor Reynolds gave me today. I know just how we are going to do this. Come on!" There was excitement in Mary's voice. She grabbed Joe's hand and led him downstairs. "Just follow my lead; God gave me a great idea!" Somewhat confused, Joe followed Mary downstairs to the living room. "Mom! Dad! The Goldstein's are coming over. Joe and I have some GREAT news that we want to share with all of you!" "OK honey." Ruth seemed a little bewildered. "I love good news," Jake added.

In just a couple of minutes Abraham and Eve arrived. Ruth greeted them at the door. "What's all the fuse about?" Eve inquired of Ruth. "I have no idea, Eve. Those two are up to something, again." Ruth laughed and nodded toward the living room. The kids were sitting on the couch and Jake was in his easy chair. Abraham strolled over to Jake and stuck out his hand. "Any idea what's going on Jake?" Abraham smiled at his long-time friend. Jake used the handshake to get assistance out of the chair. He gave Abraham a big hug and said with gusto, "I don't have a clue, buddy. But I'll bet you a steak that it is going to get into our wallets somehow!" Abraham laughed and agreed. "Joe and Mary got up off the couch and instructed Abraham and Eve to sit there. Jake plopped back down in his chair and Ruth took a seat in the rocking chair as she said, "So, what's the big news?"

Joe put his arm around Mary and smiled at each one of them. Mary was grinning from ear to ear. "Well daddy," Mary produced a piece of paper and handed it to Jake. He squinted as he tried to read it. "What is it honey?" he questioned. "It's a prescription from Doctor Reynolds, daddy. I need you to fill it for me." "How are you feeling, dear? I heard about the incident at school today." Eve leaned up in her chair. Before Mary could say anything, Ruth chimed in. "He wasn't sure what caused it exactly. However, he did say that she needed at lot of rest." Abraham's look turned to concern. "Do you think she needs more tests or something? I don't like the idea of her passing out and not knowing exactly what caused it." Jake sat quietly in his chair as the other three parents played doctor. Mary was glued to her dad's expression. There was a combination of bewilderment and seriousness in his gaze. He couldn't take his eyes off of the prescription.

After a couple of minutes of discussion, Ruth noticed that Jake was still staring at the prescription. "Having trouble reading Doc's handwriting, dear? Would you like for me to get your glasses?" "That won't be necessary, Ruth. I can read it just fine." There was seriousness in his voice, which was quite unusual for Jake. The room fell silent. The only sound that could be heard was the ticking of the grandfather clock in the hall. Joe and Mary's smiles melted into looks of fear as they scanned the room. Abraham leaned up in his chair fearing a serious illness that could be interrupted from the type of prescription. "What is it Jake?" Jake laid the prescription on the table and looked directly into Joe's eyes. A shudder ran down Joe's back as he read Jake's look. There was anger in his eyes. Jake cleared his voice as he rose to his feet. "This prescription is for prenatal vitamins." Ruth laughed nervously. "Why that is the silliest thing I've ever heard. There must be some mistake." "Of course it's a mistake," Eve added. "Doctor Reynolds is getting older. Maybe he was thinking about another patient when he wrote that. If it were correct, that would mean that Mary is...." Her voice trailed off. "There has got to be an explanation." "I'm sure there is." Jake looked at his daughter for an answer. Mary looked into the pleading eyes of her father. He was silently begging her for any explanation other than the obvious.

Mary looked at Joe who still had his arm around her. It seemed as if the announcement was not turning out the way she had anticipated. She decided to keep trying to be positive. She forced a smile. "That IS the great news, daddy; I'm going to have a baby!" Eve gasped and Ruth sat back in her chair and fanned herself. Abraham groaned and buried his face in his hands. Jake's pleading eyes turned to fire as he glared at Joe. He started toward Joe with clenched fists. Mary had never seen her dad this angry. "Why you slimy, little, snake, get your hands off my daughter! I'm going to tear you apart!" Abraham was on his feet ready to step in but Mary jumped in front of Joe. "Daddy! Calm down! You don't understand!" "For heaven's sake Jake, get control of yourself!" Eve interjected.

"Don't you tell my husband to control himself!" Ruth glared at Eve. By now Abraham was standing next to Mary and was chest to chest with Jake. "Now Jake, don't do anything you'll regret. Let's get our wits about us and figure this out." Abraham was stern but reasonable. Jake tried unsuccessfully to reach between Abraham and Mary to grab Joe. "I would NEVER regret beating the tar out of him!" Jake snorted. "Daddy please sit down. You don't understand. It's not Joe's fault. Give us a chance to explain. "NOT HIS FAULT?" Jake yelled at the top of his voice. "WHAT ARE YOU TALKING ABOUT?!"

By now, all four of the adults were on their feet and staring holes in their children. After a few seconds of silence, Joe spoke in a whisper. "Look, I realize how this appears on the surface. However, you know us. We are not bad people. If you will just calm down and give us a chance to explain, I think you will be happy about this. Please, let's take a minute and discuss this as adults. I'm positive that you will change your mind once you've heard the truth."

"TRUTH?!" Jake bellowed. "The truth is that you knocked up my daughter!" "How dare you take advantage of our little girl," Ruth added. "Now wait just a minute," Abraham snarled back at Jake. "You are treading on thin ice. Don't jump to conclusions. I'm as upset as you are. But, I'd like to hear what they have to say." "Yeah," Eve smirked. "Maybe your 'little girl' took advantage of Joe!"

That remark was all it took. All four adults began arguing at once. Mary and Joe couldn't tell what anyone was saying because they were all talking at the same time. Mary felt faint and grabbed Joe by the arm. He quickly glanced at her and realized that she wasn't doing well. He put his arm around her and helped her to the couch. She sat down and leaned back. Joe sat down next to her and held her hand. Soon, Mary began to sob which caught the attention of the adults. They immediately stopped arguing as Ruth sat down on the other side of Mary. "Are you OK, dear?" "You all are making me crazy. Please sit down and let us explain." Eve and Abraham glared at Jake but decided to oblige. Jake, still furious, and red faced couldn't hold back. "There's nothing to explain, Mary." He pointed at Joe. "That weasel got you pregnant and now you have to live with the consequences!"

Abraham started to get up in protest to the insult but Joe looked at his dad and gave him a slight head movement as if to say, 'hold off for a moment.' Jake's comment about Joe caused Mary to lose control. She jumped up and shouted through her tears. "How dare you call my fiancé names, daddy! I love him more than anything in the world! He wants to marry me!" She held out her left hand so that everyone could see the engagement ring. "Besides, he ISN'T even the father!"

The room fell silent. Jake slumped down in his chair. Abraham rubbed his forehead trying to absorb the statement. Ruth and Eve sat there with their mouths wide open. All that could be heard was that grandfather clock ticking away in the hall. The seconds melted into minutes which seemed like hours. Finally, Jake sighed and calmly asked Mary, "Well honey, if Joe isn't the father, who is?" Mary looked at Joe who smiled slightly at her. Mary returned the smile and looked at each parent intently for a few seconds. "God."

Ruth and Eve gasped in a way that caused Mary to assume that they were excited. Abraham stared at Joe with a thousand questions in his mind. Jake rubbed his eyes as he contemplated what to say next. "Mary, I realize that we are all God's children and that baby is no different. However, we want to know who the earthly father is. If you are just trying to protect Joe, don't worry. I promise I won't hurt him. We just need to know."

"I know this may be difficult to believe," Mary said as she leaned back on the couch and smiled at all of the parents. "I am giving birth to the Savior." There was a calm and peaceful air about her that amazed everyone, except Joe.

Ruth got up and went over and sat down on the couch next to Mary. She put her arms around her and Mary leaned into her mother's embrace. Mary assumed this was a show of pride and endearment but she soon realized that it wasn't. As she examined the expressions of each of the adults in the room, she didn't see pride; she saw pity in their eyes. "Oh honey," Ruth gently stroked Mary's hair. "I know this is a lot to handle, but you aren't making any sense. You have to face reality." "The poor child is delusional." Eve spoke to no one in particular. "Mary, I want you to listen to me very carefully." Jake leaned up in his chair and placed his elbows on his knees. "Everyone in this room knows that you two made a mistake. You cannot deny it. You MUST face the truth. Claiming to be pregnant with the Savior is bordering on blasphemy. Please, tell us the truth and we'll figure this out. Now, let me rephrase the question. Have you and Joe had sex?"

Mary shuddered and bristled as the question resonated through her brain. She leaned forward out of her mother's embrace, looked her dad squarely in the eye and said emphatically, "No." "Well if not Joe, then who? Is it that Gary guy you have been working with in the 'Teens for Abstinence' program?" Ruth gasped at the sound of her husband's words. Not only the accusation that Mary may have slept with someone else, but how would this affect Mary's status in that organization. She had been so proud of Mary for remaining pure to her convictions; and now, all of that seemed to be fading away. She glanced at Eve who gave her a sympathetic look as if to say, 'I'm sorry that Mary is a disappointment to you.' It made Ruth a little angry. "No Daddy! How could you think such a thing?" Jake got angry. "Well then who? Were you raped or drugged or something?" Mary just glared at her dad with no response, just fire in her eyes.

After several seconds of awkward silence, Abraham spoke up. "Joe, you are awfully quiet. I would like to hear what you have to say. Let me ask you a direct question for which I want a direct answer." Abraham paused and cleared his throat. "Have you and Mary had sex?" The tone in his voice was soft, but stern. Joe knew the tone and what it meant. No messing around, come to the point. Joe stammered a little as he looked Abraham squarely in the eyes. "Uh, no Dad, I've never touched her, but…." Joe was about to back up Mary's story but Abraham interrupted, a little louder this time. "I don't want to hear any 'buts'. I'm going to ask you again; do you swear that you are not the biological father of this child? Yes or no?" Joe looked at Mary, then his mother, and back at his dad. "It's complicated. I need to be able to speak…." Abraham stood up, fists clenched, red-faced, he looked like he was going to explode as he approached Joe. "Abraham!" Eve knew her husband. He had had enough and he wanted a direct answer. She feared that he was going to do something he may regret. "You need to get yourself under control." She barely got the words out of her mouth before Abraham shot an angry look at her and held up his index finger which demanded silence. He positioned his face within inches of Joe's. He whispered through clenched teeth. "One last time, one word answer, no 'buts', understand?" Joe nodded slightly. "Have you had sex with Mary?" Joe paused a moment and took a breath. "No."

After staring intently into Joe's eyes for a few seconds, Abraham backed away, turned around and faced his wife. "I guess that's it," he spoke in a whisper. Eve nodded her head slightly and looked at Mary who, by now, had tears streaming down her cheeks. Eve felt sorry for Mary; after all, she was like a daughter to her. The look in her eyes was one of sadness and pity. Jacob took all of this in and could no longer remain silent. He grabbed Abraham by the arm and spun him around. "What do you mean, 'that's it'?" he bellowed. Abraham looked at his long-time friend with a combination of emotions boiling up inside. He stared at Jake for several seconds and then slowly moved his eyes to the point on his arm where Jake was still clinging. The silent but clear message was a stern, 'please remove your hand from my arm.' Jake slowly released his grip but his glare remained fixed on Abraham. "What I mean is this," Abraham spoke slowly. "We have been friends longer than we have been married and I love your family as if they were my own. I will support you through this ordeal in any way that I can; however, if Joe says that he isn't the father, then I believe him. I will not allow Joe to take the blame for the fact that Mary made a mistake with some other boy!" "You've got to be kidding!?" Jake bellowed. "How dare you suggest that my daughter has been sleeping around!" "I'm not SUGGESTING anything! I am merely repeating what your daughter and my son have admitted; which is that they hadn't had sex. So here are the facts. Mary is pregnant. She and Joe haven't had sex. That tells me that she has to have had sex with at least one other guy."

"At least! How dare you call my daughter a whore!" Ruth jumped in like a lioness protecting her cub. "It's obvious that they are both lying to protect Joe. Poor Mary has no defense since he took advantage of her." Mary burst into tears again and buried her head in Joe's chest. Eve could no longer control herself. "Well if she is protecting him enough to blaspheme about being the mother of the Messiah she is not only a loose liar, but she needs some psychological help as well!"

Joe could not remain quiet any longer. "Mom! Don't talk about Mary like that! She is my fiancée. She is telling the truth. She is carrying the Messiah. Angels have appeared to both of us confirming that it is actually true! If you don't believe her then I guess I am blaspheming too!" "Be quiet Joe," Abraham warned his son.

"Don't you talk to your mother that way." "Sounds like little mister perfect isn't so perfect after all. In fact, I seem to remember that while Mary was away, he was running around with that Melissa girl who everyone knows will sleep with anybody! Maybe Joe got a little taste of something that he liked and forced himself on Mary when she got home!" Jake retorted.

That was all it took. All four parents began yelling at the same time. Arms were waving and fingers were pointing. Each was trying to be heard over the other. Mary began shaking and sobbing uncontrollably. Joe whispered into Mary's ear, "Let's get out of here." He slowly backed out of the room with Mary still in his arms. The kids slipped out of the house unnoticed by the arguing parents. As Joe carefully closed the door he could here Jake yell something about rape and a blood test. Things were heating up and he knew that his dad was about to explode. Joe helped Mary into the car and got in. "Where are we going?" Mary managed to get out between sobs. "We're just going to get away for awhile. They need to calm down and I don't want you upset. Maybe they will come to their senses and maybe they won't. I just know that I MUST take care of you and the baby. Being in an environment like that isn't good for either of you." Joe eased down the street. "What's going to happen to us, Joe? I'm scared." Joe reached across the seat and took her by the hand. "I don't know Sugar Plum, I just know that we are doing God's will and as long as we keep it up, He will take care of us." Mary smiled at him through her tears. She never grew tired of being called 'Sugar Plum'. "I love you Joe." "I love you too, Mary."

CHAPTER TWENTY-FOUR

Joe and Mary drove in silence for a long time each of them caught up in their thoughts and worries about what was going on. One thing was for sure; their lives had changed permanently. As he turned off the main highway onto a country road, his cell phone rang. He glanced at the time; 9:45. They had been gone for nearly an hour. Mary picked up the phone; "It's your mom." "Turn it off," Joe replied with no emotion at all. Two minutes later, Mary's phone rang. "They must still be together; that is my mom." Joe stared straight down the road and said, "I guess they figured out that we aren't there." There was a snide tone to his voice. Mary giggled a little and turned her phone off.

They drove for a mile or so before they came upon a bonfire about 50 yards from the road. Even though it was dark, Joe could tell that there was a tractor and a bulldozer setting near the fire. Mary could see someone walking around the fire. Joe stopped the car. "I think I know him," Joe said with a little cheerfulness. "I'm pretty sure that is Mr. Robinson." "Who?" "He farms a lot of ground around here. His son, Adam was a senior when we were in 7th grade. Adam was always real nice to me. He was a great baseball player. Adam sort of took me under his wing and taught me some cool pitches. Come on, let's go say hi." Joe threw open the door and ran around to Mary's side to let her out. "You don't think he will shoot us or anything, do you?" Joe laughed out loud. "I'm pretty sure that God isn't going to allow a farmer to shoot the Savior."

Joe cupped his hands around his mouth, "Mr. ROBINSON?" "Hello," the reply came from the darkness. Joe and Mary started out across the field and watched as Mr. Robinson came toward them. As they got within a few yards of each other, Mr. Robinson said, "I can't see as well as I used to; who's there?" "It's Joe Goldstein, Mr. Robinson." "Little Joey Goldstein? No kidding. Abraham's boy?" Mary giggled. 'Little Joey,' she repeated. Joe squeezed her hand and whispered, "Please keep that to yourself." "We'll see," she whispered back. Just then the three of them came together. They were just close enough to the fire that they could make out each other's faces. Joe stuck out his hand but Mr. Robinson grabbed his arm and pulled him in for a big bear hug. After he released Joe he looked at Mary and said, "Why Joey, aren't you going to introduce me to this pretty little lady?" "Of course, Mr. Robinson, this is my fiancée, Mary Reubenowitz. Mary, this is Mr. Robinson." "It's nice to meet you, sir," Mary said shyly. "You kids getting' married?" Wow, I'm getting old. I can remember when little Joey here was following Adam around like a puppy. Seems like only yesterday. Say, you wouldn't be related to Big Jake down at the drugstore would you?" "Yes sir, he's my daddy." "I knew it! You are the spittin' image of your momma." After exchanging some pleasantries about family and friends, Mr. Robinson said, "Say, what are you kids doing way up here, anyway?" "We were just driving around talking and enjoying the evening when we spotted you. I thought we'd stop and say hi," Joe offered. "Oh I see," Mr. Robinson said with a sparkle in his eye. "You two lovebirds were out planning and romancing? I'm not so old that I don't remember when the Mrs. and I were engaged; we spent plenty of time snuggling and such." He chuckled as the memories came back to him. Mary blushed and pulled her jacket closer around her. Mr. Robinson noticed and said, "It is getting a bit chilly out here; why don't you kids come over to the fire and warm up a little?"

Mr. Robinson led the kids over to a couple of lawn chairs. "Sit down right here. I'll be right back, I've got to push the fire up a little." Mary and Joe obediently sat down and watched as he masterfully operated the dozer and pushed the logs and brush into a tight fire. Sparks flew up into the night air as he stirred the coals. The flames rose higher as he carefully pushed the remaining logs and brush up into the fire. After he finished, he walked over to the kids who seemed to be mesmerized by the fire. "Are you two planning to stay awhile?" Joe awoke out of his trance and looked at Mary for approval. She nodded. "Well, it is awfully peaceful out here tonight. Would you mind if we stayed awhile?" "Mind? No way! I was hoping you'd stay until the fire died down. That way I can get to the house and have my dinner." "We would be glad to keep an eye on things for you Mr. Robinson, Joe replied and squeezed Mary's hand. "Thanks kids, just let me know if things get out of hand. I'll come out and take care of things." Then he thought for a moment. "Shoot, I forgot who I was talking to for a minute. You've run dozers haven't you Joe?" "Yes sir," Joe replied. "I had a little seat time working for my dad." "OK then, I'm off to the house. The key is in it. You kids have a good night." "Thanks Mr. Robinson, good night." The kids watched him disappear into the darkness.

Mary scooted her chair close to Joe's and snuggled into his arm. The warmth of the fire felt good in contrast to the chilly evening air. Joe noticed how warm he felt on his chest in comparison to the coolness on his back. It was a beautiful Montana evening. The sparks from the fire rose into the air and led a trail into the stars. There wasn't a cloud in the sky. The only sounds were the crackling of the fire which was occasionally interrupted by the howl of a coyote or the hoot of an owl.

After a few minutes, Mary sighed deeply and said, "Do you think they have calmed down yet?" Joe paused as he considered his answer. "Maybe, it's hard to tell but I kind of doubt it. I've never seen them like that before. They were pretty worked up." Mary giggled slightly. "Did you see the look on my dad's face as he was reading the prescription? I thought he was going to have a stroke." Joe laughed a little at the mental image. "Yeah, and did you see how our moms were snarling like lionesses protecting their cubs? I've never seen either of them that upset." Mary and Joe chuckled at the thought. The humor of the moment quickly faded into concern. They both realized that their laughter was a result of nervous tension. They knew that they were right. But it felt so weird contradicting their parents. They had never done that before. Both kids resumed looking at the fire. "Do you think they will ever believe us, Mary?" "I don't know, Joe. I'm beginning to wonder if ANYONE will ever believe us." Joe considered Mary's statement. "You may be right, Mary. It might just be the two of us. Are you ready for this?" "Do we have a choice?" Mary's voice cracked with fear. "I suppose not. But, you know Mary, I don't want a choice. We are blessed to be in this position. This is the greatest of all responsibilities. I'm proud to be the earthly father of the Savior! And I don't care what other people think! Not even our parents! As long as I have you and the Lord on my side, I don't need anyone else! Choice?! My choice is God and His will for my life!" By now Joe was on his feet and speaking loudly as if addressing an audience. Mary stood up and faced Joe. She put her arms around his neck and beamed at him. "We can do this, Joe! I love you." Joe's face fell from the 'audience' to his fiancée. She looked absolutely radiant. There was a crystal-like glow around her face. It was so striking that Joe forgot to breathe for a few moments. "I love you, too, Mary."

Just then the fire popped loudly and the kids instinctively looked in the direction of the blaze. Mary gasped and Joe held her tighter. Through the flames they could see two individuals on the other side of the fire. They couldn't see who it was as they were in the shadows. The figures began to move around the left side of the fire in the direction of the kids. Mary nudged even closer into Joe's arms as he held her tight trying in vain to see who it was. As they moved closer, Joe decided to confront the intruders. "Who's there?" He tried to muster up his most manly voice. No response came from the shadowy figures. They just kept methodically moving closer to the kids. They didn't move in a hurry; just steadily, almost floating around the fire. Joe's mind was racing. He was trying to figure out the best thing to do. Whoever it was were between he and Mary and the car. The Robinson house was at least a half mile away. Joe decided that he would have to confront whoever it was and protect Mary as best he could. He prayed silently, "Father please help me to protect my family." Just as he finished his prayer the two figures came out of the shadows so that the kids could see their faces. Mary gasped. Joe relaxed his hold on Mary and smiled, then laughed. He recognized one of them. Mary began to giggle and turned to face the intruders. Mary recognized the other one. "Hi Gabby! You nearly scared the daylights out of me!" "Sorry about that," Gabby apologized as she hugged Mary. "It was all Guardian's idea." "Oh that's right, blame it all on me." Guardian grinned as he greeted Mary. "It's nice to meet you Guardian, Joe has told me a lot about you." "Nice to meet you as well. Hi Joe." "Hi Guardian. You must be the famous Gabby." Joe flashed his signature smile and extended his hand toward Gabby. "My name is...." "Joe, I know," Gabby interrupted. "I've known you, like, forever." Guardian interrupted. "Literally FOREVER." There was sarcasm in his voice. "She really is older than she looks." Gabby shot Guardian a fake scowl and everyone laughed. "It's good to know that angels have a sense of humor," Joe observed. "Laughter is very important and is a precious commodity in this dreary world," Gabby stated emphatically. "Oh by the way," Joe had a thought come to him. "Thanks for the dinner at Keith's the other night That was quite a surprise." "Oh, you are quite welcome," Guardian replied with gusto. "You two were so cute. We just wanted you to know that God is always watching out for you. Besides we just put it on our expense reports; our boss is loaded."Guardian pointed to the sky. Gabby rolled her eyes. "Guardian, you are such a ham."

After the laughter died down, Mary spoke up. "So what are you two doing out here?" "Gabby looked intently into her eyes. "I guess we could ask the same of you. Truth is, we know that you had a pretty rough evening. How are you holding up?" Mary looked down and then at Joe. He took the hint. "Well, it wasn't what we expected. We sort of assumed that our parents would understand and be supportive. But it didn't quite work out that way." "We noticed," Guardian said sympathetically. "That's putting it mildly," Mary interjected. "Our parents were downright mean. I can't believe some of the things that they said to us. It really hurt." "I know honey, we were right there. We heard everything." Gabby patted Mary on the shoulder. "You were there?! Both of you?!" Joe was bewildered. Gabby turned her attention to Joe. "Of course we were there! God is ALWAYS with you; remember, He promised." Gabby almost looked hurt as she made her point to the kids. Joe felt bad. "I'm sorry," he apologized. "I know God is omnipotent and He is everywhere; it's just hard to believe that He is always specifically looking out for me. There are billions of believers out there, how can He possibly want to spend His time looking out for the little details of everyone's life? I know that He can, I just don't feel like I deserve that much attention from Him." Guardian spoke up. "I understand how you feel, Joe. Most believers feel the same way. In fact, you are correct; no one deserves His attention. He WANTS to give it to you. He loves you more than anything. Let me give you an example. Do you remember how you felt a few minutes ago when Gabby and I were approaching and you didn't know who we were?" "Yeah, I was ready to do whatever it took to protect Mary and the child." "Why?" Guardian questioned. "Because I love them more than anything." "Well, multiply that feeling of love and protection a million times and that is how God feels toward you. Once you decided to follow Him, you became part of His family. You are His son and Mary is His daughter. Do you begin to understand now?"

Mary and Joe just stood there grinning. Both kids nodded. Gabby continued. "You have no idea how much God loves His children. Just know that He does. He loves your parents too. They are His children too. He is saddened that the 'common sense' of this world has caused them not to believe you, but He loves them none the less." "Thanks," Joe said as he felt a surge of energy flow through his body. "I'm just not sure what to do next," Gabby spoke up. "Whenever you feel confused or bewildered, God says that you should get quiet and listen. He will lead you. Listen to your subconscious; your heart. Read His Word. Ask for His guidance. He will never ignore you as long as you sincerely seek Him. Stay in His will and you will be fine. There is no guarantee that it will be easy. After all, you live in a sinful world dominated by Satan. He will attempt to throw you off the course of your charge in any way that he can. Be careful and watchful. Trust in the Lord and He will guide you through." The conversation fell silent for a few minutes. The four of them just stood there watching the fire disappear into the cloudless sky.

All of a sudden, two shooting stars appeared; one from the east, and the other from the west. They were streaking toward each other at an amazing rate of speed. Each star left a beautiful white trail as it raced across the sky. As they approached each other, they seemed to gain speed. The white glow of each star turned red as their speed intensified. All four of them stood there speechless for what seemed to be hours but in reality was only a few seconds. In an instant, the stars collided with a huge burst of energy. The red flames turned into a beautiful display of colors. Whites, blues, oranges, greens, reds, yellows...the collision turned into a heavenly display of fireworks that would make the greatest 4th of July celebration pale in comparison. After a few seconds, the color spectacular still going on, the earth trembled and a low, but powerful boom overtook them as a wave of sound washed over the kids. The force of the noise caused the kids to step back in order to keep their balance. Then, as quickly as it occurred, it was gone. It had only lasted a few seconds, but now, it was as if it never happened. Mary spoke first, "Did you see that?" "Yes," he whispered still staring at the sky. "What was that?" Mary tugged on Joe's arm. He turned to look at her inquisitive stare. Before he could answer, Gabby interjected, "That was God's power. That was God speaking to you. Are you listening?" The kids turned to look at Guardian and Gabby but they were gone. Both kids looked all around, but neither of them could be seen. "What are we going to do? What does this mean?" Mary looked up at Joe. Joe smiled down at Mary, put his arms around her and said, "We are going to do exactly what Gabby told us to do; we are going to get quiet, pray, and listen to God." They both sat down and Joe led the prayer. "Dear Father in heaven, thank You for loving us and trusting us with this task. We promise to do our best to fulfill Your expectations of us. We ask for Your guidance and power as we give ourselves to be the tools for Your plan. Amen." The kids leaned back in the chairs and allowed the love and power of God to completely envelop them.

The crackling of the fire combined with the feeling of totally giving this up to God made the kids relax in a way that they had never felt before. The stress was totally gone. Mary sighed peacefully and Joe closed his eyes to absorb the moment. His right hand found Mary's left hand and they were lost in the love of God.

Joe sat up with a start. "Mary! I've got it! I know what we are supposed to do!" Mary had drifted off to sleep. She had been dreaming of living with Joe in a little cottage in the woods. They had children, horses, a garden, and stream flowing through the backyard. It was wonderful. "What? Huh?" Mary tried to wake up and join in Joe's enthusiasm. "Those stars! The beautiful colors! I know what God is saying to us." Mary had shaken the cobwebs out of her mind by now and was giving Joe her full attention. Her eyes gave her thoughts away, 'Well, are you going to tell me?' By now, Joe was on his knees in front of Mary. The excitement in his eyes reminded her of how he used to be on his birthday when they were children. She smiled at the memories. "The collision of the stars means that our journey through this event is going to have some rough times. However, in the end it is going to be magnificent. The result of the Savior coming to this world will be the most beautiful and amazing thing that anyone has ever seen. It won't be easy, but God will prevail. We can do this, along with God of course." Mary glowed with happiness at her future husband's excitement. She looked over Joe's shoulder. "Uh, Joe? What time is it?" "I don't know, 10:30 maybe 11:00. What makes you ask?" "I think it may be later than that; look at the fire." Joe turned around and was shocked at what he saw. What once had been a 40-foot circle of blazing logs with flames shooting 30 feet in the air was now reduced to a pile of glowing ashes. Mary and Joe both pulled out their phones and turned them on. "I must have fallen asleep too," Joe said doubting what he was saying. To him, it seemed as if he had only closed his eyes for a second or two. Both phones beeped. "What time do you have, Mary?" Mary groaned, "2:45, please tell me my phone is on the fritz." "I wish I could," Joe replied. But if it is, mine is too. How many missed calls do you have?" "Seven; all from home. How many do you have?" "Six; three from home and three from dad's cell. They must be getting worried. We'd better get going."

The kids ran across the field and Joe helped Mary into the car; he ALWAYS held the door for her. He got in and fired it up. As they headed down the road Mary looked forlorn and said, "Daddy is going to kill me. Do you think we should call?" "Well, first of all, your dad isn't going to kill you, he is too mad at me to do that." Mary laughed. "Second, they may be asleep and we'll be home in twenty minutes. Maybe we can slip in and deal with this in the morning when everyone has had a chance to calm down a little." Good point, Joe. Let's hope that they are asleep."

Joe eased up in front of his house and turned off his car. The kids looked at both houses. The hallway light was on in Mary's house. That wasn't unusual; Ruth always left the light on when Mary was out. However, the light in Abraham's den was on and he was up. "Looks like I'm going to have to face the music tonight." Joe lamented. "You may be in the clear. Come on, I'll get you inside before I have to talk to dad." Joe walked Mary up to the door and gave her a kiss good night. Mary eased the door open and said to Joe, "Good luck, I'll see you tomorrow." "Good night Sugar Plum."

Mary eased the door closed and started for the stairs. "Are you OK honey?" Mary nearly jumped out of her skin. Jake's voice was quiet but stern. It came from the darkened living room. "Daddy, you almost scared me to death. I was fine, until now." "I'm sorry, dear; we were just worried about you. You weren't answering your phone." Now it was her mother's voice coming from the living room. "I'm sorry that I turned off the phone. I just couldn't deal with all of the arguing. I just needed to get away from it. Things were just so crazy around here." Mary could hear her mother sobbing slightly and Jake sighed. "Go on to bed honey, we'll talk about this tomorrow. Maybe you should skip school. It's only a couple of hours before you have to get up and you need your rest. After all, you ARE pregnant with SOMEONE'S CHILD." The sarcasm in her dad's voice stung terribly. Tears ran down Mary's cheeks as she slowly climbed the stairs.

Joe decided to take the direct route and confront the problem head-on. He closed the door behind him and hung up his coat on the hall tree. He took a deep breath and walked into the den. "Hi dad; up a little late tonight aren't you?" Joe tried to be casual. Abraham was reading a book about architecture. He slowly and deliberately lowered the book and removed his glasses. "I suppose I could say the same thing about you," Abraham whispered. Joe looked at the floor. "Is mom asleep?" Abraham nodded in the direction of the couch in the den. Joe saw Eve curled up with a throw over her. "She took a sleeping pill about two o'clock. She just fell asleep. Is your phone not working?" Joe knew that the question was his dad's way of scolding him for not returning his calls. "It's fine dad. I just didn't want to talk to anyone. I needed to clear my head." "Well?" "Well what, dad?" "Did you get your head clear?" Joe looked his dad straight in the eye. "Yes sir." "Then I assume that you have come to your senses about this whole mess." Joe hesitated. "Uh, I'm not sure what you are talking about." Abraham slowly rose to his feet. His voice, although still in a whisper, was strained and angry. "I am talking about this crazy idea of you taking responsibility for someone else's baby! Joe, I know you love Mary, we all do; but IF you are telling the truth and this baby is not yours, you are ruining your future! I know you have more sense than that." The tick tock of the grandfather clock in the den sounded like thunder in the dead silence that followed. Joe decided that he would try to make his father understand, again. "Dad, I know it sounds crazy. It did to me at first. But it's true. All of it. I am not the biological father of the baby. God is. And I have been given the task and privilege of being the earthly father of the Savior. It's scriptural, dad. Our religion has been looking for the Savior for hundreds of years. He is here and I will do God's will and take care of Him AND Mary." Abraham sat back down in his chair and buried his head in his hands. He couldn't believe what his son was saying. He tried to reason with him. "But what about your future? If you do this, everything changes. How will you get through your senior year as a father? Where do you intend to live? What about college? Joe, you may be giving up everything that you have worked for; for what? Someone else's baby!?" "I already told you, dad." Joe was getting angry. "It is not just someone else's baby. It is...." "Stop right there! Don't you dare blaspheme in this house again." Abraham was almost yelling. Eve stirred on the couch and both men calmed down. "Joe, it's obvious that you have had some kind of emotional break-down. I don't blame you. The girl you love has cheated on you...." Joe rolled his eyes and started to argue. Abraham stopped him before he could start. "Let me finish. You must be in some kind of denial. Perhaps she has convinced you that this crazy story is true. Joe, I love you, more than anything but you are sick. Let me help you get better. Would you do that for me, please?" Abraham's eyes were pleading. Joe glanced at his mother who was sitting up listening to everything. "I assume you are talking about seeing a therapist or something. It won't do any good, but, I love you, both of you. And if it will make you feel better if I do this, so be it. However, I must tell you; I will not change my mind, ever." The grandfather clock struck four times. Joe groaned. "If it's OK, I'd like to go to bed."

"Good night son," Abraham sighed. "Good night sweetie." Eve's voice cracked through some tears. "See you in the morning." Joe headed for the stairs.

Joe woke up to his alarm as soon as his head hit the pillow or so it seemed. He couldn't believe that it was 7 a.m., already. He headed for the shower and heard his phone beep. Someone had sent him a text message. He flipped open his phone to see who it was; Mary. It read, 'Staying home today 2 rest, see u 2 nite, I luv u.' 'Good', Joe thought to himself, 'if she feels anything like I do, she needs to sleep in, after all, she IS pregnant.' Somehow the thought of that made him perk up a bit.

Joe finished getting ready and headed down the stairs. He dreaded the idea of facing his parents this morning. The whole idea of seeing a shrink made him a little angry. But, if that's what it took to keep the peace, he'd do it. Anyway, the experience might be interesting. The kitchen was quiet, no aroma of bacon, pancakes, nothing. As he entered he saw his dad in his usual place, drinking coffee, and reading the newspaper. "Good morning dad, where's mom?" "Good morning Joe; she's still in bed. I'm afraid you'll have to fend for yourself. I've got to shove off to work." Abraham's tone was distant and matter-of-fact. He got up and headed for the door. Joe decided to ignore the chilly atmosphere. "No problem, I'll grab some cereal and toast. Have a good one, dad." Abraham almost got out of the door when Joe spoke up. "Say dad, how did it end up with the Reubenowitz's last night?" Abraham froze in the door. He turned around to face his son, the cool April wind rushed past him. "Well I don't know when you left and what you did or didn't hear. Truthfully, it is kind of a blur. There was a lot of shouting and name-calling. It wasn't pretty. Everyone, including me, lost their temper. Things were said that were extremely hurtful. The last thing I remember was telling Jacob that I would never allow you to take the fall for some 'tramp' who has slept with God-knows-who." Joe cringed at the mental picture that his dad was painting. He couldn't believe that he had called Mary a tramp. "That's when Ruth threw us out and told us never to come back. Your mom obliged with a snide remark about not wanting to associate with trash anyway." Abraham paused, "I guess the only thing we agreed on was that we never wanted to see each other again." Joe sat there speechless. He couldn't believe what he was hearing. "Joe, it's over between us and the Reubenowitz's. We are finished with them. I know this is difficult to hear, but you are a Goldstein. And as long as you live in this house, I expect you to respect our decision. You are not to associate with those people, ever. Do you understand?" Joe started to protest but he could tell by the tone of his father's voice and the look in his eye that there was no point in it. Joe nodded slightly and opened the frig so that he wouldn't have to face his father. "I'll see you tonight, Joe." Abraham closed the door without waiting for a response from Joe. That was a good thing because Joe was so choked up with emotion that he couldn't have responded anyway. The cold air stopped rushing in and Joe heard his dad start his truck and pull out of the driveway.

Mary woke up but kept her eyes closed. She didn't want to wake up because the dream she was having was one of those dreams that you never want to end. She was sitting in a rocking chair holding her baby. They were on the porch of a cabin on a mountain with a breathtaking view. The baby was cooing and smiling. The feeling of elation and total peace engulfed her like a cloud.

After a few minutes of daydreaming, her thoughts turned to the events that took place last night. She decided that it was time to get up and face the day. She was overwhelmed at the amount of things that happened. Gabby, Guardian, Mr. Robinson and all of the 'fireworks' that they saw by the fire was the most spectacular thing she had ever seen. Then there were the 'fireworks' with the parents that also occurred last night. That wasn't so pleasant. She wondered how it all turned out. She was still angry at her father for saying some of those things. Maybe he would calm down and apologize today. She sat on the edge of the bed and looked at the clock; 12:30. She wondered how Joe was getting along at school. He had to be exhausted. She wondered how he would manage baseball practice. Her stomach gurgled and felt queasy. Was there another bout of morning sickness in store for her? She hoped not; that was one thing she didn't like about being pregnant.

She headed down the stairs to see if anyone was home. The house was strangely quiet. It was kind of weird. She assumed that no one was home. She glanced in the living room and saw her mom sitting in a recliner staring up at the ceiling. Ruth looked terrible. Her eyes were sunk into her head and she was very pale. "Are you OK, mom?" Ruth was startled by the sound of Mary's voice. "Oh! I was off in another world. I didn't hear you honey. What did you say?" "Mom, you look awful, are you OK?" "Well, I've been better. It was a rough night. I expect that there will be a lot more. I just can't believe that this is happening. How could you do this to us? And then to add insult to injury, you come up with that lie about being a virgin carrying the Savior!" Mary felt like she was losing her battle with the morning sickness. "I'll be right back." She ran to the bathroom. Ruth could hear her throwing up all the way down the hall and felt terrible about it.

Mary emerged from the bathroom in a few minutes to discover her guilt-riddened mother standing outside the door. "I'm sorry honey," Ruth said as she put her arms around her daughter. "I'm just so confused. My mind has been going faster than a bullet. What will the people at the synagogue say? What about our customers; our neighbors; our relatives!? You have to understand that our family reputation will be permanently damaged! I don't know if I can ever show my face around here again." Mary hugged her mother tightly as she sobbed on Mary's shoulder. Mary actually felt sorry for her mother. She knew that Ruth had always been proud of her family and the respect that they had earned in the community. Not that Ruth ever flaunted it; on the contrary, Ruth was proud, but humble; always giving God the glory for all of their blessings. Now, all of the blessings seemed like distant memories to Ruth. She felt as if she had lost it all.

"I wish you could trust me mom, I am telling you the truth. I know it seems crazy. How do you think I felt when it was first revealed to me? But, it's true, every word." Ruth pulled back from their embrace and looked at Mary; she was smiling. "You poor thing, you must be in denial. The shock of all of this has caused you to go to some kind of surreal world." Ruth had a pathetic look on her face. "You know, I blame Joe for all of this. I know how boys can put pressure on girls these days; and I know how much you love him; and now, after all he has done to you, you are protecting him with this crazy story." Ruth was getting worked up again. "I could just choke him! Honey, you don't need to defend him. We don't need him. We can handle this on our own!'"

Mary couldn't believe her ears. She was trying to be understanding, but, after all; SHE was the one who was pregnant! Mary became indignant. "Mother, I don't WANT TO HANDLE THIS ON MY OWN!" Mary held her fingers up in quotes mocking her mother's statement. "What I WANT is to ENJOY this with Joe; who, by the way is not the earthly father because there IS no earthly father! I AM a virgin! I am not crazy, I have complete control of myself, and I am in total touch with reality. You know, you and daddy have preached to me all my life about the power of God and how He performs miracles every day. Now that He has performed one of His greatest miracles, right in front of your noses, YOU refuse to acknowledge it! I have never lied to you. Joe and I have ALWAYS been good kids; you, daddy, AND the Goldsteins have always said so. But now, when we need you the most, you choose not to believe us; just because it doesn't make sense." Mary's fists were clenched at her sides as she breathed hard glaring at her mother.

Ruth had never seen her like this. She was surprised and angered at the notion that her daughter would defy her in such a manner. Ruth wanted to give Mary a piece of her mind, but she thought better of it. No matter what, Mary was pregnant; and it would do her no good to get any more upset at this time. Ruth bit her tongue. "I can see that you are too upset to discuss this right now. Maybe you should go lie down and rest for awhile." "I don't want to rest!" Mary was beside herself. "I want to clear all of this up right now. Where do you and daddy stand on all of this? Are you with Joe and me or are you against us? What's it going to be? And what about the Goldsteins? How did everything turn out last night? When we left you all were arguing like a bunch of children!" That was all it took. Ruth lost her cool. "Children! Are you kidding me?! It's you and Joe or whoever you slept with, that acted, and are STILL acting like irresponsible kids! So you want to know where we stand? First, it's over between us and the Goldsteins. They said some terrible things to us last night and we don't ever want to see them again. THAT INCLUDES YOU, MISSY!" Ruth was shaking her finger at Mary. "You are NOT to see, talk to or associate with any of them; ESPECIALLY JOE! In addition, your father and I do not believe your silly story and cannot believe that you will not own up to your mistake. Either you have 'flipped out' and can't face reality or you are too 'prissy' to admit a major mistake and take responsibility for your actions. Either way, you are in no condition to raise a child. Your father and I have decided that you will give the baby up for adoption." Sarcasm dripped from Ruth's lips.

Mary was in shock. She couldn't breathe; heart barely beating, eyes wide open, she just stood there. After a few seconds she came to her senses and said a silent prayer: 'Dear God, I don't know what to do. Please help me handle this in the way that You want me to. Amen.' All of a sudden she felt peace cover her like a silk blanket. "Thank you for being honest with me mother. I know it must have been difficult. It's good to know how we stand with you as we enter into this most glorious event. I love you and daddy; and the Goldsteins and I wish that you all would choose to be a part of it, but you haven't. So Joe and I will deal with this on our own. I think I will go rest awhile. You have given me a lot to think about." Mary turned and walked toward the stairs. "Don't you walk away from me!" Ruth yelled. "I told you not to see Joe anymore and I mean it. You are giving that baby up for adoption and that's final! You are still 17 and a minor and you will do as you are told! DO YOU HEAR ME?" By now, Mary had reached the middle of the stairs. She stopped and smiled at her mother. "Yes mother, pregnancy has not affected my hearing. You do not have to yell. You are correct; I am a minor, for now. And as long as I'm in this house, I will attempt to follow your rules, as long as they don't contradict God's rules." Mary continued up the stairs without further comment. At first, Ruth was confused about what Mary meant; but as she thought about it she realized, Joe and Mary were both born in July. They would be 18 and considered to be adults before the baby would be born. Ruth shuddered at what Mary might be thinking.

CHAPTER TWENTY-FIVE

The next few weeks went by relatively uneventful. Mary got over her morning sickness and the pregnancy was rarely discussed. The only mention of it was when Mary had gone to the doctor for a check-up. Jake would grumble something like, "Everything OK?" and Mary would respond, "just fine daddy" and that was it. Ruth never brought it up which hurt Mary's feelings. She had hoped that her mother would calm down and accept the situation, but this hadn't happened. Mary longed to talk to her mom about what she was feeling, baby care, and other mother daughter discussions that normally are associated with these types of intimate celebrations.

The atmosphere at the Goldsteins was equally chilly. Eve rarely left the house and looked horrible. Normally, a pretty woman, she never fixed herself up, and the stress of the situation was taking its toll. She never cooked, the house was a mess, and she spent much of her time curled up on the couch staring out of the window. Abraham immersed himself in his work. He spent all of his daylight hours on the construction sites and in the evenings he was either caring for Eve or working in the den. Joe's attempts at light discussions were met with silence and apathy. Occasionally, Joe would try to bring up Mary, hoping that they would lift the sanction against seeing her. But that was met with a fierce look from his father and sobs from his mother. They viewed that request as a betrayal to the family. Joe was devastated.

School was the only thing that kept Joe and Mary in contact with each other. They were always together; but that wasn't unusual. They soon realized that spending time together was not something to be taken for granted. They learned to cherish the walks between classes, sitting together at lunch, meeting in the library; all of the things that they so easily assumed to be to be a given had evolved into special, cherished events. A lesson they would never forget.

Allen and Angie noticed that Mary and Joe weren't riding to school together and brought it up at the lunch table. The question caught Mary by surprise. She became visibly flustered. They didn't want anyone to know that they weren't allowed to ride together. Joe observed the awkward atmosphere and jumped in to rescue Mary, "Since Mary has finished cheerleading, there is no need for her to wait for a couple of hours while I finish baseball practice." Allen and Angie looked at each other and silently agreed not to pursue the conversation. The 'excuse' didn't hold water because in the past, Mary would either work in the library or go home with Angie until Joe finished. Allen changed the subject. "I've got an idea, why don't we all go out Friday night. There is a great movie playing downtown." Now Joe got nervous. How could they go out on a date? If their parents found out, and they would, it would be a disaster. Mary spoke up, "That sounds like fun, but Friday is out for me. My parents have planned something and I have to go." "How about Saturday night?" Angie offered. "We have a double header Saturday afternoon." Joe was relieved that he had a legitimate excuse. The bell rang and all four of them got up from the table to head for class. "Well, maybe next weekend." Allen was fishing. "Yeah, maybe," Joe replied as he and Mary disappeared into the crowd. Angie looked at Allen. "Is it just me or are they acting kind of strange lately?" "You noticed it too? Something is definitely on their minds. I guess it isn't any of our business." "I know," Angie said as she walked out of the cafeteria. "I'm just worried about them."

The final bell rang and Joe walked Mary out to her car. He had to make it quick because he had to get to practice. "Joe, I don't know how much longer I can take this. Allen and Angie have got to notice that something's going on. Pretty soon, I'm going to start showing. This secret is going to come out sooner or later." Joe held

Mary's hands. "I know, Sugar Plum, but we have to lay low as long as we can. Maybe no one will notice before we are out of school. It's only four weeks before summer vacation. The only thing our parents agreed on was to keep it quiet as long as possible. They made it clear that we are to mention this to no one." "It's not fair, Joe! This is a blessed event. I want to share it with the world! Jews have been looking forward to this moment for thousands of years. They need to know that the time has come!" "Look Mary, I feel the same way, but, this is God's decision, not ours. We need to keep our eyes on what He wants, not what we think is best." Joe glanced at the time. "Mary, I have to get to practice. I'll text you later." He kissed Mary on the cheek and sprinted to the locker room.

Abraham walked into the kitchen and was met with the dead silence that he had experienced every day since the fallout with the Reubenowitzs. He remembered the 'good ol' days' when he was greeted with music playing, Eve singing along and the smell of dinner on the stove. But that was history. He knew Eve was likely lying on the couch in the den. He peaked around the corner and confirmed it; Eve was asleep. Abraham returned to the kitchen, and threw a TV dinner in the oven. While he was waiting, he began looking at the mail. There was a letter addressed to Dream Builders. The return address read, 'Witz Drugs'. Abraham froze for a second as he pondered what Jake was up to. "Oh well, might as well open it," he said out loud to no one. As he scanned the letter a few words and phrases leaped out at him. 'Sorry to inform you but…we're not the lowest bidder….' Abraham turned red with anger. Several months ago, Jake decided to renovate the store and had asked Abraham to do the work. That's the way that they had always done it; no bids, no contracts, just come and do the work and Jake trusted him to be fair. He had never even given Jake a bid! He sat there and burned. He wasn't about to do the work anyway. But the letter was a formal slap in the face.

Just then Joe walked in. "Hi dad." Joe's tone was flat but hopeful. He missed talking to his dad. "How's it going?" Abraham ignored the question. "Where have you been? Practice is usually over at 6 p.m. It's almost 7:00." "I stopped to get a burger. I'm getting a little tired of TV dinners." Joe grinned as the timer on the oven went off. He hoped that the attempt at levity would change the mood. "I'm sorry that the cuisine in this house doesn't meet your expectations." Abraham snarled. "Whoa!" Joe held his hands up as if to signify take it easy. "I was just kidding. I know mom is sick and that you have been working hard lately. I'm fine with what we have to eat." "You had better be satisfied with the way things have turned out." Abraham was really red in the face now. "After all, you ARE the reason for the conditions around here. Your mother is sick because of YOU!" Joe cringed at the words that were coming from his father. "I don't even know why you are still playing baseball. It's not like you have a career any longer. If you persist in taking care of that child, baseball is a thing of the past. You should be looking to get a job so that you can support your family!"

Joe swallowed hard. He held back the emotions that were inside and yearning to come out. He had mixed feelings of guilt, sorrow, and anger. He wanted to argue with his dad, but thought better of it. He tried to change the subject. "Speaking of work, school will be out soon and I am looking forward to working with you again this summer. What kind of projects do you have planned for me?" Abraham put his head in his hands. "Work is really slow, I'm not sure I have a position for you." Joe knew this wasn't true. He had witnessed his father tell his mother just a few weeks ago that he was expecting a record year. Joe decided to challenge his father. "I thought I heard you tell mom that things were going great a few weeks ago." Abraham didn't respond. He merely shoved the letter from Jake in Joe's direction. Joe picked up the paper and read it slowly. When he finished he looked at his dad and said, "OK this is one job I know for a fact that you have at least 20 projects going. What is it really?" Joe knew the answer but he wanted to see if his father would actually say it. Abraham confirmed Joe's suspicion. "Fact is Joe, I really don't want you on the crews this summer. Mary is going to start showing soon and, frankly, Dream Builders has a reputation to maintain. How do you think it is going to affect our testimony if the owner's son has become such a moral loser?" Joe's jaw dropped. "That's right Joe I just don't think I can stand to work with you. You are an embarrassment to this family and Dream Builders." Joe couldn't hold back his emotions any longer. "OK dad, have it your way. I have tried very hard to get along for the past couple of weeks; but it is now obvious that you do not want to have a relationship with me. I'm done. You and mom figure out when you want me to leave and I'll go. I certainly don't want my convictions to get in the way of our precious family reputation!" Sarcasm oozed from Joe's lips. Joe walked out of the kitchen ignoring his dad's command to stay right where he was. Joe took the stairs three at a time and slammed his door shut before Abraham could get out of the kitchen.

He sat down on the edge of the bed. Emotionally drained and physically sick, he felt like he was going to throw up. He flopped across the bed and closed his eyes. "Lord, I know that you are in the middle of this and I know that you have a reason for what's happening. I turn it all over to you. I don't know what to do. Please give Mary and I guidance and perseverance. Amen." He sat there with his eyes closed. He pondered his dad's words. They cut him like a knife. If his own parents didn't believe him, how could he expect anyone else to? He concluded that it was going to be him, Mary, and God. No one else would believe them. The thoughts of facing the ridicule alone bothered him. He worried about Mary. There would be no amount of explanations that would satisfy anyone. The persecution would be relentless. Maybe he should quit the team and get a job. But that would draw too much attention and questions. His mind whirled.

His phone beeped with a message. It was Mary. 'Can we talk?' Mary was hoping that Joe was in his room by now. They would talk on the phone whenever they could. He called. "Hi Sugar Plum." He tried to be 'normal' but Mary saw right through it. "What's wrong, Joe." "Aw, nothing really." Joe tried to play it off but Mary wouldn't have it. "Joe, don't play with me. Tell me what's going on." Joe relented. "Dad and I got into an argument a little while ago...." Joe recounted the events that had just taken place in the kitchen. After he finished the phone was silent. "Are you still there, Mary?" "Yes, I'm still here. I'm sorry, Joe. That must have been hard." "It was difficult. But at least now we know where we stand. Hoping that our parents would come to their senses seems impossible. So I guess it's you, me and God." Joe's tone was despondent. Mary tried to cheer him up. "We also have Gabby and Guardian on our side." Joe laughed a little. "I guess we do."

CHAPTER
TWENTY-SIX

It was the last week of school and Mary had managed to keep her secret. It was getting a little tougher as the weather got warmer. When it was cold, she could cover her expanding stomach with layers of baggy sweaters. But now the weather was getting warmer and the girls were wearing shorts and T-shirts. Her shorts didn't fit any longer and the selection of baggy blouses in her closet was limited. She looked at herself in the mirror each morning to ensure that everything was covered. She was going to need maternity clothes soon. Ruth had promised to take her shopping for clothes over at Helena, but they hadn't gotten around to it. Helena was two hundred miles from Pleasantville and that was where Ruth had insisted on shopping for maternity clothes. She refused to shop locally. That would be too humiliating.

Mary walked into the school and was immediately met by Joe who had been talking with Allen and Angie. The four of them chatted about plans for the summer. Joe and Mary were noticeably non-specific about their plans. The bell rang and the kids started off to class. "What are our plans for the summer, Joe?" "I'm not sure. I need to find a job and we need to get set up, somehow, to take care of this baby." "I don't know how long this secret will last. I'm putting on weight and my belly is getting bigger every day." "I know, Mary. But we have four days left. Maybe we can make it through the week."

The bell rang and it was finally time for lunch. It was none too early for Mary. She was starving. Joe had to go to a brief baseball meeting. He was going to catch up with Mary in a few minutes. As Mary was going through the line selecting, she heard Jimmy's voice down the line from her. "Hey, Mary! Save a little for the rest of us. You already have enough junk in your trunk." Mary ignored the insult and kept her cool until she sat down at the table with Angie and Allen. Then the tears came. "What's wrong, Mary?" Angie put her hand on Mary's shoulder. "It's just Jimmy. He was just saying some awfully mean things in line." "He is such a jerk." Allen stated with confidence. "What did he say?" Angie continued. "He was just making fun of how much food I had on my tray and he made some comment about my weight." Allen looked at Angie who shook her head ever so slightly. They both had noticed Mary had been eating more than normal and that she was putting on weight; however, they were never going to say anything; that would be just plain mean.

Joe walked up carrying his tray. He sat down and noticed that Mary had been crying. He looked at Allen with questions in his eyes. "It's just that idiot, Jimmy. He was making rude comments about Mary." Allen related the story to Joe. After Allen finished, Joe deliberately got up from his chair and looked around. He spotted Jimmy a few tables over. He slowly strode over to Jimmy who was laughing at some dirty joke that had just been told at his table. He didn't see Joe coming and wasn't aware of him until Joe whispered in his ear. "Rumor has it that you were making fun of my girlfriend." Jimmy froze at first but his cockiness returned in a few seconds. "Oh you mean, Shamu over there. I was just pointing out that she had put on a few tons. That's good for you, Joe, I'm no longer interested in her. You have no competition, now." The rest of the guys at the table busted out laughing. Joe lost his cool. He grabbed Jimmy's chair and pulled it out so quickly that Jimmy landed on the floor. This made the boys laugh even harder. Joe picked Jimmy up by the back of his shirt and spun him around. Joe towered over Jimmy. Joe took hold of the front of Jimmy's shirt with one hand and lifted him a few inches off the ground. Joe's other hand was clenched in a fist. The grin on Jimmy's face disappeared immediately. "Wait a minute, Joe," Jimmy pleaded. "There's no need for violence. I was just teasing. Put me down and we'll talk it through." "I've got nothing to say to you, maggot. I'm going give you the beating that you have been asking for. This is going to be great. This is for everyone you've offended." Joe drew back his fist and Jimmy closed his eyes not wanting to see what was going to happen to him. Joe felt a hand on his arm just as he was starting to take the first swing. "What's going on here?" Joe recognized the voice. It was his baseball coach. By now, Allen had joined his friend in order to back him up if this turned into some sort of brawl. "I saw the whole thing, sir. Jimmy fell out of his chair and Joe was just helping him up." Allen blurted it out. No one believed it, especially the coach. Joe lowered Jimmy to the floor and looked him square in the eye. Nobody wanted to admit a fight. Jimmy was already on probation and this would get him kicked out of school. Joe and Coach didn't want it because Joe would be suspended from the team for four games if he was caught fighting. Coach looked at Jimmy. "Is that what happened?" "Yes sir." "OK then, everyone back to your lunch. Nothing to see here. Joe can I see you for a minute?"

Joe followed Coach into the hall. No one was around. "Joe! What are you thinking?" A fight? In the middle of the cafeteria? With a kid like him?" "Sorry Coach; I just lost my cool. He is a real piece of work." "That's right Joe; he is a piece of work. But guess what. There are a million others just like him. Do you plan to beat up every one of them?" Joe looked down and said, "No sir." "Son, you are going to face many challenges as you get older. You can't allow the scum of the earth to bring you down. It is only harmful to you. You must rise above that level and fulfill your destiny."

The word 'destiny' rang in his ears. Coach was right. His destiny was not to get caught up in the insignificant things of this world. His destiny is to be the earthly father of the Savior! His thoughts were interrupted by Coach. "Are you listening to me? Joe, do you understand?" Joe nodded. "Good, now get back to lunch. You are going to need it for tonight's practice." Coach grinned fiendishly. Joe knew what that meant; practice was going to be brutal. "Aw, Coach; really? Sectionals start in a couple of days." Exactly!" Coach slapped him on the back as he headed down the hall. "That's why we need to be in shape!"

Joe rejoined the kids at his table and finished eating. Mary looked at the clock on the wall; five minutes before the bell would ring. "I'm going to powder my nose." Mary stood up. "I'll go with you." Angie volunteered. Joe looked at Allen. "I don't suppose the male species will ever figure out why girls have to go to the restroom in pairs." Both guys laughed as they took the lunch trays and placed them on the conveyor.

Both girls were touching up their lipstick when Mary asked, "Angie, do you think I'm fat?" Mary knew that her best friend wouldn't lie to her. Angie paused, "I have noticed a little weight gain here and there recently, but you are definitely not fat. I just figured you might be going through a stage or something. After all, we are still teenagers. I fluctuate all of the time. You look fine. You'll take it off over the summer. After all, it isn't like you are pregnant or anything!" Angie laughed at her own joke and Mary smiled politely and thought to herself, 'If you only knew.'

Friday afternoon came and everyone was glad to be out of school for the summer; that is, everyone but Mary and Joe. School had been the only way that they had been able to see each other. Now, it was going to be more difficult. They slowly walked out of the school and headed for their cars. Joe opened the door to Mary's car to let her in. Before he closed the door Mary asked him to get in. Joe obliged and got in on the passenger side. "What now?" Mary's question was straight to the point. Joe scratched his head, "I'm not sure, do you have any ideas?" "No, not really. I just know that I can't go through the summer without being able to see you." "I feel the same way, Sugar Plum; however, I do know that we are doing the right thing and that God is on our side. He will get us through somehow. I do know that I need to find a job; dad doesn't want me working for him this summer and I am going to have a family to care for in a few short months. In fact, we have a lot of decisions to make." Joe's face expressed concern. "Like when are we going to get married? What about college? Where will we live? 'Teens for Abstinence'? How will I provide for my family and remain in school? What about my scholarship? How can you go to school AND care for a baby?" Joe was beginning to panic. "Calm down Joe, it will be alright. Let's attack this one step at a time." "But Mary, we need a plan and we need to be able to spend some time figuring it all out; and that will be difficult considering that our parents refuse to let us be together." Mary started to reassure Joe that things were going to work out OK, but she was interrupted by a knock on the window. It was Allen. Joe rolled down the window. "I'm glad I caught you. We are having a party at Angie's house tonight to celebrate the end of school. Can you guys come?" Joe grinned at Mary who returned the smile. They both knew what the other was thinking. "Well, I have a game tonight, but I could stop by after. How about you, Mary?" "I would like to go to the game, but it is supposed to rain. Do you care if I meet you at Angie's?" "I think that is a great idea." "Good, I'll see you both tonight." Allen waved as he jogged to his car. "God sure worked that one out didn't He? I told you that it would be alright, didn't I?" Mary teased Joe. "Oh great," Joe said dramatically. "We aren't even married yet and you are already giving me the 'I told you so' speech." Mary punched him in the shoulder as he got out of the car. "Ow! I think that may be considered spousal abuse." Joe faked pain and grabbed his shoulder. "That's right mister, and don't you forget it," Mary teased. "I'll see you tonight, Sugar Plum." Joe shut the door and walked around the front of Mary's car. Just as he passed in front of the car, Mary laid down on the horn. Joe nearly jumped out of his skin. Mary rolled down the window and said, "Hey, you forgot something." "Oh yeah, what?" Mary laughed and pointed to her lips. "Oh, THAT!" Joe walked up to Mary's window and planted one on her. "That's better." Mary acted as if she was scolding a three year old. "Just don't let it happen again." "No ma'am." Joe flashed his signature grin.

"I love you, Sugar Plum." I love you too, Joe." Mary put her car in drive and headed home. It was good to see Joe's smile again. She hadn't seen it for awhile.

While Mary was waiting for traffic to clear so she could pull out of the parking lot, she noticed a little red sports car coming down the road. The top was down and there were two people in it. Just as they passed in front of Mary, both the driver and the passenger were waving enthusiastically in Mary's direction. Mary chuckled to herself as she recognized that it was Gabby and Guardian. She sat there for a few seconds remembering God's promise to look after them. He was the one who 'arranged' the party at Angie's. He was the one who was going to ensure that every little detail would work out. All it would take is faith. Her thoughts were interrupted when her cell phone rang. "Did you see that?" Joe was astonished. Mary looked in her rear view mirror and saw that Joe was right behind her. "See what?" Mary said shyly. "That red sports car that just went by; Gabby and Guardian were in it!" "Oh yeah, that." Mary was being coy. "Yes, I saw them. Didn't you see them waving at me? Why are you surprised to see them? They did say that they would be watching over us. "Yeah I know," Joe admitted. "I just didn't think that angels could drive!" Mary laughed. "See you tonight." She closed the phone and pulled out on the road.

Joe entered Angie's house to the sounds of gasps and 'oh no's'. He wasn't walking normally; he was on crutches. Mary, who was in the kitchen at the time helping Angie with snacks, peeked around the corner to see what the commotion was all about. When she spotted Joe, she pushed her way through the crowd that had gathered around him. "What happened?" She asked as she clung to his arm. "Well," Joe sat down on the couch, "We were winning 5-0 in the bottom of the 5th inning. I had a no-hitter going. I was fortunate that my curve ball was working well. I hit one down the right field line and rounded second on my way to third. On any other occasion, it would have been a stand-up triple, but the field was muddy from the rain and it caused everyone to run slower. Anyway, Coach gave me the sign to slide. As I slid into the base, I got my spikes too low and my left one got stuck in the mud causing my ankle to roll. Coach took me out of the game." "Are you OK?" One of the kids asked. Joe hesitated. "Uh, I'm fine, nothing broken, just a sprain." "Did we win?" Allen inquired. "No," Joe answered flatly. "They beat us 6-5." Several of the kids groaned. This was not supposed to happen. All of the sports writers had picked them the favorite to win the state championship. "Let me see your ankle." Mary demanded. She knelt down and gently removed the sock and the bag of water that once was ice. As soon as the ankle was exposed, a couple of the girls gasped. Mary put her hand over her mouth so that she wouldn't say anything. There was so much swelling you couldn't see the ankle bone. It looked like Joe had a grapefruit under his skin. It was black and blue halfway up his calf all the way down to his toes. "Can I get you anything?" Angie offered. "A bag of ice would be deeply appreciated." "Mom is already on it." Angie's mother emerged from the kitchen with an ice pack. "Thanks." Joe turned red. He didn't like being the center of attention. He didn't want the fact that they lost or his injury for that matter to put a damper on the party. He looked at Allen for help. Allen read his mind. "Hey everybody, this ain't no freak show. We all seen this nerd banged up before. We are here to party!!" Allen turned the music up loud and the party resumed. Joe gave Allen a 'thumbs up' which Allen acknowledged with a slight nod.

As soon as the focus was off Joe, Mary settled in next to him. "I guess we won't be dancing tonight." Mary mused. "Well, you can, but I'll have to sit this one out." Joe laughed which caused him to wince with pain. "How bad does it hurt?" "To be honest, it hurts pretty bad. I can't put any weight on it and it throbs every time my heart beats." Joe's answer caused Mary to be concerned. Being an athlete, Joe had experienced his share of bangs and bruises; in fact this isn't the first time she had seen him on crutches. However, it WAS the first time that he had ever admitted that it hurt. His usual answers were, 'it's not bad' or 'no big deal' or any comment to play it down. "So that comment you made earlier, 'it's just a sprain' was a bunch of bologna?" "Yep, pretty much." "Do you know for sure that it's not broken?" "No, not for sure." Joe couldn't look at Mary. He felt her stare; it seemed to pierce his brain. The silence was awkward; just like Mary wanted it to be. After a very long minute or maybe two, Joe finally said, "What?" "You know what, Mr. Goldstein." Mary was using her scolding voice. "Why are you here instead of the emergency room?" Joe mustered up the courage to look at Mary. Her coal black eyes were blazing holes into him. Joe stammered, "I, uh, uh, we, uh, really just me: it's like this, the trainer wanted me to go to the ER and Coach agreed. They think that it is probably more than a sprain. But I, uh, felt like, I mean decided that I...." "That you WHAT!?" Mary's nose was just inches away from Joe's. "Mary, I just wanted to be with you tonight. We won't get many chances to be alone and I didn't want to miss this one. I have an x-ray and an MRI scheduled for tomorrow. OK? Please don't be angry." Mary's glare turned to tears. She felt bad for getting angry at Joe. All he wanted to do was be with her. "I'm sorry, Joe. I just know how you are. I love you and hate to see you in pain." Joe put his arm around Mary. "No problem, Sugar Plum, no problem."

After about 15 minutes of watching the party and chatting with some of the other kids, Joe suggested that they go out on the porch. "Good idea," Mary replied. She helped him to his feet and they quietly slipped out of the living room, through the kitchen, and out to the porch. It was kind of chilly, but there was no wind and the stars were shining brilliantly in the Montana sky. They sat down in the swing and enjoyed the peacefulness of the evening. Both kids knew what was coming; they had to discuss the future, their plans, all of the things that were brought up earlier in the day. However, neither of them wanted to change the mood.

Finally, Joe spoke up. "Where do you want to start?" "I don't know," Mary sighed. "How about a wedding date?" "I've been thinking about that. You know the scriptures say that the Savior will be born of a virgin; that's you by the way." "Very funny." "So I think we should make it very clear that you remain a virgin until the baby is born. Therefore, we don't get married until January." "I'm not sure I like the idea of being an unwed mother. It's going to be bad enough having everyone think that it's a shotgun wedding as it is." "I know it will be hard but we have to think of God first. What newlywed couple doesn't have sex?" Mary thought for a moment. "You are right, Joe," Mary lamented. "We'll wait. What's next?"

Joe looked up at the stars. "Where are we going to live and how will we pay for it?" "What do you mean?" Mary was confused. "I don't know what's been said at your house but my dad has made it clear that 'Since I've decided to enjoy the pleasures of a married man, I must accept the responsibilities of a married man.'" Joe held up his fingers in quotes to imitate his dad. "That means no help, including financial help." Mary's face showed concern. "My parents have given me an ultimatum. They will help me as long as I give up the baby and never see you again." Mary's statement made Joe cringe. "I guess we could stay at home until the baby is born and then move into an apartment or something," Mary offered. "IF my parents don't throw me out of the house first." Joe reminded Mary of how angry his father was. "That would also mean that you would have to lie to your parents about giving up the baby." That statement bothered Mary. She had never lied to her parents before. "Joe, this is getting too complicated. I think we need to make a plan and present it to our parents and see how they react." "Oh no!!" Joe groaned. "Got a better idea?" "No." "How about this?" Mary was thinking and talking at the same time. "Let's stay at our homes until the baby is born. Then we will get married and move into a place of our own." "Assuming that our parents would agree to this, which I doubt, what do we do for money?" Joe was being practical.

"You know, food, gas, utilities, diapers, furnishings, car insurance, medical bills...the list is endless." Mary frowned. "I wasn't thinking about all of that other stuff. Could we get by on our savings for a couple of months?" "Two, maybe three at the most; assuming that everything goes smoothly. I know, I'll skip sports next year and get a job after school. Maybe that will be enough to support us until we graduate." Joe tried not to be too pessimistic. Mary looked dejected at the thought of Joe giving up sports. Joe continued. "How are we going to go to school and look after the baby? Daycare?" "I don't want anyone raising my baby but me!" Mary was emphatic. "I'll just quit school and get my GED."

The two of them sat in silence for a few minutes. They were realizing the ramifications of everything they had just said. Mary spoke first. "What about 'Teens for Abstinence'?" Joe put his face in his hands. "This is getting overwhelming. I don't know what to do." After a couple of seconds, they simultaneously looked at each other and smiled. "Pray!" they both said at the same time. Joe took Mary's hands. "Dear Father in Heaven, we feel blessed that You have given us this opportunity to do Your work. We accept this commission with great humility and ask that You take all of our burdens from us. Please guide and strengthen us and give us the wisdom to make good decisions. Please give us peace and protect us from evil. Amen."

Right after Joe closed the prayer, a gentle breeze enveloped them like a blanket. It was cool enough to make Mary shudder and snuggle closer to Joe. He put his arm around her and squeezed her tightly. "I feel better already," Mary whispered. "Me too," Joe responded. As they looked out into the darkness, both of them saw shadows moving among the trees. "Did you see that?" Joe pointed in the direction of the woods. "Yes." Mary, who was just a little bit frightened, moved in closer to Joe. He couldn't tell if it was dust or maybe leaves or someone moving around. In an instant, the breeze died down and the shadowy figures became apparent. "It's Gabby and Guardian!" Joe leaped to his feet and waved. He had forgotten about the pain in his ankle. He yelped when he put his weight on it. Mary could see them now and waving and smiling, motioned for them to come over. Gabby waved back and Guardian gave them a 'thumbs up'. Then, as quickly as they had appeared, they were gone.

The kids sat back down in the swing. "I guess they wanted us to know that putting this in God's hands is a good idea," Joe observed.

"I agree," Mary added. "We must remember that in the future. I know this is going to be rough, but He will see us through, IF we allow Him to do so."

Just as Mary finished her sentence, Joe's cell phone rang. 'Unknown caller' showed up on the screen. Joe shrugged, looked at Mary, and opened the phone. "Hello?" "Hello?" The voice on the other end of the phone replied. "Is that you, Abraham?" Joe hesitated, "Uh, no, this is Joe Goldstein, I'm Abraham's son." "Oh, hi Joe!" The voice on the other end of the line sounded familiar. "It's Jack Robinson, you know, from the bonfire the other night." Joe smiled. He was always getting some of his dad's calls. Their telephone numbers were similar. "Hi Mr. Robinson, let me give you dad's number. It's…." "I know your dad's number, I must have misdialed. Say, maybe you can help me." "I'll certainly try." "Well, I was calling your dad to see if he knew of anyone looking for some work. I know he gets applications all the time. You see, I fell off of my tractor and broke my arm. I need some help around here until it heals up. The doctor says it should be fine in two or three months. Are any of your buddies looking for long hours, hard work, and a decent wage?"

Joe looked at Mary who had heard the entire conversation. She smiled and nodded. "Well, Mr. Robinson, it just so happens that I am looking for a summer job. I would be glad to help if you think I can." "You? Joe! Are you kidding me? I'd love to have you around here this summer! I just figured that you would be working for Abraham." The statement caught Joe off-guard. "Well not this summer, Mr. Robinson." Joe looked at his ankle. "I do need to tell you that I messed my ankle up in the game tonight. I'm on crutches." Joe braced himself for the 'I'm sorry' that he assumed Mr. Robinson would say. After all, he needed someone to do physical labor. Mr. Robinson paused a few seconds. "How bad?" "I don't know for sure, I'll find out tomorrow." "Can you get up into a tractor?" "I think so?" Joe was getting hopeful. "Do you know of anyone else looking for a job? I could really use two." Joe immediately thought of Allen. He had mentioned that he hadn't found work yet. "Yes sir, I do." Joe was getting excited. "Mary, go get Allen please." Mary, having overheard the conversation was already heading for the door. Joe spoke into the receiver. "My friend Allen is looking for work. He is here with us. Would you like to talk to him?" Just then Mary appeared with Allen in tow. "It's not necessary," Mr. Robinson replied. "If he meets your standards, I'm sure that he'll be fine. I just need to be sure that I have two guys. If your buddy is ready to do all of the hard work while you recover, that's all I need. You can operate the equipment and he can be the ground man." "I'm sure that won't be a problem, Mr. Robinson." Allen came over to Joe. "What's up?" "How would you like to work for Mr. Robinson this summer?" "You mean up on the ranch? Don't tease me, Joe. I'd love too." Mr. Robinson laughed into the phone. "It's seven days a week, 12 to 14 hours a day. My wife will feed you and you can stay in the bunkhouse if you like. That way you don't have to drive two hours a day getting here and back home. Is that OK with you two?" "That's great!" Allen yelled. "Sounds like we are all set, Joe. When can you two start?" Allen heard the question. "We'll be there in an hour!" "Tomorrow morning will be just fine," Mr. Robinson chuckled. "See you in the morning, good night boys!" "Good night Mr. Robinson," Joe replied. "One more thing, Mr. Robinson, I have a appointment to get my ankle checked in the morning. Is it OK if we come after that?" "No problem," the voice on the other end replied. Joe continued. "And thanks a lot. You are a Godsend." "That's funny; I was thinking the same thing about you boys!"

Joe hung up the phone and grinned at Allen. "Looks like we are going to see a lot of each other this summer," Joe observed. "Yeah, and we can stay in the bunkhouse or come home to see our ladies whenever we want!" "That better be quite often." Angie appeared from the door and had heard the conversation. She hugged Allen and Mary sat down next to Joe. "You do know that God was in the middle of all of this, don't you Joe?" "You bet I do." Joe leaned back into the swing. Angie spoke up. "Let's go inside. I'm getting cold." Allen and Angie headed for the door. "You guys coming?" Allen said over his shoulder. "We'll be in shortly," Joe answered. "The cool air feels good on my ankle."

"Well, you are set for the summer, Joe, Mary said quietly. I wonder what the Lord has in store for me. I'm not looking forward to being here when you will be gone so much." "I don't like it either, Mary." Mary was smiling but had tears in her eyes. "I hope that you can make it home once in awhile." Joe kissed her on the cheek. "Wild horses couldn't keep me away."

Mary's phone rang. She looked at the caller ID, "It's Aunt Liz." Mary sounded excited. "Hi Aunt Liz! How are you doing?" "I'm fine sweetie. I was just sitting here thinking about you and it occurred to me that I haven't seen you in a long time. I just feel the need to spend some time with you. I know it sounds silly. But I can't get you off of my mind." I miss you, too, Aunt Liz. Why don't you and Uncle Zac come down for a visit?" "Oh honey, I wish we could, but Zac is busy with the farm right now and we can't get away. However, I was thinking that maybe you could come up here and visit if you are not too busy." Mary held her breath. "I'd love too, Aunt Liz!" "Great!" Liz giggled like a school girl. "My belly is getting too big to get much done and I could use a little help. How long can you stay?" "How long do you need me?" "For as long as you like, Mary. You can stay all summer if you want." Mary laughed with excitement. "How about if I head up there Monday and we can figure the rest out when I get there?" "Sounds good to me. See you Monday, thanks Mary. You don't know how much this means to me," Mary smiled into the phone. "You don't realize what this means to me. Bye."

Mary hung up the phone. She knew that God had set this up so that she and Joe could get out of town for awhile and she was grateful. However, it also meant that seeing Joe would be more difficult. "What's going on?" Joe's words interrupted her thoughts. "I'm going to go visit Aunt Liz. I leave on Monday." "How long will you be staying?" "I don't know for sure, maybe all summer." Mary lamented. "That's good news, Mary! Why are you so glum?" "Don't get me wrong, Joe; I am happy to be getting out of here for the summer. I wasn't looking forward to being around for all of the ridicule and teasing that I would be getting once I start showing. But I am NOT happy about being three hours away from you all summer." Joe's expression indicated sadness, but soon he perked up. "It is three hours from HERE," he said happily. "It is only two hours from Mr. Robinson's place. "I'm sure that I can work something out with Allen and Mr. Robinson for a day away now and then. Allen can cover for me and I'll cover for him when he wants to come home to visit with Angie. It actually might be easier! Don't you see God is working on all of our problems? We just have to remain faithful." Mary's concern faded into peacefulness as she laid her head on Joe's shoulder.

"What about my 'Teens for Abstinence' rally in July? There's no way that I won't be showing by then." Joe thought for a second. "Listen Mary, do you think that Gary and Karen can handle it without you?" "I suppose so," Mary replied tentatively. "Then let them do it. Just call them and your contacts in Washington and tell them that you can't go. Tell them the truth; there are some things that you must personally address." "I don't know, Jim, you know, the president's aide isn't the type of guy that you just blow off." Mary got worried again. "I know it will be difficult." Joe was trying to be encouraging. "But we have God on our side. If they will let you off for this one conference, we are in the clear until school starts. Why don't you give Gary and Karen a call?" Mary got quiet. Joe could feel her brain go into overdrive. "So I guess this is it for 'Teens for Abstinence'," Mary said sadly. "What do you mean?" Joe questioned. "What I mean is that I'm done, finished, it's over. I will never be a part of it again." What makes you say that Sugar Plum?" "There is no way that they will let me be in charge of it any longer. Once they find out that I'm pregnant, they will remove me immediately. July was the one and only event for the summer. Once school starts, I will be obviously pregnant. How would that look; a pregnant girl challenging teens to abstain?" Joe knew how much this organization had meant to her. She really felt like it had been her calling. Joe hated to see Mary in such anguish. "What if we tell them the truth?" he offered as a weak idea. "Yeah right," Mary mocked. "Our own parents don't believe us, let alone thousands of kids, AND JIM! Face it Joe, it's over." "I'm sorry Mary; I wish it could have turned out differently." They sat there in the swing for a couple of minutes neither one of them saying anything. Mary was thinking and Joe was praying for her.

All of a sudden, Mary jumped up with a big grin on her face. "What's the matter with me? I'm giving birth to the Savior! Nothing compares to that! 'Teens for Abstinence' can find a new spokesperson. I'm going to call Karen and Gary right now and get them thinking about running the July event. I'll deal with Jim later. He is intimidating, even scary at times, and sometimes I get a weird feeling around him, something kind of evil; but I'll deal with him." "That's my girl!" Joe said as he struggled to his feet to give Mary a hug. "I'm going to go get some more ice for my ankle. Make the call and I'll be right back." Mary was already dialing.

In a few minutes, Joe returned carrying a bag of ice. Mary was standing in the yard talking on the phone. Joe overheard Mary's end of the conversation. "So you're sure that you guys can handle it? Great. I really appreciate this. Thanks guys, goodbye." Mary bounded up the stairs to Joe. "No problems with Karen and Gary. I'll have to spend some time on the phone with them, coaching them along, but they both are sure that they can do it. They did ask what was up but I avoided the question. We are in the clear until school starts." Joe sat down relieved. As he struggled with the ice Mary bent down to help him position it. "I guess this is our last night together for awhile." Mary groaned but kept her focus on Joe's ankle. "I guess it is," Joe agreed. "But we can do this. It won't be that long. God will help us through it." Mary finished with the ice and sat down next to Joe. He put his arm around her and she leaned into his chest. "I know, Joe, I know."

CHAPTER TWENTY-SEVEN

Allen knocked on the door at Joe's house at 6:30 in the morning. He didn't wait for an answer, he never did. He always just knocked and went on in. As he walked inside he heard Abraham say, 'Good! I won't have to look at you this summer. Maybe your mom won't be so embarrassed if you aren't around.' Obviously, they hadn't heard Allen's knock. He cleared his throat. "Allen? Is that you?" Joe's voice came from the kitchen. "Yeah buddy, it's me. Are you ready to go to work?" Joe emerged from the kitchen and crutched his way over to Allen. "Hey, man, would you mind waiting in the car for a few minutes. We are in the middle of something here." "So I heard. No problem I'll be in the car. Take your time." Joe returned to the kitchen. Abraham was glaring at him and Eve was crying. "I'm sorry this came up so suddenly. But after you said that I couldn't work for you, I had to find something else. After all, I'm going to have a family soon." Abraham cringed and Eve sobbed louder. "I guess you had better get going then." Abraham snorted as he stared at the microwave. "Will you be coming home at all?" Eve pleaded. "I don't know, mom, right now I don't feel welcome. Give me a call if you want to see me. I guess I'd better get going. He walked over to Eve and hugged her. As he released her he started toward his dad to give him a hug. Abraham held up his hand as if to say 'no' and Joe obliged. "Goodbye dad, I hope you can get over this someday." Joe turned and made his way out of the kitchen. He grabbed his suitcase and headed for the door. Eve cried as she heard the door close.

Joe got into Allen's car. He was visibly upset. "Is everything OK?" Allen read Joe's expression. "No, not really; my parents aren't very happy with me right now." "Want to talk about it?" Joe looked over at his friend. Allen had always been his best friend, that is, except for Mary. He could tell when Joe was upset. Joe smiled, "No, I don't want to talk about it. It's a bummer and I don't want to bring us down. My parents and I had a disagreement and for the first time in my life, they are wrong. They will just have to get over it. What I do want to do is listen to some music and spend the summer working with my best friend." "Well it just so happens that you ARE working with your best friend and I do have music." Allen flashed a CD in front of Joe who immediately recognized it. They had put this CD together as freshmen. It had all of their favorite songs on it. Joe laughed. "We are going to have a great summer." "You can count on that, buddy." They high-fived each other and pulled away, music blaring.

Mary woke up around 10 a.m. She had slept soundly for the first time in a week. She stretched as she looked out at the sunshine. It was going to be a good day. Then it hit her, Joe was gone. She felt all alone. She decided to go downstairs and visit with her mom. Ruth usually stayed home on Saturday mornings so that she and Mary could have some girl time together. "Mom? Are you home? Is anybody here?" Her question was met with silence. She stumbled into the kitchen and found a note. It simply read, 'At the drugstore'. She sat down at the table. 'So this was how it was going to be,' she thought to herself. 'I can handle this. If my parents don't agreed with me and my life choices, then fine. They have their right to be wrong.' Mary was gaining confidence in herself. She knew that she was standing up for the Lord. Nothing was going to stop her. She decided to call Joe.

Joe flipped open his phone, "Hi Sugar Plum!" "Good morning, sweetie!" Mary's voice almost sang with enthusiasm. "Sounds like you're in a good mood," Joe observed. "I AM in a good mood. I am carrying the Savior, I am engaged to the greatest guy on earth, and I am feeling very confident." "That's my girl." Joe reassured her. "By the way, Joe, are you out of your appointment yet? What did they say?" "I just got out and we are on our way to the ranch. Good news, my ankle is not broken. I have some torn ligaments and tendons and a pretty bad sprain, but I'm going to be OK. When I told them what I was going to be doing this summer, they decided to put me in a walking cast so that I won't do any further damage. The cast comes off in three weeks." "That's great, Joe. What did your parents say about your new job?" Joe paused for a moment. He didn't want to upset Mary, but he didn't want to lie to her either. "Well, they are happy that I'm not going to be around. At least dad is, I'm not sure about mom. All she did was cry." "I'm sorry Joe; I know that had to be rough." Mary felt bad for Joe. He had always idolized his father and now, this? "I'm OK with it. I mean it would be nice if they were on board, but, they aren't. So we will continue to do God's work and they can worry about themselves. How about your parents? Have you told them that you are going to Aunt Liz's for the summer?" I haven't seen them yet. They were in bed when I got home and they both went to the store before I got up. I plan to break it to them tonight. I suppose they will be OK with it but who knows. However, I have decided to take the same approach as you regarding all of this. I have been called by God to do a specific work. And NOBODY IS GOING TO STOP ME!" "Good for you, Mary. Well, we are just pulling into the Robinson's driveway. I'll call you tonight. I love you." "I love you too, Joe."

Mary spent much of the morning talking to Gary and Karen about the July event. After lunch, she decided to take a walk. Just as she got to the end of their sidewalk Abraham came out of his garage. Mary froze. She didn't know what to do. There she was thirty feet from a man that she had called 'dad' all of her life. Abraham looked at her as if she were the devil. Their eyes met and Mary started to say hello but Abraham turned around and walked back into the garage. Mary's eyes welled up but she threw her shoulders back and headed down the street. NO ONE was going to kill her spirit. She was on a mission.

Mary was tired by the time she got back so she turned on the TV and laid down on the couch. The next thing she remembered was voices coming from the kitchen. Her parents were home. She glanced at the clock; 6 p.m. She sat up, collected herself, and walked into the kitchen. "How are things at the store today?" Mary put on her most chipper voice. Neither parent answered. They both continued on with their activities. "Uh, hello? Is anybody here?" Mary teased. "It was just fine, Mary," Jake snorted. "Really!? You don't say? Then how come all we did was fight today?!" Mary looked at Ruth. "The only reason that we fought is because of what Delores said. That's all." "What did she say, mom?" Mary wanted to know. "Oh you know what a gossip she is." Ruth tried to be calm. "She was just talking about lack of morals in young people today. She was going on about teenagers having sex and stuff. It just struck a nerve with your dad." "You bet it did," Jake added. "That woman will have a hay day spreading the news of your pregnancy all over town. I can't imagine the humiliation that we will have to endure just because of you." He pointed directly at Mary. Tears ran down Mary's cheeks as she silently took the wrath of her father. Ruth tried to stop Jake but he just kept going on about how bad it was going to be. How they had worked so hard to build a reputation for the family and in a selfish instant, Mary took it all away.

After Jake finished his tirade, Mary pulled herself together and announced with finality, "Well I guess this is your lucky day." How's that?" Jake snarled. "Aunt Liz called and she wants me to come and visit with her for the summer and I'm going." Ruth spoke up, "Now honey, let's not overreact. You dad didn't mean all of that, did you Jake? "It doesn't matter, mom. I decided to go last night when she called me. Daddy just confirmed my decision. I will not be pregnant in such a hostile environment. I'm leaving Monday morning." Mary didn't wait for a response. She turned on her heels and headed for her room. Ruth burst into tears. Jake yelled at Mary, "Don't you dare walk away from me! I'm not finished with you! Come back here right now!" Mary ignored her father. She was taking control of the situation and it felt good. Jake started after her but Ruth grabbed his arm. "Don't, not right now, we all need to cool off. Please?" Jake snarled but relented. He spun around and went out to the garage.

Mary woke up Sunday morning feeling alive and refreshed. The sun was shining and she noticed that some flowers were blooming. 'What a wonderful day, thank you Lord,' She thought to herself. Having skipped dinner last night, her stomach growled with hunger. 'I can't stay in my room forever. I might as well go face the music.'

Mary walked through the living room on her way to the kitchen. Her dad was in his chair reading the paper. "Good morning, daddy." Mary tried to act as if everything was OK. Jake ruffled his newspaper but didn't respond. Mary, determined to keep a good attitude, kept on going to the kitchen. Sunday mornings usually meant a big family breakfast; sometimes the Goldsteins would join them, but not today. Ruth was nowhere to be found and the lack of aroma of food being prepared indicated that there was no intention of breakfast. Mary slipped a couple pieces of bread into the toaster. It was then she noticed a note from her mother. 'I've gone to the cemetery to check on mom and dad's graves. Don't know when I'll get home.' Mary knew that her mom was distraught. The cemetery was where she always went to clear her head.

It was then that Mary realized something. She had a choice to make. She could feel guilty for her mother's sadness and wind up depressed or she could choose to fight that feeling and remain happy. It dawned on her that life is simply made up of a series of choices. If you do something wrong, then make it right. If you are in the right to begin with, then don't let other people bring you down. A person is not responsible for the happiness of others. That is not to say that we are to be selfish and not help those in need, it merely means that we are to determine what God's will is for our lives is and be happy about executing His commands. 'I choose to be happy. I choose to do God's will in my life. I will not allow the negative feelings of other people ruin my day.'

After she finished breakfast, Mary decided that she needed to get out of the house. There was no telling when Ruth would be home and it was obvious that Jake was in no mood to socialize. She wanted to enjoy the day. "I'm going over to Angie's," Mary announced to her father as she walked toward the door. No response. Mary hesitated a moment pondering the silence from her father. "Oh well, I tried," she said loud enough for Jake to hear. She closed the door behind her and actually skipped down the sidewalk to her car. Nothing was going to steal her happiness; nothing.

Mary pulled up in front of her house at 7 p.m. She and Angie had a great day. They had gone for ice cream, went for a walk in the woods, and generally talked about how much they would miss their boyfriends. They laughed at the thought of Joe and Allen cleaning out horse stalls. Angie was saddened that Mary was going away for the summer. She couldn't realize why she would want to be away for the entire summer. Mary understood Angie's confusion; she didn't have all of the information. Mary wished that she could tell Angie that she was pregnant, but there was no way that could happen. The time was not right.

Mary entered the house not knowing what to expect. She forced a smile and a big 'hello' as she walked through the door. The lights were on, but there was no response. "Mom? Dad? Is anybody home?" "In here," Jake said flatly. Mary walked into the den. Jake was sitting at the desk. "Where's mom?" "Down at the synagogue. She is praying for you." Mary fidgeted. She didn't know what to say. "Is she OK?" "What do you think?" Jake snarled. "She hasn't been OK since you gave us the 'good news'." "I'm sorry that she feels bad about such a wonderful event, but I can't help that. I will pray for her as well." Jake didn't know what to say. His face reddened and stress was written all over his face. Mary continued, "How about you, dad, are you OK?" Mary already knew the answer. "NO! I AM NOT OK!" Jake stood up and leaned on his fists. "You just don't get it do you?!" Jake hissed through clenched teeth. "This family will never be the same, EVER!" Mary prayed for composure. "I know daddy, things will never be the same again. They will be BETTER! I wish you and mom could see it the way I do. If you could you would be so happy. But I can't control how you feel. That is up to you." Jake sat back down and looked out the window. "You are right, Mary." Jake said in a somewhat normal voice. "I can't see it your way because I believe in reality. You way is some kind of fantasy. It's not real. You will come to your senses someday. I just hope it's not too late." Mary shifted her weight. She felt sorry for her dad. But she knew that discussing it further would produce no positive results. She just smiled at her dad. "Are you still leaving for Liz's tomorrow?" "Yes, bright and early." "Well, at least you being gone will delay the impact of this news on the family. I wonder how Liz will react? I suppose I will be getting a call from her. That will be humbling." Those words hurt, but Mary continued to smile through the pain. "I've got to go pack. Good night, daddy, I love you."

Mary woke up to the sound of her alarm. She was a bit groggy because she hadn't slept well. She couldn't take her mind off of her parents. She stumbled down the stairs and headed for the kitchen. Both of her parents were in the kitchen. Things seemed somewhat normal, although there was a sense of awkwardness in the room. "Good morning mom, good morning dad." "Good morning Mary," Jake and Ruth said simultaneously. Ruth was preparing breakfast and Jake was milling around looking for things that he wanted to take to the store. Things seemed a little more normal and Mary was thankful for that. Ruth spoke up as Mary sat down at the table. "Are you still planning to go to Liz's?" "Yes." Ruth paused. "Are you sure that is a good idea? What about doctor appointments?" "I have already thought about that. I'll just use Aunt Liz's doctor." Mary was proud of herself for being responsible. Ruth looked dejected. Mary could tell that Ruth didn't want her to go. Ruth started to put food on the table. "Jake, breakfast is ready." Jake appeared from the living room and took his place at the table. Mary offered to say the blessing. "Dear God, thank you for always being with us. I ask that you protect and comfort my parents. Please help them to be at peace with me. Amen."

They ate in silence. After they had finished, Mary got up from the table and announced that she was going to finish getting ready and head out to Liz's. Jake ignored the announcement and said, "I'm off to the store." Mary walked over to her dad and hugged him. "I'll see you in a couple of months. I love you." Jake hugged her back and said, "I love you too, honey. That's why this hurts so much. He looked at her with tears in his eyes, turned around, and walked out.

Mary finished getting ready and dragged her suitcase down the stairs. Ruth was waiting for her when she reached the bottom. "I absolutely hate all of this," Ruth said with streams of tears running down her face. "Are sure that you want to go?" Tears welled up in Mary's eyes as she hugged her mom. "I think it will do everyone some good. Besides, Aunt Liz needs the help." Mary tried to play off the emotions of the moment. Ruth released her hold on Mary and looked deeply into her eyes. "I don't know how you can be so happy?" Ruth mused. "I see nothing but peace in your eyes. How can that be?" "Because I am right with the Lord. I am doing His work. I wish you could see that. Hopefully, you will someday. I love you, mom. Goodbye." "Please be careful, Mary, I love you too." Mary walked down the sidewalk while Ruth watched her get into the car. She waved at Mary until she was out of sight.

CHAPTER TWENTY-EIGHT

Mary rang the door bell to Liz's house just before lunch. The trip had taken longer than expected, but she had passed the time talking to Joe on the phone. She smiled to herself as she remembered the stories that Joe had related about life on a ranch. He and Allen were working hard, learning a lot, and having fun at the same time. Joe had mentioned how relieved he felt getting out of town. Mary loved the sights, sounds, and smells of her aunt and uncle's farm. The air was clean and refreshing. Childhood memories returned to her as she remembered playing in the barn, helping Uncle Zac with the chores and following Liz around the kitchen. She was suddenly hungry as she reminded herself that Aunt Liz was a great cook.

Liz opened the door and squealed. Aunt Liz was very obviously pregnant and looked radiant. "Mary! It's so good to see you!" She pulled Mary close to give her a hug. Suddenly, without warning, Liz's baby kicked like it had never kicked before! It was like it was rolling over and over in her stomach. It seemed to be jumping for joy.

"Wow!" Liz laughed out loud grabbed Mary's hand and held it against her stomach. "Do you feel that?! The baby has never kicked like that before. This is amazing!" Mary felt her aunt's stomach and giggled at the acrobatics that was going on in there. A distinct, but gentle breeze blew across the porch. It was both chilling and warming at the same time. Liz stepped back and looked at Mary.

Her laughter faded into a look of astonishment. She just stood there gazing at Mary, looking at her up and down. "Is something wrong, Aunt Liz?" Mary asked. "Why Mary! Nothing is wrong! In fact, everything is great! You are pregnant! With the Savior! You are the chosen one! How blessed I am that the mother of our Savior would come to visit me!" Liz jumped up and down and hugged Mary so tightly that she couldn't breathe.

"How could you know?" Mary questioned her aunt. "I don't know how I know. I just know that I know; and apparently my baby knows too. Praise God!" Mary felt a brush against the back of her neck. She immediately knew who it was. "Thanks Gabby." "What did you say, hon?" Aunt Liz asked. "Oh nothing." "Well come on in and tell me all about it! How far along are you? When is the baby due? What does Joe think? How did Jake and Ruth take the news?...." Mary laughed. "Hold on just a minute. One question at a time." "I'm sorry hon. I'm just so excited I can hardly stand it. You must tired. Are you hungry?" "It seems like I'm always hungry nowadays," Mary laughed. Liz laughed along. "Well you are in the right place. Let's go to the kitchen and see what we can find."

As the ladies were milling around the kitchen, Zac came in the back door. "Uncle Zac!" Mary ran over and gave him a big hug. "How are you?" Zac pick up a piece of paper and scribbled on it. 'Lost my voice, can't talk. It's great to see you." Mary smiled and looked at her aunt. "He's been that way ever since he found out that I was pregnant. I thought I sprung the news on him while we were in the supermarket, but he claims that he already knew. The old coot won't tell me how he knew. Says it's a secret." Mary laughed and looked her uncle. There was a gleam in his eye that made her feel good. "Have you been to the doctor?" Zac scribbled on the paper. 'No need to, I know what caused it. It is part of the secret.' Zac grinned at Mary. He continued, 'I'll get my voice back when John is born.' "John?" Mary said out loud. "You've already named him?" Zac wrote some more on the paper. 'I didn't name him, God did.' Zac pointed upward. Mary smiled. "I think John is a good name," Mary mused.

"Tell your uncle about your good news," Liz suggested to Mary. 'Let's talk over lunch,' Zac said producing another note. 'I'm starved.' They all sat down at the table and Liz said to Zac, "Would you like to say the blessing, Zac? Oh that's right, you can't." Zac wrote again in big letters, 'VERY FUNNY!' All three of them laughed. Mary immediately felt at home here. She missed family. Coming here for the summer was definitely a God thing. "Thank you Lord," Mary whispered under her breath.

As they finished up what Mary thought was the best apple pie that she had ever tasted, she finished her story. She even went into detail about Joe, Gabby and Guardian. Liz and Zac sat there amazed. "I'm so excited!" Liz exclaimed. Zac nodded eagerly in agreement. He was smiling liked a kid opening a present. Mary was glad to be around people who believed her. She relaxed for the first time in a few days.

"I'll bet your parents are excited," Liz exclaimed. "Not really." Mary's face saddened. 'Why not?' Zac wrote down. "It's a long story, but the fact is, they don't believe me. They think I'm crazy or covering up for Joe or something. When Joe and I told our parents we assumed they would react like you guys, but, it ended up with a lot of yelling and arguing. Mom and dad refused to associate with the Goldsteins and vice versa. They even forbid me to see Joe." "Oh, I'm so sorry, Mary." Liz tried to console her. Zac got up and began to rub Mary's shoulders. Liz continued. "They will come to their senses soon, I'm sure." "It doesn't seem like it," Mary spoke softly. "Would you like for me to give them a call?" Liz offered. "I think things are better left alone, for now. There is just too much negative feeling in the air at home. People are not thinking properly. Hurtful things are being said. That's why I am so glad that you invited me up for the summer. I don't think I could stand it around there right now." "We are glad to have you, Mary. You can stay as long as you like." Liz touched her hand and Zac nodded in agreement. "Thanks. I really appreciate it." Mary yawned. "I'm kind of tired. I think I'll lie down for awhile if you don't mind." "You go right ahead, dear. Make yourself at home." Mary got up and headed for her room. She always stayed in the same room when they visited. Uncle Zac had called it 'Cinderella's room'. They had decorated it just for her. Mary looked around; nothing had changed. It felt good to be in a happy place.

"I could just kick my brother!" Liz fumed to Zac when she was sure that Mary was out of earshot. "Do you believe them?! How could they be so mean to Mary? I have half a mind to go down there and give them a piece of my mind!" Zac looked at his bride. He motioned for her to calm down. Getting upset is not good for their baby. Then he wrote on the paper. 'Mary asked us to leave it alone. We should honor her wishes. Let's just be there for her. She needs us now.' "Oh I know; I'm just frustrated. Jake and Ruth are missing out on a miracle!" Zac nodded in agreement.

June flew by. Mary enjoyed being on the farm with her aunt and uncle. She and Joe talked every night after Joe finished with the chores. He was out of his cast and had started to help Allen with the manual labor. He was enjoying the summer as well. Both kids agreed that getting out of town was God's idea, and it was a good one. Even though they missed each other tremendously, each one was happy for the other.

It was now the middle of July. Joe and Allen had gotten into a good routine getting the chores finished each day and Mr. Robinson was happy with their work ethic. Both of the boys had gone home for the evening on a couple of occasions. Allen wanted to see Angie as well as his folks. Joe, on the other hand, was worried about his parents and felt the need to check on them occasionally. The air in the Goldstein's house was still icy. Joe had tried to be 'normal' but the underlying tension and general somber mood made it easier for him to leave to return to the ranch.

It was Friday afternoon and the boys had just finished putting up hay. The work was hard and the weather was hot, but Joe and Allen kept a good attitude. Mr. Robinson walked up to the boys as they were laughing about nothing in particular. "Good job, boys!" he remarked. "I can't remember when I've gotten this much accomplished by the middle of July." Then he chuckled just a little. "I am worried about you two. I've never seen anyone work as hard as you two and laugh about it." "Thank you Mr. Robinson," the boys said in unison. "I've been thinking," Mr. Robinson continued. "Why don't you two take the weekend off?" The boys looked at each other and grinned. Joe spoke up. "That would be great, but what about the daily chores?" "I know that I'm getting old," Mr. Robinson quipped. "But I think I can handle the basics until Monday. Besides, how do you think I got along without you before this summer? Now get out of here before I change my mind!" Mr. Robinson smiled and waved them in the direction of the bunkhouse. Joe and Allen yelped and took off running for the bunkhouse.

Within thirty minutes, both boys had showered and packed. "I'm heading home," Allen announced. "Which direction are you going?" Allen had sensed all summer that something was on Joe's mind. He had noticed that Joe didn't talk much about his trips home. He figured something was wrong, but every time he asked Joe about it, Joe played it off. "I'm heading north!" The excitement in Joe's voice made Allen smile. He knew what 'north' meant; Joe was going to see Mary. "See ya Sunday night. Tell Mary I said hello." "I will, give Angie a big kiss for me," Joe teased. "Aw Joe, you are my best friend. I'll give her two for you!" Both boys laughed as they got into their cars and sped away.

Joe made it to Zac and Grace's about 5 p.m. Zac was walking across the barnyard toward the house when he noticed Joe pull up. At first he didn't recognize him. It had been about three years since Joe had visited them and he had grown quite a bit. Joe walked directly over to Zac. "Hi Uncle Zac! It's me, Joe." Zac grinned as soon as he heard Joe's voice. The two shook hands and gave each other a hug. Zac removed a small notepad from his pocket and wrote on it. "I lost my voice, can't speak. Boy, it sure is good to see you, Joe. You have grown up since you've been here.' "It's nice to see you, too, Uncle Zac. You are looking good. How did you lose your voice?" 'It's a long story, sort of a God thing,' Zac wrote. 'So what are you doing way up here?' Zac knew the answer but wanted to tease Joe a little. "Well, I, uh,...I came to congratulate you on the baby! How is Aunt Grace doing?" Joe played along. "She looks like she swallowed a basketball and is as happy as a pig in a mud puddle." Zac was very fast with the pencil. Joe laughed. "Is that the only reason you came?" Zac had a silly grin on his face. "Well," Joe tipped his hat back on his head and stroked his chin as if to indicate that he was deep in thought. "There is a rumor going around that you are harboring a dangerous person in your house." Zac grinned. "She is pretty dangerous. Would you like to see her?" Joe nodded eagerly. "I imagine that they are on the back porch. They usually start dinner and sit out there while it's cooking. Come on, we'll sneak in through the house and surprise them." Uncle Zac had lost his voice, but not his sense of humor.

Zac and Joe slipped through the house unheard. Liz and Mary were just as Zac had described. They were sitting in rocking chairs while snapping green beans that Mary had picked from the garden earlier. Zac flung open the door which startled the girls. Zac made a grand gesture as he waved. He made some motions as if to say, 'How are you two this afternoon?' "We were just fine until you nearly made us jump out of our skin." Liz acted angry but smiled as she said it. 'What's for dinner? It sure smells good.' Zac scribbled as he ignored Liz's fake anger. "We're having spaghetti," Mary announced proudly. "I made my special sauce just for you Uncle Zac." Zac continued writing. 'Why that's mighty sweet of you Mary. I was wondering, do you think that there is enough for another one at the table tonight?' "Of course there is." Liz never turned anyone away. Who's coming?" Zac kept writing. 'A friend of mine just dropped in and I thought he might join us for supper. He's in the kitchen.' "Well for heaven's sake, Zac, bring him out here so that we can meet him," Liz urged. Zac opened the door and motioned for Joe to come out.

Joe walked through the door and locked eyes with Mary. She shrieked and jumped up almost spilling the pan full of beans. Joe had reached her by then, and picked her up and swung her around like she was a feather. They hugged for what seemed like a second to them but in reality was almost a minute. "Uh excuse me," Liz teased. "How about a little hug for me?" Joe laughed and Mary blushed. Joe released his hold on Mary and wrapped his arms around Liz. "It is good to see you Aunt Liz. How are you feeling?" I'm doing well, thank you." Mary jumped in, she was so excited she could hardly stand it. "How did you get off work? How long can you stay? Do your parents know you are here? Why didn't you call?" "Whoa, whoa there Sugar Plum! Slow down a minute."

Mary began to cry happy tears. It had been so long since she had seen Joe. She had missed him terribly. Then came the words, 'Sugar Plum'. She smiled through her tears as she reached up to Joe for a second hug. Joe wrapped his arms around Mary, gently this time, as if he was holding a hummingbird. Mary sighed and remembered the comfort of having Joe around. Suddenly, she released her hold on Joe and grabbed her stomach. "Oh!" "What's wrong?" Joe's grin turned to concern. Zac and Liz moved closer to Mary. "I'm not sure, but I think the baby just kicked!" Liz smiled. "Mine too!" Zac put his arm around his wife. "This is the first time, Joe. Oh, there it goes again! Here give me your hand." Mary grabbed Joe's hand and placed it on her stomach. "Do you feel it,

Joe?" Joe giggled like a school girl. "Wow! He's going to town!" Joe replied almost yelling. Mary laughed at Joe's giddiness.

After the kicking stopped, they all sat down on the porch and caught up on what had been going on. Joe spoke up after a pause in the conversation. "I'm sorry to barge in on you like this, but...." Zac reached out and squeezed Joe's shoulder while Liz interrupted. "No buts about it Joe, you are family. You are welcome here any-time for as long as you want. Besides, we are honored to have the earthly parents of the Savior in our home." Joe was stunned by Aunt Grace's statement. He looked at Zac who was smiling and nodding in agreement. Then he looked at Mary. "You told them?!" He was stunned that Mary would reveal it to anyone after experiencing how their parents took the news. Mary smiled. "Aunt Grace knew it the minute she laid eyes on me Joe. It's OK. They know everything; the dreams, Guardian, Gabby, all of it. They are on our side, Joe." Now it was Joe who got choked up. They all stood up and joined in a group hug. "Thank you Uncle Zac and Aunt Grace. It means more than you know to have someone believe us."

Mary couldn't believe that it was Saturday evening already. It seemed as if Joe had just arrived and he would be leaving tomorrow. She wished that time would stop. The four of them had just finished dinner, which had turned into a birthday celebration for Mary and Joe, and were sitting on the back porch enjoying the view of the big Montana sky. They all silently watched as the sun set over the hill to the west and disappeared into the Canadian Rockies. Liz spoke first. "You know, no matter how many times I watch the sunset, I am amazed at the beauty of it all. God's creations are perfect." "I haven't felt this kind of peace in a long time," Joe observed. Mary snuggled a little closer to Joe. "I wish it would never end." "I'm sorry to put a damper on the evening, but I need to go to bed." Liz struggled to her feet. "This little guy has been kicking up a storm today." Liz stroked her sizeable belly. Zac got up and indicated that he was going to bed as well. After 'good night' greetings, Mary and Joe settled into the swing.

"Are you ready for this, Joe?" Mary broke the silence. Joe knew what she meant. School started in four weeks. Mary was going home the week before and Joe was going to work until school started. He figured that they would need the money. He knew that once Mary returned home, everyone would know that she was pregnant. She was already showing. Even though they had been separated, it had been great being away from all of the controversy all summer. Soon, it would be over and the reality of Mary's pregnancy would become common knowledge. "As long as we are together and with God on our side, I am ready for anything," Joe assured Mary.

Mary's telephone rang. It was Karen. "I forgot all about the conference." Mary opened her phone. "Hi Karen, how's it going?" "It's going great, Mary. It has been busy without you, but Gary brought a buddy with him who has been a tremendous help." The two girls talked about details of the event, number of kids there, activities, speakers...then the conversation fell silent. There was awkwardness in the air. It was one of those feelings you get when talking to someone. Something had been left unsaid; something that needed to be said. Mary decided to blow it off. "I guess I'll let you get back to the fun." "Wait a minute Mary." OK, finally, Karen was going to reveal the reason that she called. "I just wanted you to know that Jim, you know, the president's aide, was asking about you. He was disappointed that you aren't here. He seemed almost angry. Gary played it off as best he could, but...." Mary interrupted. "Thanks for the heads up Karen. I suppose Jim will be calling soon." "I just wanted you to know, Mary." Mary closed her phone slowly after they had said goodbye. Joe had heard the whole conversation. "I'm sorry, Mary. I know how much 'Teens for Abstinence' means to you." Mary smiled at Joe. "I'm over it. I guess I need to tell Jim the truth so that he can find a replacement for next year." She shuddered at the thought of confronting Jim. "I suppose so," Joe replied. "It's going to come out sooner or later. I know the rumors are already spreading all over town." "How do you know that, Joe?" "Allen goes home to see Angie once in awhile. According to her, people are talking about where we are and what we are doing. After all, you did miss cheerleader tryouts and I haven't been in the weight room working out with the football team. Allen says the cheer coach and the football coach have been asking about us." Mary's face turned sour. "I wonder why Angie hasn't said anything to me. I talk with her a couple times a week." "Angie is a good friend, Mary. I think she is trying to protect you. She doesn't want to upset you when you are so far away and can't defend yourself." "I guess you're right, Joe."

Mary's phone rang again. Mary recognized the area code as being from Washington DC She figured that Gary was calling. "Hello?" "Hello Mary; this is Jim Donavan. I'm an aide to the president. We met in Washington?" Mary's heart sank. "Of course I remember you, Jim. How are you?" "Frankly, Mary, I'm a little confused, extremely disappointed, and slightly angry." Jim's voice was terse. Mary held her breath. "I'm sorry Mr. Donavan. Is there anything that I can do?" "In fact, there is. You can explain why you aren't here. This is the biggest rally that 'Teens for Abstinence' has had so far and the chairperson decides to blow it off." Mary could hear the anger in Jim's voice. "Something came up, Mr. Donavan and...." "Something came up?!" Jim's voice got louder. "I specifically remember scheduling this event around your schedule. YOU picked the dates! I don't mind telling you that the president is more than upset. You know this was one of his pet projects." "Once again, Mr. Donavan, I'm truly sorry." "SORRY DOESN'T CUT IT! I NEED TO KNOW WHY YOU BLEW IT OFF!" Mary was visibly upset. Joe had heard Jim yelling on the phone and he didn't like it. Mary was shaking so badly that she could barely hold the phone. Joe grabbed the phone and put it to his ear. "Mr. Donavan, I would think that a president's aide would have more manners than to speak to a lady like that. You should be ashamed of yourself." "HOW DARE YOU TALK TO ME LIKE THAT! WHO IS THIS?" "My name is Joe Goldstein." Joe spoke calmly into the phone. "Oh yeah," Jim snarled. "The boyfriend. Let me tell you something, Mr. Goldstein. This is none of your business. Put Mary back on the phone." "I will not do that, Mr. Donavan. However, I will tell you this. The reason that Mary didn't come is that she is pregnant! I am submitting her resignation effective immediately. Now, leave us alone!" The phone went dead for several seconds. Joe wondered if the connection had been lost. He started to hang up when Jim spoke softly. "You have no idea who you are talking to. I will not accept her resignation. I will not allow some teenage whore to ruin this project. We have plastered her face all over the country as the spokesperson. She WILL CONTINUE TO DO AS I SAY UNTIL I SAY DIFFERENTLY! I will handle this in my own way. I am coming out there to fix this so stay out of my way. And, Joe, the next time you try to tell me what to do I will crush you like a bug." "Is that a threat Mr. Donavan?" Joe stood his ground. "No, "Jim whispered into the phone. "It's a promise." "Bring it," Joe challenged as he closed the phone.

Joe laid the phone down and put his arm around Mary. They both had heard the entire conversation. They knew that there was a tough road ahead of them and that the serenity of the summer was fading fast. "Why wouldn't he want to accept my resignation?" Mary wondered innocently. Joe rubbed his forehead. "He said that he was coming out here to 'fix it'. When you consider that statement in combination with him being so adamant about you remaining the chairperson, it can only mean one thing." Mary held her breath. "You don't mean...." her voice trailed off. "That's the only thing it can mean. He wants you to have an abortion." "NEVER! Mary stood up and clenched her teeth. "I will never do that! Never! Ever! Ever! NEVER!" "I know Mary, I know. God won't allow that to happen. I won't allow that to happen. Don't worry. He will get us through this. Come on, we need to pray." They both got on their knees and prayed together.

When they finished, they both felt better. Joe looked at his phone; 11:00. "We had better get to bed. We have a lot coming at us and we need our rest." "I hate to give it up Joe." Mary never wanted any evening to end when she was with Joe. "Me either, Sugar Plum. But we have to do what is best for the baby." Mary kissed him on the cheek. "You are going to be a great father."

The next afternoon Mary stood in the driveway and waved at Joe's car until it disappeared over the hill. Zac and Liz were standing on the front porch watching the entire event. They felt bad for the kids. They knew how much they loved their parents and how terribly hurt they were when their parents rejected them. Mary turned around and faced them. Tears were streaming down her cheeks. "I'm going to go for a walk." There was despair in her voice. "OK sweetie," Aunt Liz acknowledged.

Mary strolled through the barnyard out to the pasture. There were cows grazing peacefully among sheep and horses. Mary marveled at how the different animals got along so well. They had to know that they were different. They just accepted each other for who they were. Mary wished that people could be that way. She headed for the pond that was located in the middle of the field. There was one lone oak tree next to the pond. Mary remembered when she and Uncle Zac had spent many days fishing in that pond.

He had even built a bench for them to sit on when they were there. How she longed for the simpler life of a child. She sat down on the bench and watched the frogs jump, fish snapping at water bugs and a family of geese cruising around the pond. It was then she noticed a pile of rotting lumber lying next to the water. She closed her eyes and remembered one specific day when Joe had come along with her family to visit. They must have been about ten years old. They had decided to build a raft so that they could 'sail across the ocean' as Joe had put it then. They had spent the better part of the day building that raft. After they completed it, they decided to try it out. They had gotten about halfway across the pond when the raft began falling apart. Within seconds, they were both in the water with pieces of lumber floating all around them. They made their way back to the house, laughing all the way. Mary, eyes still closed as she relived the event, smiled to herself.

"Those were special days, weren't they?" A familiar voice startled Mary. It was from someone sitting next to her. She flinched and opened her eyes. "Gabby! You nearly scared me to death!" Mary hugged her and felt the warmth of God's love rushing into her. Gabby smiled, "You know, I've been doing this a long time and I still haven't figured out how to approach people without startling them." After they finished laughing at Gabby's comment, silence replaced the laughter. Gabby broke the quietness. "How are you doing, Mary?" "Pretty good, I guess. I mean the baby is fine, my health is good, Joe is doing well, but...." "But what, Mary?" Gabby knew the answer. But she also knew that it would be good for Mary to verbalize it. "I'm just worried; maybe a little scared. It's like I'm starting my life all over again. Don't get me wrong. I am honored to do it. I am the most blessed person in the world. It's just that I don't know what to expect. How are we going to live? Where are we going to live? Should I finish high school? How do I take care of a baby let alone the Messiah?!" Mary was getting anxious. "Now Mary," Gabby squeezed her hand. "You are getting worked up and that isn't good for the baby or for you. This is exactly what Satan wants. Don't let him win." Mary nodded and tried to calm down. "I know it's a lot to handle and I also know what you have given up for the Kingdom...cheerleading, college, 'Teens for Abstinence', a normal senior year in high school; basically, God has asked you to change your entire life for Him." "And I'm OK with that, Gabby. In fact, I'm happy about it. All of those other things don't mean a thing in comparison to what God has asked me to do. It's just so overwhelming." "I know honey. It's OK to feel a little frightened. In fact, it's normal. But try to relax. God has seen you through this so far and I promise that He will see it through to the end. Trust in Him, Mary." "I know Gabby, I do trust God. I just miss my parents. I wonder what the kids back home will think when they find out." "I didn't say it would be easy, Mary. However, I do promise that God will give you everything you need to be successful at this." Mary sat back against the bench and relaxed. "Thanks Gabby. I feel better now. I'm sorry that my faith is so weak." "Honey, don't apologize. Your faith is just fine. You just need to remember that Satan is working hard to make you worry. That is one of the main weapons that he has against people. He lures them to his side with feelings of fear and inadequacy. Don't forget, God is always right here ready to help. All you have to do is ask." Mary sighed with relief. She looked out over the pond toward the sun that was low enough in the west to indicate that supper wasn't too far off. "I'm fine now Gabby." Mary turned to look in the direction of her guardian angel, but she was gone. Mary stood up and headed for the house. "I'll see you soon, Gabby." The warm breeze coming from the pasture suddenly shifted to the north. A cool refreshing wind blew across Mary's face for a few seconds. Then as quickly as it came, it left and the warm air from the pasture resumed. Mary looked into the sky. "Nice one, Gabby."

CHAPTER TWENTY-NINE

T hree weeks went by and it was time for Mary to go home. There was one week before school and she needed to get some maternity clothes. She had gotten by thus far with what she had, and that was OK for the farm, but now she was going back to the real world. She hated leaving Uncle Zac and Aunt Liz. They had been lifesavers for her this summer. It had been a wonderful summer except for the harassing messages from Jim that occurred on a daily basis after he had spoken with Joe. She had ignored the calls on the advice of her aunt and uncle as well as Joe. After a tearful goodbye, Mary climbed into her car and headed home.

After about an hour on the road, she decided to call Joe. "Hi Sugar Plum! How ya'll doing?" "Boy, you HAVE been on the ranch for awhile. What's with the 'ya'll' stuff?" Joe laughed. "Guess what, Mary. Mr. Robinson just told us that we were finished for the summer. He is going to pay us for next week as gratitude for a job well done. Allen and I are packing right now. I should be home in an hour or so." "That's fantastic, Joe. You just made my day." Mary wasn't looking forward to facing the townspeople alone. She was dreading the sneers, ridicule, and judgmental stares from everyone "Say Joe, have you told Allen yet?" "No, have you told Angie?" "No." Joe thought for a minute. "How far are you from home?" Mary did some quick calculations in her head. "I should be home in an hour and a half; two hours tops. Why?"

"I was thinking, I'd love to see you before you get to the house as I doubt that your parents will allow me to come over. Why don't we meet at Angie's? I know for a fact that Allen is going straight there." "That's a great idea Joe. I'll call Angie and make the arrangements." Mary paused. "Do you think that they will believe us, Joe?" "I don't know Mary. I hope so. But I just don't know."

Joe noticed Allen's car in Angie's driveway. He looked for Mary's car, but it was nowhere in sight. He pulled up in front of the house and called Mary. "Hi sweetie!" Mary's voice sang into the phone. "Hi Sugar Plum. Where are you?" "I'm just coming into town. I should be there in ten minutes." "Good! I'll wait for you outside. See you in ten. Bye." Joe hung up the phone and laid his head back against the headrest. 'Dear God, this is it. Tonight we begin revealing to the general public that the Savior is coming. Please give me the right words to speak on Your behalf. As your servant, I ask for wisdom and discernment for the privilege of raising Your Son. I know that many people may react like my parents have. Help me to have compassion toward them. Please guide me through this mission. Amen.' He kept his eyes closed and remained deep in thought regarding everything that was coming. He knew that this was going to be difficult. He felt as if he were in the middle of the ocean treading water. How was he supposed to provide for a family? He hadn't even graduated from high school. Would anyone believe them? Everyone is going to think that we are crazy. His mind swirled.

"Is Satan getting to you?" Joe snapped out of his trance with a start. Guardian was sitting in the passenger seat. Joe collected himself. "Hi Guardian, you startled me." "That happens sometimes, especially when we get off track from God. I know what was going through your mind just now. Satan is trying to get you to doubt yourself. He wants you to think that it is all up to you and that God is some abstract being who is not interested or too busy to be with you. When that happens, we get scared, we feel alone and helpless. Is that where you are now, Joe?" Joe felt ashamed. "Yes, it is Guardian. I feel overwhelmed with the task that is ahead. I have to admit that sometimes I feel like it's unfair of God to ask this of me. I mean, don't get me wrong. I am humbled that God selected me for this mission, but I don't know, it is all too new and different. I feel ashamed even verbalizing it. I should be excited and most of the time I am. But occasionally, I wish that things could go back to normal. After all, I'm just a country high school kid. Does God really think that I can do this?" Guardian smiled. "First of all, God not only thinks you can do this, He KNOWS that you can. He wouldn't have selected you if He didn't. Secondly, it's OK to be a little apprehensive. God understands how the physical circum-stances of this world can conflict with the spiritual world in which He reigns. That is when faith takes over. When His will conflicts with common sense, He expects us to rely on Him. He yearns for us to trust Him by ignoring the worldly rationale and putting our entire faith in Him. Satan knows this and is constantly trying to interrupt the flow of consistent faith. That is when you get scared. You see the world through Satan's eyes instead of God's eyes." Joe relaxed. "Thanks, Guardian."

"Who are you talking to?" Mary's voice came from outside his window. He turned his head toward Mary. "I was talking to Guardian." He turned back in Guardian's direction but he was gone. "Honestly, Mary, he was just right here." Mary laughed. "You don't have to convince me, Joe. Don't forget, I invented crazy." By now Joe was out of the car and hugging Mary. "I sure have missed that pretty face." Mary beamed. "Let's go in, I can't wait to tell Angie."

Angie and Allen answered the door. "Hi you guys!" Angie squealed and headed for a big hug from Mary. "Long time no see," Allen teased Joe. Angie felt Mary's belly rub up against her own causing her to withdraw from the embrace and look instinctively at Mary's belly. Angie's astonishment got Allen's attention. He followed her eyes to Mary's belly. The moment instantly trans-formed into silent awkwardness. Angie and Allen were speechless. Joe put his arm around Mary. He and Mary smiled at their friends. Joe spoke first. "I suppose you two have questions." Angie raised a finger and pointed to Mary's belly. "Are you, uh, is that uh, I mean, is that what I think it is?" Mary smiled. "If you are asking if I'm pregnant, the answer is yes." Angie gasped and looked at Allen. He was as white as a ghost. Joe spoke up. "Relax Allen. It's OK. We have some news for you guys. Can we come in?" Angie came to her senses. "I'm sorry; of course you can come in." The four of them entered into the living room where Angie's parents were watching TV. "Let's go up to my room." She tried to lead them past her parents unnoticed but was unsuccessful. "Well hello strangers!" Angie's dad spoke from the couch. "Hi kids!" her mother chimed in. "We've missed you being here. How was your summer?" "It was great," Joe offered. We're going up to my room to visit, Mom." Angie herded everyone in the direction of the stairs. "OK honey." After the kids had disappeared, Angie's dad said to her mom. "I haven't seen Mary in awhile. It looks like she's put on some weight." "I noticed that too," her mom replied. "I suppose there is some good home cooking up in the country." They both laughed and returned to watching TV.

Angie closed the door to her room. "How long have you been pregnant? When are you due? How did this happen? What are you going to do?" "I can't believe you two are having sex; after all of our discussions about abstaining. How can you do this? Do your parents know?" Angie was chattering like a magpie. Allen was looking at Joe with disappointment written all over his face. "Let's sit down and take this one step at a time. There is a lot of information to absorb," Joe urged. Everyone took a seat and looked at Joe.

"I know this is hard to believe, but you guys are our best friends and we want you to try and keep an open mind. It is important to us that you listen to our story before passing judgment on us." Joe waited for an acknowledgment of his request. Allen and Angie nodded their heads in agreement. They looked like they were in shock. Joe began with Mary's encounter with Gabby and continued with the story in detail all the way through his most recent conversation with Guardian out in the car. "So you see, Mary is still a virgin and is giving birth to the Savior sometime in December." After he finished, Angie and Allen sat there in astonishment. Joe sat down next to Mary. They both knew that Angie and Allen needed time to process this information. Finally, Allen spoke up. "This is a lot to absorb, Joe. After all, we are not Jewish. Of course we have a limited knowledge about your faith; and we know that the Messiah is supposed to come. But, the scriptures have always seemed so abstract. Like it doesn't really apply to our world. I can't comprehend that what is written in the scriptures is actually happening, right here, right now," Angie added. "You have to admit, it does appear off the wall. Most people will think that you are crazy." Mary laughed out loud. "I know they will. I thought that I was crazy for awhile. We don't blame you for being hesitant about it. We just wanted you two to know first. We wanted you two to be able to decide for yourselves before everyone knows and begins talking about it."

The four of them sat without speaking for a few minutes. Allen broke the silence. "Joe, I have known you all of my life. We have been through a lot together. You've always had my back, and I love you like a brother. So, I don't really care if it's true or not. Time will determine that. However, in the meantime, I refuse to turn my back on you. If this is true, it will be the greatest event in the history of the world and I want to be a part of it. On the other hand, if you are crazy, you need me now more than ever. I guess what I am saying is that 'I've got your back'. I am here for you and Mary; no matter what." "The same goes for me," Angie affirmed. "I am here to help. Just let me know what I can do." Joe looked at Mary who was beaming. "Thanks guys," Joe replied humbly. "That really means a lot to us." Mary jumped up. "Time for a group hug."

Joe followed Mary home. It was 9:30 when they both pulled up in front of their houses. Joe walked over to Mary's car. "Well, this is it. Time to face the parents. Are you OK?" "I think so." Mary sounded unsure of herself. "Do you think that they have mellowed any?" "It's hard to predict. I hope so. I miss your parents as much as I miss my own." "I feel the same way Joe. I miss your parents too." "They are all upset with the situation. I don't have any hard feelings. I can see where they are coming from. We'll just keep on praying for them." He kissed her good night and headed for the house.

Joe opened the front door and quietly entered the living room. "Hi mom, hi dad. I'm home." Eve got up from her chair and hugged Joe. "We sure have missed you, Joe." "I've missed you too, mom." Abraham was sitting in his chair reading a book. He hadn't acknowledged Joe's greeting or his presence. Joe looked at his mother and both of them shrugged in ignorance about Abraham's indifference. Eve waved Joe into the kitchen. "Are you hungry, dear?" "Actually, I'm starved." "Good, I'll make you a sandwich. Tell me about your summer." Joe sat at the breakfast bar and told his mom about some of the funny things that he and Allen had experienced this summer. Eve giggled. "I wish I could have seen that."

"Sounds like you've had quite a summer," Abraham's voice bellowed from the kitchen door. "Did you have time to get your head on straight?" "I'm not sure what you mean by that dad?" Joe hoped it wasn't the whole Mary issue. "I mean, have you decided that it is not your responsibility? That it is not your baby? That you need to let go and lead your own life? That is, unless you are ready to admit that you ARE the father." Joe stood up straight and faced his dad. "It's just the opposite dad. I am more convinced now than ever. That baby is the Messiah and I have been commissioned by God to take care of Him." Abraham put his hands to his ears as if he didn't want to hear it. "Blasphemy! Spoken in my own house by my own son! Well, if that is how you feel, then you are no longer welcome in this house!" Eve began crying and tried to protest. "Be quiet Eve. I'll not have it. If he won't respect our wishes then he needs to get out!" Joe's face reddened. Anger welled up in him like he had never experienced before, but he kept his cool. "If that is your wish, I will honor it. I'll be back tomorrow for the rest of my stuff. Goodbye mom; goodbye dad." "Good!" Abraham yelled. "Go screw up your life! May God have mercy on your blasphemous soul!" Joe gently closed the front door on his way out. Tears trickled down his face as he walked to his car. Eve sat down at the kitchen table and broke down. Abraham turned around and went into the den. He sat down at his desk and prayed. 'Father in heaven, I need help. I don't know what to do. I have never seen my son act like this. I love him and I want to do what's best for him. Please give me some direction, some kind of sign. I need your help. Amen."

Mary walked into her house not knowing what to expect. She soon found out. "Mary! You're home!" Ruth's voice shouted from the living room. After warm greetings, Mary asked, "Where's daddy?" "Oh he's out in the garage. He has spent a lot of time out there this summer." "Has everything calmed down around here?" Mary wanted to know what she was walking into. "I don't know for sure," Ruth admitted. "I have been coming to terms with it, but I'm not sure about Jake. We don't talk about it." "How about the Goldsteins?" Mary was feeling bold. "Nothing has changed. We don't speak, and they don't speak. Your dad hired a different contractor for the store expansion and they don't come in the store. The only time we see them is when we both happen to be in the front yard at the same time. Then we just ignore each other." Ruth had just a hint of sadness in her voice. "Let's go out and see daddy." Mary wanted to change the subject.

The girls walked into the garage. Jake had his back to them fiddling around on the workbench. "Hi daddy!" Jake froze for a few seconds and then he slowly turned around. There were tears in his eyes. He held out his arms and Mary came running into them. "I've missed you, daddy." "I've missed you too, honey. Let me look at you." Mary stepped back and spun around slowly. "Wow! That baby is really growing. You look great." "Thanks daddy. How have you been?" "OK, I guess. Things are a lot different around here. It is difficult getting used to it. How are you feeling?" I'm great, daddy. I can't wait to be a mother!"

Jake frowned and Ruth looked at the floor. "So you haven't changed your mind about keeping the baby?" Ruth was surprised. Mary's expression changed. "No, I haven't. I am going to raise my baby. It is what God expects." "So I am to assume that you also plan to marry Joe?" Jake growled. "That's right daddy. I'm 18 now and I can make my own decisions." "Even if it means crushing your mother and I?" Jake couldn't believe Mary would do that. "Yes daddy, I must do as God has directed. I'm sorry that you can't accept that. I pray every day that you and mom will see the truth. Oh!" Mary winced a little and smiled. "The baby is kicking. Want to feel it?" Ruth's hand went immediately to Mary's belly. She beamed. "Jake, come over here and feel this! Your grandbaby is trying to say hello." Jake slowly walked over to Mary. His huge hand trembled as he slowly moved it toward Mary's belly. Mary took his hand and placed it in the correct position. "Do you feel it daddy?" Tears ran down his cheeks as he nodded. He was too emotional to speak. All three of them stood there as a family for the first time since Mary had made the announcement. It was a special moment.

After the baby stopped kicking they all went into the house. "So, do you guys think you can at least accept the fact that Joe and I are getting married?" Jake got quiet. Ruth spoke up. "I just don't know, Mary. I don't want to rehash everything you are claiming about your child. That won't do any good. The whole story about your virginity and the baby being the Savior is hard to believe. It's very difficult for your father and I to acknowledge the Goldsteins now. And I especially have hard feelings toward Joe. I don't care what you say; we blame him for all of this." Jake joined in. "We need some time honey. We love you and that will never change. But, accepting this whole deal is more than I can handle right now. Let's drop the subject, for now. How are Liz and Zac?" Mary took the hint; this had to be difficult for her parents. She went into a 15-minute speech about her aunt and uncle and all about her life on the farm this summer. "So what's new around here?" Mary said as she finished talking about the summer. "Oh nothing much," Jake muttered. "The store expansion has been a disaster. The contractor I hired is a real piece of work. He drives me crazy." "He won't admit that Abraham had spoiled him in the past. He always went above and beyond when doing work for us," Ruth said in a scolding voice. "I don't care!" Jake's face reddened. "I'll never speak to that man again! EVER!"

Mary decided to change the subject. "What you been up to, mom?" "I've just been working at the store and working in my garden. Say, that reminds me. I was working in the garden a couple of weeks ago and a man pulled up in some kind of black limo. He walked right up to me, didn't introduce himself or anything. He asked me if you where home. He was really rude; gave me the creeps. I told him 'no'. Then he asked where you were. I flat out told him that wasn't any of his business. He turned on his heels and walked back to the car. He did say something over his shoulder, "Tell Mary that Jim stopped by" and that he would be back. Do you know him?" Mary's expression told it all. Yes she knew him and Jake could tell that she didn't like Jim. "Who is that guy and what does he want with you?" Mary cleared her throat. "He is an aide to the president. He is in charge of 'Teens for Abstinence.' I missed the rally in July at Washington. He called to ask why and I, no actually Joe told him that I was pregnant. Joe told him to leave us alone and that I would resign. But, Jim wouldn't hear of it. He said that he wouldn't accept my resignation and was coming out here to take care of the situation. We are afraid that he wants me to have an abortion! He is creepy."

Ruth gasped and Jake put his arms around his little girl. "We won't let that happen, honey. I'll keep that weasel away from you." A thought snapped into Ruth's mind. "Wait a minute; you said Joe talked to him. When were you with Joe?" "He came out to see me at Aunt Grace's. He wanted to celebrate our birthdays. That's when Jim called. When Joe saw how upset I became after talking to him, Joe grabbed the phone and told him off. I think Jim threatened Joe because I heard him say to Jim, "Bring it." "He stood up to the president's aide? I'm not sure that was a good idea." Jake shook his head. "Yes daddy, he loves me. He just wants to protect me. Not only that, he loves you guys. He said he misses you and continues to pray for you and mom." A hush fell over the house.

The only sound that could be heard was the tick tock of the grandfather clock in the hall. It had belonged to Jake's father. Jake remembered when he brought it home after Jake's father died. Joe had helped him bring it in the house. "It wouldn't work," Jake whispered. "What wouldn't work?" Ruth asked. "Jake motioned in the direction of the clock. "The grandfather clock, Joe helped me move it in here when dad died a few years ago. It was late in the evening. We set it up and it wouldn't run. I remember being so disappointed that I just went to bed." Mary smiled as she remembered the rest of the story. Jake, who was having a difficult time holding back his emotions, continued. "The next thing I remember is hearing it strike six times the next morning. I had forgotten about it so I leaped out of bed to see what was going on. I headed down the steps and saw Joe polishing the woodwork." Jake broke down. Mary picked up where her father had left off. "Joe had stayed up all night working on it. I fell asleep on the couch. All I remember is that he wanted to surprise you by fixing it. He kept saying that he wanted to repay you for being such a great dad to both of us." Jake's huge shoulders bounced up and down as he sobbed. Ruth rubbed his back in an attempt to console him.

After a few minutes, Jake calmed down. He looked at Mary through red, swollen eyes. "Even after all of the terrible things that I said about him, he said that he loved us? Missed us? Is praying for us?!" "That's right daddy. He told me that just a few minutes ago." "Wait, what did you say?" Jake questioned. "Where is he?" Mary was frightened. "He's, uh, he's at home." Jake held his forehead. He was visibly shaken. He turned to Ruth. "Could all of this be true? Is it possible that the kids are telling us the truth!?" "I suppose so, Jake. But it does seem like quite a story. It's hard to believe, but, maybe...." Her words trailed off.

Jake started to pray. 'Dear God, I'm in way over my head. I don't know what to believe. I don't want to stand in the way of the Kingdom, but this is so difficult. I know You can do everything and I know that the Savior is coming. Could it really be that Mary is the chosen one? Please help me. Amen." As soon as Jake finished, the clock in the hall stopped ticking. It was so quiet that you could hear your own heart beat. Mary heard a voice whisper in her ear.

"Go touch the clock." It was Gabby. Mary slowly backed away from her parents and walked over to the clock. "Thank you Lord," she said loud enough that her parents could hear. As soon as she touched the clock, it began ticking again. Mary's face became encircled in a white light. She absolutely glowed. Jake and Ruth were speechless. They just stared at Mary. Then as quickly as it appeared, it was gone. Jake and Ruth went over and embraced their daughter. "I'm so sorry that I didn't believe you, honey." "Please forgive us, sweetie." Mary laughed out loud. "No worries mom and dad. It's OK. How does it feel to be the grandparents of the Messiah?" They all smiled, giggled and hugged each other. Mary was happy again.

Allen's cell phone rang. "Hi Joe! What's up?" "I need a place to crash tonight. Can I stay at your house?" "Sure buddy, no problem. Is everything OK?" Joe simply replied, "No." The phone went dead. Allen met Joe in the driveway. "I'm guessing that it didn't go so well at home," Allen observed as Joe got out of the car. "Good guess." Joe looked awful. Allen could see the stress all over his face. "My dad threw me out." Allen was speechless. He hugged his friend. Joe couldn't hold back any longer. He broke down into sobs.

After Joe collected himself, the boys headed for the house. "Do your parents know that I'm staying?" "Not yet, but they won't care. You know that mom and dad love you to death." "It seems like there are less and less of those people anymore." Joe tried to break the tension with a weak attempt at humor.

The boys walked in the door. "Well hi Joe. This is a nice surprise." Allen's mom got up and hugged Joe. Allen's dad was sitting on the couch watching a baseball game. "I thought you two might be sick of each other by now," he teased. "Come on in, have a seat. It's tied in the bottom of the seventh." Joe obliged. Allen's dad continued. "Don't get me wrong, it's great to see you and you know that you are welcome here anytime. However, I am a little curious, Joe. You haven't been around all summer and I know you must be missing Mary. How come you are sitting in my living room instead of hers?"

The question caught Joe off-guard. He quickly analyzed his options. He could fabricate a story to play off the question or he could tell the truth. 'I am not going to lie. I'm proud to have been chosen for this task. Let's just see how regular people are going to react.' "Well sir, the truth is that I am no longer welcome at Mary's house. Her parents have made it clear that they do not want me to see her anymore." Allen's dad turned off the TV. His mother asked, "I've known Jake and Ruth longer than you have, Joe. This can't be right. Why on earth would they treat you like that?" Joe looked at Allen for advice. Allen shrugged as if to say, 'you might as well tell them.' "Mary is pregnant." Joe looked Allen's parents in the eyes. His mother gasped and his father frowned. "Is Mary OK?" Allen's mom wanted to know. "She's fine." "What are your plans?" Allen's dad got right to the point. "We are going to get married as soon as the baby is born. Joe prepared for the next question. "Why wait until the baby is born? Why not get married now? Have you thought about giving it up for adoption?" Joe smiled. "Those options have been suggested by several people. However, we refuse to consider them. We must raise the child ourselves." "You must? Why?" Joe continued. "I know that you are not Jewish, but I'm sure that you know that the Jews believe the Messiah is coming." "Yes, I am aware of that. I believe it too." "Good," Joe continued, "because Mary is carrying the Savior. She is a virgin. The chosen one." Allen's parents' facial expressions shifted from amazed to a look when one witnesses a car wreck. It is a look of pity and sympathy. "How do you know this, Joe?" Allen's mother questioned Joe. "An angel told me." "So let me get this straight." Allen's dad was trying to understand it all. "Mary is a virgin who is pregnant with the Messiah. You have been commissioned by an angel to be the earthly father of this baby." "Correct." Joe looked at Allen's parents hoping for validation. "What do your parents think about this?" Joe hesitated. "They don't believe me. Dad threw me out of the house about an hour ago." "So you need a place to stay?" "Just until I figure things out. I was hoping to stay with my parents and graduate at the end of the semester. Then, after the baby is born, we could get married and I could get a job. I wasn't planning on being thrown out of my house."

Allen's parents looked at each other. They had been married long enough that they could communicate without saying a word. "You can stay here as long as you like, Joe. Your story is difficult to believe. I'm sure that you know that. I need some time to get my head around all of this, so forgive me if I'm skeptical. I wonder if the stress of this whole thing hasn't made you lose touch with reality. Having said that, you have always been a good, honest, trustworthy person. I admire your commitment to take care of the baby. We will help you in any way that we can." "Thank you, sir," Joe said relieved. Allen's mom spoke up. "There's one more thing. I must call your mother, Joe. I know Eve must be worried sick about you. I need to be a friend and tell her that you are here." "I understand, tell mom that I love her."

Mary looked out of her bedroom window across the street. She was just about to call Joe and tell him the good news about her parents when she noticed that Joe's car was gone. She sent him a text, 'Where r u?' In a few seconds, Joe returned a text, 'Allen's.' Mary sensed that something was wrong. She hit speed dial. "Hi Mary." Joe's voice was solemn. "Hi Joe, why are you at Allen's?" "Dad threw me out of the house." Joe's voice cracked a little. "I'm sorry, Joe. Maybe they will come around." "I'm not sure anyone will come around, Mary." "Well, sweetie, I have to disagree with that." "What makes you so sure?" "My parents believe, Joe! They are totally on board!" "Don't tease me Mary, I'm not in the mood and it's not funny." Just then Jake came into Mary's room to say good night. "I'm not teasing, Joe. It's true," Jake interrupted. "Is that Joe?" Mary nodded. "May I speak to him?" Joe heard the conversation and groaned. 'Here we go, I'm going to get chewed out, again!' Mary handed the phone to her dad. "Hey Joe!" Jake's voice seemed happy. Joe was confused. "Hello?" Joe said cautiously. "Joe, I owe you an apology. I'm sorry that I didn't believe you and Mary before. God has opened my eyes and I am sure that you two were telling us the truth. I am going to be the grandfather to the Savior! Please forgive me." Joe looked at the phone as if maybe it were broken and was giving him bad information. "Joe? Are you still there?" "Yes, I'm here." "Why don't you come over for a few minutes? I want to apologize in person." "Uh, I guess so. It's getting pretty late, though. Is Mary up to it?" Jake looked at Mary who was beaming back at him. "Mary, are you up to having my future son-in-law come over for a visit?" Mary shrieked with joy, "Yes!" Joe heard her over the phone. "I'm sorry, Joe, Mary says that she has a date. Maybe some other time." Mary playfully slapped her dad on the shoulder. Joe grinned to himself. Jake was back to his jolly ol' self. "Very funny, dad. I'll be there in ten minutes." Jake smiled when he heard Joe call him 'dad'. "Thank you, Lord." He closed the phone and hustled down the stairs to tell Ruth the good news.

As soon as Joe got out of the car, he saw Jake, Ruth and Mary sitting on the front step. Jake jumped up and ran over to Joe. He held Joe by the shoulders and looked at him as if he had never seen him before. With joyful tears in his eyes he said, "I'm sorry Joe. Can you ever forgive me?" "I already have, dad, I already have." Jake hugged him so hard that Joe thought he might break some ribs. Ruth and Mary had gotten to the men by now. "Do you have any room for us in there?" Mary tapped her dad on the shoulder as if to 'cut in' on a dance. "Absolutely," Jake reached out for Ruth while Joe pulled Mary in the circle. They all laughed, teased, and prayed out in the yard. It was a glorious moment for Joe and Mary. Finally, someone else believed.

Meanwhile, across the street at the Goldsteins, a single light came from the den. A silhouette of a man watched the celebration that was going in the Reubenowitz's front yard. No one noticed Abraham in the window. 'I wonder what is going on,' Abraham mused. 'I thought they hated us, especially Joe.' He watched until the four of them entered the house. He turned off the light and went to bed. 'That just doesn't add up. It makes no sense.'

CHAPTER THIRTY

Mary woke up the next morning and looked at the clock; 9:30. She had slept in because the celebration did not end until about 1:30 last night. She smiled to herself as she remembered the events of the party. There had been laughing, toasting, teasing, worshipping, and a lot of fun in their home last night.

Her peaceful thoughts were interrupted by reality. "Oh no! I forgot that mom and I were going shopping today!" She crawled out of bed and headed downstairs. "Good morning sweetie." Ruth was working in the den. "Good morning mom. I'm sorry that I slept so long. Do you still want to go shopping?" "No problem honey. We have plenty of time. Why don't you get ready and I'll make you some breakfast?" That sounds good, mom, thanks."

In less than 30 minutes, Ruth and Mary were in the car. "Where do you want to go, Mary?" Ruth was in full mother mode. She was going to spoil her daughter today. "I'd like to go to Helena if that's OK." Ruth felt guilty. Her mind returned to a conversation they had had when she had stated in anger that Helena was the only place she would go with Mary because she was ashamed of her. "Mary, if you are suggesting Helena because of what I said about being ashamed of you, I'm sorry. I'll walk into any store in Pleasantville with you and I'll be as proud as a peacock." Mary smiled and said. "Thanks mom. But I'm not ready to deal with the public yet. School starts in a few days and I will have no choice then. I would prefer to stay out of the mainstream until then. Besides, there is a store in the mall that specializes in maternity clothes. They will have a better selection." "I understand completely. I know that people are going to gossip and spread rumors like crazy. But we will get through it. For now, however, it is just you and me heading for Helena looking for a good time." Ruth held up Jake's credit card. "And this little jewel right here will insure that we will have a great time!" Mary burst out laughing as they headed for the interstate.

Ruth and Mary were having a great time shopping. It was getting close to 1 p.m. when Mary suggested that they take a break and have some lunch in the food court. Just as they sat down Mary heard a familiar voice several yards behind her. "Isn't it a small world." Ruth looked up and groaned. She whispered, "I can't believe that Delores is here." Mary turned red. "Just stay put, maybe she won't notice." Delores walked up to their table. "What a coincidence to bump into you two here." "Yes, what are the odds?" Ruth tried to be cordial. "Mary! How are you? I heard you spent the summer out of town?" "I'm fine, thank you." Mary said politely. Delores pulled up a chair and began doing what she does best; gossip. Mary and Ruth said very little as they ate other than nodding and smiling at what they thought were the correct instances.

Delores became more animated as she continued to talk. She was waving her hands around like an orchestra conductor. Then it happened. In a sweeping gesture intended for effect, Delores knocked a drink over right into Mary's lap. Mary instinctively stood up. The water had drenched her belly causing the material to cling to her stomach. Delores didn't notice her immediately. "I'm so sorry Mary." She grabbed a handful of napkins. "Let me help you." As she moved her eyes from the napkin holder to Mary's midsection, she noticed Mary's belly. "OH! I'm sorry; I didn't know that you were...I mean, uh...." Delores was shaken at the obvious news. However, she quickly regained her composure. Mary stood there humiliated. Ruth was furious. There was awkwardness in the air. Delores smiled like a fox. "I didn't know there were congratulations in order!" Her fake sincerity was apparent. She was loving this. "When are you due, Mary?" Mary ignored the question. "I'm going to go dry off." Mary slipped away to the restroom. Ruth was biting her tongue. She wanted to rip into Delores; but that would only make it worse. "I'll go with you Mary," Ruth announced as she got up and followed Mary. "Well, I've got to get going," Delores said with a fiendish grin. "I'll being seeing you." Ruth ignored her and kept walking. "Ruth!" Delores' voice echoed in the food court. Ruth spun around and glared at her as if to say, 'What?' "Let me know when you are having a baby shower, I'd love to help." Sarcasm dripped off of Delores's lips. Ruth kept her cool. "I'm sure you would, Delores." Ruth headed for the restroom and Delores disappeared into the crowded mall.

Ruth found Mary in the restroom trying to dry off. "Boy, that was fun." Ruth picked up on the sarcasm in Mary's voice. "That woman drives me nuts." Ruth was still fuming about the baby shower comment. "Are you OK, honey?" "I'm fine. I suppose it will be all over town in a few hours." "I'm afraid so honey; there's no stopping her now. She can't wait to get home and get rumor mill churned up. I'm sorry." Mary looked at her profile in the mirror and stroked her stomach. "It had to come out sooner or later. I guess I would have preferred later, but God wanted it to come out now. So be it. God's will comes first. I'm not ashamed, I'm proud. I know people won't understand and will think the worst, but that is not my problem; it is their problem." Ruth beamed. "That's the spirit, Mary. We will not allow gossip to drag us down. Now come on, we have more shopping to do!" Mary laughed. "You're the best mom." They exited the restroom arm-in-arm.

Joe had spent the day working on his car. Allen had come and gone a couple of times to go to two-a-day football practices. Joe missed football. He had briefly considered playing this fall, but dismissed the thought quickly when he realized that he needed to get a job after school. He was going to have a family to support. There was no longer time for boys' games. He was a man now; a man with a lot of responsibilities. Coach had called him a couple of weeks ago while he was still on the ranch. He was concerned when Joe didn't show up for practice. He had been relieved when he found out that Joe was working out of town. Joe had assured him that he would be in touch when he returned. He didn't have the heart to make it official. He hoped that, somehow, God would work it out.

Allen pulled up, fought his way across the driveway and collapsed in the grass. Joe was polishing his wheels. "I assume that you had a tough one?" Allen moaned. "I'll take that as a yes." Allen didn't look at him but confirmed Joe's supposition with a 'thumbs up' sign.

"Coach was asking about you." Allen sat up in the grass. "He knew that we worked together this summer. He figured that since I was there, you would be too." "What did you tell him?" Before he could answer, Allen looked up at a car coming down the street; it was Coach. He nodded in the direction of the street. "I told him that you were at my house. It appears like he wants to confirm that." Joe stood up. "Well here goes. He walked over to Coach's car. "Hey Coach, what's up?" "Well Joe I'm not sure. You tell me. I kind of figured that you would be at practice today. What's going on?" Joe looked down. "Truth is, Coach, Mary is pregnant. I won't be playing this year. I've got to get a job." Coach sat there a minute and allowed the news to absorb. After he got over the shock, he got out of the car and went around to Joe. 'Here comes the lecture.' Joe thought to himself. Coach stuck out his hand. Joe shook it and Coach pulled him close for a hug. "I guess that explains why Mary didn't try out for cheerleading this year. I can't say that I'm not disappointed. The team won't be the same without you. We'll miss you, Joe. But I can say that I am very proud of you. You made a mistake and are owning up to it like a man." Joe wanted to explain to Coach that Mary was pregnant with the Savior but he held his tongue. It just wasn't worth it. "I'm sorry Coach." "Don't worry about it, Joe. Take care of yourself and your family If you ever need anything, give me a call." "Thanks Coach." Joe watched Coach drive away. "Are you OK?" Allen asked. Joe wiped a tear from his cheek. "I'm good," he lied. "I just realized, again, that this isn't going to be easy."

Mary and Joe tried to spend the next few days out of sight. They drove out to a secluded park for a walk or a picnic or hung out at Angie's, but mostly they stayed at Mary's house. Mary and Joe discussed the option of going public before school started. But, with the help of Jake and Ruth, they decided to lay low this week. The rumor mill was in full swing thanks to Delores. She had been all over town telling whoever would listen about the encounter with Ruth and Mary at the mall. She justified her gossip by saying things like, 'We need to support the family' or 'Just thought you might like to know so that you aren't shocked when you see Mary'.

No one would directly say anything to Jake or Ruth when they saw them around town or in the store. They would merely look at them like sideshow freaks. They were the same looks people get when they pass a car wreck; either interested, pathetic or judgmental. Occasionally, someone would boldly ask if everything was OK or 'How's Mary?', and Jake and Ruth would hold their heads up, respond with, 'Everything's great! Why do you ask?' Then they would stare holes into the person until he or she slithered away.

Eve was so depressed that she never left the house. She would stay in bed until 11 or 12 o'clock and then would move into the den and lay on the couch until Abraham came home. She tried to make idle conversation with her husband, but it would end in a discussion about Joe. Invariably Eve would cry and Abraham would snarl.

Abraham received several inquiries from employees and customers. It was always the same, "Hey Abraham, I heard a rumor the other day. Is Mary Reubenowitz pregnant?" Abraham never answered. He would always ignore the question and move on. However, the look on his face told it all. The rumor was true. Usually, that was all it took. The conversation was over. Occasionally, however, someone would press the issue with an 'innocent' comment like, 'Is Joe going to marry her?' Abraham would respond angrily, "How do you know it's Joe's?" The shock of that response would end the conversation abruptly.

Mary and Joe also had their share of harassment. There was always someone calling their cell phones. On the rare occasion in which they actually answered, there was always some comment about not being able to fit into a cheerleading uniform or some crude insult about Joe being a stud. These calls hurt. Both kids decided not to answer unless they were sure that it would be someone civilized.

It was Saturday afternoon, school was to begin on Monday, and Joe and Mary had gone to Helena to see a movie. It was one last chance to get away. As they started for home, Joe's phone rang. "It's Cindy." Joe's tone asked Mary for advice regarding whether he should answer. "Who's Cindy?" Mary asked. "She's the freshman who flew out to Boston on the same flight as mine over spring break. You know, she is into architecture and construction. She worked for my dad this summer." "Oh yeah, I remember now. She and I had a few girl talks before school was out last year. She's cool, go ahead and answer it." "Hello?" Joe spoke into the receiver. "Hi Joe, it's Cindy." Her tone was flat, no emotion. "What can I do for you Cindy?" "I just heard a rumor and I hope it isn't true, but I must ask you; is Mary pregnant?" Joe looked at Mary who had overheard Cindy's question. Mary shrugged her shoulders as if to say, 'You might as well tell her.' Joe spoke softly, "Yes." Cindy didn't respond. "Are you still there, Cindy?" "How could you, Joe!? After all that junk you told me on the plane during spring break. You know, abstinence, sex is for married couples only, all that God stuff. It's just a bunch of bologna isn't it?!" Cindy was almost hysterical. "I believed you Joe, I really believed you. And I believed Mary. She fed me a load of bull about the same thing! You know, a lot of people look up to you two. Or should I say, 'looked' because they won't any longer. You have no idea how many people you have hurt. I hope you two are proud of yourselves!" The phone went dead. Joe looked at Mary. "I'm sorry, Joe." "Me too, I can understand how she feels. I probably would feel the same way. How do we tell people that things aren't always the way they seem?" "I don't know, Joe. I do know that it stings when people say that stuff. We must get tougher. We can't let it get to us. We are on a mission." Joe squeezed Mary's hand.

Joe pulled up to Mary's house just as the sun was going down. There was an unfamiliar car in front of the Goldstein's that neither Joe nor Mary recognized. They went on into Mary's house and sat down on the couch. Joe's phone rang; he rolled his eyes and looked at the caller ID. "It's my mother!" Joe was astonished. He hadn't talked to either of them since his dad had thrown him out. He opened the phone and spoke, "Mom?" "Joe, I don't have much time." Speak up mom, I can barely hear you." "I can't speak up; I'm upstairs in our bedroom and I don't want anyone to hear me. Now listen, there is a man downstairs asking your father a lot of questions about you and Mary. He wants to know where you are; if Mary really is pregnant; who's the father; lots of personal stuff. I can tell that your dad doesn't like him because he is evading the questions. He says he's from the government." Did he give you a name, mom?" "Yes, Jim Donavan. I've got to go, Joe. I don't want him to get suspicious." "Thanks mom, I love you." "I love you too."

Joe grabbed Mary's hand. "We've got to get out of here! Jim Donavan is over at my house. It is just a matter of time before he shows up here." "Who is Jim Donavan?" Jake asked. "He's the jerk who barged in on me this summer asking me a lot of questions about Mary." Ruth clenched her jaw. "He's the president's aide in charge of 'Teens for Abstinence' daddy. He is the one who is here to 'fix it'." Jake's face reddened. "You two get out of here," Jake ordered. "Spend the night somewhere else. I'll tell him that you are staying with friends. That will buy us some time."

Ruth was already at the door. "I don't see any sign of him, he must still be inside. You'd better go, now." "Mary," Joe looked her in the eyes. "You get in the driver's seat and put the car in neutral. I'll push us down the block and around the corner. That way, Jim won't hear the car start and get suspicious." "Got it." The kids slipped out the door and into the night.

Fifteen minutes later, the doorbell rang at the Reubenowitz's front door. Ruth opened the door. "I'm Jim Donavan, we met...." Ruth finished his sentence "earlier this summer. What can I do for you?" Ruth was extremely short with him. "Who is it dear?" Jake's voice came from the hallway. He headed for the door with the determination of a lion moving in on a kill. "It's that man I told you about who stopped in this summer." Jake stepped in front of his wife. He towered over Jim. Jake looked down at the man on his porch. "Do you mean the rude little weasel that claimed to be working for the president?" Jake knew the answer. He just wanted Jim to know where he stood on the subject," Ruth nodded. "What do you want?" Jake acted agitated. "I just need to ask you a few questions, may I come in?" "Do you have a warrant?" Jake growled. The question surprised Jim. "Well, no; I just wanted to visit with Mary for a few minutes." Jim changed his tone. Jake was intimidating him. "First of all, Mary isn't here. Don't know when or if she's coming back. Second, unless you have a warrant, don't ask to speak with my daughter. Third, visiting hours are over!" Jake slammed the door.

Mary and Joe came home around noon the next day. Mary walked into the house and flopped down on the couch. Joe closed the door and sat down next to her. "You two look horrible!" Ruth observed. Jake came in from the kitchen and looked them over. Mary was pale and Joe had dark circles under his eyes. "Bad night, huh?" Jake patted both of them on the back. "You can say that again, daddy. I couldn't sleep at all. Angie sat up with me most of the night. I couldn't get that man off my mind. I can't believe that he wants me to have an abortion!" "What happened to you, Joe?" Ruth asked. "I couldn't leave Mary. I wanted to be there if for some reason Jim found out where we were so I spent the night in the car outside Angie's house." "Aw, you poor kids, you're safe now," Ruth consoled. "Are you hungry?" Both kids nodded. "I'll give you a hand." Jake followed her into the kitchen.

A few minutes later, Jake and Ruth emerged from the kitchen with a tray of food. "Here ya go!" Jake started to announce but stopped when Ruth shushed him. She pointed to the couch. Mary was lying down with her feet on Joe's lap. Apparently, he had been giving her a foot massage when they both fell asleep. Jake and Ruth tiptoed back into the kitchen. "I'm worried about them, Jake," Ruth whispered. "I know, and this is just the beginning. Just wait until tomorrow when they go to school." Jake winced at the thought of what they would have to face.

CHAPTER THIRTY-ONE

Mary and Joe walked into the school fifteen minutes before the bell was to ring. They were immediately met with stares and whispers. A few boys giggled and the girls were caddy. The judgmental looks followed them everywhere. The kids looked at them like they were lepers. Joe and Mary stopped in at the office to pick up their schedules. There was a long line and the office was packed. Joe could see Jimmy up in front. He tried to position Mary so that they might not have to run into him but there was no way. They were stuck in the door. Jimmy grinned fiendishly at Joe as he headed in their direction. He purposely brushed up against Mary's extended stomach. "Oh, excuse me!" Sarcasm flowed from his mouth. "You must be in the wrong line. If you are trying to enroll your kid in school, the line for kindergarten is over at the grade school." Everyone in the room heard it and laughed; even the office staff. Mary turned red and Joe started for Jimmy. Mary grabbed his hand. "Don't." Joe stopped and looked around. Everyone was laughing and pointing at Mary's belly. They were humiliated. Just then the principal walked out of his office. "What's going on here? You kids have about ten minutes before class starts. I suggest you get your schedules and get going." The fierceness in his voice demanded an end to the ruckus. "Joe, Mary, please come into my office." They made their way through the crowd ignoring cat calls and fat jokes. When they made it to the principal, he showed them to his office and closed the door.

"Sorry about all of that, kids," he apologized. "I'll try to keep it under control but I have my limits. You had to know that this was coming." "We knew," Joe replied. "We just hoped that it wouldn't be this cruel," Mary added. "I'll get your schedules so that you can get out of here." "Thank you," they said in unison. In just a minute, he returned with two slips of paper. "Here you go. Good luck, kids."

As they walked out of the office and through the crowd, they heard someone say, "Since when do pregnant students get special treatment?" Another spoke up, "If I say I'm pregnant can I cut in line too?" The laughter and the looks continued. Joe was furious but he kept his cool. He knew that's what Mary wanted.

They walked down the hall in silence. Kids continued to stare and make rude comments. Mary sighed with relief when she noticed the cheerleaders had gathered in their normal place. She pulled Joe in the direction of the group. "Hi guys!" Mary tried to sound normal. Congratulations Lisa, I heard you made captain." That was difficult for Mary. Everyone knew that Mary would have been captain if.... All of the girls looked at Mary like she was from outer space. Then, one by one, without speaking a word, they turned their backs to Mary. Then Lisa said, "Shouldn't you be at a 'Teens for Abstinence' meeting? Oh that's right. I forgot that you don't abstain any longer." All of the girls laughed. Mary began to cry and Joe pulled her down the hall. "I can't believe they said that to me," Mary exclaimed between tears. "They are supposed to be my friends!" Joe stroked her forehead. "I guess you find out who your friends really are when you go through something like this."

He no sooner had spoken those words when a few guys from the football team walked by. "What's up guys?" Joe said hopeful that they would be decent. "Sorry you aren't playing this year, Joe." One of the guys who was a lineman said as they kept moving. He continued. "But it looks like you've been doing some other kind of playing there big guy. I can protect you on the field but I can't protect you in bed! You should have asked me about a different kind of protection!" Everyone within earshot busted out laughing. Another guy said, "Oh well, you can't do her any more harm, tag her once for me!" "Let's get out of here." Joe held Mary's hand. Mary eagerly followed tears still flowing down her cheeks.

The rest of the morning was miserable for the kids. In between classes, during classes; all of the time there were rude comments, pathetic looks and disappointed expressions from the teachers which followed Joe and Mary everywhere they went. When the lunch bell rang, Mary and Joe bristled again. They would be exposed to the entire school, all at the same time. They silently and slowly walked toward the cafeteria. Then a voice spoke from the intercom. "Mary Reubenowitz please report to the office immediately." Mary looked at Joe with fear in her eyes. "I'm going with you." "Thanks."

As they walked down the long hallway in the direction of the office, they could see several men wearing dark suits standing in the lobby. They could also see the principal talking with them. He spotted Mary and walked to meet her. "Mary, what's going on? These men are federal marshals and they have a warrant for your arrest." Mary squeezed Joe's hand so hard it hurt. As they walked closer, Mary could see the faces of the men. She stopped as she recognized one of them. "Jim," she whispered to Joe. "Don't worry, Mary, I won't let them hurt you."

"Hello Mary," Jim smirked. "I told you I would be back to fix this. This young man must be Joe." Jim stuck out his hand in a fake attempt to be civil. Joe glared at him and folded his arms over his chest, refusing to comply with the offer to shake hands. "Well let's get down to business." Jim rubbed his hands together as if to prepare them for some dirty work. "We have a warrant for your arrest, Mary. You must come with us." Joe spoke up. "What are the charges?" "This is none of your business, son." Jim tried unsuccessfully to push Joe back. "First of all, I am not your son, second, I am making this my business. So answer the question." "OK," Jim snickered. "The charge is obstruction of government. Now, we have worked out a plea agreement with the Department of Justice. If you agree to the terms, you will be free by the end of the day with no criminal record. If you don't agree, well, let's just say that prison will be involved." Mary gasped and Joe reddened. The veins on his neck were as tight as a rubber band. Mary caught her breath. "What are the terms of the agreement?" "We'll discuss that in the car." Jim looked at one of the agents who immediately pulled out some handcuffs. "Now, we can do this the easy way or we can do this the hard way. It's your call Mary." Jim's beady eyes narrowed as he smirked at her. "There's no need for handcuffs," the principal interjected. "Is there Mary?" "No." She gave in. "I'm going along," Joe demanded. Another agent stepped in between Jim and Joe. "Wait, just a minute," Jim said to the agent. "It might be a good idea if Joe goes along. His presence would indicate he agrees with the terms. Sure Joe, you can come along. There is just one catch. For your safety and mine, you must be handcuffed." Jim displayed an evil grin. Joe held out his hands and the agent slapped the cuffs on his wrists. The two were immediately taken to the car and swept away. The principal watched in disbelief.

"OK, we are in the car, what are the terms?" Joe demanded. He glanced at Mary. Her eyes were red and swollen from crying and she was trembling. Joe, still in handcuffs, gently bumped her arms with his elbow. "The terms are as follows." Jim's voice was monotone. "Mary agrees to have an abortion and will continue as chairperson of 'Teens for Abstinence' for a period of one year. She will deny ever being pregnant. If she agrees to those terms, the charges will be dropped." Mary injected a question. "What about the people from around here who already know?" "First, you live in the middle of nowhere. So we are not particularly interested in what a couple hundred people think. Second, you will tell anyone who questions you that it turned out to be a tumor. Thirdly, if anyone tries to make too much of this, we," Jim nodded to the silent thugs in the car. "Will speak to them on a personal level and provide incentive for them to drop the discussion. My friends can be VERY persuasive." One of the thugs chuckled.

"What if I don't agree to your terms?" Mary had collected herself and became bolder. "Then you disappear into prison for a very long time. I have known of cases like yours taking years to settle." Jim's evil grin was dreadful.

The car swung into the parking lot at the hospital. "Take those handcuffs off of Joe," Jim ordered. "We don't want to draw attention to ourselves." Jim focused on Joe. "You won't give us any trouble will you Joe? I'd hate to have you thrown in jail for the night." Joe didn't respond. His icy stare penetrated Jim. The agent removed the cuffs. They led the kids into the ER and Jim walked up to the lady behind the desk. After a couple of minutes of discussion, the lady disappeared through a door and within a few seconds reappeared with someone who looked like a doctor. He spoke with

Jim for a few seconds and then the two of them walked over to Mary and Joe. The doctor's demeanor was kind and pleasant. "Hello, I'm Dr. Sheppard. I'll be taking care of you tonight. Would you please come with me into the patient rooms?" Mary looked at Joe, "Can he come too?" "Are you the father?" Joe nodded. "Of course he can come." Mary and Joe got up and followed the doctor through the double doors. Jim was right behind them. "I'm sorry, Mr. Donavan, only relatives are permitted beyond this point." Jim started to protest. "Do you know who I am?" Dr. Sheppard turned around looking Jim straight in the eye. "Yes, you made it very clear who you are. You are an aide to the president who brought me a patient. However, I also know who you aren't. You are not a relative, so I will repeat. Only family members are allowed past these doors. I will keep you posted on the progress of the procedure." The doctor spun around and closed the doors behind him.

Once the kids got settled into one of the patient rooms, Dr. Sheppard excused himself with a promise to return shortly. "What are we going to do?" Mary was panicking. "I don't know, Mary. But there is one thing that I am sure about. This is God's child and I know that He is going to lead us out of this mess. I don't know how, but I do know that He will. I believe that with all of my heart." Mary relaxed a little. "I'm still scared." "Me too, Sugar Plum, me too."

Doctor Sheppard reappeared through the door carrying a clipboard. "We have some paperwork to fill out, standard stuff, most of it is legal mumbo jumbo, but we still have to do it. What is your name?" Mary's voice cracked. "Mary Reubenowitz." Doctor Sheppard hesitated and looked at Mary, then Joe, then back to Mary. "You wouldn't happen to be related to Jake Reubenowitz, would you?" Mary blushed with embarrassment. "He's my father." "I thought I recognized you. Your pictures are plastered all over that store." Then he looked at Joe. "You wouldn't happen to be the boy that I've seen in a lot of those pictures?" "Joe stood, smiled, and extended his hand. "Yes sir, my name is Joe Goldstein." Dr. Sheppard shook his hand. "Goldstein, Goldstein…hmm…it sounds familiar but I just can't place it…." He thought for a moment. "Is your dad Abraham from Dream Builders?" Joe nodded. "You dad put a room addition on my house last year. He is a wonderful man."

Joe continued to nod. The moment quickly became awkward as the three of them remembered why they were there.

Dr. Sheppard returned to the paperwork. After he filled in the address, birth date, and standard information, he looked up at them. "I need to ask you a few questions and provide some you with some information so that you understand exactly what is going to happen. Ready?" Mary nodded. "Do you understand what an abortion is?" Mary began to cry. Joe put his arm around her. "Yes," she said between sobs. "It's murder!" Dr. Sheppard looked up astonished and confused. He took Mary's hand and looked into her swollen eyes. "Mary, it's obvious that you have been carrying this baby for quite awhile. That tells me that you have struggled with this decision. Are you sure that you want an abortion?" Mary sobbed uncontrollably. Joe answered for her. "No, Dr. Sheppard, neither one of us wants an abortion. We want to have the child, get married, and raise Him ourselves." "I don't understand." Dr. Sheppard was really confused. "Why are you here?" "Do your parents know you're here?"

"It's a long story, Dr. Sheppard. Do you really want to hear it?" Dr. Sheppard sat down in one of the side chairs. "This is an important decision. From the sound of things, you may under some extenuating circumstances that may be clouding your thought processes. As your doctor, I believe it is my duty to help you fully understand the situation so that I can be sure that you are making the correct decision." Joe began. "First of all our parents do not know that we are here. They are totally against abortion. We were forced to come here by those men in the lobby. They are the ones that want Mary to have an abortion." "Why would the government care about a couple of pregnant kids from Montana?" Dr. Sheppard leaned forward in his chair. Joe continued. "Mary is the chairperson for an organization called 'Teens for Abstinence'." "Oh yeah," Dr. Sheppard interrupted. "I've seen your picture in the paper. I think we might have some of the brochures in the waiting room. It is a great organization. I've heard it is having quite an impact on some kids." Then he remembered why Mary and Joe were there. He looked at Mary's belly. "Oh, I see, that is a bit of a problem." Joe resumed his explanation. "Mr. Donavan is the president's aide in charge of the program. He is demanding that Mary get an abortion in order to save the integrity of the organization." Dr. Sheppard spoke up. "But the law says that Mary must consent to the procedure." "They have a warrant for my arrest, 'obstruction of government'. They are forcing me to consent or they will press charges. They are threatening to put me in jail if I don't go through with this!" Mary lamented.

Joe hugged her and whispered. "We're going to figure this out." "You bet we will." Dr. Sheppard was on his feet. He pulled his stethoscope from his pocket and hit the call button for a nurse. "Lay back on the pillow, I've got an idea." Just then the nurse opened the door. "You called?" "Yes, we need to do an ultrasound on this lady. Would you get the machine for me please?" "Right away." She disappeared down the hall. Dr. Sheppard put the stethoscope up to Mary's belly. "Do you know how far along you are?" he questioned as he continued moving the stethoscope around her stomach. "I am going on six months." Now it was Mary who was confused. Dr. Sheppard smiled. "Good. Wow! This little guy is going to town! I can't believe how active he is." The nurse reappeared pushing the ultrasound machine into the room. It wasn't long before she had the ultrasound hooked up and they were watching the baby move on the screen. Mary and Joe watched in astonishment as the Savior moved all around inside her stomach. The miracle of what they saw took them away from the reality of the moment. Dr. Sheppard waited patiently as he watched the kids enjoy the image. Suddenly, they snapped back to reality and looked at the doctor who was smiling from ear to ear. Joe was confused. "What?" Dr. Sheppard moved his eyes from the screen and focused on Mary. "This baby is viable!" Excitement filled his voice. "What does that mean?" Joe inquired. "It means that you are too far along to have an abortion! I couldn't do it if you wanted me to. It is against the law to abort a viable baby unless it is an immediate threat to the mother. Kids, you are in the clear!" Joe hugged the doctor and the nurse who was quite confused by now. Mary laughed out loud as she watched the baby tumble around in her womb.

When the celebration died down, Dr. Sheppard continued watching the baby on the screen. "Are you sure that you are only six months?" Joe looked at Mary who smiled. "Absolutely," Mary replied with confidence. "Why? "I've never seen anything quite like this." Dr. Sheppard observed. This baby is extremely unique. I can't put my finger on it specifically, but there is something very different about Him. Don't get me wrong. He is fit as a fiddle. But there is something about Him. He is very special." Mary and Joe smiled at each other and then at the doctor. Now it was his turn to be confused. "What?" he offered. Joe looked at Mary. "Should we tell him?" Mary laughed and shrugged her shoulders. "Tell me what?" Dr. Sheppard inquired.

"This is going to sound crazy, Doc," Joe began. "I'll begin at the end. You are looking at the Messiah, the Chosen One, the Son of God." Joe hesitated while his words sunk into Dr. Sheppard. Joe was waiting for him to react. However, his face remained stoic. "Go on." Joe continued. "Mary is a virgin who was told that she has been selected to be the earthly mother of the Messiah. We were both visited by angels who confirmed this to us. This happened in late March. I was in Boston and Mary was in Florida. We know the exact date when Mary became pregnant with the Savior." Joe waited for Dr. Sheppard's reaction. He continued watching the screen. "You probably think that we are nuts. Most people do. It took awhile for it to sink in to us. You won't hurt our feelings if you don't believe us. We are just so thankful that God sent you to us this very afternoon. You don't realize it, but God put you right here, in this moment, for this purpose. I can't thank you enough for helping us...."

"Shhh!" Doctor Sheppard interrupted Joe. "Look." He pointed to the screen. All eyes focused on the screen. There was the baby, hands together in a position of prayer and His head was bowed. Everyone in the room, including the nurse, held their breath. Time stood still as they watched the Savior pray. Warm feelings mixed with goose bumps, swirled around all of them. Then, the baby turned and appeared to fall asleep. Dr. Sheppard turned the machine off and looked at Mary and Joe. There were tears in his eyes. "I'm not even supposed to be here today. This is my day off. But the doc who was scheduled to come in got called away for a family emergency. I was in my den last night because I couldn't sleep. I was looking for something to read and I came across the Bible. I'm not a particularly religious person but my parents were. Anyway, something urged me to select it and it fell open to the Book of Isaiah, chapter 9. It speaks about the Messiah coming. Something strange happened that I couldn't explain until now. It was kind of a feeling, one of those moments when things strike you as being significant, one of those defining moments in which you realize that it is a significant point in life. Do you know what I mean?" Mary and Joe both nodded. "Anyway, I read a little more and went to bed. I still couldn't sleep but I felt the urge to pray. I hadn't prayed since I was a little kid. It's not that I don't believe in God. It's just that I kind of fell away from Him. So I followed the urge and started talking to God. Just like you and I are talking now. I asked Him to tell me what the passage in Isaiah meant. Then the phone rang. It was the other doctor. He asked me to cover his shift today." Doctor Sheppard got choked up. "Now I know why all of that happened to me last night. God was preparing me for this moment. Do I think you are crazy? No, not in the least. Just the opposite. I feel blessed, privileged, and honored to be in the company of the Savior."

Joe and Mary remained silent as the doctor quietly released his emotions. He sobbed, giggled, laughed, and cried. After a few moments there was a knock on the door. Mary answered, "Come in." A man walked in that the kids recognized immediately. Joe and Mary froze. "Dr. Sheppard, are you finished with the ultrasound? They need it up on the third floor." The man looked up at Joe and Mary as he waited for the doctor's answer; it was Guardian! He winked at the kids who grinned back at him. Dr. Sheppard snapped back into reality. "Yes, we're finished with it." "Thanks, Dr. Sheppard." Guardian backed the machine out into the hall leaving the door open. "Here you go," they heard Guardian say to someone. "Thanks, you're a lifesaver." A familiar voice sang back to Guardian. They watched the machine go by the door being pushed by Gabby. She waved at the kids as she walked by. Joe and Mary giggled. "Something funny?" Dr. Sheppard inquired. "Do you know those people, Doc?" Joe asked. "I've seen them around now and then. They seem to work unusual shifts. Sometimes they are here a lot and then I don't see them for awhile. Do you know them?" Mary smiled at Dr. Sheppard. "We've seen them around town."

"We had better get going." Dr. Sheppard changed the subject. "It's time to tell good ol' Mr. Donavan that abortion is out of the question. Come on. I'm going to really enjoy this." Joe and Mary followed Dr. Sheppard into the waiting room. "Stay here." He ordered the kids to stay by the desk. Joe and Mary stopped in their tracks and Dr. Sheppard walked swiftly over to Jim. They could see

Dr. Sheppard talking to Jim. Jim nodded for awhile and then began shaking his head. The conversation became more animated. Jim was obviously angry. He looked over at Joe and Mary and scowled. Dr. Sheppard put his hands on his hips and tried to be patient as Jim began ranting. Then Jim poked Dr. Sheppard in the chest with enough force to cause him to step back. Dr. Sheppard clenched his fists but kept his cool. "This conversation is over!" He said loud enough for everyone to hear. He quickly strode over to the kids. He smiled at them. "That went well...for me." He turned his back to Jim and chuckled. "What do we do now?" Joe asked. "Do whatever you want to do. You are free to go." "What about the obstruction of justice charges?" Mary wanted all of the bases covered. "I told Mr. Donavan that if he pressed charges against either one of you, I would go to the newspapers, TV stations, to anyone who would listen to me and expose him for exactly who he is. He threatened to have my license revoked but he is bluffing. He has no grounds. Even if he does, it would be worth it if it helps secure your safety. Just be careful. I don't trust that guy." "Thanks, Dr. Sheppard." Mary hugged him and Joe shook his hand. They headed out the door right past Jim and his thugs. "This isn't over," Jim hissed as they walked by. "I will fix this, one way or another." Joe put his hand on Mary's back and they continued out the door.

CHAPTER THIRTY-TWO

The next few weeks went by slowly, but uneventfully. The teasing at school continued which caused Mary and Joe to dread going. However, they were determined to finish the semester so that they could graduate. Joe continued to stay at Allen's but spent the evenings at Mary's. They rarely went out. It wasn't worth it. All of the kids except Angie and Allen either shunned them or said hurtful things. They had even tried going to a football game once, but the stares and pitiful looks from the parents were more than Mary could handle and they left at halftime.

Ruth and Jake were filled with conflicting emotions. When they thought of becoming grandparents, let alone grandparents to the Messiah, they were in seventh heaven. They would go shopping for baby clothes, high chairs, cribs...they were on top of the world. They had enjoyed spending evenings with Joe and Mary. Sometimes they would talk about places to live, things to expect when taking care of babies or just playing games and watching TV. The four of them had gotten very close. However, Ruth and Jake had to endure some of the similar insults that Joe and Mary had to experience. People would avoid any lengthy conversations with them at the store. In the past, their customers, who were also friends, would talk about their kids, things going on the community, what happened at the last football game, vacation plans, just general conversation. But now, they were distant, and avoided any lengthy discussions. Once in awhile, someone would ask, 'How's

Mary getting along?' with a pathetic sound in their voice. The tone sounded as if Mary had some terminal illness. Ruth would hold her head high and say, 'She's doing great, we are so excited'. That resulted in surprised looks and quick exits. They could handle that OK but it really hurt them to see Mary so upset when she came home from school. Joe did his best to protect her, but there was no way to shield her from everything. Besides, he got his share of comments as well. It really hurt Jake and Ruth to watch the kids go through such misery. They also really missed Abraham and Eve. They longed for their friendship and companionship. The history between the two families dated back to before they were married. They had been inseparable ever since. Jake understood how they felt. After all, he had felt the same way, that is, until God opened his eyes. Several times he tried to bump into Abraham. He would stay out in the front yard waiting for Abraham to come home or he would drive by some of his construction sites. But when Abraham saw him, he would turn away and ignore him. He had even thought of going over and knocking on their door but Joe had talked him out of it. If his dad reacted poorly, it would be hard on all of them, especially Mary. Jake prayed every night that God would give him a chance to talk to Abraham.

Mary usually drove her car to school. It was out of the way for Joe to come by and pick her up so they would meet in the parking lot and walk in together. However, Joe had decided to give Mary a ride on this sunny Wednesday morning late in October. Joe had already picked Mary up and Jake was heading out the door to the store. He was running a little late because he had overslept. He hurried to his car, jumped in, and tried to start it; nothing. It was dead. He hustled into the house and yelled to Ruth, "My car won't start; I'm taking Mary's car to the store." Ruth came out of the bedroom to the top of the stairs. "That's fine honey, I have a few errands to run and then I'll be there." "OK sweetie, got to go, I'm really late." Jake grabbed Mary's keys and ran out the door. Jake shuffled through the stuff in his car and placed what he thought would be necessary in Mary's car.

He jumped in Mary's car, fired it up and threw it in reverse. He sped down the street faster than usual trying to make up for lost time. He suddenly remembered a purchase order for some medicine that he had filled out the night before. It had to go out today or they would run out before the next shipment arrived. He searched through his briefcase as he drove down the street. In his distraction, he failed to notice a traffic signal change from green to red.

He looked up and saw that the light had changed. There was just enough time to stop but when Jake slammed on the brakes the pedal went all the way to the floor. The brakes were not working. Jake braced himself. "Wham!" He broadsided a pickup truck right in the middle of the passenger door. The airbag deployed and engulfed him causing him to be thrown back against the seat. Jake couldn't see anything because the airbag was all around him. He sat there for a moment, stunned, attempting to collect himself. All he could think about was the other driver. He had to get out of the car and check on him, her or even them. He tried to open his door but the impact had caused his door to jam. He pushed as hard as he could but to no avail. He finally gave up and sat back in the seat. All he could do was wait.

Someone came running up to the car shouting "Mary! Mary! Are you OK?" The voice was muffled but sounded familiar. Jake fought through the airbag and finally came face-to-face with the voice. Abraham was pounding on the window yelling Mary's name. As Jake maneuvered the airbag so that his face was revealed, Abraham stopped yelling and said, "Jake? Is that you? Are you OK?" Jake smiled weakly as Abraham tried to open the door. "Wait right here, Jake," Abraham ordered. "I've got a crowbar in the truck." A crowd was starting to gather by now and the sounds of sirens could be heard coming in their direction. Abraham returned and stuck the crowbar in the door. He pulled with all of his strength but couldn't open the door. "Let me help you." A stranger came up behind him. "Maybe we can do it together." "Thanks," Abraham replied. The two men pulled and strained until finally, almost magically, it popped. Abraham pushed the door open. "Are you OK, Jake?" "Never better." Jake smiled at his former friend. "Never thought I'd run into you here." Abraham shook his head in disbelief. How could he crack jokes at a time like this. "We need to get you out of here, Jake. I smell gas." "That might be a bit of a problem." Jake pointed to his legs. The force of the crash had caused the dashboard to jam into Jake's knees. "I think my leg is broken." "I'll lift you out, Jake." Jake laughed. "I know you're a big strong guy Abraham but there is no way. Let's just wait for the ambulance. "I think we can both get him out." It was the same guy who had helped Abraham pry open the door. "OK then." The two of them gently twisted and turned, pried a little here and there, but eventually got Jake out of the car. They helped him over to the grass and sat him down. The ambulance turned the corner and headed toward them. The gentleman who helped Abraham waved the ambulance over. The EMTs started looking Jake over and assessing the situation. They gently cut open his pants to reveal the leg; there was no doubt, it was broken. His bone was sticking out through the skin just above the knee. Abraham was busy directing the EMTs, trying to help them get Jake into the ambulance. Someone kept tapping Abraham on the shoulder, "Sir, sir." Abraham ignored him but the man was persistent. "Sir?" "Just a minute, fella," Abraham scolded him. Jake motioned for Abraham to come over as they were loading him into the ambulance. "What are you doing here, Abraham?" Abraham chuckled. "I'm the one you hit you big goofball." Jake chuckled along with his friend. "That explains the blood running down your head." Abraham felt the area just behind his temple. He hadn't realized it, but there was a six-inch gash in his head and blood was running down his neck and onto his shoulder. Again there was tapping on his shoulder. "Excuse me sir but I really think you should let someone take a look at that." Abraham turned around to identify the annoying voice. It was the stranger who had helped him with Jake. "You're bleeding pretty badly. You have been so busy taking care of your brother that you don't realize how bad you are hurt." An EMT began to examine his wound. Abraham looked at the middle-aged man and smiled. "He's not my brother." The man shrugged and began to walk away. "You could've fooled me." Abraham watched him take a few steps. "Hey, thanks for the help. What's your name?" The man stopped and faced Abraham. "Guardian, my name is Guardian. See you around." He disappeared into the crowd. Jake's voice resonated from inside the ambulance. "How 'bout it buddy. Want to share an ambulance? I can't afford it by myself." Abraham laughed and looked at the police officer who was investigating the accident. Abraham knew him. Dream Builders had built his house a few years ago. "Hey Bill, would you mind if I go get this taken care of? I'm feeling a little...." He never finished his sentence. He passed out into Bill's arms.

Fifteen minutes later the doorbell rang at the Goldstein's house. No answer. Ruth rang it again. Still no answer. She pounded on the door as hard as she could. "Eve! Open the door!" Ruth, not to be dissuaded, knew where they hide the spare key. She opened the door. "Eve, where are you? It's Ruth." The sound of Ruth's voice both angered and frightened Eve. She came out of the den. Ruth gasped. Eve, normally a very pretty, well-kept person, looked awful. "How dare you come barging into my house uninvited?" Ruth ignored Eve's tone. "Eve, there's been an accident. They're OK, but both of the guys are in the hospital. Come on, we've got to go." "What?!" Eve felt weak in the knees. Ruth steadied her as she led her to a chair. Jake and Abraham were in a wreck. It is not life threatening, but it is serious. We have got to go to the hospital. Now let's get you fixed up." Ruth brushed Eve's hair and helped her get dressed. Ten minutes later the girls were in the car. "We need to call the kids," Ruth said to Eve who remained silent since Ruth had told her the news. Eve seemed to be in shock. "Pleasantville High School;" it was a familiar voice on the line. "Hi Carol, it's Ruth." "Hello Ruthy! How are you doing?" Carol was always perky. Ruth got straight to the point. "Carol, Jake and Abraham have been in an accident. They are OK but both of them are in the hospital. Can you find Mary and Joe and tell them to call me?" "Consider it done, Ruth. Let me know if I can do anything." The phone went dead.

A few minutes later, Ruth's phone rang. It was Mary. "Mom?" "Hi honey." "Carol said that daddy and Abraham were in a wreck. Joe and I are on the way out to Joe's car. What's going on?" Mary's voice was shaken. "The police said that they are both OK. That's about all I know. Eve and I are pulling into the hospital right now. We'll see you two in a few minutes. Tell Joe I have Eve and you two, BE CAREFUL! I don't want you two to get in a wreck."

Mary and Joe found their mothers in the waiting room of the ER. Ruth had her head in her hands and Eve was crying. Both women sensed the presence of their children and stood up as they approached. Mary hugged Ruth and Joe held his mother. After a few seconds, both children released their grips on their mothers. Joe immediately reached for Ruth who hugged him tightly. Mary didn't know what to do. She wanted to hug Eve but she was unsure of how she would react. Eve's eyes looked sunken into her head.

She seemed to be a shell of a woman compared to what she looked like a few weeks ago. This ordeal had taken its toll on her. Eve slowly raised her arms in Mary's direction. Mary smiled and stepped into the embrace. Eve noticed Mary's belly during the embrace. A strange feeling came over Eve as she hugged Mary. It was peaceful and serene. Then the baby kicked. He kicked so hard that Eve felt it. She laughed for the first time in weeks. She stepped back and looked at Mary. Then it hit her. "It's true! I know it's true! You ARE carrying the Savior! I know it now!" Mary nodded as all four of them joined in a group hug.

A couple of minutes went by as the four of them basked in the moment. "I'm so sorry that I didn't believe you kids." Eve searched their eyes for forgiveness. "No problem, mom. We're just glad to have you back." Eve looked at Ruth. "Do you believe them?" Ruth grinned and hugged her friend. "I do believe Eve, and so does Jake. God revealed Himself to us in an amazing way. We are going to be grandparents to the Messiah!" They jumped up and down like school girls.

Joe came back to reality. "What's going on with the dads?" Ruth spoke up. "Jake is in surgery. He has a compound fracture in his leg. The doctor said that he should be OK. He should be out in a couple of hours." "How's dad?" Joe inquired. Eve jumped in. "He has a deep cut on the side of his head. He lost a lot of blood but they say he is going to be fine. They are stitching him up right now." "Can we see him?" Mary wanted to know. Eve squeezed her hand. "He is unconscious, honey." Mary gasped. "I guess he did lose a lot of blood," Joe's voice cracked.

About thirty minutes later, a lady wearing surgical garb emerged from the double doors. "Mrs. Goldstein?" Eve stood up. "I just finished stitching up your husband. It took 73 stitches. He is still unconscious. He has a pretty severe concussion. We gave him the last pint of AB negative blood that we have but that is a rare blood type. Anyway, we expect him to regain consciousness within a couple of hours. If we had more AB negative, he would wake up sooner and recover quicker." Joe spoke up. "I'm AB negative; I can spare a gallon or so." "Great!" the doctor said. "Come on in and we'll get the IV started." "Can we see him?" Eve spoke softly. "Are you all family?" Eve looked at the other three and beamed. "You bet we are!" The doctor led them to Abraham's room. She began hooking Joe up and continued. "He took a pretty bad whack on the head. He's going to wake up with a tremendous headache. But we will give him some pain medication for that when he wakes up. We are moving him to Intensive Care so that we can keep an eye on him. I expect him to be fully recovered in a couple of weeks."

The four of them sat around Abraham's bed in silence. Joe had a direct line from his arm to his father's arm. Abraham was pretty banged up. Both of his eyes were black. His head was bandaged and his left jaw was swollen. His arms were all cut and scratched. Eve sat with her head on the edge of his bed and held his hand. Even though the doctor had told them that he was going to be fine, she was worried. She didn't like how he looked or the fact that he was unconscious.

None of them had known how long they had been there. It was like time stood still. On the one hand, it felt like they had just sat down, like they had been there for only a few minutes. At the same time, however, it was as if they had been there for days. Their trance was interrupted when the doors to the IC unit opened. The orderlies were pushing a gurney through the doors following a doctor. "Mrs. Reubenowitz?" Ruth stood up and noticed that it was Jake in the gurney. The orderlies positioned him in the area next to Abraham. "The surgery went fine. I was afraid that we were going to have to reconstruct the femur in order to set it properly but it snapped right back in place. We secured it with a couple of screws. He should be fine. He won't be able to get around very easily for a few weeks, but I would guess that he'll be walking in three to four weeks." Ruth shook the doctor's hand. "Thanks, I really appreciate it. How long before he wakes up?" "I'm not sure." The doctor looked at Jake. "He's a pretty big guy; it took a lot to knock him out. He should wake up in an hour or so." She hesitated and then added, "Your husband is a lucky man, and this could have been worse; a lot worse." Then she smiled at Ruth and retreated back through the doors.

The four of them just stood there in between the beds. They would look at Jake, and then at Abraham. Both of them seemed to be sleeping peacefully. One of the nurses came up to them and said, "I know this is hard on you all. It's getting close to 12:00. Maybe you should go to the cafeteria and grab some lunch. I'll call you if either of them wakes up." She, Ruth and Eve started to protest but Joe sensed that a diversion may be good for all of them. "That's a good idea. After all, Mary needs her strength, she's eating for two. Come on, moms, the lady said that she would call. He held up his arm with the tube in it. "Besides, I'm kind of tied up here."Joe winked at the nurse as she ushered the girls out of the room.

When they returned there was no change; both men were still asleep. They all made themselves comfortable in some chairs that the nurse had brought in for them. Joe had been correct; the lunch break had been good for them. Eve and Ruth discussed everything about the baby. It was good to see the two women back to normal. Mary sat there and grinned at them.

Abraham stirred slightly. Eve jumped up to the side of the bed. Then he moaned. The nurse came over. "He's coming out of it." "Abraham, it's Eve. I'm here. Can you hear me?" Abraham blinked a few times and groaned. He put his hand to his head. Eve repeated, "Can you hear me Abraham?" He opened his eyes and looked at his bride and smiled. "Sounds like an angel. Am I dead?" He chuckled ever so slightly. Eve returned the smile and kissed him on the forehead. "No honey, you're not dead. I'm not through with you yet." Abraham, still groggy, looked around the room. Then he remembered, "Is Jake OK? He was pretty banged up. I remember getting him into the ambulance but it gets foggy after that. Wow, my head is killing me." The nurse jumped in. "I am giving you something for that right now. You should feel better in just a few seconds." "He's going to be fine, dad. He's in the bed right here next to you." Joe stepped aside so that his dad could see Jake. Abraham noticed the tube running from Joe's arm into his. Abraham got choked up. "I throw you out of the house and you give me blood!?" Tears ran down his cheeks. Joe played it off. "No big deal, dad, we checked your oil and you were a couple of quarts low. You always taught me to keep plenty of oil in the engine." Joe's wit broke the awkward moment. That's when Abraham noticed Ruth and Mary. "Hi Ruth, is that true? Is the big lug going to be OK?" Ruth sighed; relieved that Abraham wasn't angry, at least for the moment. "That's what they tell me and I believe it. He's too ornery to be hurt too bad." Abraham smiled at the thought. Then he looked at Mary who had been keeping her distance, halfway hiding behind Joe. Abraham held his hand out to Mary. "Come closer, honey." Mary slowly approached his extended hand. As she took it, he sighed. "I'm sorry, Mary. I should never have doubted you and Joe. I now know that you were telling the truth. You are carrying the Savior." Abraham searched Mary's teary eyes for forgiveness. Mary smiled and nodded. Abraham looked at Eve and said, "It is true honey, I swear." Eve, tears of joy streaming down her face said, "I know, Abraham, I know." Joe squeezed his dad's hand. "What changed your mind, dad?" Abraham relaxed and looked deep into Joe's eyes. "Ever heard of a guy named Guardian?"

Joe nodded and Mary held her breath. Abraham related the story of how Guardian had helped him at the accident. "I thought he was just a good Samaritan until just now. But he spoke to me while I was out. I mean it was as real as if he were standing here right now. Anyway, he told me the truth about you two and the baby. It was amazing." Everyone just stood there. No one knew what to say. All they could do was grin. The silence was broken by a voice from behind them. "Welcome back, buddy." Jake was leaning up on an elbow smiling at the group. "Daddy!" Mary hugged her dad. Ruth came over and kissed her husband. Eve patted him on the arm. "I missed you Eve," Jake whispered. "How long have you been awake?" Joe inquired as he greeted Jake. "Long enough to know that Abraham has finally come to his senses. How's it feel, Grandpa!" Abraham laughed out loud and then grabbed his head. "Don't make me laugh, you old goat!" Everyone burst out laughing. Mary bubbled up on the inside. The baby was doing flip-flops inside her. She placed Abraham and Eve's hands on her stomach so that they could feel. Tears filled Abraham's eyes. "Praise God!"

The celebration was cut short when a nurse appeared with a police officer. "Hi Bill." Abraham recognized him. "Hello Abraham, Hi Jake. How are you guys doing?" Jake spoke up. "We're fine, Bill. I suppose you're here to tell me that the accident was my fault. No problem, I admit it," Abraham interrupted. "I'm pretty sure it's my fault Bill. Everyone knows what a bad driver Jake is. I should have known better than to be out on the roads with him!" Everyone laughed except Bill. "Seriously Bill," Abraham continued, "there's no need to file with our insurance companies. We'll work it out between ourselves, right buddy?" "That's right." Jake added. "I'm sure it will at least cost me dinner!" Everyone laughed again. But Bill remained serious. "I'm afraid it isn't that simple. You see, this is now a criminal investigation." "Criminal investigation?" Abraham repeated in disbelief. "Are you tied up with the some bad actors there, Jake?" Jake picked up on the tease. "I'm busted. I confess. I've been involved with drugs for over thirty years." He howled at his own joke. "We've determined the reason for the accident." Bill continued. "It wasn't an accident. The car was sabotaged. The brake lines were cut. There was no way that you could have stopped that car." In an instant, the smiles faded into looks of concern. No one spoke as the words of the police officer sunk in.

Bill broke the silence. "Jake, do you have any enemies? Anyone angry enough to want you hurt or dead?" "I don't think so, Bill." "Have you sued anyone for lack of payment at the store?" Ruth answered. "No, he never does that. If they don't pay, he just writes it off." Have you fired anyone, argued with a supplier, gotten into it with a neighbor? Anything?" The only neighbor that I have had a disagreement with is Abraham here. But I am sure that he wouldn't do anything like that." Everyone considered the possibility for just a second and then dismissed it as impossible. Mary spoke quietly. "It isn't daddy's car; it's mine. Daddy never drives my car. I don't think they were after daddy. They were after me."

A hush fell over the room. Joe looked at Mary. They knew what each other were thinking; Jim. He had said that it wasn't over. Mary's expression was a look of helplessness. Joe shook his head slightly to let Mary know that now was not the time to tell a local police officer that an aide to the president was attempting to kill her. "Mary?" Bill spoke kindly. "Is there anything that you want to tell me?" Mary shook her head. Ruth read her daughter's body language. "Bill, this is a lot to absorb. A lot has happened today. Give us some time to think about it. If we come up with anything we'll call you." "I understand. I'll leave you all alone. But be careful. I can tell this was a professional job. Whoever it is means business, and they are very good. Call me anytime."

After Bill left the room, Ruth looked at Mary. "I can tell by looking at you that you have a pretty good idea who might be trying to hurt you." "So do I," Jake interrupted, leaning up on his elbow with a scowl on his face. Ruth had a pretty good idea as well. The four of them had discussed Jim's threats on more than one occasion. However, Eve and Abraham were clueless. They hadn't had the benefit of being involved in the details. "Anyone care to fill us in?"

Abraham looked at Eve who had a confused look on her face. Joe spoke up. "The president's aide, Jim Donavan, wasn't too pleased with the idea of the chairman of the 'Teens for Abstinence' being pregnant. He drummed up a bunch of false charges against Mary and came to school and arrested us." "Oh, no," Eve gasped. "They hauled us away to the hospital and said that they would drop the charges if Mary got an abortion." Abraham got very upset and tried to sit up. The pain in his head was too great; he leaned back against the pillow and moaned. Joe continued. "Luckily for us, the ER doc stood up for us and told Jim that Mary was too far along for an abortion. That's when Jim left and told us that this wasn't over. We think he's trying to kill Mary. He wants to save the face of 'Teens for Abstinence' and is willing to murder in order to do it."

No one said a word for a long time. Everyone was trying to absorb the craziness of what Joe had verbalized. Abraham looked at the ceiling and spoke softly to his friend. "Jake, you know what we have to do." Jake shared Abraham's upward stare. "I know." He slowly turned to look at Abraham who by now was looking back at Jake with tears in his eyes. Jake choked up and said, "We have to get these kids out of here. They are in danger and it isn't safe here. For all we know, Jim and his thugs are outside right now." Eve went over to the window and looked outside. Ruth tried to protest. "But they need us, Jake! Who's going to look after them? How will they manage? WHERE will they go?" Jake held out his big hand toward Ruth. She took it and he pulled her close. I don't like this either, Ruth, but it's the only way. We have to get them out of town; tonight." "The sooner the better," Eve added through some sobs. "I see a couple of limos parked at the main entrance down there. I've only seen that kind of limo once before and Jim was the one in it!" It's only a matter of time before they figure out that their plan failed." Joe walked over to the window and looked out. He saw Bill, the police officer who had just left their room walk up to Jim and begin talking. Joe could see that Bill was waving his arms in disagreement with Jim. Soon a couple of the thugs walked up and the conversation stopped. They walked by Bill who stood there shaking his head.

"Mary, we've got to go right now!" Joe started gathering his things. "Jim and his henchmen are on their way up here right now! Come on!" Joe and Mary hugged all of the parents briefly and started to leave. "Wait a minute." Jake's voice was concerned. "You kids are going to need some cash. Ruth, get my wallet." "Good point." Abraham agreed. Eve was already digging through his clothes. All four of them pulled out all of the cash that they had and handed it to the kids. Joe looked at the money; astonished at the size of the wad. "There must be over three thousand dollars here!" Mary exclaimed. "Thanks." "Where are you going?" Eve asked quietly. Her saddened voice reminded everyone that they might not see the kids for a long time. "I don't know." Joe replied, "but we'll call you when we get there. We love you all." "Joe," Abraham stopped them. "Don't be afraid to use the credit card. We'll get you more cash when we find out where you are and Joe." Abraham smiled at his son. "I'm proud of you, both of you." Joe and Mary waved goodbye as they closed the door. Ruth looked at Eve through teary eyes. Eve returned the same helpless stare. "We need to pray for those kids," Jake whispered. Abraham sat up, swung his legs around to the side of the bed, and took four steps in order to get to Jake. All four of them bowed their heads and prayed.

Joe and Mary walked quickly down the hall. "We had better take the stairs," Mary offered. "We don't want to run into them on the elevator." "It's four floors down, Mary. Do you think you can make it?" Mary walked through the door marked 'stairs' and said, "Watch me." Joe followed her down two flights before they heard someone coming up. Both kids froze. Could Jim be coming up the stairs? "Can you see who it is?" Joe whispered. Mary peaked over the railing and shook her head. The steps were coming closer. It sounded like they were running. Mary moved closer to Joe. He put his arms around her and waited. The footsteps rounded the landing and they came face-to-face with the person who had been running up the stairs. "Well, fancy meeting you two here!" Dr. Sheppard hugged Mary and shook Joe's hand. "What are you two doing in the stairwell?" "Let me give you the short version, Doc." Dr. Sheppard could tell that Joe was in a hurry. Joe recounted the accident, the results of Bill's investigation, and the fact that Mr. Donavan was in the hospital. "We think he's here to make sure his plan worked," Joe concluded.

Dr. Sheppard's face turned red with anger. "I just spoke to Bill in the lobby. He seemed out of sorts; kind of frustrated. Come with me, maybe I can help." He led the kids down the remaining two flights of stairs. "What kind of car are you driving?" "It's a 1967 Shelby GT, black with a white racing stripe. Why?" "Nice car." Dr. Sheppard smiled. "Thanks," Joe returned the smile. "My dad and I rebuilt it." Mary interrupted. "Really guys? You want to talk about cars at a time like this?" "Right. Sorry." Dr. Sheppard apologized. "You stay here. I'm going to go out and make sure that they aren't watching your car. I'll be right back."

Dr. Sheppard walked into the lobby and nodded in the direction of a man wearing a black suit. Joe could see through the small glass window that it was one of Jim's men. Dr. Sheppard walked through the double doors and out into the afternoon sky. It wasn't difficult to pick out Joe's car. Dr. Sheppard strolled around the lot as if he were on a break and occasionally stopped to stretch. In just a few minutes he walked into the stairwell. "There is one guy in the lobby and two guys in the parking lot.I'm convinced that they are watching your car, Joe. You guys cannot go out there." Mary looked despondent. Joe tried to console her. "I've got an idea." Dr. Sheppard grinned at the kids. "This is my lucky day." He held up the keys to his car. "Want to trade?" "What?" Joe was confused. "Look, Joe. The hospital staff parking lot is right out that door." He pointed to a door behind them with an exit sign above it. "My car is sitting in the front row. Just take my car. It's no Shelby but I think it will work for you. It's the only way you two can get out of here unnoticed." Joe grabbed his keys and tossed them to Dr. Sheppard. "I don't know what to say, Dr. Sheppard. How can I ever repay you?" Dr. Sheppard held up his hand. "Tell you what, just put in a good word for me with the Messiah, OK?" Mary and Joe hugged Dr. Sheppard and started out the door. "Oh, Dr. Sheppard, what kind of car is it?" Joe asked as he scanned the parking lot. "It's that little silver one right in front of you." Joe looked at the car next to him. "This one?!" "Yes, it's a little smaller than yours, sorry. You'll just have to make due." Mary's jaw hit her chest and Joe grinned at the doc. "I'm sure that a brand new Porsche Carrera will be just fine." Joe and Mary slid into the seats, waved at the doc and drove away.

"Where are we going to go, Joe?" Mary's voice trembled. "We need to run by the house and get some stuff and then we are getting out of town." "Do you think it's safe to go back to the house? They may be there." Mary was scared. "They are at the hospital looking for us. I think we'll be OK for a few minutes. Besides, it's beginning to get dark; hopefully, no one will see us." Joe stopped in front of Mary's house. "You go get some clothes and stuff. Just get bare necessities. I'll do the same thing. I'll meet you back here in five minutes." The kids jumped out of the car, looked around for anything suspicious, and walked quickly up the sidewalks to their homes.

Five minutes later Joe came out of the house carrying two bags. He threw them into the car and waited for Mary. After a couple of minutes, he became worried. 'Where is she?' he wondered to himself. 'Could they have been waiting for her inside the house?' Surely he would have noticed something. He looked at his cell phone; it had been ten minutes. He started to panic. He ran up the sidewalk and just as he got to the door he heard some struggling going on inside. There were a few thumps and bangs and then he heard Mary; "Ow!" she cried. Joe threw open the door ready for a fight. He could barely see because it was almost dark and there were no lights on. He strained his eyes, "Mary?" "Down here, Joe." Joe looked in the direction of the voice. It was coming from the bottom of the stairs. "Are you alone? Are you OK?" There was a long silence. Then Joe heard Mary quietly sobbing. "Turn on the light, Joe," Mary whispered between sobs. Joe found the light and flipped the switch. Mary was sitting on the floor. There were four suitcases scattered all around her. Much to Joe's relief, she wasn't sobbing, she was laughing. "What happened?" Joe was confused. "I was trying to bring all of these down at once. I slipped on the last step. That's when you came in." Joe helped Mary to her feet. "What did you think happened?" Joe collected himself. "I thought someone was in here. It sounded like you were being attacked." Mary laughed harder and Joe began to giggle. "Are you sure you're OK, Sugar Plum?" "I'm fine, Joe. My hero," she mocked. "I can't wait to tell the baby about the time you saved me from some ferocious stairs!" "Very funny." Joe began picking up the suitcases. "Say, what happened to "bare necessities, and five minutes?" he teased. "These aren't even all of the bare necessities and you know that there isn't any such thing as five minutes when it comes to a girl getting ready." She kissed him on the cheek and said, "Come, quit fiddling around, we need to get going." Joe shrugged and followed Mary to the car.

CHAPTER THIRTY-THREE

Mary and Joe rode silently for a few minutes. The levity of the moment back at Mary's house had temporarily allowed them to escape the looming realities. Joe headed for the interstate. "North or south?" He broke the silence and answered Mary's question at the same time. He didn't know where they were going either. Mary said a one-word prayer, "Help." The answer came to her immediately. Go north Joe; I don't know why, but I do know north." "OK, Sugar Plum; north it is."

Joe turned on the radio. He felt like it may reduce the tension. Occasionally, one of them would sing along or make an attempt at small talk; but both realized that they were trying, unsuccessfully, to console the other. The kids continued down the interstate both wondering where they were heading. After about 45 minutes, Joe tried again. "I haven't been this way in I don't know how long." He hesitated. "I guess it's been since I went with you and your family to...." Mary looked at Joe who was grinning back at her. "Aunt Liz and Uncle Zac's!" they said in unison. Mary flipped open her phone and hit speed dial. "Hi Aunt Liz, it's Mary." "Well hi yourself, sweetie. This sure is a coincidence. Zac and I were just talking about you. I was saying how much I missed having you around and Zac mentioned that he had been having a funny feeling about you. We were just praying for you." Mary laughed into the phone. "We sure need it Aunt Liz." Mary heard rustling in the background. "Yes Zac, it's Mary." Mary listened as Liz hit the button. "You're on speaker sweetie." "Hi Uncle Zac. How are you?" He gave Liz a 'thumbs up'. "He still can't talk, Mary but the old coot is fine. But the bigger question is 'How are you?' I haven't been able to get you off my mind all day. I just got a funny feeling down in my stomach. Can't quite put my finger on it. I just don't feel right about things. Are you OK?"

Mary paused for a moment. "Mary? Are you still there?" "Yes, Aunt Liz, I'm here." "What's wrong honey?" "It's a long story," Mary sighed. "The short version is that someone is trying to hurt me. Joe and I are leaving Pleasantville. We don't know where…." Aunt Liz interrupted. "You kids head straight here. Right now! I mean it! I won't take no for an answer. Where are you?" "Thanks Aunt Liz. You don't know how much this means to us. We should be there in a couple of hours." "We'll be waiting, honey," Aunt Liz soothed. "Don't worry, it will be OK." "Thanks Aunt Liz. Oh, by the way, we are in a different car; another long story, it's a Porsche. Don't shoot us Uncle Zac." Aunt Liz chuckled. "You sure know your uncle. He's getting his shotgun out of the closet as we speak!" Mary heard Uncle Zac shuffling some papers in the background. He gave Liz a note. She read it to Mary. "You pull that little car in the barn. I'll be on the porch with my Winchester. Don't you kids worry. We'll take care of you. Ain't nobody gonna hurt my niece and nephew." Joe could hear the conversation. He smiled when he heard Zac call him a nephew. Aunt Liz spoke up. "Don't stop for anything. I bet you're hungry. I'll fix something for you kids and have it ready when you get here." Mary giggled. "Bye Aunt Liz."

An hour later Joe looked at the gas gauge; it read half full. "I'm going to get some gas. I don't want to get to your aunt's house on empty." He exited the interstate and pulled up to a pump at a gas station. "I'm going inside," Mary announced. "I'll be in after I fill up," Joe replied. "I need some coffee." There were several cars in the other spots at the station that had customers filling their cars. The gentleman across from him overheard Joe's statement and said, "I know what you mean, it's getting late, I could use a little coffee myself." After Joe filled the tank he went inside. 'That's odd,' he thought to himself. Even though there were cars in the parking lot, there was no one in the store. There wasn't even anyone at the cash register. "Hello?" No response. 'Mary must be in the restroom.' He walked over to the coffee counter and began pouring himself a large cup. Mary walked up behind him carrying a bottle of orange juice and squeezed him on the arm. Her touch startled him so much that he spilled the coffee. "I'm sorry, Joe. Why are you so jumpy?" "Isn't it kind of weird that no one is in here?" Joe said as he grabbed some napkins and began cleaning up the spill. Mary looked around. "I didn't notice it when I came in, but it is kind of strange. It gives me the willies." Joe finished cleaning up the spill. "Let's get out of here." He grabbed his coffee and headed for the counter. "Hello?" Joe almost yelled. A muffled female voice responded from the back room. "Be right there." Joe rolled his eyes at Mary. "It's a good thing we are honest. We could have walked right out of here." Now the voice came from behind the cash register. "I was pretty sure you wouldn't do that." Startled, because they didn't see the attendant appear, Mary and Joe whirled around. "Gabby!" Mary shouted with surprise. "What are you doing here?" Gabby chuckled. "I suppose that I could ask you the same question. But, I already know the answer. You two are heading to Liz and Zac's. That's a good move. But the Boss," Gabby pointed skyward, "wanted me to let you know that it is not where you will give birth to the Savior." Mary and Joe looked at each other. "What are you talking about? Where are we supposed to go?" Joe sounded desperate. Gabby smiled. "He will guide you. You just need to have faith. Don't get impatient. God will lead you. Just wait for His signal."

The bell rang indicating that someone was coming through the door. Joe and Mary instinctively turned to see who it was. The gentlemen who had spoken to Joe outside nodded and smiled at the kids. When Mary and Joe turned back around to Gabby there was a young man standing in her place behind the register. "That'll be $37.73," he said without looking at the kids. Joe looked at Mary who was staring straight ahead in disbelief. He pulled out two twenty dollar bills, laid them on the counter, got the change and ushered Mary out of the door.

Once they got into the car and started to drive away, Mary said, "Didn't see that coming." Joe laughed. "We need to start writing this stuff down. I want the baby to know what we went through to get Him into this world!" Mary chuckled and searched her purse for some paper. "Good point. Even if nobody believes us, we will be able to recall quite a few memories when we get old! I can't fathom it, Joe; it's just crazy. I'm scared, humbled, blessed, comforted, excited, and anxious all at the same time!" Joe smiled at his future bride and squeezed her hand. "I know, Sugar Plum, I know."

Joe turned into the long driveway belonging to Aunt Liz and Uncle Zac. It seemed like every light in the house was on. The glimmer of the yellow lights against the backdrop of a full moon on a cloudless night made the house look like a painting. The image was so impressive that both kids sighed as they approached the house. They finally felt safe; at least for awhile.

Joe stopped in front of the house and the kids got out of the car. "Hey kids," Aunt Liz's voice came from the shadows. "It's good to see you." The rocking chairs creaked as Liz and Zac stood up. Even though it was dark, Mary and Joe could tell that Zac was holding his shotgun. Mary skipped up the stairs and threw her arms around her aunt and uncle. Joe followed closely and joined in the hug. "Thanks for letting us stay with you, Uncle Zac." Joe's voice cracked. He broke down as he spoke. The adrenaline rush was over. He was relieved to be around people he could trust. Zac sensed Joe's emotions. He hugged both of them tightly. Zac scribbled on a notepad. "You are welcome kids. We wouldn't have it any other way."

Joe stepped back from the hug and pointed to the shotgun. "Expecting company?" Joe knew why Zac had the gun. He used the question as an excuse to collect himself. Zac stepped back and held up the gun in a mock defensive position. Zac wrote on the notepad. His grin turned serious. "You never know when varmints are going to show up." Everyone knew what he meant. He intended to protect the kids. No matter what had to be done. Zac wrote more. "You had better get that car in the barn. A car like that will draw attention in these here parts. We don't need for anyone to be asking a bunch of questions." Joe nodded, headed to the car, unloaded their bags, and put the car in the barn.

Joe entered the house and was greeted by the mixed aromas of good food. He suddenly realized that he was very hungry. He followed his nose into the kitchen where everyone had gathered. "We got leftover roast beef and potatoes. Here are some salads and I just took an apple pie out of the oven. Help yourself Joe." Aunt Liz smiled and handed him a plate. Mary was already busy filling her plate. "Apparently you are as hungry as I am," Joe teased. Mary turned around and grinned at Joe. She was chewing on a carrot. "You have no idea, Joe." They all sat down and ate while Mary and Joe filled Zac and Liz in on the details of what had been happening. Aunt Liz gasped several times during the conversation and Zac turned red several times. He wrote on the pad. "Try not to worry. God will take care of you kids. You are safe here."

Mary looked at Joe who knew what she was thinking. 'Should we tell them about what Gabby had said at the gas station?' Mary read Joe's mind; 'No, there is no need to alarm them.' They both smiled appreciatively and then Mary yawned. "I'm getting sleepy. I think I'll turn in." "Me too," Joe added as he got out of his chair. Both kids said good night to Aunt Liz and Uncle Zac.

Joe followed Mary out of the kitchen. "We should call our parents. I know they will be worrying." "Good idea, Joe. We can call them from my room." Mary sat down on the edge of the bed and hit speed dial. Ruth's phone rang. She shuffled through her purse, found the phone, and looked at the caller ID. She looked around the hospital room and panicked. Her face turned white. Abraham, Jake, and Eve read her look and figured out it was one of the kids. Ruth opened the phone. "Hi Delores!" Ruth mustered up a cheerful voice. "How are you?" Mary held out the phone and looked at it as if there were something wrong with it. "Mom?" Mary spoke curiously into the phone. Ruth continued. "It's so nice of you to call." "Mom, what's going on?" Mary was still confused. "Oh yes, the guys will be just fine. They are a little banged up. But they will heal up quickly. How is your family?" Mary figured out the charade. "Can't talk right?" "That's right Delores. You are welcome to come over but there is a room full of people here." Ruth wasn't lying, there were several people in the room. "Mom, you are acting weird. Is everything OK?" Mary quizzed. "Who's here? Oh you know, many friends and relatives. I guess everyone came over after work. Some folks are in jeans and some are in suits." Even though Ruth was cheerful, Mary sensed that her mother was in an extremely awkward situation. There was something wrong. Ruth NEVER described people by how they were dressed. In addition, Ruth disliked Delores. IF Delores had called, Ruth would be cordial but cool. The fact that Mary had called her 'mom' and she didn't respond meant not only that she couldn't talk; she was under some duress. Ruth's voice cracked a little. "Oh, Mary and Joe? They are fine. We expect them to get here any time now." Now Mary was convinced that there was trouble. Joe, who had overheard the entire conversation, looked at Mary and gave her the slashing signal across his neck indicating that Mary should end the conversation. "I get it, mom. I'll call back tomorrow. I love you." "Thanks for calling, Delores, I'll tell the boys. Take care."

Mary hung up the phone. "That was weird." Joe sat there thinking. "There is obviously someone there that she is uncomfortable with." Joe said as he looked at the floor. "Someone whom she didn't want to know that she was talking to you. Who could that be?" "I don't know Joe; and that comment about what everyone was wearing was off the wall; my mother never does that." Something came to Joe. "That's it!" He turned to face Mary. "She was giving us a clue! It's the suits! No one wears suits during the week in Pleasantville. At least no locals." Joe hesitated waiting for the information to sink into Mary. In a few seconds, it came to her. She spoke softly. "It's Jim, he and his thugs are in the room waiting for us." Joe had been so determined to figure out the puzzle that he had temporarily forgotten the seriousness of the situation. His shoulders slumped. "And I guess that comment about us getting to the hospital anytime was for their benefit." Mary nodded in agreement and put her head on Joe's shoulder.

Ruth slowly and deliberately closed her phone. She looked directly at Jake. "That was Delores; she heard about the accident and called to check on you two." Jake, Abraham, and Eve knew that she was lying. So did all of the other people in the room; that is everyone but Jim and his crew. They had no clue. It was a small town and most people looked after each other in Pleasantville. The friends and relatives who were in the room had sensed tension when Jim was in there. They didn't know why, they just knew that he made Ruth, Eve, Abraham, and Jake uncomfortable; and that was all they needed. They were loyal friends. No one said a word.

Jim spoke up. "Tell me again, Mrs. Reubenowitz, where is your daughter?" Jake started to interrupt but Ruth put her hand on his. She glared at him and spoke sternly. "Like I told you several times before, Mr. Donavan, I called the school as soon as I found out about the accident. Mary and Joe came directly to the hospital and were here for several hours. We sent them out to get some supper and they haven't returned." "That's been several hours ago; aren't you worried?" Jim snarled right back. Eve jumped in. "Look! You've stood right there and watched us attempt to call our children several times." The 'attempts' had been staged. Both Ruth and Eve had called their homes when they had claimed to call the kids. "They are not answering their phones! Of course we are worried. But we trust our kids, and more importantly, we trust God to look after them. It is not unusual for us to have poor cell phone service. We live in a mountainous and remote part of the country. We don't have all of the luxuries that you Washington folks enjoy. Why don't you mention that to the president, Mister Donavan?"

Jim was stunned for just a second. He wasn't accustomed to be challenged. His eyes narrowed. "Maybe if you hadn't been so trusting," Jim held up his fingers and signed quotes around the word 'trusting'; "of your children, they wouldn't have wound up in a family way." Jake turned red and clenched his fists. Abraham threatened Jim and started to get out of bed. A deep voice from the back of the room spoke. "I got this." Everyone from Pleasantville recognized the voice. It was Mark.

Mark was a good ol' boy who lived in the mountains. He was raised on a farm but made his living as a lumberjack. He was a huge man—six foot, eight inches, and three hundred twenty-five pounds of sheer muscle. He had long black hair and a beard to match. He had fierce, piercing green eyes and was intimidating to anyone who didn't know him. To those who did know him, he was a big teddy bear. Known all over town as, 'Uncle Mark', he could often be found in the park playing with the children. Piggyback rides were his specialty. He could carry three at a time. Everyone loved him.

Mark slowly walked toward Jim. His thugs snapped to attention as Mark approached their boss. The air was filled with tension. No one breathed. Mark stopped about three feet from Jim and held up his hand in the direction of the thugs who were making their way to Jim. They stopped. Mark glared into Jim's eyes. "Relax boys, ain't nothing going to happen to this here little weasel. Besides, if there was, there ain't enough of you all to stop it." Mark smiled fiendishly at Jim as he towered over him. He deliberately took a step toward Jim, who by now had his back to the wall. Mark leaned down so that their noses were just inches apart. Mark spoke in a soft but firm voice. "Didn't your momma teach you any manners? If I had said what you just said to these nice people, my momma would have slapped me into next week." Several people chuckled quietly. Mark continued. "Now I think that these folks have had enough for one day. I suggest that you and your little band of wannabes ought to call it a day. Don't you?"

Jim slid out from Mark's glare and motioned for his men to follow. He paused as he opened the door. "You have no idea who you are dealing with. I'm going to overlook this evening due to the circumstances of the accident. However, know this; and make no mistake about it, I will find your daughter and justice will be served," Jake yelled at the top of his lungs. "If you so much as touch my daughter I'll hunt you down and...." "You'll do what?" Jim snapped back. "Attack a federal agent? Obstruct justice? Send your goon," he nodded at Mark, "to take care of things?" "Maybe," Mark interjected with a slight grin. Jim turned his focus to Mark. "I'll deal with you later." "Looking forward to it." Mark was now smiling. Jim walked out the door followed by his goons.

CHAPTER THIRTY-FOUR

The next two weeks went by without incident. Abraham and Jake got out of the hospital and were spending the days renewing their friendship as they recovered. Jim's men hung around the hospital for awhile, but quickly figured out that the kids were not coming back. Mary and Joe had contacted their parents a couple of times. Everyone was glad that the kids had gone to Zac and Liz's. Jim would never find them there.

It was Friday afternoon and Mary was talking to her parents on the phone. The conversation was cut short because of a poor connection. There was an annoying clicking sound that made it almost impossible to hear. Just as Mary was saying goodbye, Joe and Zac walked in the house for lunch. "How's your mom and dad, Sugar Plum?" "They are OK, I guess. We couldn't talk long, we had a bad connection."

Eve was getting lunch ready for Abraham when the house phone rang. "Hello?" Eve didn't recognize the number. "Hi Eve, this is Roberta." She whispered into the phone. Roberta was a close friend who worked at the telephone company. "Hi Roberta, what's up? Why are you whispering?" "I'm calling from a secure line here at work and don't want anyone to hear me. Listen, I need to tell you something; if I get caught, I will lose my job and might be prosecuted so keep it under your hat, OK?" Eve became concerned. "Sure thing, Roberta." "Good, I just wanted you to know that your phone line has been tapped. Yours and the Reubenowitz's both have an indefinite order to record any and all conversations. I don't know what's going on, but this came from high up. I just happened to see an e-mail on my boss' desk." Eve couldn't speak. "Eve? Are you still there?" "Yes, I'm here, Roberta. I can't tell you how much this means to me. Thank you for calling." Then Eve panicked. "If the phone is tapped, aren't they listening to THIS CONVERSATION?" "No Eve. This line is secure; that means it can't be tapped in either direction, either incoming or outgoing. It's the ONLY way anyone talking on your phone will not be recorded. Just thought you should know." "Roberta, does this extend to our cell phones as well?" Roberta thought for a moment. "I can't say for sure. You cell phones are on a different carrier. But I would assume so. I've never seen an order like this before. Someone REALLY wants to hear what being said in your houses. Oops, gotta go. Here comes my boss." The line went dead.

Eve hung up the phone. The shock of what she had just heard resonated in her mind. 'Could this all be actually happening? Could the government be so upset that they are willing to tap phones and attempt murder just because some program might have a little egg on its face? Really? The fact that Mary is in charge of 'Teens for Abstinence' and has become pregnant has cause for embarrassment; no one would dispute that; but murder?' The thought made her shiver. She walked out the front door and headed across the street. Abraham had gone over to visit with Jake. Ruth and the guys needed to know this.

"We have to let the kids know what's going on," Jake announced after Eve had finished filling them in. "I agree," Ruth added. "If they call here and happen to mention where they are, Jim will be there before you know it." "But how do we contact them without using the phone?" Eve questioned. All four of them looked at each other as they quietly searched for the answer. "Probably can't trust e-mail either," Jake offered. Abraham shook his head. "We also have to assume that Mary and Joe's phone are tapped as well. In fact, they could be tracing their phones via satellite. I've heard that as long as a cell phone is in use, its location can be tracked." Ruth groaned and Eve became frightened. Abraham perked up. "I've got an idea. What if we borrowed a phone and called Liz and Zac. More than likely their phone isn't tapped." "Good idea, buddy." Jake slapped Abraham on the back. "I'll run next door and borrow Candy's cell phone," Ruth volunteered. "She won't care." Ruth zipped out of the back door and was gone.

Liz, Zac, Mary and Joe were finishing lunch when all of a sudden Liz cringed; "Oh!" Mary giggled. "Is that little guy kicking again?" "I suppose so." Liz said as she collected her breath. "He's never kicked that way before." They all got up and began clearing the table. A few minutes later, Liz bent over a chair, clutched her stomach, and cried, "Owww!" Zac ran to her side and motioned for Joe to help him get her to the living room. Once on the couch, Liz calmed down a little and smiled at Zac who was sitting next to her holding her hand. "Zac, it's time." Zac misunderstood Liz. He thought that she was asking what time it was. He pointed to the clock on the wall. Liz laughed. "No dear, it's time. My water just broke. The baby is coming." Zac hugged Liz and Mary screamed with excitement. Joe, who was in the kitchen, heard the commotion and came out holding a piece of apple pie in his hand. "What's all of the ruckus about?" "Aunt Liz is having her baby!" Mary yelled as she jumped up and down with excitement. Joe dropped the pie and said, "I'll get the car. Mary, you get Aunt Liz's bag. Uncle Zac, can you get Aunt Liz outside to the car?" No response. "Uncle Zac? Are you OK?" Zac turned and looked at Joe. With a smile on his face, tears of joy streaming downing his face, he nodded. Joe shot out the door and Mary skipped up the stairs.

Thirty minutes later they arrived at the hospital. They wheeled Liz into the ER with Zac in hot pursuit. Joe and Mary parked the car and headed into the waiting area. "I guess this is a good dry run for us Sugar Plum." Joe put his arm around Mary and gave her a squeeze. "Looks pretty easy so far," he teased. Mary playfully slapped him. "Yeah, easy for YOU!"

Ruth tapped her fingers on the kitchen table as she listened to the phone at Liz and Zac's ring. Abraham, Jake, and Eve watched anxiously. Three rings, four rings, five rings; the answering machine picked up. Ruth looked at Jake for help. He waved his hands telling her not to leave a message. She hung up. "I don't think it's a good idea to leave a message like that on their machine," Jake suggested. "It wouldn't make sense and it may scare them." Abraham shook his head in agreement. "We'll try back later."

Candy's phone beeped. "No we won't, at least not with Candy's phone. The battery is dead."

Mary and Joe sat down in the waiting room; both wondering how Aunt Liz was doing. After a few minutes Mary laid down the magazine that she had been looking through. 'I think I'll call mom and daddy. I'm sure that they would like to know that Aunt Liz is in labor." Joe nodded in agreement. He was watching a news channel on the TV in the waiting room.

Ruth nearly jumped out of her skin when the phone on the kitchen rang. She jumped up and looked at the caller ID. "It's Mary! What should I do?" "Don't answer it." Jake offered the obvious. "But she knows that we are here. I told her so when we spoke briefly this morning. She'll worry if we don't answer." "It could be possible that you are out and Jake can't get to the phone." Eve offered a weak excuse. Abraham spoke up. "It's better for her to worry than for Jim to find out where she is." Five rings later the phone went dead.

"That's funny, there's no answer," Mary said to Joe. "Maybe they are on the porch or something," Joe suggested. "Did you leave a message?" "No, there was this clicking sound in the background that was really annoying." "Why don't you try your mom's cell phone?" "Good idea Joe, mom ALWAYS has her cell phone."

Ruth's cell phone rang. "Is it Mary?" Eve asked knowing the answer. Ruth nodded. "There's that clicking again." Mary was frustrated. There must be something wrong with my phone." She shook it in a feeble attempt to fix it. "Any suggestions, now?" Ruth's eyes pleaded with the rest of the parents. "Mary knows that I always have my phone." "Let me talk to her." Eve held out her hand. Ruth gave up the phone. "Hi Mary!" The clicking got louder. "This is a terrible connection. I can barely hear you. How's the weather down in Nevada? Are you enjoying your vacation?" Mary looked at the phone as if it were broken. "Eve? Is that you? Where's mom? What's all this talk about Nevada? You know good and well we are in...." Eve yelled into the phone. "What's that dear? I can barely hear you!" Click, click, click; the noise continued in the background. Mary became angry and confused. She yelled into the phone. "Tell mom that Aunt Liz is in labor!" Eve panicked for a second. "So you called your Aunt Liz, that's nice; I'll tell Ruth. Goodbye." The phone went dead. Mary closed her phone. Joe spoke first. He had heard it all. "Something is wrong. That conversation was weird. My mom doesn't act like that unless...." his words trailed off. Then a thought occurred to him. He flipped open his phone and called his mother.

Meanwhile, the parents were trying to figure out how to safely call the kids. "Well, we know they aren't at Liz and Zac's," Jake stated analytically. "And we know that Liz is in labor," Abraham added. "Then most likely, Liz and Zac are at the hospital." Eve's face lit up. "They must be at the hospital!" Ruth yelled, jumped up and hurried over to the counter. She fumbled through the drawer and found her address book. As she was flipping through it looking for the hospital's phone number, Eve's phone rang, it was Joe. She opened her phone, click, click, click.... "Hi Joe! How are you?" Joe hesitated, and said a quick prayer. "Please God, let mom remember." "Hi mom, I was just thinking about Uncle Noah. How's he doing?" Eve looked confused. Uncle Noah had passed away before Joe was born. Why would he ask about.... Bang! A light came on in Eve's mind. This was Joe's way of suspecting that something was wrong. This was a code that she and Joe had set up when he was a small child. If something were ever wrong, she could call him and ask about Uncle Noah. If everything was OK, he was supposed to say, 'Why momma, you know Uncle Noah is gone'. But, if there was something wrong, he was to respond, 'Uncle Noah is just fine, momma.' That would be her clue that she needed to get to him ASAP. Joe was just turning the tables. Eve spoke softly into the phone. "Uncle Noah is just fine sweetie." Click, click, click, the background noise continued. "I didn't hear you very well, mom, did you say that Uncle Noah was fine?" Eve smiled and said in a loud voice. "Yes, Joe he's fine!" "Thanks, mom, I was just wondering." He slowly closed his phone and continued looking at it. "There is something wrong," Joe finally offered. "What are you talking about, Joe? And what is all that stuff about your Uncle Noah?" "That was a code my mother and I worked out when I was a kid. Uncle Noah died before I was born. But if I was ever in trouble and talked to mom, I was supposed to tell her that Uncle Noah was fine. That's exactly what mom told me. Her answer tells me that something is wrong. And all of that nonsense about Nevada tells me that they want someone to think we are someplace other than where we are. I just can't figure out why they won't come out and tell us plainly. Why all this mystery and code?" Joe looked at Mary quizzically. "I think I've got it, Joe." Mary had sadness in her eyes. "They are afraid to talk to us on the phone because the phones are bugged. That would explain the clicking noise every time we talk. Our conversations are being recorded or something." Mary got quiet. "Joe, I'm scared. Do you know what I am thinking?" Joe nodded his head. "I believe I do, Mary. Jim is trying to track us down."

Mary and Joe sat there for a long time. Both of the kids were trying to absorb this information and figure out a solution. "Well at least our parents are on to them. They have Jim thinking that we are in Nevada somewhere," Mary said resolutely. "I hope you are right, Mary." Joe sounded less sure. "What makes you think differently?" "I don't know for sure, but I think I heard that it's possible to track cell phones through satellite transmissions. I remember now, that's how they found that lost hiker in the mountains last year. He kept his phone on and they traced the signal right to him." "Do you think Jim would go to that kind of trouble just to find us?" Mary hoped the answer to her question was 'no'. "He went to enough trouble to cut your brake lines, didn't he?" Just then the doors to the emergency room burst open. Uncle Zac came striding out with a huge smile on his face. Joe reached for a piece of paper and pen to hand it to Zac so he could communicate what was going on. Zac wrote on the paper, "It's a boy!" Joe asked, "What's his name?" Zac took the paper back and wrote, "His name is John." Immediately Zac was able to speak and he began praising God. Mary shrieked with joy and Joe hugged Uncle Zac. "How is Aunt Liz?" Mary wanted to know. "She and John are doing fine, honey." Suddenly, it dawned on Joe. "Uh, Uncle Zac, do you realize that you are talking? What happened to your voice?" Zac laughed a big hardy laugh that made everyone in the waiting room look in his direction. "Boy, I missed laughing out loud. Anyway, I got my voice back as soon as John was born. Come on, Liz wants to see you two." He led the way through the doors and into her room.

Mary followed her uncle into the room. As soon as she laid eyes on her baby, he kicked, and kept kicking. Liz offered to let Mary hold John and Mary readily accepted the offer. She sat down in a rocking chair and looked deeply into John's eyes. Then, miraculously, John smiled directly at Mary and placed his tiny hand around Mary's finger. Mary felt like John was trying to communicate with her. A tingling sensation began in her womb and radiated up through her arm and down into John's little hand. Just as it reached John, he giggled and squeezed a little tighter. At that point, Mary knew that John was communicating with the Savior. As Mary and Joe were admiring the baby, Liz mentioned to Zac that he should call Jake and Ruth. Zac fumbled through his pockets. "I guess I left my phone at home." Then he saw where Mary had laid her phone down when she had picked up John. Zac grabbed her phone unbeknownst to the distracted kids and dialed. Ruth looked at the caller ID; Mary. "I guess the kids haven't figured out what the problem is yet. I suppose I'd better answer." She picked up the phone. "Hi Mary." Click, click, click, "Listen, don't talk. I need to tell you something...." Zac interrupted. "Ruth, it's not Mary, it's Zac! Good news! It's a boy! His name is John! He and Liz are doing great!" Click, click, click.... "Boy, this is a terrible connection. Can you hear me?" "That's wonderful, Zac." Ruth related the news to everyone at the table. "I just wanted you all to know!" Zac was as excited as Ruth could ever remember. "Well, you said that you needed to tell Mary something so I'll turn the phone over to her. Bye Ruth!" "Wait! Zac? Don't!" Too late. "Hi mom." Mary's voice cracked. Click, click, click. "Hi sweetie, are you OK?" "Yes." "We need to talk, honey, but not now. I'll get to you somehow, but we had better hang up now." Suddenly, the clicking stopped. "But mom," Mary protested. "That awful noise just quit I really need to ask you some questions." "I know, Mary. But not now; goodbye." The phone went dead.

Somewhere, in a small motel just outside Pleasantville, a man took off his headset, switched off the computers and other equipment that he had been operating and made a call. "Yes?" The voice on the phone spoke as if he were being interrupted. "Location is confirmed. They are about three hours away in a rural community upstate. I have pinpointed the location to within 100 feet." There was a short pause. "How sure are you?" "Very sure, sir. The conversations that they have had confirm the satellite signal. Both are coming from the same place." "Thanks Doug." "You are welcome, Mr. Donavan. Oh, by the way. They may be suspicious. You may want to hurry." "We are already in the car, Doug. Can you upload the coordinates into my portable GPS, please?" "Already done sir." "Good, keep listening and tracking through the satellite. We can't let this one slip through our fingers." Jim hung up the phone and switched on the GPS. "We got them, boys. Let's go." The limo sped out of the parking lot. "How long until we get there?" Jim asked. "We should be there in about two hours, Mr. Donavan." "Make it faster, Doug says that they may be on to us. I don't want to lose them." "Shall I notify the state police, sir?" "Yes, tell them that we are on official government business and to leave us alone." "Do you want an escort?" "No! I don't want to roll into that town looking like a circus. That's all we need. Just keep the police off of our tail. We don't have time to deal with speeding tickets." "Yes, sir."

The doorbell rang at the Reubenowitz's house while all four parents were still sitting at the kitchen table. "Who could that possibly be?" Jake got up from the table and started for the door. He looked through the peephole and saw that a police officer was standing there. He had his back to the door so he couldn't tell who it was. "Good evening, officer," he said as he opened the door. The policeman turned around and smiled. "Why hello Bill." Jake pounded his friend on the back. "Come on in. Ruth, Eve, and Abraham are in the kitchen." "Good," Bill said. "I would like to talk to all of you." He hesitated. "Say, do I smell some of Ms. Ruth's apple pie?" Jake laughed. "Boy, I knew that you cops could sniff out donuts, but pie too?" Bill played along. "We have reason to believe that Ms. Ruth's apple pie may be dangerous to the public. I've been sent here to inspect it and make sure it's safe for consumption." "And how do you propose to do that, my friend?" Jake teased. "Well Jake, you know that I am dedicated to insure the safety of the citizens of our community. I am willing to sacrifice myself in order to absolutely insure that the pie is safe. I may be forced to taste it!" Jake bellowed as he led Bill into the kitchen. "Hi Bill!" Ruth, Eve and Abraham said in unison. "To what do we owe the pleasure of this visit?" Abraham stood up to shake his hand. "Bill is here," Jake spoke in a hushed, spy-like type of voice, "on a highly sensitive mission." He is here to investigate the potential dangers in Ruth's apple pie." Eve rolled her eyes and Abraham chuckled. Ruth jumped up and brought Bill a piece of pie. Bill popped a bite in his mouth and savored it like it was a slice of heaven. After he swallowed a second bite he looked around at the four people around the table. "How's the investigation going?" Abraham blurted out. Bill swallowed and got serious. "The FBI took it over. It was the weirdest thing I've ever seen in all my years on the force. Within 24 hours after the accident, they came in, took my files and ordered me never to discuss it with anyone." All four parents exchanged looks of confusion. Eve spoke the obvious question. "Why then, are you discussing it with us?" Bill finished his pie and looked at his watch. "Would you look at that. My last shift is over. I am officially retired." "What do you mean, retired?" Abraham asked. "I thought you had four more years to go?"

Bill smiled wryly. "It appears that I have become "uncooper-ative" as of late." Bill leaned back in his chair. "I argued with my captain about the FBI taking over my case. I don't mind help; I've worked with those boys before, but, for them to just take it away without an explanation just didn't seem right. So I bucked the system. I started poking around in some classified computer files and such. I didn't like what I found and went straight to the captain. That's when I was "offered" early retirement. The kind of offer I couldn't refuse so to speak. But I will tell you this, that government guy, Jim Donavan is up to no good. He has been bullying his way around headquarters like some kind of king or something. I believe he's tied up with your accident somehow." Bill paused a moment. "There are a couple of other things you may want to know," Bill continued. "Your phones are tapped." "We know," Ruth confided. Bill looked confused. "How did you know?" "Roberta over at the phone company told me." Bill busted out laughing. "That's great! I love our town. We do stick together." "What was the other thing you thought we should know, Bill?" Eve asked. "I just heard an all-points bulletin telling all officers to allow a government limo to speed north on the interstate. We are not to stop them under any circumstances I recognized the plates; it's the same car that Mr. Donavan is using. Listen folks, you all are like family to me. I want to help but I need to know why they are after Mary. What could that sweet little girl have done to cause so much expenditure of manpower?"

"Thanks Bill," Jake said quietly. "You have just confirmed what we have been assuming." Jake looked at the other three parents for approval. They all nodded. "Well Bill, it's kind of a long story but I'll give you the highlights." "Sounds good to me." Bill leaned back in his chair.

"You might have heard by now that Mary is pregnant." Bill looked at the floor in embarrassment. "Yes, I've heard. But kids make mistakes!" He said defending Mary and Joe. "The last time

I checked, being pregnant isn't against the law!" Jake held up his hand in an effort to calm Bill down. "That's not all there is to it. Mary is chairperson for a national organization called 'Teens for Abstinence' supported by the president and a bunch of other high-powered people in Washington. Well it doesn't look good for the chairperson of such an organization to be pregnant." "Why doesn't Mary just quit?" Bill was looking for easy solutions. "She tried, they won't accept that. Something about having too much invested in her personally. Mr. Donavan doesn't want the organization embarrassed. They tried to force her to have an abortion but she is too far along and the doc wouldn't do it. That really made Mr. Donavan angry. Then a couple of weeks went by and we thought that was the end of it. That's when we had the accident." Bill leaned forward in shock. "Are you telling me that you think Donavan cut Mary's brake lines?! That he is so proud of his 'organization's' reputation that he would be willing to kill someone?!" Bill's words resonated through-out the room. It was the first time that anyone had actually verbalized what everyone was thinking. After a long silence, Abraham was the first to speak. "That about sums it up, Bill. Kind of crazy isn't it?"

Bill was lost in thought. It took awhile for Abraham's words to sink in. "Crazy isn't exactly what I was thinking. This is downright evil. But it sure does explain a lot; the secrecy at the office, the FBI taking over the case, the fact that Donavan's goons are tracking you all by bugging your phones, the fact that I got fired! It all fits! As weird and twisted as it sounds there is no other explanation for it. Our government is out of control." Bill put his head in his hands and moaned.

Jim Donavan's limo was just about to pull onto the interstate when he noticed an unusual car coming at them from the opposite direction. "Isn't that a 1967 Shelby?" he asked the driver. "It kind of looks like one," the driver replied. One of the goons spoke up. "That is Joe Goldstein's car, sir. I am sure of it." "Turn around. Follow that car!" Donavan ordered. "But Mr. Donavan, Doug said that they were in...." "I don't care what Doug said!" Donavan bellowed. "At least one of them has to be in that car! The limo spun on a dime and began to follow the Shelby. "Not too close," Donavan ordered. "We don't want him to spot us."

The limo followed the Shelby all the way up to Joe's house. "Pull over at the end of the block," Donavan ordered. "We can watch from here." A person got out of the Shelby and strolled up to Mary's house. Donavan couldn't see who it was but assumed that it was Joe. He watched as the person rang the doorbell or so it seemed, he stuck his hands in his pocket as if he were looking for keys. Donavan couldn't quite tell. In a few seconds the person stuck a key in the door and went inside. "We've got him!" Donavan said gleefully. "She can't be far away. Let's give them a few minutes, maybe she'll show up too." The goons nodded and settled back in the seats.

"Well, hello Dr. Sheppard," Ruth said as she closed the door. "This is a pleasant surprise. Come on in the kitchen. We were just having a little desert. Would you care for some apple pie?" Dr. Sheppard stopped in the middle of the living room and looked at Ruth. "Ruth, I'm here to tell you all something very serious." Ruth's smile turned sour. "Well, this must be the night for serious discussion. Bill is in the kitchen filling us in on what he knows about...." "Let me guess," Dr. Sheppard interrupted. "Jim Donavan and his plan to hurt your kids." Ruth was astonished. "How did you know? Come on in the kitchen and we can all share some information."

After polite greetings, Dr. Sheppard sat down at the table. "What's going on Doc?" Jake went straight to the point. "Well, first of all, I am sure that Jim Donavan is out to hurt your kids, at least Mary. I was the attending physician the day they brought Mary in to force her to have an abortion. I was the one who told Donavan that she was too far along and that the baby must be allowed to come to full term. He was furious. I remember he threatened them as they left the hospital. That's when I decided to remain involved." "What do you mean by that?" Ruth questioned. Doctor Sheppard smiled. "I am sort of a nerd when it comes to electronics. I am a ham radio operator which allows me to communicate with people all over the world. Since I have been doing this since I was a kid, I have developed friends everywhere including Washington DC. I also have police scanners and other equipment that tells me what's going on locally. I have these so that I can track emergencies where I may be called into the hospital." "Very interesting," Abraham interjected. "What have you learned?" "First, there has been a lot of chatter in the DC area about a 'situation' in Montana. The phrase

'Teens for Abstinence' comes up frequently as does Jim Donavan's name. Unofficial channels say that he has complete authority to rectify the problem in whatever way he deems necessary."

"That's all interesting Doc," Bill spoke up. "But you have just confirmed what we all have suspected anyway. Did you know that their phones are bugged and that we have reason to believe that Donavan has found the kids and is heading there right now? We are trying to figure a way to warn them so that they can get out of there." Doctor Sheppard grinned and said, "I didn't know that the phones were bugged, but it doesn't surprise me. However, I did suspect that Donavan was on to the kids' location. Like I said, I have a scanner. I heard the APB a few minutes ago about letting a limo speed north on the interstate. I suspected it was Donavan. So I created a diversion." "What kind of a diversion?" Eve asked.

"There is another piece to the puzzle," Doctor Sheppard continued. "I ran into the kids in the stairwell the other day when Abraham and Jake had the accident. They told me what Donavan was up to. So I went out in the parking lot to see if those thugs might be watching Joe's car. Well they were, so Joe and I switched cars. The kids slipped out the back into the employee parking lot and took my car. That's how they got away that night."

"That's awfully nice of you, Doc. I can't thank you enough, really," Jake spoke up. "But that doesn't help us now. Donavan has figured out where the kids are and is on his way there as we speak." "That's where my diversion comes in." Dr. Sheppard smiled wryly. "When I heard the APB I figured that they were looking for Joe's car. So I jumped into it and took off for the interstate. I was hoping they would see me and figure that it was Joe. Well, it worked. I met them about a quarter mile from the interstate. They turned around like bloodhounds and followed me all the way here. They are parked right down the street. I'm pretty sure they think that I'm Joe. They are probably waiting for Mary to show up before they move in."

All six people around the table breathed a sigh of relief. "We are not out of the dark," Eve observed. "It's only a matter of time until they figure out that the kids aren't here; then they will head north. Doctor Sheppard has bought us some time, but we still need to find a way to warn the kids without Donavan finding out." "Where are the kids right now?" Dr. Sheppard asked. "They are with my sister and her husband," Jake replied. "But they are not home. My sister just had a baby a couple of hours ago. Joe and Mary are at the hospital with them." Doctor Sheppard perked up. "I've got an idea. What is the name of the hospital?" Ruth slid her phone book over to the doc. "It's Community Hospital. The number is right there." "No kidding?" Doctor Sheppard was amazed. "Community Hospital right on the Canadian border?" "That's the one," Jake replied. "Why?" "I just so happen to have a good friend from med school who is chief of pediatrics there." He flipped open his cell phone and dialed the hospital.

"This is Doctor Sheppard from Pleasantville. I need to speak with Dr. McKee. It is an emergency." Two minutes later Dr. McKee answered the phone. "Hey Shep! How are you doing? I was just leaving the hospital when I got your page. What's up?" "Hi Mac! Not much time here. We have a situation. There are a couple of kids there in the hospital who are in danger. You haven't had any newborns today have you?" "Just one baby today but the parents aren't kids. They must be pushing 50. I just left their room. The baby is doing fine." "The names of the parents wouldn't be Zac and Liz would they?" "Yeah." Mac seemed surprised. "Are they in danger?" "No Mac, not them, we think that they had some visitors who were kids. Did you see anybody around? The girl has long black hair and is pregnant." "Yeah!" Mac remembered. "That little girl was holding the baby and grinning from ear to ear. There was a boy there too; big kid, good looking." "That's them Mac. We need to talk to them ASAP. These are good kids and they are in big trouble." "I'll head to their room right now Shep. They forwarded your call to my cell phone so hang on. I'll get to them in a few." "Thanks Mac."

Dr. Sheppard could hear his buddy running up the stairs. A couple of people tried to stop him but he blew them off. "Can't stop, I've got an emergency!" A few seconds later Mac came back on the line. "They are all here, who do you want to talk to?" "Can you put me on speaker and close the door, Mac?" "Sure thing, Shep." Dr. Sheppard put his phone on speaker as well. "OK Shep, you've got Zac, Liz, Mary, Joe, me and baby John here. Who's on your end?" "Ruth, Jake, Abraham, Eve, Bill, and me here. OK folks, we've hooked you all up. You need to start talking."

Mary spoke up. "Mom? What's going on? Why won't you talk to me? Why are Bill and Dr. Sheppard there?" Abraham took charge. "Listen kids, we don't have much time. Donavan has bugged our phones and apparently has figured out where you are. He was on his way up there but Dr. Sheppard has thrown them off course for now, but we don't know how long that will last. It's only a matter of time before he figures out that you aren't here. You have got to get out of there." "Where is he now?" Joe asked nervously. "He is sitting right down the street," Dr. Sheppard replied. "I drove your car here when I heard that he was heading north on the interstate. He spotted your car and thinks I am you." Jake jumped in. "We don't have time for details kids. You have got to leave now. Donavan could figure things out any minute. Then he is just a couple of hours away." Bill spoke up. "Joe? Mary? Listen carefully. Under no circumstances are you to use your cell phones. That's how they tracked you. In addition, do not call your parents' phones; not the house, the office or their cell phones." "Yes sir." Joe understood. "But mom! How are we supposed to talk to you?" Mary protested. "I don't know honey." Ruth tried to sound soothing but her voice cracked. "We'll figure it out somehow."

Just then the doorbell rang startling everyone at the table. Jake ran to the window and peaked out to get a glimpse. He sprinted back to the kitchen. "It's Donavan! Kids you need to leave right now! We'll stall them as long as possible." "Let's go Mary." Joe attempted to sound confident. "We love all of you. Doc, Bill, thanks for the help." "We love you too." Eve spoke through sobs. Joe nodded at Dr. McKee who shut the phone off.

The doorbell rang again along with a sturdy knock. "I'll get it," Jake growled. He threw open the door and came face-to-face with Donavan and his goons. "Hello Mr. Reubenowitz. May we come in?" Donavan had fake politeness in his voice. Jake gave him a one word answer. "No." "I assumed you would react in such a manner." Donavan sneered as he produced a piece of paper from his pocket. "This is a warrant allowing me to search your home. We have reason to believe that you are harboring fugitives." Jake grabbed the warrant from Donavan and examined it carefully. After he finished, he didn't say a word. He merely stepped back and opened the door. Donavan took the warrant and walked past Jake as if he were a king. The goons followed and refused to make eye contact with Jake's glare. Donavan scanned the living room as he walked straight into the kitchen. "Good evening everyone." His voice was all business. "I hope I am not intruding." "Well, since you brought it up, Donny boy, you ARE intruding," Bill snorted. "But I assume that you really don't care." Donavan winced at the nickname. Everyone at the local police station had tagged him with the name and he hated it feeling he deserved more respect. "Why Bill, I'm surprised to hear you speak to a fellow officer in such a manner." Donavan tried to regain his composure. "I am not a fellow officer any longer," Bill replied. "In case you've forgotten, I was forced to retire thanks to you. By the way, thanks. It's the best thing that ever happened to me. If being in law enforcement means identifying with people like you, I would just as soon not be a cop." Bill's words both surprised and infuriated Donavan.

Abraham changed the subject. "What are you doing here?" Jake answered from the kitchen door. "He has a warrant to search the house. He thinks we are harboring fugitives." Dr. Sheppard spoke up. "You got me. I confess." He held up his wrists as if to surrender. "I have a library book that is two weeks overdue." Everyone at the table snickered.

Donavan's goons appeared at the kitchen door. "We've searched the entire house, sir. No sign of either of them." Donavan's face turned red with anger. He slammed his fist on the table rattling the dishes. "WHERE ARE THEY!?" he demanded. "Where are who?" Eve asked innocently. Veins were sticking out of Donavan's neck by now. He was furious. "YOUR CHILDREN! MARY AND JOE!" "I really don't know," Abraham answered in a straightforward manner. "I haven't seen then lately. You know how kids are these days. They go here and there, check in once in awhile, and then they are gone again. Do you have kids, Mr. Donavan?"

Donavan knew they were lying. After all, he had listened to their telephone conversations. But he couldn't give that secret up. He turned around abruptly, looked at his goons and ordered, "Come on!" Jake showed them to the door and as they left he said, "Thanks for stopping by, come back and see us." He laughed as he closed the door.

CHAPTER THIRTY-FIVE

Joe and Mary hugged Aunt Liz and Uncle Zac goodbye and headed out to the car. "We need to get back to the house, get packed, and get out of here." Joe had stated the obvious. Mary squeezed his arm as he opened the car door for her. "It'll be OK, Joe. God will take care of us." He kissed her, shut the door and sprinted to the other side of the car. 'Dear God, I know Mary is right. Please give me faith.' He jumped into the car and headed for the farm.

Thirty minutes later they were eastbound on the interstate. Neither of them had said much while they packed. Each one knew what the other was thinking. They wouldn't be seeing or even speaking to their friends or relatives for a very long time. Finally, Mary spoke up. "Where are we going?" "I don't know." Joe was bewildered. Mary sensed his despondence. "You know, Gabby told us that we wouldn't be staying long at Aunt Liz's." "I know," Joe replied. "I just assumed that it would be longer than this. I'm in unchartered waters here, Mary. I don't know what to do." Joe's response scared Mary. He had always been her rock. She could always depend on him. To see him doubting himself, unsure of a plan, unable to make decisions, made her extremely uncomfortable. She started to cry. Joe looked over and saw the tears running her cheeks. He immediately felt bad. He reached over and took her hand. Their eyes met and each gave the other a pathetic smile. It was a feeble and unsuccessful attempt at encouragement.

Joe noticed a sign saying there was a rest stop ahead. He knew that Mary needed a break so he pulled in. He shut down the car and both kids walked in. Joe got a cup of coffee while he waited for Mary. When she came out of the bathroom he put his arm around her and said, "Do you want to stretch for awhile?" "No thanks, Joe. We had better keep going. I want to get as far away from here as fast as we can. There's no telling where Donavan is."

The kids got in the car and Joe turned the key to start the engine; nothing. It was dead. He tried again and got the same result. Frustration set in as he slammed his hand on the steering wheel with his hand and got out of the car. He opened the hood but couldn't see very well because it was dark. He knew about engines because he had worked with his dad on his Shelby. But new cars were much more complicated. He squinted as he tried to make out anything but it was just too dark.

After a couple minutes, a flashlight appeared over his shoulder. "Having a problem there young fella?" Joe turned to face a man who appeared to be in his sixties. He was wearing a baseball cap, a light jacket and jeans. "I was sitting in my rig over there and noticed that your hood was up." He pointed to a semi in the lot as he spoke. "Mind if I take a look?" "Be my guest." Joe was thankful for the help. The man scanned the engine quickly with the flashlight. After a few seconds, he pulled a pair of pliers from his pocket. "Hop in the car and give it a shot when I give you the signal." Joe obliged but didn't have much hope. How could this guy look at things for a couple of seconds and fix the problem? Thirty seconds later he heard the man say, "Turn her over." Joe rolled his eyes and expected nothing but dutifully turned the key. Bang! It fired right up. Joe was amazed as he ran up the RPMs to make sure that it would stay running. The man closed the hood and came around to the window. Joe couldn't see his face because the light from the rest area shadowed his face. Joe rolled down the window. "Thanks mister, I can't believe you fixed it that quick. What was wrong?" Joe gasped as the guy leaned the window and said, "You just had a loose connection on the battery. You are all ready to go." Mary looked over at the man to thank him. "Guardian!" she squealed. "But, how...that wasn't you out there?" Joe muttered to himself. Guardian laughed. "Pretty good trick huh?"

After the kids collected themselves Joe said, "Get in, we are in a mess and could use some help." "First of all, I know all about your situation," Guardian assured them. "However, there isn't much time. You need to keep going. I will tell you that you are heading in the right direction and that God has your back. Try to relax and follow His guidance." "But we don't know what to do or where to go?" Joe protested. "Just follow your instincts, pray a lot, He likes that, and remember that you have friends all over the country. I've got to go now and so do you. I'll be in touch." Guardian took off in the direction of the semi. Joe looked at Mary who smiled and said, "You heard the man, let's get going." Joe, still bewildered, shrugged his shoulders and put the car in reverse.

"How much longer?" Donavan snarled from the back seat of the speeding limo. "We should be there in 45 minutes, sir." "Step on it. I don't want to lose them again." He spoke into the phone. "Doug, do you still have a fix on their cell phones?" "Yes sir, Mr. Donavan, we have a very clear reading on their position." Donavan leaned back in the seat of the limo. "Gentlemen, I believe that we have them."

Joe pulled out onto the interstate. He was more confused than ever. When he saw Guardian, he had been relieved. He assumed that Guardian would give them a clear direction about what to do. He, being an athlete, was used to being coached, guided, and directed. He felt like Guardian had left him up in the air. He looked over at Mary. She had her head back, eyes closed, and grinning from ear to ear. This really confused him. "Penny for your thoughts?" Mary opened her eyes and smiled at Joe. "I was just praying, Joe. That's what Guardian said to do. He said that God likes that." Suddenly, Joe felt guilty. "How about praying out loud? I could use it right now." Mary bowed her head. "Dear Father, thank you for guiding us this far I know that You have a plan for us and that You will reveal it to us when the time comes. Please give us peace and comfort while we wait for Your direction. Amen." "Thanks Mary. I feel better."

Donavan's limo swung into the hospital parking lot and pulled up to the front door. "Doug, do you still have a signal?" Donavan barked into the phone. "Yes sir, you should be less than 500 feet from them." "Thanks Doug, are we close enough that the handheld tracker can lock on to the signal?" "Yes sir." "Good, switch the satellite over to our portable unit." One of the goons switched on the portable device and waited a few seconds. "Got it sir. It looks like they are upstairs." They all followed the signal up the stairwell. "They entered the third floor and followed the signal down the hall. The signal became stronger with each step. Each agent looked in every room as they walked briskly past. "Wait a minute." The agent with the unit stopped. "The signal is weaker, we must have passed it." They turned around and slowly followed the signal until it was loud and strong. "They've got to be around here somewhere." All of the agents began frantically searching the rooms, including Donavan. The agent with the tracking unit slowly moved around the hall. After a few seconds he yelled, "Got it!" Donavan and the other agents came out of the rooms toward him. "Where?" Donavan barked. The agent didn't respond. He merely pointed to a trashcan near the nurse's station. Donavan looked in it and saw two phones. He slowly reached down and retrieved the phones. He moved them closer to the portable unit which created a series of beeps and alarms from the unit. Donavan, enraged, looked at the agents and said, "Apparently they have been tipped off! Find out who did it! I want his or her head on a platter!" He slammed the telephones on the floor and stomped down the hall. The agents followed at a distance.

Mary and Joe drove east on the interstate for a couple of hours. They passed the time talking about nothing in particular. Both of them were attempting to ease the tension that loomed over them. After awhile, Mary became quiet and Joe realized that she was asleep. He looked at the clock in the dashboard; 12:30. He decided that it had been quite a day for his eight-month pregnant fiancée and that she deserved to sleep in a real bed. He saw a roadside motel and pulled in. Mary woke up as they came to a stop in front of the motel. "Where are we?" "I'm not sure," Joe replied. "Somewhere in North Dakota. I figured we both could use some sleep." "No arguments from me." Mary rubbed the sleep out of her eyes. "I'm hungry. How about you?" Joe grinned. "I could stand a little something. There's a diner across the street from the motel. Let's check in and get some food." The kids went inside and walked up to the desk. "Do you have any rooms available?" Joe asked. The night clerk looked up and said. "Sure do, would you like a king size or one with two double beds?" The question hit the kids like a ton of bricks.

They didn't know how to answer. They had never been in this situation. They had never slept together or even in the same room. They looked at each other in bewilderment. Joe spoke up. "We would like to have two adjoining rooms please." The clerk looked at Joe, then at Mary's protruding belly and then back at Joe as if to say 'really'? "Joe, I know what you are thinking but can we afford two rooms?" Joe looked dreamily down at Mary. "Sugar Plum, we can't afford not to be in separate rooms. I simply refuse to allow there to be any chance the Savior's reputation would be tarnished." Mary smiled up at Joe and said, "I love you more than ever." The clerk shook her head and shrugged as she slid two keys over the counter. Joe paid in cash and the kids headed across the street for some dinner.

It started snowing as the kids enjoyed a leisurely dinner. There was no one else in the diner except for a couple of truckers drinking coffee at the counter. In a strange way, both kids had a kind of peace come over them as they ate. There was something magical about being in a remote location where no one knew them and no one knew where they were. They were isolated in the middle of North Dakota and were totally dependent on each other, and God. After they finished, they started back across the street to the motel. The wind picked up and the snow started falling faster. Arm in arm, they strolled across the parking lot. "Isn't the snow beautiful?" Joe observed. "Yes! It is so romantic! I feel like we are in a movie." Mary snuggled in closer to Joe. They reached the door to Mary's room and the baby started kicking. "He's kicking again!" Mary squealed with delight. Joe felt the Savior's enthusiasm and smiled. "I love you Sugar Plum." He kissed her and waited for her to go inside. "Lock the door and call me if you need anything," Joe ordered. "I'll be fine sweetie, good night."

Joe awoke the next morning and looked at the alarm clock; 7:30. He wanted to roll over and go back to sleep but something told him to get up. He walked over to the window and opened the curtains. He rubbed his eyes because he couldn't believe what he was looking at; two feet of snow and it was still coming! He looked at the Porsche. It was covered. For just a second he felt bad. A car like that shouldn't be left out in the snow. He walked over to the TV and found a local station. The weather report was bad. All roads were shut down and a travel warning was in effect. They were predicting snow for the next three days. Joe figured that only a high rise 4x4 pick-up would have any chance of making it through something like that.

The phone in his room rang. "Joe! Have you looked outside?" "Yes Mary, I think we got a little dusting last night," Joe teased. "I guess you could put it like that," Mary responded. "Looks like we aren't going anywhere for awhile." "I've been watching the local TV station and you are correct. We aren't going anywhere for quite awhile. They are predicting snow for the next three days." Mary started to worry. "Three days? What are we going to do?" "Calm down Mary. We didn't have any plan or place to go anyway. It looks like God wants us here for awhile." Mary sighed. "You're right, Joe. Thanks. I'm just worried about the baby. What if I go into labor early? I don't want to give birth in a motel." Joe laughed. "That's not going to happen, Sugar Plum. We'll just chill around here for a few days and then head somewhere else. Maybe God wants us to be still and listen to His voice." "Well, we certainly are in a good position for that!" Mary relaxed. "I'm hungry." Joe laughed into the phone. "You eat more than I do now, Sugar Plum!" Mary snorted into the phone. "For your information mister, the Savior has quite an appetite. Do you think the diner is open?" Joe peered out the window. "I can't tell but it looks like the lights are on." "Let's hope so," Mary replied. "I'd hate to have to clean out the vending machine! I'll see you in 30 minutes." The phone went dead. Joe walked over to the nightstand and picked up his wallet; $500 left. That wouldn't last long. He needed to get a job.

The North Dakota wind blew the kids across the street toward the diner. Joe noticed that the interstate was totally closed and that drifts were over six feet high. There were a couple of trucks in the parking lot but Mary noticed that the diner had about 20 people inside. The wind nearly blew the door out of Joe's hand as he opened it for Mary. The gust that came in caused the customers to shiver as they looked up to see who had let the wind blow in.

"Grab a seat anywhere, kids." A middle-aged lady spoke to them from behind the counter. "It's just me and the hubby today. None of the employees could make it in. I'll get to you as soon as I can." Joe could tell by the way she moved that she was frazzled. "Take your time, ma'am, we aren't going anywhere." The lady smiled in appreciation, waved, and kept working. Joe and Mary watched the activity in the diner. Some of the patrons were getting upset because of the delay in service. The lady was running around frantically trying to please the customers; but she was fighting a losing battle. She zoomed up to the kids and said, "Sorry, I'll get to you ASAP, I promise. It's just that some of these people are so impatient." Joe flashed his smile. "Don't worry about it. Where did all of these people come from? There aren't any cars in the lot." "They're from the motel across the street. As the snow got heavier last night the motel filled up. We weren't even going to open today but my cousin owns the motel. He called this morning asking us to open because they didn't have any other place to eat. My husband and I decided that it was the right thing to do. It isn't right letting people go hungry if you can do something about it. I am worried about him. He just had a heart attack and is in the back cooking and washing dishes. I had back surgery a few months ago and it's killing me." She paused. "Oh, I'm sorry kids. I didn't mean to vent to you. Can I get you something to drink?" Joe looked at Mary who read his mind, smiled and nodded. "You know ma'am, you are right. A person should help those in need," Joe said as he and Mary stood up. He looked at Mary. "You work the counter, I'll help in back." The lady looked bewildered. "What are you saying? Are you offering to help us?" "That's right Ms...." Joe waited for her to give her name. "Uh, I'm just Kate. None of that Mrs. stuff. My husband is Ken. Kids, I don't know what to say." "Just put us to work, Kate. I'm Joe and this is Mary. All I ask is that Mary doesn't carry anything heavy." He pointed to her stomach. Kate smiled and nodded knowingly. "Well Mary, if you will take orders and keep the coffee cups full, that would be a great help." Mary went straight to the counter and began conversing with some truck drivers as she filled their cups. "She'll get big tips as cute as she is," Kate whispered into Joe's ear. She led Joe into the back room where Ken was working frantically over the grill. "Ken this is Joe. He's here to help." Ken looked over his shoulder at Joe and was overcome with emotion. "I don't know where you came from son, but you probably just saved my life." No problem sir. Just glad to help. What can I do?" "Well you can call me Ken to start. And if you don't mind, you could start on that mountain of dirty dishes by the sink." "I'm on it." Joe headed to the sink, rolled up his sleeves, and dove in.

Kate walked over to Ken. "Where did they come from, Kate?" "I think they are staying at the motel. They came in to eat and when they saw how busy we were they offered to help." Ken sighed with relief. "I was just praying for a miracle. I feel bad that I really didn't think it would happen." Kate kissed him on the cheek. "Don't ever doubt God, Ken." She returned to the front of the store.

Within an hour and a half, everything was running smoothly. Joe caught up on the dishes and was running the grill under the watchful eye of Ken. Joe's whole goal was to allow Ken to sit on a stool and rest while he instructed Joe in what to do. Meanwhile, Mary was out in front having a ball with the customers. The truck drivers were laughing and teasing Mary, who gave it right back, which caused the entire mood of the restaurant to change. She had found out that four of the drivers tried to run together whenever they could. Some people even cleared their own dishes and brought them into the kitchen. Kate moved around taking orders and delivering food while singing along with the jukebox that played in the background.

A half hour later there were only a couple of customers left. Mary sat down on a stool realizing how exhausting the restaurant business could be. Joe came out of the kitchen and sat down beside her. "Are you OK Sugar Plum?" "Yes, I'm fine. Just a little tired and definitely hungry." Kate overheard the conversation. "I'll bet you are honey. You were hungry two hours ago when you came in here. I believe we can take care of that. What would you kids like?" Neither Joe nor Mary hesitated. They replied in unison, "Pancakes!" Kate yelled over her shoulder into the kitchen. "Two extra large VIP orders of pancakes, please." Ken replied, "Did you say VIP?" "Sure did. VERY VIP!" "You got it boss." Ken mocked his wife.

Within ten minutes, two huge stacks of pancakes appeared from the kitchen. They were covered with strawberries and whipped cream. Mary and Joe dove into them like they hadn't eaten in weeks. Ken came out of the kitchen as the kids devoured his creation. "From the looks of things I guess the VIP cakes are acceptable." Joe looked up with his mouth full and mumbled, "These are the best pancakes I've ever had!" Mary nodded in agreement but was too busy eating to say anything.

After they finished, they sat back and sighed. Joe looked at Mary and could tell she was exhausted. "Mary would you like to go lie down for awhile?" "As a matter-of-fact, I am kind of tired." Joe pulled out his wallet and said, "What do we owe you for the wonderful breakfast?" Ken laughed out loud and Kate flipped Joe playfully with a towel. "Are you kidding me? What do we owe YOU?" You two are the sweetest kids I've ever met. I don't know how we would have gotten along without you this morning." "Why don't we call it even?" Mary offered. Kate protested. "But it isn't even, honey. We owe you something." "We just did what God told us to do. We need to help people when we can. Call it even. God will make it up to us. He already has in so many ways." "Ken leaned on the counter. "Are you two believers?" "Yes we are!" Mary said proudly. "So are we!" Kate hugged Mary. "Well it's nice to meet you." Joe tried to wrap up the conversation. "I'm sure we'll be back." "OK kids, see you later," Kate said as she turned to Ken. "Well, they got us through the breakfast rush but what are we going to do now? You know all of those people will need to eat again." Joe overheard their conversation as he was putting on his coat. "I couldn't help but overhear, I need a job until the roads clear. I could help if you want." Mary spoke up, "I'll help whenever I can. We could use the money." Ken breathed a sigh of relief. "There is just one condition young lady." His voice was serious. "That baby comes first. You only work when you feel like it. Now Joe, you take her to the motel and get back here ASAP. Mary here's the phone number at the restaurant; you just call if you need us." The kids grinned at their new employers and headed for the motel. Kate looked at Ken. "Do you think that they are angels or something?" "I don't know Kate. There is something special about them. I do know that God sent them here for a reason; and I believe that it isn't just to help us in the restaurant."

"We have got to find those kids!" Donavan slammed his fist down on the table in the motel room near the hospital where Liz was recovering. "It's been almost two days since anyone has seen them. They can't just drop off of the face of the earth!" The veins were sticking out of Donavan's neck. "Has Doug picked up on anything?" "I spoke with him an hour ago," one of the agents responded. "He hasn't heard anything." Donavan took a deep breath and tried to control his temper. "OK, let's review; what do we know?" Another agent flipped open a laptop and began reading. "They were last seen at the hospital. The aunt and uncle claim not to know where they are as do the parents. We do not know what their mode of transportation is because all of the family vehicles are accounted for." "Wait a minute," Donavan interrupted. "Who was in that Shelby when we followed them to the girl's home?" "We suspect it was Dr. Sheppard, sir." Donavan smiled fiendishly. "Find out what the good doctor drives. Maybe there's a connection." "Yes sir."

Joe had helped Ken and Kate through the lunch rush and had gone back to check on Mary. She was still asleep so he decided to take a nap. He was asleep as soon as his head hit the pillow. He dreamt that he was walking through a snowstorm and could barely see where he was going. Suddenly, he could make out a figure heading in his direction. He stopped and shielded his eyes in an effort to determine who it was. The figure waved as he came closer but Joe still couldn't make out a face. Joe half-heartedly waved back. "What kind of a wave is that for an old friend?" The gentleman laughed as he came into view. "Guardian!" Joe ran the last few feet and threw his arms around his friend. "Now that's a proper greeting." Guardian returned the hug. "What are you doing here?" Joe asked. In his confused state, he couldn't tell if he was still dreaming. Everything seemed so real. "Am I dreaming?" "Does it really matter?" Guardian smiled. "I need to tell you something." Joe tried to focus. "You and Mary need to get out of here; tonight if possible." "TONIGHT!? How am I supposed to do that?" The roads are shut down and that Porsche won't get through a heavy dew, let alone all of this snow." Joe panicked. "Calm down Joe. Wait for the Lord. He will provide a way. Use your instincts and watch for His clues. He won't leave you." A gust of wind blew up which began to cause the snow to get into Joe's eyes. He covered his face for a few seconds to avoid the blowing snow. When the wind died down he looked up to continue his conversation with Guardian; but he was gone. Joe yelled as loud as he could for his friend to come back; but all that he could hear was the howl of the wind. He tried again, but this time he found himself back in his room lying on the bed.

Mary came running into his room. "Joe! Are you OK? You've been yelling like a crazy man!" Joe sat up and attempted to make sense of everything. "I must have been dreaming. What was I saying?" "You were yelling Guardian's name over and over. You sounded like you were in trouble. Did Guardian tell you something in your dream?" Joe looked at Mary sadly and nodded. "He said that we need to get out of here ASAP." Mary gasped. "How are we going to do that?" "We'll figure it out." He looked at the clock; 4:15. "I've got to get back to the diner. Maybe something will come to me over there." "I'm going with you," Mary stated with authority. Joe started to protest but he realized by the look on Mary's face that it would do no good. "OK, just promise me that you will take it easy."

Joe and Mary entered the diner fifteen minutes later. It wasn't too crowded. There were just a few guys at the counter. Joe assumed that they were truck drivers from the motel. However, he did notice a snowplow and a state police 4x4 SUV in the parking lot so he assumed that there was some attempt at opening up the interstate. "You're just in time." Kate grinned from behind the counter. Mary smiled and put on an apron. Mary recognized one of the truck drivers from this morning. He winked at Mary and said in a loud voice, "If Mary is going to work the counter, I believe I'll stay awhile. I'd rather look at her than that mean old Kate!" Kate rolled her eyes at the tease and Ken yelled from the kitchen. "Me too!" Everyone laughed as Kate faked anger and headed for the kitchen. Ken pretended to run in fear.

"Say, who's driving the snowplow?" Joe asked the crowd. "How are the roads looking?" A middle-aged man in coveralls spoke up. "That's my rig; and it is tough out there. We're doing the best we can but it is going to be a couple of days before traffic is moving." The policeman who was sitting by himself at the end of the counter added, "It took me two hours to get twenty miles in my 4x4. I wouldn't plan on going anywhere soon." Mary looked at Joe with helplessness in her eyes. Joe smiled warmly back at her in reassurance. She read his mind. 'It will be OK, I promise.' Mary started humming and filling coffee cups.

One of Donavan's agents smiled as he put down the phone. "Doctor Sheppard drives a new Porsche, sir. We've got the color, make, VIN, and plates." "Great!" Donavan sneered. "Put out an APB on that car. They've had enough time to get out of state so make it apply to all of the surrounding states as well." "Yes sir." "And have our man back in Pleasantville go visit the Doc and see if he has any explanation why he was driving Joe's Shelby and where that Porsche may be."

Thirty minutes later an agent had found Dr. Sheppard in the hospital. "Dr. Sheppard, I'm a federal agent. Do you mind if I ask you a few questions?" The doc recognized him as one of Donavan's goons. He wanted to say no because he suspected that it was about Joe and Mary but he thought better of it and decided to play along. "Sure, but you'll have to walk with me. It's busy around here and I need to keep moving." "I understand. I'll get straight to the point. We have determined that the only car registered in your name is a brand new Porsche. Is that correct?" Dr. Sheppard was stunned by the question and the agent could tell it. Dr. Sheppard quickly collected his thoughts. "Yes, that is correct." Could you please explain, then, why you were driving a 1967 Shelby when we saw you at the Reubenowitz's the other night?" Dr. Sheppard's face went white. The agent was glaring straight at him. Dr. Sheppard reached for the elevator button as his mind raced. "Sure I can. When Joe's father and Mary's father got into the accident a few weeks ago, the families had too many cars here. The wives had both driven separately. Mrs. Goldstein was in no condition to drive so the kids took her car home and I offered to bring the Shelby when I was going to be in their neighborhood." "Why then were you seen driving the Shelby around town?" The agent wasn't buying it. "Alright, you got me. I kept the car for a few days with the permission of the Goldsteins. After all, who wouldn't leap at the chance to drive one of those cars for a few days." Dr. Sheppard laughed and the agent chuckled. The elevator doors opened and Dr. Sheppard got in. "I've got to go into surgery now, is there anything else I can help you with?" Innocence dripped from Dr. Sheppard's tongue. "The agent stuck his hand in the door. "Just one more thing. Where is your car now? I didn't see it in the parking lot." "It's in my garage at home. I didn't want to drive it in the snow." "What did you drive?" "I am driving my mother's SUV." Dr. Sheppard acted inpatient. "Is there anything else?" "No, not right now, thank you Dr. Sheppard." The doors to the elevator closed and Dr. Sheppard sighed. 'Maybe that bought those kids some time but they are on to us. I wish I knew how to get in touch with them.' The agent let the elevator doors close before sprinting for the doors. 'We'll just see if that Porsche is in the garage.'

Joe and Mary were busy in the diner. The supper crowd from the motel had shown up and the 'party' had begun. They called it a party because everyone had become familiar with each other and there was music playing, family conversations between what had been strangers the day before, and even some dancing going on. Everyone was having a great time.

Joe was working the cash register when the state police officer left. "Was everything OK?" Joe asked. "It was just fine son," the officer replied. "I've never seen anything like this. When people are stranded and cooped up like this, they are usually cranky and short tempered. These people are acting like this is a family reunion. I've been watching you and that young lady behind the counter. You two have had a lot to do with helping these people get through a tough time. I'm sure that everyone appreciates it." "Thank you sir, be safe out there."

Joe returned to bussing tables. As he looked outside, he noticed a 4x4 pickup with big mud tires parked in back of the diner. It had been jacked up about three feet higher than normal. If anything could get through this storm, that truck could. Joe got an idea. He walked up to the counter. "Who's big four by is that out back?" Everyone shrugged and looked around. "That's Ken's truck," Kate said. "If that's what you want to call a ten-year-old pile of junk." Joe laughed and carried a tub of dishes into the kitchen. Joe wandered over to Ken. "Kate tells me that you own that four by out back?" "Ken smiled at Joe. "I sure do, it's kind of my hobby. I buy old trucks and fix them up. That one is my baby. I've been working on it for about 18 months now." "Does it run?" Joe's face turned serious. "Why sure it runs. It is just about finished. All that I'm waiting for is a chrome roll bar with desert lights. They would have been here by now if it hadn't been for this storm. What makes you ask?" Joe got quiet, said a quick prayer, and whispered. "Would you like to make a trade?" "Trade?" Ken was confused. "You mean my truck? Trade for what?" "A brand new Porsche," Joe said proudly. "Do you mean that Porsche that has been sitting over at the motel?! I have been admiring it for a couple of days now. Is that your car?" "Well, yes and no."

Joe didn't know where to start. "It's not stolen or anything. You see, I traded my car for it a couple of days ago. It was kind of a rushed transaction and we haven't had time to change the title yet." Ken held up his hand. "Wait a minute Joe. You are a nice kid and all and I really appreciate all of the help you have been giving me, but I don't want to get mixed up in any kind of shady deal or something." "I understand Ken." Joe thought for a minute. "What if I could put you in contact with the original owner? What if he convinced you that this was all on the up-and-up? Would you be interested then?" Ken rubbed his chin. "Well, I guess so. But why would you want to trade a brand new Porsche for a ten-year-old pickup? It doesn't seem like a very fair deal for you." "I need to get out of here tonight, Ken. There are some bad people chasing us and they want to kill Mary. I'm afraid they might catch up with us if we stay here too long." Joe waited for Ken to absorb what he had just said. Ken rubbed his jaw for what seemed like eternity. He finally looked at Joe and said, "Kate and I agreed last night that there was something special about you two kids. In addition, you said that you were believers. If you put me in contact with the original owner to confirm your story, I'll make the trade." Joe jumped for joy and hugged Ken. "I've got his name and number in the glove box, I'll be right back." Joe ran out of the door. "Where's he going?" Mary asked Ken. "If my gut feeling is correct young lady," Ken put his arm around Mary. "He is going to prove just how much he loves you." Mary blushed as the truckers whooped and hollered at what Ken had just said.

In just a minute, Joe came running through the door with the car's registration and a business card. "Here's the registration. It's made out to Doctor Elijah Sheppard. Here's his business card with his cell phone number hand printed on the back. Go ahead and call." Ken headed for the kitchen while Mary silently quizzed Joe with her stare. He flashed his smile and followed Ken into the kitchen. Kate looked at Mary, shrugged her shoulders, and smiled. "Men, you never know what they are up to."

Three rings went by. "Hello, this is Dr. Sheppard." "Dr. Sheppard, my name is Ken Sherwood. I am standing here with Joe Goldstein...." "YOU'RE WITH JOE? IS HE OK? HOW'S MARY?..." Dr. Sheppard interrupted with a string of questions. "Well, Doc, obviously you know them. Joe here wants to trade what I believe is your car for my pickup truck. "This seems a little strange. Can you fill me in on what's going on?" "Sure, I traded my car, the Porsche, to Joe for his car, a '67 Shelby. There isn't any paperwork because there wasn't time. You see Mr. Sherwood, Mary and Joe are very special kids and through no fault of their own, there are some bad people trying to kill them, at least Mary. They want that child dead and they'll stop at nothing to get the job done. If Joe needs to trade that car for your truck please do it. I promise I'll make it good to you." "Why in the world would anyone want to hurt Mary's baby?" Ken asked trying to figure things out. "Well, Mr. Sherwood, this may be hard to believe. I had trouble with it myself at first, but, try to keep an open mind and believe me. Without going into details, Mary is carrying the Savior, the Messiah, the King of Kings." Ken couldn't believe his ears. He was speechless. "Mr. Sherwood? Are you still there? May I talk to Joe please?" Ken didn't say a word. He just handed the phone to Joe. "Hello?" "Joe!" It is so good to hear your voice! Are you guys OK?" "Hi Dr. Sheppard. We are fine. Just stuck in the middle of a snowstorm somewhere in North Dakota." "Listen Joe, you've got to get out of there. One of Donavan's goons came around here asking a bunch of questions about your car, er...my car, and where it is. I don't know why you decided to trade it but do it and get out of there. It's just a matter of time before they put out an APB on my car." There was urgency in the doctor's voice. "Let me talk to Mr. Sherwood and convince him to trade." "OK Doc, but can you get word to our folks for us? Tell them we are OK and that we love them." "Sure thing, Joe. You guys be careful. You take care of the Savior." Joe handed the phone in Ken's direction. "He wants to finish the deal." Ken was still in a trance. He was looking past Joe in the direction of the door. Mary and Kate were standing there. Mary was smiling, glowing at Ken who couldn't take his eyes off of her. He walked slowly over to Mary and said to Joe as he walked, "There's no need, Joe. You have a deal. Tell the doc." Joe put the receiver to his ear. "Doc?" "I heard Joe. We have a deal. Now get out of there!"

Ken walked over to Mary with tears running down his face. He hugged her as if he were holding a hummingbird. Kate was confused. "What in the world is going on here?" Ken looked at his wife. "Do you remember last night when we said that these two kids were something special?" "Yes," Kate replied cautiously. "Well, that was the understatement of the year. You see Kate, Mary is going to be the mother of the Savior! She is carrying the Messiah!" Kate looked at her husband as if he were crazy. Then she looked at Mary and noticed the most serenity in a woman she had ever seen. "May I?" Kate asked as she reached for Mary's stomach. Mary nodded. As soon as she touched Mary's stomach the baby kicked her right in the hand. The feeling sent shock waves throughout Kate's body causing her to jump back. Kate started laughing and crying at the same time. "Can this really be happening to us, Ken? Is it possible that we are witnessing the greatest miracle that man has ever known? Right here in this little old dirty diner?!" Ken nodded with excitement as he hugged his wife and jumped all around the kitchen.

Back in Pleasantville, the agent who had questioned Dr. Sheppard shined a light into his garage; no Porsche. He flipped open his cell phone and hit speed dial. "Mr. Donavan, Dr. Sheppard's story is inconsistent. His car is not, repeat, not in his garage as he alleged." "Thanks, good work." Donavan hung up the phone. "We were right boys. The kids have run away in the Porsche. FIND IT!"

After Ken and Kate settled down Joe spoke up. "I hate to break up the party but we really need to go." "Oh yeah, right." Ken returned to reality. "Come on, we had better get you two on the road." "Uh Ken, you might want to hide that Porsche for awhile. Dr. Sheppard thinks that the feds are going to put out an APB on it if they already haven't." "The feds!? Are they the ones who are after you? "Yes," Joe answered honestly. He was afraid that Ken would back out of the deal once he found out about the feds' involvement. "Our government has gone nuts! What possible reason could they have for wanting to hurt the baby?" Joe gave them the short version about Mary's involvement in 'Teens for Abstinence' and Jim Donavan. "So that's why they want the baby dead?!" Kate asked in disbelief. Mary nodded and Joe said, "That's why we need to get going. And if you could hide that car for awhile, they won't track us to this location." "OK then, we need some help. I've got an idea." He led the three of them out into the diner.

"Listen up folks. We've got a situation here. Mary and Joe need to get going; and they need to do it now. We need some help." There were several sad moans from the folks at the counter as they focused their attention on Ken. "What do you need Ken?" "First, I need someone to gas up my pickup." "I'm on it." One of the drivers was putting on his coat. Ken threw him the keys. "Next, we need to hide that Porsche that's parked over at the motel." One of the other drivers spoke up. "My trailer is empty and I've got a set of ramps. We could put it in there. I'm not in a hurry to go anywhere for awhile." "Good," Ken replied. Joe flipped the Porsche keys on the counter and several guys headed out to take care of that project. "What else?" one of the ladies asked. "We need to fix these kids up with a care package for the trip." Several ladies got up and followed Kate into the kitchen. Now the only people left in the diner were Ken, Mary, Joe, and Sam, the snowplow driver. Ken continued. "Mary, you and Joe go get packed. I'll send the truck over as soon as it gets filled up. Mary and Joe headed out the door as Ken turned to his remaining customer. "Sam, we've been friends ever since first grade. I need the biggest favor from you." "Now wait a minute, Ken. I'm all tied up. My boss doesn't know it but I have a special job to do. I'm going to be leading a pickup truck with a pregnant girl in it as far south as it takes to get out of this storm. Don't you dare ask me for a favor." He grinned at Ken who walked over and hugged him like a bear. "Thanks buddy, I knew I could count on you." Sam played it up. "It's going to cost you breakfast."

Thirty minutes later the kids were in the truck, the ladies had packed a bunch of food, the Porsche was safely hidden in the semi, and Sam was in the snowplow. Ken walked up to the window and handed Joe an envelope. "We took up a collection, it's only $700 but it should help you down the road." Joe smiled as Mary tried to refuse the gift. "Please take it," Ken insisted. "It's the least we can do." "Thank you for everything," Joe said as he took the envelope. Everyone waved as the kids followed Sam out of the parking lot. They all stayed outside and watched until the lights from the snowplow disappeared into the night. No one spoke as they returned to the diner. Everyone sat in silence for a very long time. Mixed emotions filled the air. They were happy that they had been able to help the kids but at the same time, they struggled with the thought of how empty the diner seemed without them. Everyone hoped they would be OK.

After about 15 minutes, one of the truck drivers looked out the window in the direction of the motel. "I wonder what that state trooper is doing over at the motel?" Everyone in the diner watched as the trooper slowly circled the building. He stopped in front of the entrance and went inside. Someone recognized him as the trooper that had been in the diner earlier. "I'll bet he's nosing around looking for that Porsche," Ken growled. "Kate, did you warn your cousin to keep his mouth shut about the Porsche?" "Sure did," Kate responded proudly. In just a few seconds the trooper returned to his car and drove over to the diner. Kate greeted him cheerfully as he walked in. "Are you back already? Couldn't stay away from this great food could you?" The trooper chuckled and replied, "Well ma'am, I'm here on official business. It seems as if the feds are looking for a new black Porsche. The APB covers four states so they must be pretty serious about it. Anyway, when I was in here this morning, I thought I saw one sitting over at the motel but the clerk said that he hadn't seen one. I was just wondering if anyone in here had seen it?"

There was an awkward silence in the room for a few seconds then Ken spoke up in a loud voice. "Has anyone seen a black Porsche around here in the last few days?" There were several people who shook their heads while others verbalized a collective "no." "This really isn't Porsche kind of country, officer. We're just a bunch of rednecks who drive pickups. I'm pretty sure that if a Porsche had been within twenty miles of here, someone would have noticed it." Ken was convincing. "I'll bet you've had a big day, officer. Why don't you have a seat and let me whip you up some dinner on the house?" Ken led him over to the counter and winked at the guys sitting there. They took the hint. "Sure buddy!" "Have a seat." "Nothing is too good for our men in uniform." "I suggest the meatloaf. It is great tonight." The officer, surprised by the friendly treatment, smiled and sat down among the truckers. "That's awfully nice of you guys," he said. "I usually get treated like I have the plague or something. I must have been imaging that Porsche. I get sick of chasing rainbows for those feds anyway." "Well you're among friends here, buddy. Kate, how about some coffee for the newest member of the 'counter club?' Let those feds chase their own tail for awhile. You deserve a break." "Thanks, you all really know how to treat a stranger." The officer smiled and toasted the 'counter club' with his coffee. Back in the kitchen, Ken bowed his head. "Thank you Lord. Please protect those kids."

CHAPTER THIRTY-SIX

Joe and Mary had been following Sam for a couple of hours. Neither one spoke much. Joe was concentrating on driving and Mary was worrying about where they would go next. It was slow going. Most of the time they went about 20 mph. Occasionally, Sam would spread some salt which told Joe that a hill was coming. On and on they slowly made their way south. The monotony of the trip started to get to Joe. Mary saw his head nod. "Joe!" Joe snapped out of the daze. "I'm sorry Mary. I guess I'm getting bored." "Do you want me to drive for awhile?" Mary offered. "I hate to stop. I'm afraid we may have trouble getting going again. I'm OK. Maybe we could talk awhile."

"Good idea." Mary brightened. "I have been thinking, actually wondering, do you have any idea where we are going?" Joe frowned. "No I don't. I've been thinking about it. I just know that we need to get as far away from that Porsche as possible, as quickly as we can. That means we need to get out of this snow so that we can make some time." "That's fine Joe, but that wasn't exactly what I meant. I've been wondering where we are going to settle down. The baby is due in three weeks which could mean anytime. I am beginning to get a little scared about where we are going to live. How are we going to live? We need furniture, food, clothes, baby stuff…."

Joe could tell that Mary was getting panicky. "I really don't have any answers for you Mary. I'm just trying to get us out of this snowstorm right now. Don't forget, God has a plan for us." Mary relaxed a little. "You're right Joe. Besides, I'm sure that Gabby and Guardian are around here somewhere." Both kids laughed as they pictured their angels being close by.

They drove on for a couple of hours talking about houses, dishes, how they would decorate, all of the dreams that young people who are in love discuss. They were having a good time 'planning' their life. Joe looked out of the window and noticed that the snow seemed less deep. He noticed that Sam was going about 40 mph as well. "I think we may be getting out of it, Mary. Look, it doesn't seem as deep and the drifts are smaller." "Good!" Mary agreed. "It is starting to get lighter outside. The sun should be up soon. Maybe some of the snow will melt."

Just as Mary finished talking, Sam's right turn signal began flashing. He pulled off of the road into a truck stop. Joe followed obediently and stopped the truck right behind the plow. Sam walked up to the truck as Joe and Mary got out to stretch their legs. "This is as far as I go, kids. The South Dakota border is just a mile over that hill. Sorry that I can't take you farther but...." Joe held up his hand. "Stop right there Sam. You've already gotten us farther than we ever could have on our own. I don't know how I can ever repay you." Joe shook his hand hardily and then Sam turned to Mary. "No handshakes from me." Mary grinned as she held up her arms for a hug. "Thank you so much for all of your help, Sam. We will never forget you." Sam blushed. Mary noticed tears in his eyes as he got choked up. "You kids be careful." He barely whispered as he turned and headed for the truck. Joe and Mary stood there and watched as he pulled back out onto the highway. The kids waved and he honked in reply as he headed down the road.

Mary turned to Joe. "Well, what now?" Joe looked down. "I don't know Mary; I just don't know." Mary sensed despair in Joe's voice. She knew that he needed some encouragement. "I'm hungry, Joe. And I need a break from sitting in the truck all night. Why don't we get some breakfast? Maybe something will come to us." She didn't wait for an answer as she grabbed his hand and led him into the truck stop.

Joe slung his backpack into the booth as he and Mary sat down. The waitress came over to take their order. "Have you heard anything about the road conditions?" Joe asked after he ordered. "Honey, that's all I've heard. Everything is closed north of here but there is one lane open from here heading south. Which way are you going?" "South." Joe grinned. "Got a 4x4?" "Sure do." Joe continued grinning. "Well the guys say that a 4x4 will make it, might be slow going, but you should be alright." "Thanks miss." Joe relaxed a little. "That's the best news I've heard all day."

In a few minutes, the waitress brought their food. They ate slowly, almost thoughtfully, as they watched the sun come up. It caused a relaxation to come over the kids as they sat there, mesmerized, each absorbing the revitalization of the sun's energy. Their thoughts were interrupted by a familiar voice, "Would you like some more coffee, sir?" Both kids snapped out of their trance and searched for the source of the voice. "Gabby!" Mary almost screamed. Gabby smiled at the kids and playfully said, "Shhhh! You don't want me to get fired on my first day do you?" Joe laughed and Mary smiled. "Scoot over Mary, I'm on a break." Mary slid over and Gabby sat down next to her. "I bet you two are wondering what's next." Joe looked at Mary while he answered. "This is good timing, Gabby. You are correct. We haven't a clue." Gabby giggled. "It's a good thing that my Boss," she pointed upward, "has a plan." Joe blushed and Mary smiled. "Well, how about letting us in on it?" Mary urged. Gabby started to speak but was interrupted by the other waitress. "Gabby, you have an order up and the customer is getting cranky." Gabby smiled at her co-worker and got up. "Thanks." She turned to the kids, "Duty calls." "Whoa!" Joe protested. "What about God's plan for us?" Gabby placed one hand on Mary's shoulder and the other hand on Joe's. "Use your resources, kids. You have a lot of them. I would start by looking in the bag right next to you. I've got to go. I'll be in touch." Just like that, Gabby disappeared into the kitchen.

Joe looked over at his backpack and said in a doubtful tone. "What could possibly be in there that would help us?" Mary shrugged but was more enthusiastic than Joe. "You won't know until you open it, Joe." He pulled it up off of the seat and put it on the table while Mary cleared the dishes to make room. Joe opened the zipper and began pulling things out. "Let's see here, we have a copy of 'Sports Illustrated', a blank notebook, a pair of clean socks." Mary giggled. "Oh brother, you and your socks." Joe ignored the tease and continued. "There are some pens and pencils, the cash from Ken and Kate, my Bible...." "That's a pretty good resource," Mary observed. In just that instant, the baby kicked Mary so hard that she winced in pain. She grabbed her stomach and leaned over in the booth. "Ow!" Joe jumped up and moved over to Mary's side of the booth. "Are you OK Sugar Plum?" The pain subsided quickly. Mary smiled. "Yes, I'm fine now. However, I do believe that the Savior is trying to tell us something. Open your Bible." "OK, but I'm pretty sure that we don't have time to read the whole thing right now. Where do you want me to go?" Mary bowed her head and prayed silently. 'Lord, I know that you have answers for us in Your Holy Word, please lead us to the right passage, Amen." Mary took the Bible and opened it to the Table of Contents "Let's start at the beginning," she suggested. "Genesis...hmm." She closed her eyes and allowed the events of Genesis to flow through her mind. After a few seconds she sat up suddenly and looked at Joe with excitement in her eyes. "Joe, do you remember the story about Abraham's servant who went out looking for a wife for Isaac?" Joe began to share Mary's grin. "Oh yeah, he asked for a sign from God. Something about asking a woman for a drink of water from a well." "Yes, that's it!" Mary was flipping the pages of Genesis. "Here it is! Genesis 24:12! Look Joe!" They read the passage together. After they finished, Joe prayed, "Dear God, please show us a sign." Both he and Mary had concluded that they needed to search this passage for an answer. He brushed aside his backpack in order to make more room. As he did, a small red book fell out of his backpack. Mary recognized it as his address book. Joe ignored it and continued reading the Bible. Mary, however, felt compelled to open the address book. Unbeknownst to Joe, she casually flipped through the pages. She had always been aware of the book, Joe liked to write phone numbers down because he would lose anything stored in his phone when it got lost or broken, both of which happened frequently.

As she turned the pages, something caught her eye. Joe always wrote in black ink and everything was in his handwriting; everything except this one entry. It was written in red ink, and it was in a girl's handwriting. There was a phone number and next to it was written, 'Ginger, call me if you ever need anything.' A tingling sensation ran down Mary's spine. "Joe, who is Ginger?" Joe had been so engrossed in the passage from Genesis that he hadn't noticed what Mary was doing. He looked over at Mary. "She's that girl from Harvard. She was the roommate of the girl-friend from one of the guys on the team. I told you about her." "Oh, now I remember," Mary reflected. "You fell asleep on her shoulder." Both kids chuckled as they remembered the incident. "That certainly seems like it was a long time ago," Joe observed. "Why do you ask about her?" Mary showed Joe the entry into the address book. Joe got defensive. "Now wait a minute Mary. You can't be angry about that; she just grabbed my address book one time and...." Mary shushed Joe. "I'm not angry, silly. This might be our sign! It is the only entry in your book that isn't in your handwriting; AND she is offering to help. It may be worth a try to call her. After all, Gabby said to use your resources."

Joe leaned back in the booth and thought about Ginger. "I seem to remember that she lived in Vermont; no, she was raised in Vermont but now lives in Pennsylvania...." "That's very nice Joe but I don't see how that's going to help." Mary sounded a little impatient. "I'm just trying to think it through, Sugar Plum. Maybe there was something she said or did that would give me an excuse to call her. I just don't want to call out of the blue and start babbling. Don't forget, I think she was interested in being more than friends." Joe looked over at Mary for a reaction. He did not expect to see Mary grinning and pointing to her engagement ring. "I'm not too worried," Mary teased. Joe laughed and squeezed Mary's hand.

"Maybe we should look at this another way," Mary suggested. "Let's list the things that you do well." Joe looked at the ceiling. "Well, there's sports, school, loving you...." Mary smiled. "I love you too, Joe but I doubt that you can make a living at it." "Good point Sugar Plum; the only other thing that I can think of is...." Joe's thoughts wandered off. "That's it!" he almost yelled. "I can do construction work! And, guess what? Ginger said that her dad was in the construction business! I need to give her a call." "Good idea, Joe," Mary said sarcastically. "Alright, I know it was your idea," Joe admitted. "But there is one problem," he continued as he looked around the restaurant. "I don't see a pay phone anywhere." He looked at Mary for help who was already on it. She was pointing to a display in the other section of the truck stop where there were prepaid mobile phones. Joe followed her direction and found the display. He smiled. "Beautiful AND smart. I am the luckiest man in the world." He jumped up and headed for the display.

A few minutes later Joe was back in the booth dialing Ginger. Four rings went by then Ginger picked up. "Hello?" her voice was cautious because the caller ID read 'unknown caller'. "Hi Ginger, this is Joe Goldstein." Ginger paused a minute while the name registered. Then it hit her. "Hi Joe, how are you? How's the senior year going? Are you and Mary still planning to go to Harvard?" "Well, Ginger, Mary and I have sort of had a change of plans. We won't be attending college next year. We are getting married in January." Joe didn't feel like going into details at the moment. "That's great Joe! I'm so happy for you two. Guess what?I'm engaged too! My boyfriend and I got back together and he proposed two weeks ago. We are getting married this summer." "That's great Ginger. He's a lucky guy. I'm really happy for you." There was an awkward silence for a few seconds. Joe didn't know how to bring up the subject. Ginger broke the silence. "Joe, I sense that you didn't call just to catch up. Is everything alright?" Joe paused. "Well there is just one thing that you may be able to help me with. You see, Mary and I are looking for a change of scenery. We need to get out of Montana and experience somewhere else." "I understand," Ginger agreed. "You guys need to spread your wings a little." "Yeah, something like that. Anyway, I remember that you said that your dad was in the construction business and I was wondering if he might be hiring. I need a job." Ginger paused for a moment. "I'm not sure Joe. When I was home for Thanksgiving I heard him say something about a big job starting in January. Would you like for me to put in a good word for you?" "That would be great, Ginger! I mean, if it's not too much trouble." "No problem Joe. You're a great guy and I would love to help you if I can. I'll call dad and talk to him. Give me your number and I'll call you back after I find out some more details." Joe gave Ginger the new cell phone number. "Thanks a lot Ginger, you don't know how much this means to me. Bye."

"Well?" Mary's eyes questioned Joe. "She's going to check with her dad and call back. It sounds promising. In the meantime, we need to keep moving. We have no idea how close Donavan is."

Fifteen minutes later the kids where back on the highway headed for South Dakota. It was slow going for awhile. Joe didn't dare go over 30 mph because of the snow and ice. However, after about an hour the roads cleared a little and Joe was able to step it up to around 50. "It feels like we are flying, now," Mary observed. "Finally." Joe seemed to relax a little as he leaned back in the seat of the truck. "Driving 30 mph gets real old after a couple of hours. How are you doing Mary? We've been driving all night. Do you need to stop and rest for awhile?" Mary yawned. "I'm OK Joe. Sure I'm tired; but you have been doing all of the driving. How are you doing?" Mary's yawn was contagious. Joe yawned and replied, "I could use a nap but I'd like to keep going until we are out of this snow. I'm afraid that it may start again and we'll get stranded." "I'm with you sweetie. I'll see if I can find a good radio station to help keep us awake." Mary fiddled with the dial and finally got a country station. "Good job, Sugar Plum." Mary settled back as Joe half hummed and half sang along. They drove along in silence enjoying the music and the beautiful countryside. Ten minutes later Mary was asleep. Joe turned down the radio and became lost in thought.

Mary awoke with a start. The telephone poles were going by faster than they had been when she had dozed off. She looked at the speedometer; 65 mph. The roads were clear, the sun was shining, and the snow covered landscape was breathtaking. She looked at Joe who was grinning and whistling along with a rock and roll station. "How long have I been asleep?" Mary was groggy. "At least three hours, maybe more. Feel better?" Mary tried to wake up. "I will in a few minutes, I'm still waking up. Do you mind if we stop? I need a break." "No problem, Sugar Plum. Besides, we need gas."

Mary went straight to the restroom while Joe filled the truck. When she returned, she found Joe asleep in the truck. She opened the door. "That's it for you mister. Move over, I'm driving." Joe protested. "I'm OK Mary. It was just a little catnap. Besides, I don't want you to hurt yourself." Mary smiled at her red-eyed fiancée. "Joe, I'm pregnant, not helpless." "But it's a stick shift," Joe attempted again. Mary laughed so hard that her belly shook. "Joe, you must be delirious. I have been driving your car for as long as I've had my license." Joe blushed. "Oh yeah." He got out of the truck and helped Mary get in behind the steering wheel.

Mary took off and Joe started to give her advice about the particulars of driving a 4x4. She rolled her eyes as his speech became slower and slower. He was asleep in less than two minutes. Mary found an easy listening station on the radio and continued down the road.

A few hours later, Joe was awakened by the sound of the new cell phone. Mary was shaking him with one hand and driving with the other. "Joe, Joe, the cell phone is ringing." Joe sat up quickly and tried to collect himself. "Hello?" "Hi, my name is Mac Howard, is this Joe Goldstein?" Joe stumbled over his words as he attempted to shake the sleep out of his brain. "Uh, yes, this is Joe Goldstein." "Well Joe, I just got off of the phone with my daughter Ginger. She has nothing but good things to say about you. She tells me that you may be looking for a position in the construction field." Joe was wide awake now. "Yes sir, Mr. Howard." "First of all, call me Mac. Tell me about yourself. What kind of experience do you have?" "My father owns a construction business and I have worked with him all of my life. I can operate heavy equipment, I can work concrete and I have experience in both framing and finish carpentry. I'm not saying that I don't have a lot more to learn but I am strong and willing. I promise that I will do a good job for you." "Ginger tells me that you are getting married. Most kids want to stay close to home. You do realize that Pennsylvania is a long way from Montana. Why aren't you working with your dad?" The question caught Joe off-guard. "We just need a fresh start, Mac. Besides, we kind of want to experience life outside of Montana for awhile." "I understand Joe. The Mrs. and I did the same thing when Ginger was a little girl. Listen, I would like to give you a chance. Ginger is a pretty good judge of character and I can tell from our brief conversation that you are on the level. The job is in Allentown. It starts after the first of the year. Can you be here before that?" "YES SIR!" Joe almost jumped out of his seat. "Good, I'm looking forward to meeting you. Call me when you get into town. Here's my number." Joe scrambled for a pen as he wrote the number down on his jeans. "One more thing Joe, would you mind if I called your father? I'd just like to get his opinion about your strengths and weaknesses." "Sure thing, Mac. Here's his number." When Joe had finished he said, "Thanks Mac, you don't know how much I appreciate this opportunity." "You are welcome Joe. Somehow I get the feeling that it is going to work out for me as well. I'll see you in a couple of weeks." The phone went dead and Joe closed the phone.

He laid back against the headrest and sighed. "Well?" Mary could hardly contain herself. "Well what?" Joe teased. "Don't start with me Joe." Mary smiled as she held up her tiny little fist in Joe's direction. "Who was that? What did he say?" "Oh that." Joe acted like he didn't know what Mary was talking about. "That was Ginger's dad. I'm pretty sure I have a job beginning right after the first of the year." "THAT'S GREAT, JOE!" Mary startled Joe with her enthusiasm. "Where?" "Allentown, Pennsylvania." "Where is that, Joe?" "I'm not sure," Joe responded nonchalantly.

"Well, Joe, how do we get there?" "I'm not sure; I don't know where we are." "JOSEPH GOLDSTEIN! STOP BEING COY!" Joe could tell that the joke wasn't funny anymore. "I'm sorry Sugar Plum. I'm just so happy that things are working out. Pull into the next station and we'll get a map." "That's more like it." Mary smiled at Joe as she watched for an exit.

CHAPTER THIRTY-SEVEN

Mary and Joe spent the next ten days trying to get to Pennsylvania. They spent as much time as they could on the road and then they would stop at a motel so that Mary could rest. She became more and more uncomfortable as the trip wore on. The truck was rough riding and it caused Mary to have back and stomach pain. Joe became worried about Mary. She was pale and weak.

They stopped at a 24-hour acute care clinic on the west side of Ohio so that a doctor could check on Mary and the baby. The doctor suggested that Mary should minimize her travel. He also said that the baby, although fine, could come just about any time. Mary had lost her appetite from bouncing around in the truck so much which was causing her to become weak. "Doc, we have to keep moving; I've got a job starting in Pennsylvania the first of the year," Joe explained. "I understand what you are up against kids. I'm just telling you the medical facts. If you must travel, you need to take a lot of breaks. Mary needs to walk so that she doesn't get blood clots. I recommend that you stop at least every two hours and get her feet up for a few minutes before you continue on." Mary protested but Joe stopped her. "OK Doc, anything you say. I'll make it happen."

This routine slowed the trip considerably. Even though Mary protested, Joe stopped faithfully and tried to make Mary as comfortable as possible. They would stop at rest areas, truck stops, parking lots…. They would walk around for awhile and then rest for awhile. There were even times when Mary would lay down in the truck and rest while Joe would stand outside in the cold winter Midwest wind.

It was late in the evening on December 21st when they saw the sign; 'Welcome to Pennsylvania'. Mary breathed a sigh of relief. "We are finally here." "Well, sort of," Joe replied. "We still have to cross over the entire state. Allentown is on the other side." Mary frowned at the news and Joe immediately wished that he had kept his mouth shut. It had been a long, grueling trip and it was taking its toll on them; especially Mary. Money was running short and the tension was rising. Mary was due any day and she could never get totally comfortable. They had stopped renting a room for each of them but Joe refused to sleep in the room. He remained adamant about maintaining the integrity of the Savior. He would sleep in the truck.

"It's time for a stop." Joe changed the subject. Mary groaned. "I don't feel like walking." "I know Sugar Plum, but we have to. We must do all that we can for you and the baby." Mary nodded in submission. "I know. I just ache all over." "I'm sorry, Mary. I wish that I could fix it somehow." He felt helpless. Mary smiled at him and squeezed his arm. "You are Joe, just your understanding and being with me is all I need."

Joe pulled off of the interstate into a gas station. "We need gas. I'll fill up while you stretch. I'm out of cash. I need to make a withdrawal from the bank," Joe announced. Mary had been designated to keep the money and Joe had called her 'the bank' ever since. Mary searched through her purse. "All we have left is $75." She started to panic and Joe sensed it. He smiled and chuckled. "Plenty of money. It takes $50 to fill up and that will get us down the road quite a ways. We'll figure something out by then. Are you hungry?" "You are amazing, Joe. I can't believe how you can take a difficult situation and make it seem OK. That's one reason why I love you. And yes, I am hungry." Joe flashed his signature smile. "You go on in and get you some food for the road while I fill up the truck." "What do you want to eat, Joe?" Mary asked as she climbed out of the truck. "Nothing for me, thanks. I'm not hungry." Mary headed for the mini-mart thinking it strange that Joe wasn't hungry. Joe watched her go into the store and began filling the truck. His stomach growled. He was starving. He hadn't eaten in 24 hours.

But there was no way that he was going to 'waste' money on himself. He had a family to take care of.

An hour later, they were back on the road. Although both of them were tired, they were in a good mood. They had found a good country station on the radio and were singing along and acting silly. It felt good to forget about their problems for a few minutes and be kids again; even if it was only for a short while.

Thirty minutes later the radio became fuzzy and the mood changed. Mary searched for another station but was unsuccessful. She yawned. "Are you OK, Joe?" "Sure am!" he lied. "I think I'll take a little nap if you can drive without company for awhile." "Well, I'll miss the company, but I'm fine. You just rest and I'll get us a little further down the road." Mary leaned the seat back and was asleep in a few seconds. Joe shook his head and rubbed his eyes. He felt like he could sleep for a week solid, but he knew that he had to keep going. He fought sleep for two hours as they rolled down Interstate 80 in the darkness.

Suddenly, Joe felt someone tap him on the shoulder. Joe realized that his head was down and that he had dozed off. He snapped back into an alert state and realized that he had crossed over into the passing lane and was about to run off into the median. "You are doing some pretty fancy driving there Joe." A voice came from the cargo area behind the seat. Startled because he was afraid that he was dreaming instead of driving, he looked in the rear view mirror to see a grinning Guardian in the reflection. "Guardian! You nearly scared the socks off of me!" Guardian laughed. "Sorry Joe. Just doing my job. Better sockless than dead. Do you think it may be time for a break?" Joe looked at the clock; 2:15 a.m. They had been driving for over three hours. "I guess it is, Guardian. Thanks." "No problem. I'm here to help. See you later." Joe glanced at the road and said, "Wait! Guardian! I've got a problem! We are out of money and I don't know what to do." Joe looked back in the mirror. Too late, Guardian was gone.

Mary woke up as Joe pulled into the motel. "Where are we?" "We are sitting in front of a motel somewhere in the middle of Pennsylvania. I can't go on without some sleep. I almost wrecked awhile ago." Mary rubbed the sleep from her eyes. "Well, I hope they have a room for $25 or we'll both be sleeping in the truck."

Mary mused as they looked at the motel's sign advertising rooms beginning at $50. "Check your purse again, Mary. Maybe you missed something. I'll check my wallet and backpack." Mary reluctantly opened her purse and began to search. She was sure that there was no more cash to be found. She was always very careful with her money. Joe was busy looking through his backpack when Mary said happily, "Bingo." Joe looked over to see her holding up her dad's credit card. Joe hesitated and Mary read his mind. He said it was OK to use it. Remember, he told us right before we left the hospital," Joe grinned. "I DO remember!" "We'll use it on one condition," Mary insisted. "You MUST get a room as well. I'm tired of feeling guilty sleeping in a room and you in the truck. Deal?" Joe was so exhausted that he couldn't protest. He didn't like using someone else's money but the thought of sleeping in a real bed was extremely inviting. "Deal, thanks Sugar Plum." Ten minutes later they were both sound asleep.

At 8 a.m. the next morning, a phone rang in Washington DC "Donavan," he answered tersely. "Mr. Donavan, we have positive conformation that a credit card issued to Jacob Reubenowitz was used early this morning at a motel in central Pennsylvania." Donavan sat up in his chair. "Do you know exactly where it was used?" "Yes sir. Would you like us to move in?" "Where are the parents, uh, what are their names, uh...." "Jacob and Ruth, sir." "Yeah, them, do we know where they are? I don't want to move in on a middle-aged vacationing couple." "Well, sir, I assume that they are back in Montana...." Donavan yelled into the receiver. "DON'T ASSUME ANYTHING! Find out for sure and call me back. Also, find out if we have agents close to that motel!" Donavan slammed the receiver down.

"Witz's Drugs; how may I help you?" Ruth answered the phone at the store. "This is Jennifer from the credit card company. May I speak to Jacob or Ruth Reubenowitz, please?" This is Ruth. Is there a problem?" "This is a courtesy call to let you know that your card was used last night at a motel in Pennsylvania. We wanted to insure that you were aware of the transaction and make sure that you had authorized this usage." It took a couple of seconds for the information to soak in; then it hit her. The kids were out of money and had resorted to using the credit card. "Yes, we are aware of it and it's fine. Thanks for calling." She hung up the phone and walked back to the pharmacy where Jake was working. "Jake, that was the credit card company calling to confirm that we had authorized usage in Pennsylvania." "PENNSYLVANIA?" He thought for a second. Then it came to him as well. "What on earth are the kids doing in Pennsylvania?" "I have the same question," Ruth replied. "Do you think that we should try to contact them? They are obviously out of money and they may even be in trouble.... Jake held up his hand. "Slow down a minute Ruthy. I have all of the same concerns that you do. But you know as well as I that we can't call them. Our phones are bugged and we don't even have a number for them." Ruth's look of concerned immediately transformed into a look of helplessness. Jake reached out and pulled her close for a bear hug. "You know that I want to be there for them as much as you do. But we have to wait for them to contact us. It is the safest thing for them." "I know, Jake. It's just so hard. Our little girl is about to give birth and we can't even be there for her." She sobbed into Jake's chest.

Mary woke up and looked at the clock; 9:05. She moaned as she struggled to sit up. The big belly on her tiny little frame made it difficult to do almost anything. She picked up the phone and rang Joe's room. Six rings later, Joe picked up the phone, then dropped it, then answered with a sleepy, "Hello?" Mary laughed. "Did I wake you sweetie?" In his typical quick wit, Joe replied, "No, not at all. I had to get up to answer the phone." Mary laughed louder. "What time is it?" Joe yawned as he asked the question. "9:05. I think we should get going." Joe longed to fall back into bed. He hadn't slept in a real bed for over a week and it felt great. But, he knew that Mary was right. It was the 22nd of December and they had to get to Allentown before the 1st. "I'll be ready in thirty minutes, Sugar Plum." "Make it 45 minutes, Joe. I have a big belly to wash." "Joe laughed heartily. "I love you."

Back in Washington, Jim Donavan's phone rang. He looked at the caller ID. "You had better have some information for me," he growled. "Yes sir, Mr. Donavan. The Reubenowitzs are still in Montana. We have agents within two hours of the motel where the card was last used. Do you want us to move in?" Donavan looked at his watch; 10:30. "How much was the charge on the card?" "The charge was for two rooms totaling $117.85." "Two rooms? That doesn't make sense. The guy gets her pregnant and then sleeps in another room? These kids are weird." He thought for a moment. "They are only staying one night. Most likely they will be gone before we can get there. I don't want another botched attempt at apprehending them. Let's just continue to track the credit card. Maybe we can see a pattern and catch them when they arrive at wherever they are going." He hung up the phone, sat back in his chair, smiled, folded his hands behind his head, and put his feet on the desk. "It won't be long now, Miss Mary."

Three hours later Joe pulled off of the interstate into a truck stop. He filled the truck while Mary stretched and then they went inside for some lunch. There was a buffet in which both kids took full advantage. They walked out 45 minutes later stuffed and very happy. "Remind me to tell your dad thanks for the lunch." Joe helped Mary into the truck. Mary laughed. "I'm sure he won't mind." They eased back onto the interstate and settled back for more riding. "How long until we get there?" Mary asked. "We should be there tomorrow," Joe replied triumphantly. "Good." Mary was relieved. She had been having some minor abdominal pain which she assumed told her that labor was getting close. However, the baby hadn't 'dropped' so she didn't tell Joe. He was stressed enough.

Ruth hung up the phone at the store with a confused look on her face. Jake walked by and noticed. "What's wrong honey?" "I'm not sure. That was the credit card company again. They called about some more charges on our card in Pennsylvania. Of course I approved the charges but when I told the representative that I had spoken with them earlier today, she told me that it was policy to call the cardholders on all out-of-state purchases when their account has been flagged." "Flagged?" Jake asked. "What does that mean?" "I'm not sure. When I asked the representative, she told me that she was new but she thought it had to do with the government somehow." Jake rubbed his forehead as he tried to figure it out. He looked up and walked to the phone. "Who are you calling?" "Bill, maybe he knows what 'flagged' means."

"Donavan here." He answered from his limo. "Mr. Donavan, the Reubenowitz card was used 30 minutes ago at a truck stop along I-80. There were two purchases, one for gas and one at the restaurant." Donavan smiled. "It looks like they are headed east. Good work, stay on it and keep me posted. They will have to stop soon. That girl must be about to pop."

"Thanks Bill, you've been a big help." Jake hung up the phone. The look on his face told Ruth that the news wasn't good. "'Flagged' means that someone in the Federal Government has deemed it essential to monitor the card. Bill says it is usually used by the FBI when they are tracking stolen cards." Jake paused to look at the floor while Ruth absorbed the information. When he did look at her, there were tears in her eyes. "Donavan is tracking our cards hoping to find the kids isn't he?" Ruth hoped that the answer was 'no'. Oh how she wanted to be wrong. "That's what Bill thinks," Jake admitted. "What are we going to do, Jake?" "I don't know, Ruth. I just don't know."

Later that evening, Jake and Ruth were at the Goldstein's filling them in on what was going on. Eve turned white and Abraham frowned as he spun his coffee mug around and around. "I wonder if Dr. Sheppard could shed any light on this," Abraham thought out loud. "Let's call him." "That's not such a good idea." Ruth remembered what Jake had said in the store. "Don't forget that our phones are bugged." Abraham grinned and fumbled around in his pocket. A couple of seconds later he pulled a different cell phone out of his pocket. "I switched phones with my foreman for a couple of days. I thought we might have a little fun with our friend Mr. Donavan." Jake laughed out loud. "Pretty sneaky old buddy. I'm only sad that I didn't think of it first," Eve spoke up. "I'm sorry to rain on your parade but how do you know that Donavan hasn't tapped all of our employees' phones?" "Good question," Abraham observed. "I had Bill check it out. This phone is clean." "How about Dr. Sheppard's phone?" Eve persisted. Abraham got quiet. He hadn't thought about that. "There's only one way to find out." Jake took the phone from Abraham and dialed Dr. Sheppard. "This is Dr. Sheppard," he answered. "Hi Doc, this is Jake Reubenowitz." "Hi Jake." Click, click, click. Jake immediately knew what that meant. "I'm sorry Jake, we have a terrible connection." "That's OK, Doc. I'll make it short. We are across the street at the Goldstein's playing cards and stuff and wondered if you and the Mrs. might want to come over and join the party." Dr. Sheppard wasn't married and he knew that Jake knew it. He sensed that Jake was speaking in code for some reason. "You know what Jake? That sounds great. I've been meaning to get the little woman out of the house. We'll be right over."

Twenty minutes later Dr. Sheppard walked into the Goldstein's home. "My wife couldn't come," he teased as everyone greeted him. "Sorry about that Doc," Jake confessed. "I was hoping that you would get the hint." Dr. Sheppard observed the somber looks from everyone in the room. "So what's up? I assume this has something to do with Joe and Mary?" "And you." Jake added. "First, we are pretty sure that your cell phone is tapped. That clicking sound was one of the first things we heard on our phones before we confirmed that our phones were bugged." Dr. Sheppard's first reaction was denial, then shock, and finally anger. "It's been doing that since I had a visit from an agent at work the other day. I should have known. If Donavan were here right now, he'd be a patient of mine before I got finished with him!" "I'm sorry Doc," Abraham interjected. "It's our fault that you are involved in this." "Don't apologize," Dr Sheppard disagreed. "I am happy to be a part of getting the Messiah into the world." Everyone smiled and agreed. "So is there anything else?" Ruth spoke up. "We are pretty sure that the kids are in Pennsylvania. The reason we suspect this is that the credit card company called to insure that we had authorized the purchases made in Pennsylvania. We assumed that the kids ran out of cash and have been using our credit card. The strange thing is that the company has called two days in a row. When I questioned them they told me that it was 'policy' to call on all out-of-state purchases when a card has been flagged." Dr. Sheppard's face became quizzical. Jake jumped in. "We asked Bill what 'flagged' meant. He said that it usually means that the government is tracking a card. Normally, when it has been reported stolen, however we believe...." Dr. Sheppard interrupted. "Donavan is tracking your cards." "Exactly." "When is that snake going to give up?" Dr. Sheppard shook his head. "Do the kids know?" "I don't think so." Abraham sounded dejected. "Eve spoke up. "That's why we asked you over. You are the only one who has talked to them recently. Do you have their number?" Doctor Sheppard shook his head. "No, he called from a land line in North Dakota. I have no idea how to get in touch with them."

Just then Abraham's cell phone rang. He looked at the caller ID and recognized the area code as being from Pennsylvania. "It may be the kids but I'm afraid to answer. You know that Donavan is listening." "Just write the number down and call them right back from the clean phone," Eve suggested. "Good idea."

In just a few seconds Abraham dialed the number. An unfamiliar man's voice answered. "Hello?" Abraham was caught off-guard. "Uh, hello, this is Abraham Goldstein. I believe that you just attempted to call me." "Well, uh, yes." The voice was hesitant. "The caller ID doesn't match with the number that was given me." "My cell phone is on the verge of giving out." Abraham was thinking quickly. Maybe this guy knew something. "This is my alternate number." The voice on the other end of the line relaxed. "I understand completely. I've just recently replaced my phone for the same reason." Abraham chuckled in agreement. "My name is Mac Howard. Your son, Joe, and my daughter became friends while he was at Harvard last spring. She speaks very highly of Joe." "Thank you Mr. Howard, we are proud of Joe. How can I help you?" "First of all, please call me Mac." "OK Mac, as long as you call me Abraham." Mac chuckled. "Sounds like we are cut out of the same mold. OK Abraham, Joe called me asking for a job. I'm in the construction business as are you according to Joe." "That's right Mac." "I'll get straight to the point. I know you are prejudiced, but can you give me an idea of his capabilities?"

Abraham went into detail about what Joe could do well and what his experiences were. "That's all I needed to hear, Abraham. That and the fact that you knew what he was up to. As one parent to another, I'd like to know what my kids are up to if they are far from home." "Thanks Mac, I really appreciate it. Speaking of which, we haven't been able to contact the kids recently. We suspect they have lost their cell phones or something. Do you have a number where they can be reached?" "Sure, Abraham, in fact I seem to remember that Joe said something about calling from one of those phones where you pre-pay for minutes. Here's the number." "Thanks Mac, I appreciate you giving Joe a chance. If he doesn't work well for you, give me a call. I'll straighten him out." Mac laughed. "I don't think I'll have any trouble with him. I'll talk to you later. Bye."

Abraham hung up, put the phone on speaker, and dialed the number. "Thank you, God," he said out loud while holding back some tears.

Mary and Joe were cruising somewhere along I-80 when the phone rang. "Who could that be?" Mary looked over at Joe. "I don't know. The only person I've called is Mr. Howard. Maybe you should answer it." Mary panicked. "It may be bad news, maybe he has changed his mind, maybe you don't have a job, maybe...." Joe took the phone. "There's only one way to find out. Hello?" "Joe?" He immediately recognized his dad's voice. "DAD!" He could tell that he was on speaker. "Wait a minute; I'll put you on speaker so Mary can hear." Joe hit the speaker button. "Dad, it is so good to hear your voice. Are you alone?" "No son, your mother, Ruth, Jake and Dr. Sheppard are here." The kids heard a collective 'hello' along with some sobbing from their mothers. Mary, almost yelling into the phone said, "Hi everyone! I love you!"

After a couple of minutes of catching up, Jake went straight to the point. "Have you kids been using the credit card?" Mary answered. "Yes daddy. I didn't think you would care. We ran out of cash." "We don't mind at all, honey. But you must stop using it. We are pretty sure that Donavan is tracking you as you use it." "How can he do that?" Joe asked. Just then his phone started to beep. "I am running out of minutes." Joe panicked. "There's no time for explanations, son," Abraham interjected. "Just stop using that card!" "OK dad but we are down to about $12. What are we supposed to do?" Dr. Sheppard spoke up. "Can you get to Allentown on what you have?" Joe looked at the gas gauge and thought for a moment. "I don't think so, it would be very close." "OK, look for a place that will cash checks. Some truck stops will do that. When you find one, see if they have a way of accepting wired money. If they do, call us on this number and we'll wire you some money. I have a friend in Allentown. I'll call him and he can help you when you arrive." Joe's phone started beeping faster. "My phone is about dead. I'll call you as soon as I...." The phone went dead. Eve looked at Abraham. "What do we do now?" Abraham paused. "Wait."

Joe closed the phone and tossed it behind the seat. He and Mary rode in silence for awhile. Both kids were deep in thought. Finally, Mary spoke up. "A penny for your thoughts." Joe sighed. "I was just thinking about the state championship game last year. Remember? We were down ten points halfway through the fourth quarter. I remember Coach telling us; 'Fourth quarter, boys, fourth quarter. Don't quit. Never give up.' We didn't quit and we won." "What does that have to do with us now?" "Mary, this is our fourth quarter. It may seem like things are closing in on us but we can't give up; I refuse. I intend to protect you and the Messiah no matter what it takes. It may be tough, but, with God's help, we will win." Mary sighed and leaned over into Joe's arm. "You make me feel so safe. I love you."

Joe didn't respond; he was scanning road and exit signs as they traveled along. He was looking for a truck stop that may cash checks. After about twenty miles, he spotted one. "There it is!" He pointed to a sign. "Do you see it Mary?" "Yes Joe. I see it. Good job." Joe pulled off of the interstate and up to the doors. Both kids scurried out of the truck and up to the counter.

A big, burly, tattoo-covered, scary-looking man about forty years old came up to the counter and growled. "What do you kids want?" Mary stood behind Joe who was as intimidated as she was by the tattooed giant. "Well, uh, I'm uh, I mean, uh...." "Well spit it out boy!" The man glared at Joe, occasionally glancing at Mary who was peaking around Joe's shoulder. "I don't have all day!" Joe gathered his courage. "Do you cash checks here?" The man sighed in disgust and pointed to a big sign behind him. 'Checks cashed, $50 limit, two forms of ID required, $5 service fee.' "Well sir, I don't have a check but I wonder if I could have money wired here from my dad's account." The man's face reddened and he acted as if Joe had requested that he give up his kidney. He raised his huge hand and ran his fingers through his hair. Joe was afraid that the guy was going to reach across the counter and smack him. Instead, he lowered his hand and started typing on the computer. "I'll need to speak to him and his bank." "Well sir, we don't have a phone, may I borrow yours please?" The man looked at the kids as if they were out of their minds. "You've got to be kidding." "No sir, we are desperate. Please help us. I'm begging you." The man leaned forward on the counter and stared at the kids. Joe stepped back just a little. After a few seconds, he started laughing. "I can't go on with this any longer." Joe looked at Mary who was looking at the guy wondering if he were crazy. "Gabby and Guardian told me to give you two a hard time." He laughed even louder as the kids stood there in astonishment. Joe finally spoke up. "How do you know Gabby and Guardian? I mean, they are, well...." The guy stuck his hand across the counter. "Angels? Hi, I'm Gus. We come in all forms. You never know when you may be looking at one." Mary, still scared, looked around from behind Joe and said, "Are we looking at one now?" Gus bowed low and smiled. "At your service. Sorry about the tease. Guardian told me that you guys were getting too serious and that I should lighten you up a little. Seems like you forget who your Boss is." He pointed upward "Stop worrying, He is on your side and guys like me are everywhere looking out for you." He handed Joe a cell phone. "Now call your dad and let's get you kids some cash." Mary and Joe relaxed and even chuckled along with Gus. "Tell Gabby and Guardian that they really pulled one over on us. Joe told Gus as they waited for the transaction to be completed. Ten minutes later the kids were back on the road $500 richer.

Dr. Sheppard dialed his friend from his house phone. "Hi Jeff, it's Shep." Dr. Sheppard was careful to listen for clicking sounds. He wanted to make sure that his house phone wasn't bugged. "Can you hear, OK Jeff?" "Clear as a bell, buddy. What's up?" "I need a favor, Jeff. It's important." Name it Shep. You introduced me to my wife and was my best man at the wedding. I'll do anything I can for you." "Good, there are these two kids heading your way. They need your help...."

"They are headed for Allentown, sir." "How do you know that?" Donavan growled into the receiver. "I just recorded Dr. Sheppard talking from the land line at his house to a Jeff Green in Allentown. He told Mr. Green about the kids heading his way. He asked Mr. Green to help them." "Have you fixed that awful clicking noise on the taps? They are driving me nuts!" "Yes sir." "Good job, get Mr. Green's phone number and address. Have some agents watch his house and tap his phone. Post agents at all of the emergency rooms in the Allentown area. I know she is due anytime. Keep me posted." "Consider it done, sir."

CHAPTER
THIRTY-EIGHT

M̲ary woke up with sharp pains in her stomach. They had stopped for the night at a little motel just outside of Allentown. The pains weren't terrible and didn't last long. She wondered if Joe was awake. She looked at the clock; 7:30. Joe picked up after the first ring. "Good morning Sugar Plum." "Good morning, Joe. Have you been up long?" "I woke up about 6:00. I just couldn't sleep. Did you sleep well?" "Not bad, but…." "But what, Mary?" "I think, I'm not sure, but maybe, I might be going into labor." Joe panicked. "We had better get to a hospital!"

Dr. Sheppard awoke to the sound of his phone ringing. It was 4 a.m. 'It must be the hospital,' he thought to himself. "Hello?" he mumbled into the receiver. "Shep, it's Jeff. Sorry to wake you but something strange is going on here." Dr. Sheppard was wide awake and on the edge of his bed in an instant. "What's going on, Jeff." "Well, 30 minutes after I hung up with you yesterday, a black SUV with Virginia plates parked across the street from my house. I didn't think much of it then but when I got up for work this morning I noticed that they were still there." "I'm such an idiot!" Dr. Sheppard spoke out loud to himself. "They tapped my phone and now they know the kids are heading for you." "THEY? Who are they? And why are they tapping your phone and sitting outside of my house?!" "Jeff, this is going to be difficult to believe, but I am going to tell you the truth." "Please do." Dr. Sheppard spent the next ten minutes explaining the story to his friend. When he had finished, he waited for a reaction. "Shep, if I had heard that story from anyone but you, I would have said that they were crazy. But, I have this tingling sensation all over after listening to it. I've never felt anything like this in my life. Could it really be true that the Messiah is finally coming?!" "Yes, Jeff, it's true. Now we have to help these kids. You have to assume that your phone is bugged, so be careful what you say. I'll get in touch with you somehow, just stand by." OK, Shep, I'm all in; and oh, by the way, in case anyone is listening, you will not win! This baby will be born and will remain safe!" "Thanks buddy, I'll be in touch."

Ten minutes later the SUV pulled away from Jeff's house. 'That's right, you had better give up,' Jeff said to himself as they disappeared down the street.

"They are on to us Mr. Donavan. Dr. Sheppard knows that the phones are tapped." Donavan scowled as he absorbed the news. "No matter, but keep on monitoring. You never know when someone will slip up. Anyway, the kids are in a bind. They can't run much longer. I'm sure they will be looking for a hospital soon. We'll find them."

Joe and Mary entered the city limits of Allentown around 10 a.m. Mary's labor pains had subsided somewhat and were about 45 minutes apart. Notwithstanding, Joe was determined to get her to a hospital so that a doctor could check on her. He spotted a sign indicating that a hospital was located near the next exit. He started to drive into the emergency room unloading area but Mary spoke up. "Joe, just park out in the lot. I don't want to go into the ER and make a huge scene." Joe started to protest, but the look on Mary's face told him that it would be futile. "Besides, they may be too crowded or they don't deliver babies here or...." Joe interrupted. "Now wait just a minute. I'll do as you ask, but your excuses are lame. What's the real reason you don't want to go in?" Mary paused. "I really don't know, Joe. I just have a bad feeling about this. Call it intuition. Please just go in and check it out." Joe looked intently at Mary's pleading face. "I'll be right back."

Joe walked into the ER and noticed that there were a lot of people in there. A lot of them were in obvious pain and the staff was running all over the place. He walked up to the reception area to discover an empty chair. However, there was a lady working at a

filing cabinet who had her back to him. "Excuse me miss, but…."
"I'll be right with you. Just give me a minute." Joe waited patiently
as the lady finished her filing. He was looking out at the crowd in
the ER when she came up to him. "I'm sorry for the delay, sir; it's
been crazy here this morning. How can I help you?" Joe spun around
to look in the direction of the voice. When he saw the lady, he almost
passed out. "Gabby?" She held her finger to her lips as she shushed
him. "Have a seat sir." Joe sat down obediently. "We just need to get
some information from you." Joe was confused. Gabby was acting like
she didn't know him. "What's going on? It's me, Joe," he whispered.
"Just fill out the form sir." Gabby looked at him and winked ever so
slightly as she pointed to the form. He followed her finger to the form
and noticed a note written on the form in large red letters. "Beware
of the men in black suits." Joe looked at Gabby quizzically. She
looked in the direction of the waiting area and nodded ever so
slightly. Joe scanned the room and noticed two men dressed in black
suits. They stood out like a piece of coal in a pile of snow. Joe realized
that they had no business in the ER. Joe met Gabby's smile and
nodded. He slowly got up and made his way to the door. His blood
was racing and head was spinning. He wanted to slip out unnoticed.
As he went through the doors, he glanced over his shoulder and
sighed with relief. The men hadn't noticed him. He walked slowly to
the truck and got in. "We've got a problem," he said as he fired up
the truck and left the lot. "What problem?" Mary asked. Joe related
what had just happened. "What are we going to do, Joe?" "We are
going to check another hospital."

Thirty minutes later the kids parked on the lot of another
hospital. Joe was more careful this time. He went in through the
main doors and peaked into the ER through an inconspicuous set of
doors. As he glance around the room his heart sank; two more men
in dark suits. He slowly closed the door and exited the hospital. "I
assume by the look on your face that the goons were there too,"
Mary observed. Joe didn't say anything as he started the truck and
drove on.

They stopped at two more hospitals and three emergency care
units with the same results. Joe got back into the truck. "They are
everywhere. Obviously, they know we are here. We need another
plan." Mary grimaced in pain as she nodded to Joe. "Another
contraction?" he questioned knowing the answer. She nodded again.

"How long has this been going on?" Joe was getting concerned. "I've had three in the last hour and a half." She started to cry. "Joe, they are getting closer." Joe prayed, 'God please help me.' When he opened his eyes he saw a hotel across the street from the hospital. "I've got an idea. We'll get a room, call a doctor, and try to get him to come to us." "That's a long shot, Joe." "I know, Sugar Plum, but we have to try."

Joe swung up to the entrance of the hotel and ran up to the front desk. "Can I help you?" the girl behind the desk asked. "Yes, I need a room, please," the girl chuckled. "I'm sorry sir, we are all booked up." "OK, could you please direct me to another hotel?" She sensed urgency in his voice and felt compassion. "I'm sorry, sir. There is a steel convention in town this week. All of the hotels for miles around have been booked for over a month. I wish there were something that I could do." Joe expression immediately changed from hopeful to dejected. "Thanks anyway." He turned and walked out of the door.

Mary read Joe's expression as he got into the truck. "No luck?" Joe shook his head. "There are no rooms anywhere in the city." His voice cracked as he gave Mary the bad news. "I figured as much." Mary pointed to the sign in front of the hotel, 'Welcome Steel Conventioneers' and just below that a sign flashed 'No vacancy'. "I'm sorry, Mary. I didn't see it when I drove in." Mary could see that Joe was dejected. "Don't worry, Joe, everything is going to work out. After all, God is on our side." She consoled as she held his hand. Tears ran down his cheeks as he looked helplessly at his fiancée. "I'm at the end of my rope, Mary. I don't know what to do." Mary had never seen Joe so dejected. She searched for the right words. "You don't realize that God is all you need until God is all you have." She forced a smile at Joe. "It's the fourth quarter, Joe. Are you going to quit?" He didn't respond. He just bowed his head and started to pray. "Dear Father, I know that You have a plan and I know that we will fulfill that plan. I ask that you reveal that plan to us and give us the courage, wisdom, and the resources to complete it. Amen."

Both kids leaned back in the seat as they let the prayer soak in. After a couple of minutes, Joe said, "Well, we aren't going to get anywhere sitting here." He sat up, started the truck, and drove out of the lot. Mary noticed that Joe showed signs of confidence. "OK, where are we going?" "We, my dear, are leaving town. It isn't safe here." "OK, but...." Mary couldn't finish her sentence. She shrieked in pain. Joe grabbed her hand. She squeezed it tightly for about 30 seconds. He looked at the clock; 1:30. It had been 25 minutes since the last contraction. He had to act fast. 'OK God, which way do I go?' he said to himself. Suddenly it came to him. He pictured Gus, the burly angel from the truck stop. He was pointing up. 'Up? How can I go up'? They came to a stoplight and Joe glanced at a map that was open between him and Mary. His eyes focused on the key. 'Up' meant north. He prayed again. 'Lord, if this isn't right, please, let me know now.' He started making his way north to get out of town.

Mary and Joe wound their way north through the avenues of Allentown. One-way streets forced them east occasionally, but Mary felt like that was God's way of directing them. Eventually, they hit the suburbs and saw a sign that said, 'Welcome to Bethlehem'. Joe hoped that they could find a hospital or hotel that was safe. All of the hotels had signs that said, 'No vacancy'. He stopped for gas and asked the attendant for directions to the closest hospital. "Two blocks down and one block over." Joe found the hospital and slipped up to the doors of the ER. His heart sank. There were goons in suits there too. He walked back to the truck mumbling to himself; "Fourth quarter, two minute drill, fourth quarter...."

Mary didn't have to ask, she read Joe's look. She held her stomach and moaned. "Joe, my water just broke!" Joe looked at the clock on the dash; 4:30. It would be getting dark soon. Mary screamed with another contraction. They were coming 15 minutes apart. He sped out of the parking lot. For some reason he felt compelled to get out of the city. He was a country boy and that's where he felt comfortable. It didn't make sense, but that's what his gut was telling him. "Where are we going, Joe?" Mary asked between contractions. "We are getting out of town. I don't know why. It doesn't make sense, but I feel strongly about it." Uncomfortable as she was, Mary collected a smile. "I trust you, Joe."

Those words hit Joe like a ton of bricks. She was telling him that he may have to deliver the baby! That thought hadn't occurred to him. He went pale. Mary giggled just a little. "Do you mean to tell me that, as smart as you are, you hadn't considered the possibility that we may have to do this ourselves?" Joe was speechless. His mind raced. They drove in silence. The only break from the quietness was Mary's shrieks of labor pains which were coming more frequently.

The suburbs melted into countryside and darkness started to fall. Under any other circumstances, the rolling hills which were interrupted occasionally by a farmhouse would have been beautiful. But there was no time for sightseeing. Mary's contractions were coming at five-minute intervals now. "Joe, we have got to stop! I can't take this anymore! I don't care where we stop! This baby is coming!" Just then Joe saw a little lane leading into the woods. Something told him to turn in. It was dark now and Joe followed the lane as it twisted through the woods. Finally, after about a half mile the lane ended. Joe stopped and looked around. The only thing in sight was a barn. Mary saw it too. "Let's go in!" Joe protested. "Are you kidding!? You want to deliver the Messiah in a barn?!" Mary opened the door as she screamed with another contraction. Three minutes apart now. "She looked at Joe pathetically. "Joe, it's not my first choice, but it is our ONLY choice. Are you going to help me or am I going to have to do this myself?!" She didn't wait for an answer. She headed for the barn. Joe grabbed a flashlight and followed obediently.

Once inside, the kids examined the place carefully. Mary found a pile of straw and lay down in the middle of it. Joe looked around and saw that there were animals milling around. Some were in stalls and some just roamed freely about the barn. All of them were a bit curious about the kids at first but soon seemed to ignore them and went about their business of settling in for the night. Joe found a couple of lanterns and lit them. The room glowed with a quiet charm.

Mary moaned again. "It won't be long now," she said through clenched teeth. Joe went into automatic mode. He ran out to the truck and brought in all of the clothes, blankets, food and water that they had. He quickly arranged the blankets to make Mary as comfortable as possible. The contractions were coming about two minutes apart now and Mary was in constant pain. In between the contractions she took Joe's hand. "We will need something to keep the baby warm and we will need a place to put him." Joe nodded and ripped open his suitcase. He began tearing soft cotton shirts into strips. He looked around and found a manger that the cows had used for eating hay. He laid a blanket in the manger and formed a makeshift cradle. Mary screamed, "He's coming!" Joe ran to Mary's side and prayed, "Lord, thank you for sending the Savior into the world. Please guide my hands as I help Mary, Amen."

Thirty minutes later, the Messiah entered the world. Joe and Mary lay in the straw with the baby between them and smiled at each other. The baby cooed and squirmed in His makeshift clothes. The cows made lowing sounds and the sheep joined in with their bawling. It sounded like a chorus from a choir. Mary looked up through the cracks in the ceiling and saw a bright light hovering directly over the barn. She pointed upward and Joe followed her finger. He noticed something move in the loft. He squinted as he made out what looked like a hologram of Gabby and Guardian. Mary saw them too. Joe and Mary waved at their angelic friends. Gabby and Guardian gave them a 'thumbs up' and slowly floated heavenward. They disappeared through the ceiling into the bright light above the barn.

Somewhere along Interstate 78 between Harrisburg and Allentown, four truck drivers walked out of a diner after finishing a huge dinner. "I'm stuffed." "Me too." "It's not too cold and it is as clear as a bell. Just look at those stars. Let's walk it off before climbing back into the rigs." "Good idea, I don't think I could fit behind the wheel right now." They all laughed and slapped each other on their backs as they started down an access road. They had been friends for a long time and they looked forward to spending time together whenever they could. They walked in silence for about ten minutes each lost in his own thoughts. All of them missed their families but were grateful for the company of good friends.

All of a sudden a bright light appeared out of nowhere. It was so bright that they had to shield their eyes until they got used to it. They feared for their lives. Could it be a UFO? A bomb? In just a few seconds their eyes adjusted and they could make out an image in the sky. It was huge and had the form of a man. It looked like it was right on top of them but at the same time it seemed like it was a thousand miles away. Then the image spoke. "Don't be afraid. I bring you good news. Be glad. Today, in the town of Bethlehem, the Messiah, who is Christ the Lord, has been born. You will find the baby in a barn, wrapped in strips of clothes, lying in a manger." In that instant, the image was joined by thousands of angels covering the entire sky. They said in unison, "Glory to God in

Heaven, peace on earth, and good will toward men." Then, just as suddenly as they appeared, they vanished.

The drivers stood there in awe. Minutes went by as they tried to absorb what they had just witnessed. Each one of them had the same thought. Was it real? Did the other guys see it? What if they didn't? Am I going crazy? What should I do? Finally, one of them attempted to speak. "Umm, did anyone...uh...." Another spoke up. "I think, maybe...something...ah." A third injected. "I can't explain, I mean, did you see...." After a short pause, the fourth guy said, "I'm going to Bethlehem, anybody want to join me?" The other three looked at their friend. He was grinning from ear to ear. They all said in unison, "I'm in." The four of them ran to their trucks.

Doctor Rogers walked out of the lecture about 8 p.m. He and two of his friends, Dr. Likens and Dr. Isaac had been attending a conference at Ohio State in Columbus. The theme of the conference centered on all of their interests; ancient history, architecture, and culture. Dr. Likens was the first to notice it. "Look at that star in the east. Is it me or is it shining brighter than anything I've ever seen." Dr. Rogers and Dr. Isaac looked up. "Wow! That is the most brilliant star that I have ever seen! Just look at that!" Dr. Isaac, who specialized in ancient history, stroked his bearded chin thoughtfully. He didn't say anything. He merely walked over to a bench, sat down, and pulled out his computer. "What are you doing?" Dr. Rogers quizzed. "Something just struck me and I want to look it up." "You want to look it up, now?" Dr. Likens added. Dr. Isaac kept pounding on his computer as he replied, "It's just a passing thought, it's probably nothing. You guys go on, I'll catch up later." Dr. Rogers and Dr. Likens shrugged and sat down on either side of him. Dr. Isaac looked at Dr. Likens with a question in his eyes. "Look, we are the three amigos; we stick together," Dr. Rogers teased. "Besides, it's your turn to buy dinner, we'll wait." All three of them laughed as Dr. Isaac returned to his computer.

Ten minutes later, Dr. Isaac looked up with tears in his eyes. "You guys are going to think I'm crazy." He looked at both of them. "Give us a try," Dr. Rogers replied. "You know that I was raised in a strict Jewish home and went to Jewish schools all the way through high school. Well, when I saw that star, I remembered one of my history teachers talking about a star in the east and how it would be an indication that the Messiah, the Christ, had come to earth. I've looked over the evidence here very quickly and I believe that the time has come. I have tried to dispute my theory, but all indications are that the Savior is here." Both of his friends just stared at him for a few moments. They had to process the information. Finally, Dr. Isaac spoke up, "I told you that you would think that I'm crazy." He started to get up to leave; both Dr. Rogers and Dr. Likens grabbed his arm. "Where are you going?" "I'm going to follow that star." Both of his friends stood up. "You're not going without us," Dr. Likens smiled. "Yeah, we want to be a part of this," Dr. Rogers added. Tears welled up in Dr. Isaac's eyes. "Thanks guys. Let's go get packed."

It was after midnight when Joe heard the barn door slowly open. Mary had snuggled down into the straw for warmth. Joe was holding the baby to keep him warm. "Who's there?" Joe spoke boldly. "Uh, nobody really. Can we come in?" Mary spoke from her makeshift bed. "Please do, but close the door, the wind is chilly." "Thanks," one of the guys said. "That voice sounds familiar," Mary said quietly to Joe. As the men came into the light, Mary's suspicion was confirmed. "Hi guys. Sorry, we are all out of coffee." She smiled. One of the guys looked at them through the shadows. "Joe? Mary? Is that really you?" Joe handed the baby to Mary and got up and greeted his new/old friends. "It's us," Joe said proudly. "It's been a long time since we were snowbound in North Dakota." Another guy stepped up and hugged Joe. "I can't believe it's you. You two are the parents of the Savior?!" Mary, now on her feet, smiled and pulled the blanket down so that they could see the baby. The rays from the star beamed brightly through the cracks in the ceiling. One of the beams appeared to encircle the child as the four truck drivers stood there awestruck at what they were witnessing. One by one they knelt before the newborn King.

After a few moments, Joe asked, "How did you find us?" They rose to their feet and began telling the events that transpired at the diner. Each one confirmed the story. Joe was amazed at what he was hearing. Mary quietly treasured in her heart the things that she was hearing and made a mental note to always remember what the truck drivers had told them. "What are you kids going to do?" "I believe we will stay right here for awhile. Mary is too weak to move, let alone ride in that truck," Mary added. "This is really quite serene and comfortable for us, guys. Just look around; this is God's creation at its finest." The truck driver who was the one who teased Mary back at the diner in North Dakota laughed and said, "That's definitely classic, Mary. I've never met anyone who sees the bright side of everything like you do." Another spoke up. "If you two are staying here for awhile, we're going to head back to town and get you some supplies. You can't expect the King of Kings to get by with nothing. Come on gentlemen, we're going to town." "That really isn't necessary guys." Joe tried to stop them. "Now Joe, you are not going to deny us the opportunity to receive a blessing, are you?" He grinned and slapped Joe on the back as they walked out of the barn. "We'll be back in the morning."

Dr. Isaac, Dr. Rogers, and Dr. Likens took turns driving through the night. They couldn't believe how the beams from the star led them along the way. It stayed on the road in front of them all night. They had no idea where they were headed; they just followed the star. The sun was coming up and they wondered how they would follow the star in the daylight. They soon found out. As the sun came up, the star remained bright. The rays remained clearly visible. It was amazing. "This truly is a miracle. I admit I was doubtful. But now I believe. The Savior has arrived." Dr. Rogers' voice cracked as he was overcome with joy. They continued down the road singing and praising God.

As the three professors entered Bethlehem, Dr. Likens noticed a sign indicating that a hospital was close by. "Let's check the hospital and see if the Savior is there." "Good idea," Dr. Rogers agreed. "We can see if any newborns are there or in any surrounding hospitals. Chances are, the mother would have gone to a hospital. But how will we know which one is the Savior?" Dr. Isaac answered. "God will tell us. Make no mistake about it. WHEN we find the Savior, there will be no doubt about who He is.

The three of them walked up to the information desk and asked the receptionist if any babies had been born there within the last 24 hours. She looked around nervously and motioned for one of Jim Donavan's thugs to come over. A huge man in a black suit came over to the receptionist, quickly observed the three professors and returned his icy stare to the receptionist. "These three gentlemen were inquiring if any babies had been born here recently."

The thug squared up with the professors, paused for a moment, and then questioned, "What is your interest in newborns in this area? Are you relatives? Who are you looking for?" His tone was flat and serious. The professors were stunned silent. Finally, Dr. Rogers spoke up. "We have reason to believe that the Messiah has been born in this area and we are trying to find Him." "Do you have a name?" The thug was terse. "No," Dr. Isaac replied impatiently. The thug snickered, mumbled "Messiah" under his breath and instructed them to wait right there. He walked away from them and flipped open his cell phone. They looked at the receptionist who expressed a combination of fear and bewilderment. Just as Dr. Isaac was about to ask her some questions, she raised a finger to her lips indicating that they should be quiet. She scribbled a note and slid it in Dr. Isaac's direction. 'These are very bad men who have been placed here to find a newborn and the parents. The government has men stationed at all hospitals and emergency care units in the area looking for them. Be careful. I am sure that they want to harm the baby and the mother.'

Dr. Isaac stuffed the note into his pocket as the agent briskly walked toward him with the phone stuck in his ear. "Make sure they understand that we want to find their Messiah too. Who knows, it may be the same kid!" Donavan yelled into the phone. "Yes sir, Mr. Donavan." He closed his phone and moved toward the professors. "I just got off the phone with my boss. He is extremely excited that the Messiah may be here. We are sure that the parents' names are Mary and Joe. So if you find them, please call me. My boss would like to pay his respects to Him." The agent handed them a business card. Dr. Rogers took the card and assured the agent that they would definitely call when they found the baby. Dr. Isaac thanked the receptionist and they walked out to the car.

"Something doesn't sound right," Dr. Rogers said as they eased out of the parking lot. "You think?" Dr. Likens agreed. "I hope the government isn't looking for the same people that we are." Dr. Isaac spoke up. "I'm not taking any chances. When we do find the Savior, we are NOT calling that guy back. Agreed?" "Agreed," the other two said in unison. "Good, now let's keep following that star."

They turned down the lane to the barn about 10 p.m. that night. They followed the beam right up to the barn. They became excited and awestruck as the beam stopped at the door. They sat there stunned not knowing what to do next. Joe noticed the star and the bright lights outside. He slowly opened the door. All he could see was the light from the star.

Dr. Rogers gasped. "I know him!" He jumped out of the car. "Joe? Joe Goldstein? Is that you?" Joe still couldn't make out who was calling his name. "Yes, my name is Joe Goldstein. Do I know you?" "This is Dr. Rogers from Harvard; remember?" It took Joe a few seconds to register. Then it hit him. "Oh yes, Dr. Rogers come on in." "I have friends with me, Joe." "Any friend of yours is a friend of ours." Joe held the door open as the three of them made their way into the barn. They stopped in their tracks as soon as they laid eyes on Mary and the baby. Dr. Isaac immediately knelt down and the other two followed his lead. Dr. Rogers whispered, "Joe, do you know that your baby is the Messiah?" Mary giggled slightly as Joe placed his hand on Dr. Rogers' shoulder. "Yes sir, we know." Dr. Likens remained reverently silent as Dr. Isaac was overcome with tears of joy. "May we approach the King?" he asked humbly. Mary walked over to the now-standing Dr. Isaac. "Would you like to hold him?" she asked innocently. Tears streamed down his cheeks as he took the child. His entire body tingled as he held the baby. "How blessed am I to be in the presence of the Savior."

Dr. Likens spoke up. "We have gifts." He approached Mary and handed her a beautiful box filled with gold. "Gold—to represent the magnificent gift that God has given the world." Dr. Rogers stepped up to Mary and bowed low. "When I met Joe, I sensed that he was destined for greatness. I had no idea that he would be the earthly father of the Messiah. I humbly offer the gift of emeralds. Emeralds represent the fragrance of spring and new beginnings." Dr. Isaac handed the baby back to Mary and produced his gift. "I offer the gift of rubies. Rubies represent the blood of the sacrifice that is in the future for this King." Mary graciously accepted the gifts and asked Dr. Rogers if he would like to hold the baby. As he approached he asked, "What is His name?" Mary replied, "His name is Jesus."

To contact the author, please visit his Facebook page at:
www.facebook.com/charlesjackson7